murder

in a
quiet
place

murder
*in a
quiet
place*

tony caxton

st. martin's press
new york

Design by Junie Lee

Library of Congress Cataloging-in-Publication Data

Caxton, Tony.
    Murder in a quiet place / Tony Caxton.
        p.   cm.
    "A Thomas Dunne book."
    ISBN 0-312-11031-6
    1. Police—England—Fiction.   I. Title.
    PR6053.A94M87   1994   94-2178
823'.914—dc20   CIP

First Edition: July 1994
10 9 8 7 6 5 4 3 2 1

murder

in a
quiet
place

She lay dead for two days before she was found. The man she had promised to marry found her lying face-down on the sitting-room rug when he climbed into her cottage through a back window.

They were going to Paris for the weekend, and he arrived just before eight on Saturday morning to take her to the airport. He parked at the bottom end of School Walk and walked briskly up the thin-gravelled way. There were nine cottages, and hers was the second. They were all alike; a porch with a ridge top, a large mullioned window downstairs, wistaria climbing up faded brick, two small bedroom windows under a low roof.

There was no answer when he knocked on the green-painted door and no answer when he called up to the bedroom window above the porch, where she might be doing last-minute packing. The curtain over the front window was drawn close, something she always did at night, claiming the neighbours were nosy.

He went 'round the side of the cottage, past a rainwater-butt, and tried the back door. It was locked, as he expected it would be. Unlocked doors were a part of a mythical past, when friends and neighbours strolled in and out, unannounced and welcome. The kitchen window gave a view of a refrigerator, a corner of an electric cooker, and a stainless-steel sink. An unwashed cup and saucer stood on the draining board.

By now he was uneasy. She ought to be waiting for him at the door with an overnight case, ready to go. But the cottage was quiet; there was no sound inside. Nothing at all stirred, not a whisper, not a breath. He thumped his fist on the back door and rattled the knob, shouting 'Lynn, Lynn!'

The man in the next cottage came out into his patch of garden to stare at him over wooden palings, where bedding plants were just starting to flower red and yellow. Stanhope had seen this neighbour once or twice before, when he had stayed with Lynn.

He didn't much like the look of him, probably because the man had a black beard and dressed like a teenager, though he wasn't far short of forty. Some sort of antiquated drop-out, Stanhope thought, pathetic, inadequate, unemployable. In all probability living on social security hand-outs.

'I think she's away,' said Blackbeard, sounding very offhand. His name was Empson Rowley and he wore washed-out jeans with an ugly yellow T-shirt. On it was printed COLLAPSING WORLDS.

'Out of the question,' said Stanhope, his tone making it clear that any information from Rowley was discounted as unreliable. 'She knows I'm collecting her. We've got a plane to catch.'

There was a lot about Stanhope that Rowley didn't like. For a start, his houndstooth cashmere jacket, his carefully casual hair-style, his silver Mercedes at the bottom of School Walk.

'I haven't seen her since Wednesday or Thursday,' Rowley said curtly, his contempt showing for people who dressed up to catch planes. 'And I've been here most of the time.'

'You've got that wrong,' Stanhope told him. 'I talked to her

Wednesday when I got back from Edinburgh. In fact, that's when I arranged to pick her up this morning.'

'Have it your way,' Rowley said dismissively. And then: 'Hey, you can't break into somebody's house!'

Stanhope was a man who knew his own mind and didn't wait for other people's suggestions. He picked up a large terracotta pot of pansies and smashed in a pane of the kitchen window. Deaf to Rowley's protesting, he reached in to turn the catch and push up the sash window. He clambered inside to the crunch of glass in the sink under his feet.

When it was built in Queen Victoria's day, the cottage had two small rooms on the ground floor. A more recent owner had taken down the internal walls to make one decent-sized sitting-room, and added a long extension to contain a kitchen big enough to serve as a dining-room as well.

Stanhope saw her as soon as he came in from the kitchen. She was lying face-down on the rug in front of the fireplace.

'Lynn!' he said hoarsely. 'Oh, my God!'

He knew she was dead before he knelt and turned her over. The back of her head was crusted black with blood. A patch the size of a dinner plate had dried hard on the rug. Her body was stiff and unyielding when he moved her; it was like rolling over a plastic shop-window dummy.

Stanhope knelt over her, making loud, moaning sounds. Finding the woman you are in love with dead—and violently dead— cracks even the best-disciplined executive heart. There were tears on his face when Rowley found him, following through the window.

'God almighty! What's happened to her?'

'She's dead.' Stanhope struggled to get a grip on his emotions. 'I think she's been murdered. Get the police.'

In Long Slaughter, 'the police' meant PC Kevin Whitelock. There was a sleek grey telephone on a writing desk over by the window, and Rowley was reaching for it when he remembered that you were supposed to touch nothing at the scene of a crime.

There was no doubt in his mind that a crime had been committed here.

'Won't be long,' he said sickly.

The phone was left untouched. Rowley went off in a shaky rush to fetch the law.

Whitelock was in the front room of his police house on Bridge Street, the room with a wooden counter for official business. He sat helmetless at a standard-issue green metal desk, reading through the thick wad of official notices the morning post had brought him. Included was a poster for his notice-board, WANTED in big letters, over an Identikit picture of a man so anonymous that he could be practically anybody.

Whitelock heard a motorbike stop outside his house. Empson Rowley rushed in a moment later. He hadn't even put on his crash-helmet, he was so staggered by Stanhope's find.

PC Whitelock knew who his agitated customer was before words were spoken. The constable had a natural suspicion of grown men with beards who wore T-shirts with silly messages. He was very likely an agitator of some sort, not that you could run him in for that. But he could very well be a pot-smoker, and he was on Whitelock's little list of locals to keep an eye on.

One of these days, Whitelock thought, as he stared blankly at Rowley, *I'll catch you, my lad.*

But he forgot about that when Rowley stammered out his story of bloody murder in School Walk.

'Are you certain?' Whitelock asked. 'Did you actually see a body yourself?'

He wanted to be sure before he took any action. To his way of thinking, Rowley was capable of wasting police time with a cock-and-bull story from a drug hallucination. He might be on an LSD trip. Whitelock knew from circulars sent to him that teenagers were found regularly in Reading discos with Ecstasy tablets on them. The Polytechnic at Henley had been raided for LSD several times lately. And in Oxford students reeled around the streets, stupefied on drugs.

Rowley took in a deep breath and went through it again. Woman next door, boyfriend calling for her, no answer, got in through a kitchen window, dead on the floor with her head smashed in.

'All right,' said the police constable at the end of Rowley's recital. 'Go and sit in my car outside. I'll be with you in a minute, and we'll have a look.'

'I've got my motorbike here. I'll ride on ahead and tell him you're coming.'

'Go and sit in the police car and wait,' Whitelock repeated, sounding very stubborn, 'I want you where I can see you.'

When he parked at the bottom of School Walk, Whitelock wrote down the registration of the Mercedes standing there, starting a clean page of his notebook for what might be an investigation of some importance. Under the porch the cottage door stood open now, on the sitting-room floor a fluffy blue blanket shrouding the dead body from sight. Of Stanhope there was no sign.

Whitelock looked around the room. He could see nothing out of place or disturbed, at least not obviously so. There was a pair of large silver candlesticks on the mantelpiece, a TV set, and a VTR on a wooden stand in a corner. A brown leather handbag lay on the broad window-seat, closed and unrifled.

If the woman had been killed because a breaking and entering went wrong, the villain had left without taking the obvious items of value. That was the constable's deduction.

He got down on one knee to examine the mortal remains of Mrs Lynn Hurst, turned up a corner of the blanket, and said, *'Bloody hell!'* under his breath when he saw her head.

He dropped the blanket and stared inch by inch all round the floor of the sitting-room. But there was no sign of a suitable weapon—a blunt instrument, to use the official classification. He checked his watch and noted the time in his book before he stood up again.

In the meantime, Empson Rowley lurked on the porch just beyond the open door, his beard masking the pallor of his face.

'Where's the man who found her?' Whitelock asked, making it sound as if Rowley were personally responsible for him.

'He was here when I came to get you. His car's still there, so he can't be far. Why don't you try the garden?' Rowley snapped back.

Shaken he might be, but Rowley did not like policemen of any sort, uniform or plain-clothes, constable or Commissioner. This was on principle, not personal. His defiance drew a cold glare.

'I don't want you trampling on evidence while I'm out there looking for him,' said Whitelock, sounding very much the voice of authority. 'You go next door into your own house, understand me? And stay there until I want you again.'

Stanhope was in the back garden, sitting on a large upturned flower-pot, his back to the cottage, his arms wrapped round his knees, a picture of misery. He stood up slowly and rubbed his face with the back of a hand when Whitelock tapped him on the shoulder.

'Come along with me, sir.'

The cashmere jacket and gold Rolex warranted a *sir,* whereas a bile-yellow T-shirt and scruffy jeans did not.

'Where to?' Stanhope asked dejectedly.

'My house, sir. It's the best place to wait while my Sergeant gets here. My missus will make you a cup of tea, and we'll get a few particulars down on paper before they slip your mind.'

Stanhope gave him a tragic look that said he'd never, never in his life forget what he'd seen that day, or the emotion he felt when he knelt beside the battered body of his intended. Then he nodded and went with Whitelock, around the side of the cottage, to the waiting police car.

The official process had begun. Whitelock telephoned from his house to report the finding of a dead woman in what appeared to be suspicious circumstances. It took twenty-one minutes by the clock on his wall for the Sergeant to arrive from town. You could hear a siren at full blast for the last mile or two.

PC Baker was driving the car and hugely enjoying the flat-out screaming ride, a desperate thing to do on the minor road which was little more than a lane into Long Slaughter.

Baker's fun was over. He was left to keep an eye on Stanhope while Whitelock took the Sergeant to School Walk and showed him the body under the blue blanket.

'Did you put that over her?' Sergeant Dobson demanded.

'No, Sergeant. That's how I found her. The boyfriend covered her up before I got here. He turned her over as well, he says.'

'So everything's been thoroughly disturbed? CID will love it when they get here. There's nothing we can do now. You stand on duty outside while I take a look at the man next door and make sure he's still there. What did you say his name was?'

'Rowley. I think he's a wrong 'un.'

From the finding of the body to the arrival at PC Whitelock's house of the Detective Inspector assigned to the investigation took three hours. It was Saturday morning, not a peak time for major crime in those parts. Inspector Bowker was off-duty, and there was a delay while he was located.

His regular Detective Sergeant was on leave. A substitute had to be found, and that took more time.

Bowker was not happy when he set off for Long Slaughter with a stranger beside him in the car.

'Do you know the area?' he asked his passenger.

'No, sir,' said Detective Sergeant Jack Knight, not a trace of shame in his voice at his confession of ignorance. 'I was only transferred here from Walsall two weeks ago. I'm finding my way 'round still.'

Inspector Bowker glanced at him malevolently and shook his head. Whatever was waiting for him out in the sticks, his weekend was already messed up. And to crown it all, he'd been given a DS wet behind the ears.

The sketchy information Bowker had was that a female had been bludgeoned to death in her own home, no sign of a break-in.

With any luck, thought Bowker, it would turn out to be a nice straight-forward Friday-night wife-bashing after the local pub closed. If the village bobby knew his job, the husband would already be in custody. Or the boyfriend, now that couples didn't bother to get married any more.

And if the killer had gone on the run, husband or boyfriend, whichever he proved to be, the local bobby would already have a description to circulate.

Seen one wife beaten to death, seen them all, Bowker thought gloomily. What varied was the degree of nastiness involved. One case he recalled was a husband beaten to death by his wife while he lay drunk on the sitting-room sofa. She'd used a brick out of a builder's skip in the street outside. Very, very nasty, that one was, she kept on hitting him after he was dead. Face smashed in and unrecognisable. There was only her word for it that it was her husband she'd killed.

'Sign-post ahead on the left, sir,' said Knight, who had been silent ever since the glare that told him where he stood.

Bowker grunted and turned off the main road into a lane where a white finger-post pointed. *Long Slaughter 6* it said usefully, and *Sandy Bottom 14,* which seemed less relevant.

As English country lanes do, this one twisted left and right, for no sensible reason, between thick green hedgerows. The gaps where there were five-bar gates allowed glimpses of fields planted with crops of some sort, Bowker had no idea what. Nothing above a few inches tall this early in the year.

Agriculture was not a topic in which he took an interest, but he had been shown the difference between wheat and barley three years ago, when he investigated the violent death of a girl not above 20 miles from where he was now. Her naked body was found at harvest time in a barley field.

Detective Sergeant Knight was observing Bowker with caution, wondering if there was any truth in what he'd been told about the Inspector.

Young coppers called Bowker the Mad Mangler because of some small resemblance to a popular wrestler on TV. But not when he was around. Coppers have a notoriously perverse sense of humour among themselves, Knight knew well, and the jokes they made up were the sort called gallows humour. From the days when they had gallows for hard cases.

Bowker was on the right side of forty, an advantage in Knight's view. Knight was never impressed by silver-haired senior officers rattling on about how things used to be a damn sight better in the Force in the old days. He imagined Bowker would turn out no worse than any other DI he'd worked with.

To look at, Bowker was a dark man, a bruiser. Dark hair and a swarthy complexion, like a fairground gypsy. It wasn't hard to see a resemblance to the TV wrestler. His shoulders were thick and hunched, as if he was squaring up to flatten an opponent. A direct stare, intimidating to wrongdoers. They would interpret it as suspicion, disbelief, accusation and condemnation, rolled up into one—without a word spoken.

That was the right word for Bowker, the DS decided eventually—he was *intimidating*. He was big and broad. Whatever he did he had a distinct air of physical menace about him, even if he sat still and said nothing. His nondescript dark grey suit, rumpled as it was, couldn't make him look insignificant.

The car swept over the brow of a low hill and the road ran to the left, down to the first houses in Long Slaughter. There was a metal sign identifying this as Bridge Street. The police house was on a corner where another road crossed it.

Bowker parked by the official notice-board, its posters a guide to rural life, dealing with Swine Fever precautions, Lost Dogs, Regulations to Prevent the Spread of Mad Cow Disease and Colorado Beetle.

And a ridiculous WANTED poster with an Identikit portrait of nobody much.

Inside the house, behind the desk, was sitting not the local bobby but a uniformed Sergeant Bowker knew slightly. He was on the phone, listening not talking. When he saw the Inspector and his DS, he announced to whoever was on the line, 'He's arrived.'

'Who was that?' Bowker asked suspiciously.

'Chief Superintendent Horrocks. He's been on every fifteen minutes to see if you're here yet.'

'So now he knows,' Bowker said with indefinable menace.

Dobson stood up to move out from behind the desk and make way for the Inspector. Bowker ignored the chair and perched himself on a corner of the metal desk. It crossed Jack Knight's mind that he looked like a buzzard on a tree branch, eyeing the terrain for something to pounce on. Knight nearly smiled, but thoughts like that you kept to yourself.

'What have we got here, Sergeant,' said Bowker, 'all they've told me is a dead woman with her head cracked open.'

'That's right, sir. Mrs Lynn Hurst, aged twenty-seven, found dead early this morning at 3 School Walk, where she's lived for the past year or two. Divorced, no children. Found by a man friend, Mark James Stanhope, who says he was taking her to Paris.'

Sergeant Dobson handed Bowker the sheet of paper on which the details were typed.

'Right, Sergeant. Very neat and comprehensive. Has the doctor seen the body yet?'

'At the cottage now. The undertaker's men are on stand-by to take the body away as soon as you say so.'

'Where's the boyfriend now?'

'In Constable Whitelock's parlour. He's pretty shocked. We didn't know exactly what to do with him till you got here.'

As if to disprove the Sergeant's assertion, the door between office and parlour was flung open and Mark Stanhope strode in. The numbness of shock had worn off, aided by hot sweet tea, and he had worked himself up into a bad temper.

'I've had enough of this!' he said belligerently. 'I've been kept here all morning for no reason. I'm going now, and you'll be hearing from my solicitor.'

Stanhope was not a man to be kept waiting about; his sense of his own worth was well-developed. Bowker stared at him hard.

'Who are you?' Stanhope demanded.

'Detective Inspector Bowker, in charge of the investigation, and this is Detective Sergeant Knight,' said Bowker, genially ferocious. 'I'm sorry you've had to wait. I need you to tell me what you saw and did, when you found Mrs. Hurst.'

'I've already told the Sergeant that; you've got it on paper. There's nothing else I can tell you. Now, can I go or not?'

It was a direct challenge, the way Stanhope said it. Unspoken words hung in the air between the two men facing each other, as it might be *Back down or I'll set my dog on you.*

Jack Knight wondered for a moment how Bowker reacted when his authority was questioned. But only for a moment. The Inspector slid off the desk and stepped forward to less than a yard from Stanhope. His arms hung at his sides, his fists bunched, a hard smile on his face. Six foot six, solid as an oak, powerful as a dray-horse, thought Knight. He'd put bets on heavyweight boxers in the ring who looked less dangerous.

'I'd like you to stay here till I've time to ask you a few questions,' said Bowker, his voice as chill as a winter wind. 'First I want to look at the scene of the crime, so I know what I'm talking about. Why don't you go and sit down in the Constable's parlour. I'm sure his wife can make you another cup of tea.'

Stanhope was backing towards the door he'd come in by, a look of shock on his face.

'Don't you dare hit me!' he said in a strained voice. 'I'm warning you! Sergeant, you're my witness!'

His appeal was addressed to the uniformed Sergeant, standing by a filing cabinet, not to Jack Knight.

'Witness, sir?' Dobson asked, playing up to Bowker. 'Witness to what?'

'You've had a bad morning and you're a bit distraught,' said Bowker, taking a menacing step forward. 'Why not take a rest in the parlour till I get back?'

Stanhope shot through the door, Bowker pulled it shut, first putting his head into the parlour for a parting shot.

'Maybe you ought to ring your solicitor,' he said, his words a cheerful threat. 'We wouldn't want you to be nervous about a few questions. We like to think of ourselves as servants of the public.'

They took Sergeant Dobson's police car to School Walk, Bowker beside him up front, Knight in the back. PC Baker stayed behind to answer the phone, maintain public order, and keep an eye on Stanhope.

Knight was puzzled.

'I don't understand why you told him to get a lawyer. They're just a bloody nuisance round the place.'

'You didn't see the look on his face,' Bowker said, with the bleakest of grins. 'He's properly got the wind up now he thinks he's top of the suspect list. He'll be lucky to get hold of his lawyer on a Saturday midday. They're all idle sods who go off golfing or laze around their weekend cottage or kerb-crawling for a young tart. Or whatever it is lawyers get up to in their spare time.'

'Psychological warfare, is it?' Knight asked.

'Just bouncing Stanhope along,' said Bowker. 'Nothing to it, really. What can you tell me about Long Slaughter, Dobson? I've never been here before.'

'Not much to tell. This is Bridge Street—it takes us down to the Thames. It's old houses and a shop or two, as you see. Down by the bridge on this side, there's a T-junction where the road goes right and left along the river.'

'Where do you get to straight on over the bridge?'

'Nowhere much. There's a row of houses, a corner off-licence, and that's the end of Long Slaughter. Keep going for twelve or fifteen miles, more than the sign-posts say, and you'll come to Sandy Bottom, which is even smaller than Long Slaughter.'

At the bottom of Bridge Street, Dobson turned right. There was a pub, the Black Swan, backing on to the river, then houses and shops on both sides, and a grey stone church set back from the road in a small graveyard with upright tombstones.

'Church Street,' Dobson said. 'We go down here a bit and turn right again into Badger Lane. There's another pub there on the corner, the Bull's Head. School Walk runs off Badger Lane. You can't drive a car up it—there's iron posts to stop you.'

A gleaming nearly-new silver Mercedes was parked by the kerb at the bottom of School Walk.

'If Stanhope parked there while he went for his girlfriend and her luggage,' said Bowker, 'he might not bother to lock the car, early in the morning. Have you had a look inside that car, Dobson?'

'No, sir, no permission and no reason.'

'Right,' said Bowker. 'Very proper. Knight, you have a bit of a quiet rummage through that Mercedes and see what you can find that interests us. I'll be in the cottage.'

'Stanhope could make a fuss if he gets to know,' said Knight, not at all enthusiastic about the assignment.

'Put things back where you find them and he'll never know. We have a serious crime on our hands, we haven't got time for nit-picking scruples.'

'You suspect Stanhope of murdering his girlfriend?'

'I suspect everybody she ever knew, including him. So see if there's anything enlightening in his car.'

'Like what?' Knight demanded, knowing he'd lost the argument and uneasy about it, 'a bloodstained monkey-wrench inside the glove-box?'

'You never know your luck. I've arrested killers who've done sillier things than that.'

'I haven't heard any of this,' Dobson said.

'I should bloody well hope not,' Bowker said, glowering at him malignantly.

PC Kevin Whitelock stood outside the cottage door, performing no useful function except to advertise the police presence. For Bowker's benefit, he stood to attention and looked serious. With him was a thin man in a baggy green Harris tweed suit and a hat suitable for stalking deer in the Scottish Highlands. His name was Pendleton, and Bowker knew him of old.

'Morning, Doctor,' he said, 'you got caught for this one, like me. What can you tell me?'

'I've been standing here over an hour waiting for you to turn up,' Pendleton grumbled, very surly, 'I'm damned if I know why. I've other things to do at weekends besides standing 'round here wasting time.'

'You get paid for it,' Bowker told him with a cheerless grin. 'The sooner you fill me in, the sooner you can clear off.'

He brushed the Doctor aside with a twitch of his shoulder and went into the cottage. Just inside the sitting-room he stopped and looked round. Dr Pendleton came up behind him, fuming silently. The blue blanket Stanhope had used to cover the corpse had been taken off and thrown over a chintz-covered couch.

The late Lynn Hurst lay on the bloodstained rug on her back, her eyes closed, her mouth open.

'There's not very much I can tell you that you can't see for yourself,' said Pendleton, who sounded offended still. 'A woman fully dressed, no indication of sexual assault. She was struck on the back of the head several times, and it killed her.'

'The bobby outside saw that much,' said Bowker, the corners of his mouth turning down sourly. 'How long dead?'

'At a guess, thirty-six hours. I'll narrow it down later.'

'Sometime Thursday evening, then?'

'Yes,' Pendleton agreed. 'She died between six and midnight on Thursday evening, I'd say.'

'Instantaneous?'

'Not with all that bleeding. After she was hit, she was deeply unconscious, irreversibly so. Her attacker probably thought she was dead and went. She might have lasted an hour or more before she stopped breathing, but she never moved.'

She looked deader than anyone Bowker had seen since the girl in the barley field, and she'd been there three weeks when they found her. When he was a young copper and saw a victim, Bowker's first thought was *why do people do this?*

He felt an unprofessional surge of compassion, just a moment of mourning for those whose lives were terminated brutally. The women raped and murdered, children abused and strangled, poor old bastards of pensioners coshed for their few quid savings, nightwatchmen and security guards blasted with shotguns. Even a ginger-haired Traffic Warden once, stabbed to death by a bloody demented motorist she'd given a parking ticket.

'It's a rough and ready world,' said Bowker under his breath, mournfully eying the dead woman. 'Too bloody rough.'

Nowadays he still felt the pang, but he didn't ask himself why anymore. He knew why people killed and raped and robbed. There was a streak of cruel and selfish wickedness in human nature, all the way through, and it never would be eradicated. Not this side of Judgement Day.

He couldn't undo the evil someone had done here in this quiet cottage. There was no restitution for a dead woman, even after he found the murderer. The idea of justice had got watered down till nobody gave a sod for it anymore. All Bowker could do was get on with his job, arrest the wrong 'uns, and see them locked up with their own kind. To vent their wickedness on each other, for however long seemed fitting to some dim old geriatric Judge wearing a pantomime wig.

No sign of disturbance in the sitting-room, Bowker noted with Sergeant Dobson's report in his hand. Curtains drawn and light switched on. Front and back doors locked, obviously someone she let in herself. Most likely a friend, as they say.

This friend had followed her from the door and bashed her head in from behind. And did that with something brought specially for the purpose and taken away afterwards. It will be in the river, I'd lay ten to one on it, Bowker thought. I'll get a diver down under the bridge and see what he can find.

'I'll have the cadaver sent to St Martha's Cottage Hospital,' Dr Pendleton said with an ill-disguised sneer. 'The pathologist there can do a post-mortem as soon as you arrive.'

'Tell him to get on with it,' Bowker growled. 'I can't waste my time watching doctors gutting dead women, there's a murderer to catch. I'll read the report.'

The truth was Bowker never went to post-mortems, and Pendleton knew it. He was not squeamish, but it made him furious to watch a human being reduced to a plastic bag of bloody innards and an empty shell; it upset his sense of the rightness of things.

The stretcher with the body under a blanket was going out as Knight came up School Walk, a worried look on his face.

Bowker's thick black eyebrows rose comically. 'Found the monkey-wrench?'

'There's a tyre-iron in the boot with the spare wheel, but it's so clean it's never been used for anything. The glove-box was locked, but I tickled it open. Two air tickets to Paris, first-class, and his passport. He was telling the truth about that.'

'That all?'

'Some papers in a thin black briefcase on the back seat. I've made a list of them.'

'We'll have a look later. The first thing we do is go through this cottage top to bottom and find out everything we can about Mrs Hurst. Especially we want to know where her ex-husband can be found and talked to.'

'What about fingerprints?' Knight said. 'Shouldn't we wait for forensic and the dabs-team before we start ferreting about in here?'

'There'll be millions of fingerprints. The ones we want won't be here. Chummy came in all nice and friendly, touching nothing and leaving no traces, caved her skull in, and buggered off.'

'All the same, forensic's important,' Knight argued.

'Forensic evidence is a snare and a delusion,' Bowker declared with savage gusto. 'Get your murderer convicted on forensic, and before he's done twelve months inside, some meddling do-gooder on TV hires his own forensic expert who makes your expert out to be a fool and a liar. Your murderer's let off on appeal, and some copper gets reprimanded or sacked. Thousands of pounds are handed over to the murderer to compensate for his mental suffering in the clink—and nobody gives a sod for the victim?'

'So what do you want, a written confession?'

'I want this case sewn up tight. Incontrovertible. No appeal, no clever lawyer's tricks, no TV smear campaign against us.'

Knight looked at the Inspector sideways. 'What's so special about this to get you agitated, sir?'

'You're a cheeky bastard, Knight, but I'll tell you. I don't know what's so special, but I've got the nastiest feeling we're looking at something a long sight more vicious than an ordinary jealous domestic bashing.'

2. .... *karma kottage*

Wearing throw-away plastic gloves, Bowker sorted quickly through the likeliest parts of the Hurst cottage for items of interest. The sitting-room, which had a writing-table with drawers by the window, the main bedroom, where there was a dressing-table with drawers and a wardrobe with a long drawer at the bottom.

He found bank statements and a Building Society savings book downstairs in the writing-table. H. Hurst paid £1500 every month into the bank account. Must be the ex-husband, Bowker guessed.

In the handbag on the window-seat were 500 French francs and £500 in traveller's cheques. All set for her weekend in Paris, he thought with a pang. Poor dead bitch.

He was more interested in the leather-bound address book from the drawer. Many of the entries were initials, not full names. Some had only a telephone number, not an address. Most of all he was interested in Lynn Hurst's Building Society book, which had a balance of £42,000.

'Look at that, Knight,' he said, 'most of it paid in over the last three years. In multiples of £100. We'll ask the boyfriend what she did for a living.'

He found a photo album. Nearly every picture had Lynn Hurst in it; on seaside beaches with striped sun umbrellas, on hotel terraces with drinks, in sidewalk cafés abroad. Four pages with Mark Stanhope, both suitably dressed in casual expensiveness.

'Good-looking woman,' said Bowker, studying the sand-and-sea scenes.

Lynn Hurst in a scarlet bikini, in a zebra-striped one-piece, topless in an acid-green thong, palm trees in the background.

'Nice,' Jack Knight agreed. 'Worth showing off those.'

'Fancy her yourself? I know I would if I'd met her like that on a beach. She always found somebody to snap her looking sexy. Does that tell you anything?' Bowker asked with a snarl.

'She had a good opinion of herself,' said Knight. 'Sexy women always do, nothing unusual in that.'

'Stanhope took her about a bit, didn't he? That's got to be the South of France—see that café sign. And here they are on a cruise liner. And skiing—that's either Switzerland or Austria because I can see half a German word on the chair-lift there in the background.'

'He spent a lot of money on her, you mean?' asked Knight, who sounded disapproving.

Bowker nodded and turned back pages in the album.

'So did this one—my guess is he's the ex-husband. There's a couple of pages of photos with him and her. Dinner jacket and strapless gown. And horse-riding on dunes. And sunbeds beside a swimming-pool with tall glasses in their hands.'

'She liked the good life,' said Knight, 'and found enough men to pay for it. There's another topless one. Nice pair she had.'

'There's quite a few loose photos, maybe taken earlier, maybe not,' Bowker said. 'Posh places, different men, five or six of them. Pity she didn't bother to put a date and place; then we'd know if she put herself about still or whether she settled down happily.'

'Not that happy, sir, couldn't be. Divorced before she was thirty and engaged to another fellow. What are you thinking, a jealous boyfriend from the past? Ex-hubby turns up in a blind rage and clobbers her?'

'Always possible when you've got a woman with these looks and that gleam in her eye. When we find out who gave her the money in her Building Society account, that may help.'

Upstairs, in the bottom of the wardrobe was a white cardboard shoe box full of old letters. Bowker took one from its envelope and checked the date and signature.

'Six years ago,' he said, grinning brutally. 'It's bloody well from Pooh-Bear! You read this lot through, Knight, then carry on searching the rest of the house. I'm going next door to have a chat with the neighbour who was conveniently on hand to see Stanhope find the body.'

He stopped for a word with PC Whitelock, still standing guard outside and looking very fed up.

'You're neither use nor ornament standing there,' he told the constable. 'While I interview Rowley, you do me a house-to-house at the other cottages in the Walk, and then the nearest ones on Badger Lane. We want sightings of Mrs Hurst Thursday afternoon and evening. And any visitors seen coming or going that day.'

From what Whitelock told him, Bowke half-expected to see a brain-damaged drop-out in the next house. The name-board outside said KARMA KOTTAGE, it seemed a fair enough hint of loopiness ahead. He was surprised when the door opened to his brisk knocking to reveal a pleasant-looking woman in a neatly ironed blue shirt and a grey skirt.

She was in her early thirties, he guessed, shortish brown hair and not very tall. Cosy-looking, the sort to cuddle up to on a sofa in front of the TV, after she'd cooked you a nice steak dinner. Not a bearded weirdo's woman.

'Detective Inspector Bowker. I'd like a word with Mr Rowley.'

He spoke in as friendly way as he knew how, but she looked at him nervously and stepped backwards. His size overawed most of the people who met him.

'You'd better come in. He's been expecting you all morning.'

Like the Hurst cottage, this one also had the internal walls removed to make a fair-sized sitting-room. Bowker noted it was well-furnished and comfortable, not at all the dingy squat, with orange-boxes to sit on, that PC Whitelock's prejudices had suggested. Empson Rowley was down on his hands and knees on the floor. He and a small boy in red dungarees were playing with a wooden train.

The happy domesticity faded when Rowley stood up to face the Inspector. He didn't like policemen; he took no trouble to hide it. In particular, he hated and despised Inspector Denis Bowker on sight. The accusation *Gestapo* trembled on his tongue, just waiting to be hissed out. The black beard almost bristled as he glared at the Inspector, fists clenched down by his sides.

Bowker gave him a hyena grin and spoke his introduction line all over again, though Rowley must have heard it from the door.

'Unpleasant business next door, Mr Rowley.'

Bowker wondered if COLLAPSING WORLDS on the yellow T-shirt had any meaning, or whether it was the usual garbage rock-fans adorned themselves with.

'Perhaps you can help me with my enquiries.'

The woman picked up the little boy, who was staring at Bowker from floor level open-mouthed, and said she'd take him upstairs while they talked. She seemed upset about something—that much was obvious to Bowker. So, too, was Rowley; it was obvious he was going to take it out on the Inspector by making the interview as difficult as he could. He was going to give *yes-no, don't-know,* and *can't remember* answers.

Without waiting to be asked, Bowker sat down on a

comfortable-looking armchair and took out his notebook, making the simple action awesomely deliberate. His combative nature relished what was to come.

'Tell me if I've got it right. At about eight this morning you assisted Mr Mark Stanhope to break into Mrs Hurst's cottage and found her lying dead on the floor.'

That got Rowley going. He waved his arms about and said he'd never broken into anywhere in his life. Stanhope was lying if he said that. Stanhope broke the window by himself, and he only followed him into the cottage to see he didn't take anything that didn't belong to him.

'Such as what? Money, jewellery? Why did you think he was a thief—surely you'd seen him with Mrs Hurst before?'

Empson Rowley's determination to stick to *yes-no* answers and be as unhelpful as possible was forgotten. He floundered about, defending his actions.

'How long have you lived here, next door to Mrs Hurst?' asked Bowker. 'How well did you know her?'

'We've lived here nearly two years.'

'*We* meaning you and Mrs Rowley and your little boy?'

'It's none of your business. We're not married, as it happens. What gives you the right to pry into people's private lives?'

'A murder next door and you at the scene of the crime. That's all the right I need to ask any questions I like,' Bowker told him with a scowl that terrified most people. It had the desired effect on Rowley. He stopped blustering.

'Where were you on Thursday?' Bowker asked, pen poised over his notebook in a menacing way, as if anything Rowley said now would be used against him in a court of law later on. 'Start at noon and take me through till midnight.'

'Thursday—is that when she was killed?'

When he got no answer he ran his fingers through his beard in an attempt at concentration.

'Thursday, let me think, I was working here all morning. Till about one o'clock. Then we had something to eat; I forget what. Judy will remember, if you want to know.'

'Judy being your lady-friend?'

'My life-partner,' said Rowley, indignant a wrong description should be used of the companion of his bed and board. 'Are you all male chauvinists in the Police Force?'

'A fair number of us,' said Bowker with genial ferocity, 'and we've got a few racists, I should think, just like the world at large. Even one or two woman-haters. What's her other name?'

'Judy Holbooth. Our son's name is Krishna—he's only four. I suppose you're going to run *him* through your computer to see if he's got a criminal record!'

Poor little bastard, Bowker was thinking, to be lumbered with a fancy name like Krishna. When he goes to school he's bound to be bully-ragged rotten if the other kids find out. Still, he can always call himself Kris.

'You haven't answered my question,' he said, letting Rowley's heavy sarcasm bounce off. 'How well did you know Mrs Hurst?'

'Not all that well,' Rowley said firmly, his eyes tight shut. 'Only as a neighbour. She was away a lot. We said *Hi* over the garden fence. Once or twice she was in here having a cup of tea with Judy. She asked us in for sherry and a mince pie a couple of days before Christmas.'

'I see.' Bowker's tone indicated he didn't believe a word of it. And he didn't. Experience told him he was listening to outright lies.

On the other hand, he could hear nothing from upstairs, where Judy had taken the boy. She'd left the sitting-room door half-open, and if she'd left the bedroom door open as well she could very likely hear every word spoken downstairs.

That would make Rowley mind his tongue. He wouldn't admit to any sort of hanky-panky with the deceased while his girl had her ears open.

'Getting back to Thursday,' said Bowker, with subdued menace. 'You got as far as lunch with your family. Where did you get to in the afternoon?'

'I rode over to Reading on the motorbike. I'd got a book on order in W. H. Smith, and a postcard came at the beginning of the week to say it had arrived. If you don't believe me, I can show you the book.'

'What time did you get back here with your book?'

Rowley fidgeted, rubbing his feet together, grubby trainers squeaking faintly. He was the least competent liar Denis Bowker had talked to for months.

'I'd been working hard. I felt like a break. So I went to Slough to the new multi-screen cinema.'

Bowker didn't even bother to ask what film he'd seen, only what time he'd got home.

'I stopped for something to eat,' said Rowley, fidgeting with his hands as well as his feet. 'About eight, I think it was.'

'And when was the last time you saw Mrs Hurst? Alive.'

It was said with such significance that what could be seen of Rowley's cheeks behind the black beard turned pallid.

'Tuesday or Wednesday, I'm not sure now,' he said, so feebly Bowker could hardly hear him. 'She was on her doorstep, coming out of the cottage as I came up School Walk.'

'*Tuesday* or *Wednesday*,' Bowker repeated with open scepticism as he wrote the words down, spinning it out to unsettle Rowley. 'And when you came past her cottage on Thursday with your book in your hand, what did you see?'

'Nothing. There wasn't anything to see.'

'At eight o'clock it would be dark. Were her lights on? Was there a car parked at the end of the Walk? Did you hear voices from inside her cottage?'

'The curtains were drawn,' said Rowley after he'd thought for a moment. 'I don't remember a car. I'm sure there wasn't one, it would have been in my way with the motorbike. Now I come to think of it, Lynn must have been out, or I'd have seen her car. It's a Volkswagen, a white one with a roof that folds down.'

'Registration number?' asked Bowker, biro poised.

'You expect me to remember somebody's car number!'

'One more question; what do you do for a living?'

In his thinking, he'd put Rowley down as some sort of com-

puter maniac. The sort who worked at home, devising programmes for a software company, as a freelance. The bolshy
manner and sloppy clothes were a dead giveaway.

'I'm an artist,' said Rowley, proving him wrong.

Bowker pursed his lips in mild wonder. Rowley mistook it for
disbelief and said, 'Come on, I'll show you.'

He led the Inspector to a small extension at the back of the
cottage, beyond the kitchen. It had no windows, just long neon
tubes on the ceiling. The walls were painted white, and on them
hung cork pin-up boards with pictures torn out of magazines
and books.

'No natural light? I thought artists couldn't do without,' said
Bowker, thinking it looked more like a counterfeiter's den than a
real artist's studio.

'My sort of work needs total concentration—I don't want any
distractions,' Rowley explained.

'I bet Michelangelo felt the same while he was painting that
chapel ceiling,' said Bowker, but his joke went unnoticed.

A large and expensive-looking drawing-board on chrome tub-
ing legs stood in the middle of the room, by it a tall swivel chair
with a circular foot-rail. On the board was an oblong sheet of
paper with a watercolour in bright tints.

Bowker glared at the picture: a dark blue dragon as big as a
Boeing, surrounded by strange trees with smooth red trunks and
black fronds like hair. From its huge black nostrils the creature
was spouting orange flames at a spectacular blonde woman in a
stainless-steel bikini.

'You draw for the comics,' said Bowker, sizing up the garish
picture.

'No, I'm into Fantasy Art,' Rowley put him right curtly. 'It
might not mean much in police circles, but I'm probably the best-
known fantasy artist outside the United States.'

'Sort of Science Fiction,' said Bowker.

'That's a typically unintelligent way of putting it. I create alternative worlds and people them with cosmic projections from the

collective unconscious. I don't suppose you understand what I mean by archetypes—I give them shape and form in my work. I vivify them as superhumans and monsters. Paradigms, you could call them, locked together in deadly combat, their existence in mortal peril and threatened annihilation.'

'Right,' said Bowker, wondering what the hell a paradigm was.

He noticed the dragon was really a machine running on tracks like a tank. Maybe it meant something to Rowley. He also noticed the blonde had a bigger chest than any living woman he ever met. And she had a purple orchid tattooed on the inside of a muscular thigh. No mystery what that was about.

'Ever tried LSD?' Bowker asked amiably. 'It scrambles your brain so you see things like this, they say.'

'Plenty of times when I was a student,' Rowley said.

On the subject of his art he was decisive. Defiant, even. The unspoken words behind his admission were *And what are you going to do about it, copper?*

Bowker had no interest in doing anything about it, but he was curious whether PC Whitelock's suspicions of dope-dealing were true or not.

'I'll be on my way,' he said, scowling at the yellow-T-shirted artist, 'but I shall certainly want to question you again. Some of your answers are far from satisfactory. I suggest you think things over carefully; second thoughts are often the best. I'll be back.'

He left Rowley twitching in anxiety and went to talk to his Sergeant next door.

'Found any car papers?' he asked. 'Insurance, something with the registration number? The victim's car should be outside, and it's not. Might be in a local garage for repair—check that. On the other hand, Chummy might have gone off in it and dumped it somewhere.'

'Vehicle papers are in that drawer in a big envelope, sir.'

'Good, get on the phone. We want to find the car fast.'

When the call was made, they drove in the police car left for them to PC Whitelock's house on Bridge Street.

'Anything useful in those letters she kept, Knight?'

'Mostly they're from her ex-husband, the one signing himself Pooh-Bear. There's a few from other chaps.'

'And?'

'Pooh-Bear's name is Harvey Hurst, and he's a doctor—private, not National Health. He put a lot of passion in his letters to her before they got married. Between the lines there's a lot of jealousy about her going out with other chaps.'

'You're telling me he could have smashed her head in?'

'The passion might have calmed down after they'd been married a year or two. We don't know what the divorce was like or which of them started it. We'd have to talk to Hurst to see if he's a runner or not.'

'And we will, we will,' Bowker assured him. 'Doctors are easy to find—get his present address and we'll have a chat. In the meantime, ring up W. H. Smith in Reading and ask if Empson Rowley collected a book-order from them last Thursday afternoon.'

'Is that what he said he was doing?'

'Our bearded loon told me a pack of lies. Said he hardly knew Mrs Hurst, but I think he's had his leg over her. Every time I mentioned her, he got that shifty something-to-hide look.'

Knight was driving. He stared at Bowker in disbelief, and the car wobbled as his hand slipped on the steering-wheel.

'Why should she bother with *him?*' He sounded puzzled. 'The local bobby says he's a scruffy clown, he's seen him round the village in one of those Mickey Mouse baseball caps with a long peak. Her style was more champagne and posh hotels.'

'There's about ten grand's worth of motorbike parked outside Rowley's house,' Bowker said malevolently, 'and in his sitting-room I reckoned up at least five grand's worth of furniture and carpets and stuff.'

'Stolen goods?' Knight asked hopefully.

'Shouldn't think so for a minute. Rowley draws comics for his living. Science Fiction, ray-guns, and naked blondes with great big boobs being mauled by creatures from outer space. The usual teenage nonsense. He's better off than the local bobby thinks.'

'Well, then, Lynn Hurst might have taken an interest in him. Does he use models for his drawing?'

'Not a chance, I've yet to meet a woman shaped like the ones he draws. But it's only wishful thinking, in real life he takes what he can get.'

'And you think he had it off with Lynn Hurst, sir? That's not bad going, if you ask me. But if he was dropping in on her for a quickie when he felt like it, why would he want to crack her skull?'

'He's *got* a very nice woman living with him. Her name's Judy Holbooth. They've a little boy he's devoted to. Motive enough to get rid of Lynn Hurst, if she threatened to spill the beans to Judy unless Rowley paid up.'

'I know what you're going to say next,' said Knight. 'Take a look at Rowley's bank account, see if he's been shelling out on a regular basis to anybody besides the gas and electric.'

Bowker nodded and showed his teeth in a friendly snarl.

'I won't say a bloody word about how bloody hard it is to get hold of a bank manager at the weekend,' said Knight, 'even when you've got a Warrant, but consider it done. You realise that if Rowley was buying books miles and miles away at the time of the murder, his live-in lady-friend won't have an alibi. Suppose she knew about the leg-over and slipped in next door to put a stop to it. Have you thought about that, sir?'

'It crossed my mind. I'm not ruling her out. The weapon's not in Lynn Hurst's place, and we'd have to get a Warrant to search Rowley's cottage and garden. There's no evidence at all yet to justify asking for one, only routine suspicion. So we'll have to leave it for now.'

By seven that evening, Bowker decided he'd done enough for one day. The local garage hadn't got Mrs Hurst's Volkswagen. It had been serviced only about a month ago, so affirmed with many an obscenity by George Hogg, sole proprietor, dragged that afternoon from a First Division football match on TV.

Mark James Stanhope had been interviewed, wrung dry, and sent home. He provided background information on Lynn Hurst, none of it with much immediate bearing on her death. She didn't have a job. Her former husband paid decent alimony, though that would end when she married Stanhope. They were in no hurry to be wed. Lynn liked her independence, and it suited him that way. She had no money of her own, as far as he knew.

'Forty-two thousand pounds in a savings account,' Bowker said sombrely, and Stanhope looked impressed. He was beginning to be just slightly bedraggled. The elaborately casual hairdo needed a comb through it; his shirt collar was crumpled.

In the two hours Bowker kept him waiting while he went to the cottage and talked to Empson Rowley, the boyfriend had lost his bristliness and sunk into lethargy. The reality of Lynn Hurst's death had sunk in. He would never again see his bright, lively, sexy, bantering fiancée, only the polished wooden coffin at her funeral.

Bowker went easy with him. He sat opposite him in Whitelock's parlour, not dominating him, and asked the questions he needed answers to. Stanhope was an architect. He was thirty-six years old and last saw Lynn alive, he said, on the previous Sunday. They had lunch in Brighton and spent the day together. And the night. He brought her back to Long Slaughter on Monday morning, before he flew up to Edinburgh to discuss a possible commission.

'Edinburgh? Bit far from home, isn't it?' Bowker said with open suspicion. 'Haven't they got any Scotch architects?'

'Plenty,' Stanhope said. 'These are hard times, you have to jump at any chance of a commission. Less than a month ago I was in Nigeria pitching for a job. And that's the sort of place where you never get paid for your work.'

He was home again late Wednesday, he said, and talked to Lynn for half an hour on the phone. That was when he suggested they go to Paris for the weekend. He rang her again Thursday about nine in the evening, but there was no answer. He assumed she'd gone out and thought nothing of it.

No, there wouldn't be an answer, Bowker thought darkly, but that's given us an end-time to work to.

Assuming there *had* been a call and Stanhope hadn't driven to Long Slaughter to dispose of his girlfriend. What motive could he have for that? His grief seemed genuine. The trip to Paris he said he'd arranged on Wednesday suggested that all was well between them then.

Suppose after he made the call Stanhope somehow found out his girl had been dropping her knickers occasionally for another—a possibility, if no more? Would that fire him up enough to drive over and kill her?

If we're talking about Empson Rowley the Fantasy Artist, then it's possible that Judy slipped the bad word to Stanhope to get her own back, Bowker thought. But there might be somebody else. We'll have to go through that photograph album again and try to identify as many men as we can.

After Stanhope had gone, Bowker sat glowering and thinking. A good ten minutes passed before Knight considered it sensible to make his presence known.

'He could have done it, if he had a motive,' he ventured.

'Everybody I've talked to so far has got a bloody motive for killing her,' said Bowker ferociously. 'Except the local bobby, and he's daft enough.'

'Nothing doing on the bank manager, sir,' Knight said with a doubtful shake of his head after taking a call. 'He's gone away for the weekend. I can roust out his Regional Director, if you say so, but it's going to take hours before we get a Warrant to see the books.'

'Leave it till Monday. Rowley won't run away, and if he does, he's our man. What have we got so far? If Stanhope is telling the truth, Mrs Hurst was dead or nearly dead by nine o'clock Thursday—which tallies with what that idle Doctor said.'

'I thought everybody knew everybody else's business in these villages,' said Knight, sounding slightly aggrieved, 'but not a soul in School Walk saw visitors to her cottage on Thursday. In fact, the only person who remembers seeing her at all that day is the old lady at number 4 who thinks she might have seen her at the baker's shop about midday.'

'Take my word,' said Bowker, 'villages aren't what they used to be. I don't think they ever bloody were. Besides, Lynn Hurst wasn't a villager; she was here only because she bought a house after the divorce. Or the ex-hubby bought it for her to get her from under his feet.'

'We know she knew a lot of people whose names she didn't put in full in her address book,' Knight suggested. 'Not all local telephone numbers.'

'If they were girlfriends, she'd have put their names,' Bowker said with gloomy relish. 'Asphodel, Buttercup, Celandine, Daisy. Get on to British Telecom, if anybody there works on Saturdays, tell them we want a name and address for every bloody number in this book, and we want them in the next thirty minutes.'

One man's name written out in full in the leather-bound book was *Harvey*. Desk research established that Dr Harvey Hurst was associated with an expensive and highly esteemed private clinic at Oxford. The phone number was for his riverside house on the Thames, not far from Abingdon.

On the phone the housekeeper said Dr Hurst was out and might be at the clinic, but she expected him back before long for a dinner-party he was giving. But at the Princess Margaret Rose Clinic, an overhelpful receptionist voice said Dr Hurst was not there.

'Oh sod it,' said Bowker when Knight relayed the news to him, 'I was hoping he'd be doing a life-and-death operation through the night on minor Royalty, or a major pop-star, maybe a brain transplant, so we could call it a day. I half-promised my wife I'd be home in time to take her out.'

Until this moment, it hadn't occurred to DS Knight that Denis Bowker could be married. It was a difficult thought to grapple with; he found himself baffled to envisage the sort of woman who would marry the Mad Mangler. The door-mat type who liked to be rolled on? Or the self-contained sort living a life of her own parallel to his? Or had the impossible happened and Bowker found a big bold woman he couldn't put down, someone like himself? Knight decided he'd find an excuse to go 'round to the Inspector's home as soon as he could, to get a look at Mrs Bowker.

'What do you want to do then, sir?' he asked.

'We'll drive to Abingdon and ruin Dr Hurst's dinner-party for him. Why should he have it good when the rest of us are working all Saturday evening to find out who murdered his ex-wife?'

'*All* evening, you said?'

'We'll put up for the night here at a pub; then we can get an early start tomorrow. There's no point driving back and forth like bloody commuters, not when we know what we're looking for is right here in Long Slaughter.'

'How do we know that, sir?'

'I'm buggered if I know how we know, but I know we know. That good enough for you, or do you want the song-and-dance version about coppers' hunches? Or the unconscious interpretation of something we've seen or been told which we didn't recognise the importance of at the time? Bloody hell, Knight, you're making me sound like our least-favourite Fantasy Artist, Mr Collapsing Bloody Worlds.'

'If you say what we're looking for is here in Long Slaughter, sir, that's good enough for me.'

Knight had heard that Bowker mostly ignored evidence and procedure and cracked his cases by glaring at people till they confessed. He thought it was a joke, like the Mad Mangler nickname, but he was beginning to change his mind now he'd seen him in action.

3. hawthorne lodge

It was dark when Bowker rang Dr Hurst's door-bell and followed up with a brisk rat-a-tat of his knuckles on the wood. He held his warrant card in his hand at shoulder level, knowing of old the effect he had on nervous householders. Sometimes they took him for a burglar; women of a nervous disposition often thought he was a rapist come to do the dirty.

Hawthorne Lodge was a big house, white-walled, with eight or nine expensive cars parked on the gravel drive. There would be a lawn at the back, was Bowker's guess, running down to the Thames, a motor-launch for picnics afloat on summer weekends. A bottle or two of cool white wine with smoked salmon sandwiches. Private doctoring was well paid, particularly Dr Hurst's end of it: the knife.

It seemed unlikely the Doctor disposed of his ex-wife to save himself a grand and a half a month, not a lot for anyone living in this style. But if the divorce was a spiteful one, plenty of other possible motives suggested themselves. Everyone who ever knew a deceased was a suspect; that was always Bowker's line of approach to murder. Finding the right one was a only a question of elimination.

The porch light was on, the door opened and a woman wearing a plain black dress stood there, most likely the housekeeper. She saw Bowker's hulking figure looming out of the dark and stepped back with a gasp of fear.

She tried slamming the door, Bowker had a foot in it to stop her, while he waved his warrant card in front of her face.

'Police,' he snarled. 'I've come to see Dr Hurst.'

She cowered as he slid past her into the entrance hall. Knight followed quickly behind the Inspector to smile at her in a reassuring way and ask her politely to get Dr Hurst.

The dining-room was off to the left, they could hear laughing and chatter through the door. The housekeeper scuttled into the jolly proceedings to get her employer.

'Nice,' Bowker said, glancing 'round slowly at the pictures on the walls and a console table with a white marble bust. 'Not my taste, but the mark of a man with money to spend. Just the sort who complains to the Chief Constable about insensitive coppers behaving disrespectfully. So mind your manners, Knight.'

'Me?' said the outraged Detective Sergeant.

Dr Harvey Hurst came out of the dining-room and stared at his visitors as if they were charity cases suffering from unsightly diseases. Knight saw Bowker's shoulders hunch aggressively and heard a muted rumble of rage. He expected an outburst of words, but Bowker said nothing, forcing the Doctor to open the bout.

'Well, what do you want?' Hurst demanded, sounding petulant. 'This is inconvenient and inconsiderate, I've a dozen guests to dinner. If you've come about the speeding charge, I've nothing to say to you. I shall be represented in Court and fully expect to be exonerated. The whole affair was a travesty of justice.'

Hurst was nearing fifty, Bowker guessed, twenty years older

than his ex-wife. The photos in her album were misleading. He was a tall, thin man, long-faced, angular chin, greying hair combed forward Julius Caesar–style, to cover his creeping baldness.

He was wearing a dark-blue silk shirt and no jacket, closely-fitting black designer jeans with tasselled Gucci shoes. Ageing trendy was written all over him. Frothy coffee and bottled Spa water. A nineteen-year-old girlfriend at his dinner-party, for sure, Bowker decided, name of Mandy or Sammy or Cindy or another left-over diminutive from the past.

He glared at the Doctor and counter-attacked.

'I'm Detective Inspector Bowker. This is DS Knight. I'll tell you why we're here,' he said with barely-controlled ferocity, making the hair bristle on Knight's neck. 'I have to inform you that your ex-wife has been brutally murdered. I think you can help with my enquiries.'

It wasn't a direct accusation but it was near enough to stop the Doctor in his tracks. He stood silent a moment, staring at Bowker in slack-jawed dismay.

'Which one?' he said eventually. 'Sally or Lynn?'

Knight very nearly laughed, but Bowker seized the opportunity to attack again.

'You're telling me you've got *two* ex-wives?' he said, and he managed to make it sounded like a serious offence, punishable by a fine and a stretch of imprisonment. 'I'm talking about Mrs Lynn Hurst of School Walk, Long Slaughter.'

'I know where she lives,' Hurst said testily; he'd recovered his usual air of superiority, 'I don't believe you. You've made some sort of stupid mistake.'

'Have I? Then you won't mind coming with me to identify the body we've found? If there's any doubt who the victim is, the sooner we know the better, so we can get after the murderer.'

'Certainly not!' Hurst almost snorted. 'What sort of country do we live in when I can be harassed in my own home by policemen? Good God!'

'No one's harassing you,' said Bowker, his voice as menacing as ever, 'I'm here to ask for your co-operation. What makes you so sure Mrs Lynn Hurst hasn't been murdered?'

He hadn't addressed Hurst as *sir* once, Knight noted, and knew he was witnessing a Bowker bravura performance. He wondered how Bowker had managed to keep his job, let alone rise to the rank of Inspector. The file of complaints about him must be at least a foot thick. There could be only one answer; Bowker solved his cases and got his man.

'Why should anyone want to kill her? It's unreasonable,' said Hurst, who seemed to have shifted his ground. 'What happened?'

'This interview may last some time. Do you want to conduct it out here in the hall?' Bowker asked.

'In here,' and Dr Hurst led the way into a large sitting-room where empty glasses and full ash-trays indicated a long stretch of before-dinner chattering.

The walls were stippled off-white; the pictures on them were large blobs of scarlet, emerald, and indigo, signifying nothing. The exposed floor-boards were polished to a honey glow, a pair of silky-looking Bokhara rugs were placed strategically. It was the sort of room Bowker had expected to find after Hurst's blue silk shirt and hair-style.

'Sit down, sit down,' said Hurst unpleasantly.

He poured himself a glass of neat whisky from a decanter on a sideboard and sat down as far from Bowker as the arrangement of the furniture allowed. He pointedly did not offer his visitors a drink, depriving Bowker of the satisfaction of refusing it. A belligerent step or two put Bowker uncomfortably close to him, looming over the Doctor like a black thundercloud.

Knight stayed well away from the action, on the other side of the room, his notebook at the ready.

'What happened?' Hurst repeated.

'Last Thursday evening, between six and nine, a person or persons unknown called at School Walk and gained access,' said Bowker as deliberately and aggravatingly official as he could manage. 'A number of blows were struck to the back of Mrs

Hurst's head, resulting in her death. The body was discovered this morning by a man friend who entered through a rear window when he got no answer.'

'My God!' Hurst sounded shocked, but not too shocked—certainly not broken up by the news.

'Where were you last Thursday, Dr Hurst, between six and ten in the evening?' Bowker asked with a scowl.

'Me? You expect *me* to account for my movements!' said Hurst in high dudgeon bordering on outrage. 'You can't possibly think I had anything to do with her death! We're divorced. I haven't seen her for two years, and I've spoken to her only once on the telephone in that time.'

'When was that? Recently?'

'Damn it all, it was last year, man!'

'Write that down, Knight. The Doctor said last year since he spoke to the deceased. When last year, exactly—spring, summer, autumn, winter?'

'This is ridiculous! In the spring, I think it was.'

'Now, Dr Hurst, I should like you to answer my question. Where were you last Thursday after six in the evening?'

'This interview is at an end,' said Hurst, almost squawking. 'I want you to leave my house at once. If there are any more of these ridiculous questions, you can address them to my solicitor at his office.'

He was on his feet, trying to shoo the policemen out. Bowker wasn't a man to be shooed; he stood immovable, like a cliff, with white waves breaking at its foot. Hurst was above average height, but Bowker's dark-clad bulk dwarfed him, and his expression was ferocious.

'I am investigating a murder,' Bowker said in a warning growl. '*I* decide when an interview is over. And this one isn't. So if you refuse to answer questions here, you will have to accompany me to Long Slaughter and answer them there. Is that clear?'

'No, it is not!' Hurst broke out angrily. 'You can't make me go anywhere with you, or answer your damn silly questions!'

'Make a note, Knight, Dr Hurst stated his intention to refuse to answer questions,' said Bowker with a cut-throat grin. 'I am now cautioning you, Doctor, that if you continue to refuse to co-operate, I have no alternative but to place you under arrest and remove you to the nearest police station.'

'What!' Hurst exclaimed.

'Oxford's the nearest with proper detention facilities,' said Bowker with vindictive enjoyment. 'You will spend the night in a cell while I obtain a search warrant to go through this house and see what you're trying to conceal.'

'You're mad, raving mad!' Hurst said, his face dark crimson.

'If you offer resistance or become violent during the arrest, I am empowered to use sufficient force to overcome you,' Bowker said with savage relish. 'You will then be taken away suitably restrained in handcuffs. Questioning will resume tomorrow after you have had time for reflection.'

Hurst stared with hate-filled eyes, not believing what he was hearing.

'Is that what you want?' Bowker demanded fiercely. 'All that for a few questions? Your dinner guests must already be asking each other what's going on. What will they think when they see you exit in cuffs between two plain-clothes coppers?'

'You're going to regret this, I promise you,' Hurst said from between clenched teeth. 'Ask your confounded questions and get it over with.'

'Where were you last Thursday evening?'

'Thursday, Thursday . . . yes, I played squash with a colleague, Dr Nigel Penwidden. You can check with him; he's at the Medical School in Oxford.'

'Till what time?'

'It must have been about six when I left him. I wasn't watching the clock. I was going to take a friend to dinner, but she rang up and canceled that afternoon.'

'You're avoiding the point,' Bowker said bluntly. 'What you didn't do is of no interest. What *did* you do?'

Hurst sat down again on one of the long facing sofas and lit a cigarette, giving himself time to think.

'I came back here.'

'Your housekeeper will confirm that?'

'I realise it must sound awkward to you, but Thursday is her day off. That's why I arranged to have dinner out.'

'Anyone phone you? Did you phone anyone? Were there callers you hadn't expected?'

'No,' said Dr Hurst, 'nothing. I settled down in front of the TV with a sandwich and a large vodka.'

'So you're telling me you were alone here all evening?' said Bowker in a tone of massive incredulity.

The Doctor nodded unhappily and stubbed out his half-smoked cigarette in an onyx ash-tray.

'Did you remain in the house the whole evening on your own? Or did you drive to Long Slaughter to visit your ex-wife?'

'Look here, I didn't murder Lynn. Is that what you want me to say? Write that down in your damned notebook. We divorced over two years ago. She was out of my life. I tell you frankly I may not have wished her particularly well, but I have no reason to want her to die. In spite of the split-up, there was a residual regard of some sort, at least on my part.'

'Someone she knew wanted her dead.'

'Yes, well, I know nothing about that,' Hurst said unhappily, flicking imaginary cigarette ash from his close-fitting black jeans. 'I can't say what sort of men she's been running round with since the divorce.'

'Before the divorce, what sort of men interested her?'

There was pure hatred in Hurst's eyes as he stared at Bowker. A painful nerve had been touched.

'She was on the make,' he said. 'She never loved me, she was interested only in money. It took me some time to realise it.'

'How would she go about making £42,000 in the past couple of years? Did you give it to her?'

'Certainly not! I bought her the cottage and paid a monthly sum in alimony, as ordered by the Court, though the whole thing was a farce from start to finish. She deliberately set me up.'

'With anyone in particular?'

'It's got nothing to do with it. It was my secretary, if you must know. She doesn't work for me now. Her name's Fiona Good.'

'We've found an address book with initials in it. Your phone number's there. Some of the others may be relatives. You'd know about your ex-wife's family.'

'There's a sister who lives in Chiswick. Mrs Myra Barton.'

Bowker had the address book in his pocket. He took it out and flicked through the pages. 'There's a Myra listed, with a London code.'

'And a brother who lives in Canada,' Hurst said. 'He was over for the wedding. No one else I know of.'

'Do you know Mr Mark Stanhope?'

'The name means nothing to me. Who is he, a friend of Lynn?'

'Your ex-wife was going to marry him. Did you know that?'

'She said nothing to me about it,' said Hurst, looking angry. 'Who is he?'

'But how could she tell you about him—you told me you hadn't been in touch with her for twelve months. Isn't that what he said, Knight?'

DS Knight made a show of consulting his notebook.

'Spring last year is what the Doctor said, sir.'

Without stirring a step, Bowker loomed over Dr Hurst like an avalanche about to crash down a mountainside. Hurst very nearly cowered away, then got a grip on his emotions and straightened his back.

'That's perfectly correct,' he said, the hint of a snap in his tone, 'but I am mildly surprised Lynn did not inform me of her plans. After all, it affects the alimony payments.'

Bowker changed tack to disconcert him again.

'The young lady you invited to dinner, who cancelled and left you at a loose end. Was it Miss Fiona Good, your ex-secretary?'

'No, it wasn't. I haven't seen her for months. And as you told me, what I didn't do has no interest for you. There is no point in naming her.'

'Thank you, Dr Hurst,' Bowker said, with a malign smile.

'You have been most helpful. I mustn't keep you from your guests any longer. There's still the business of formal identification of the deceased. You look like the best candidate.'

'I'm damned if I will!' Hurst said violently. 'I'm having no more to do with Lynn, she's caused me grief enough already. You can get her sister to identify the body.'

'We're talking about your ex-wife. Or, as you informed us, *one* of your ex-wives,' Bowker said in a voice like doomsday.

'Think what you like.' Hurst sounded very determined. 'I will not identify her body nor attend an inquest. Nor will I be involved in any other legal rigmarole. Is that clear?'

'Very,' said Bowker. 'Write all that down, Knight, we may use it later on. I've no more questions at present, Dr Hurst, but I doubt if you've seen the back of us.'

On the way to the car he grumbled to Knight there was sure to be an official complaint by Hurst.

'You went at him a bit fierce,' said the Detective-Sergeant.

'Me? What gives you that idea? He started off very bolshy, so I reminded him he has a bloody duty to answer questions.'

'But he doesn't. Have a duty, I mean. If he wants to keep his mouth shut and say nothing, that's his right,' Knight said.

'And it's my right to haul him off to the nick if I've reason to suspect he's committed a crime. Not answering questions is the surest way to make me bloody suspicious. You know what the trouble today is? Everybody's seen American movies on TV—the bit they remember best is say nothing to the police in case they incriminate themselves. Why the hell do they think we ask them questions at all, if not to incriminate them?'

'You went a bit bloody far when you offered to duff him up,' said Knight, wondering if he was going too far himself.

'I did no such thing! All I did was explain what happens if persons under arrest offer resistance. The trouble is, he's the sort who plays bloody golf with the Chief Superintendent. Or, as he's a doctor, he's bound to be the bastard who cut the Chief Constable's prostate out.'

'You don't seem all that worried about it, sir.'

'Well, of course I'm worried. It means a long moan from Chief Superintendent Horrocks about my approach to the public. I know his sermon by heart. It's very tedious, well-meaning but bloody tedious.'

Dr Hurst's pink gravel drive was cluttered with the shiny and expensive cars of his dinner guests. Bowker had been forced to leave his dusty Honda out in the road. He had parked under a lamp post, to deter any local vandals. Knight thought Dr Hurst's upmarket road an unlikely place to find teenage yobs breaking car windows to snatch radios. Bowker's bleak view of humanity did not exclude the possibility.

'As a matter of interest, sir,' said Knight, 'if Dr Hurst had resisted arrest and started a punch-up, have you got cuffs with you?'

'You think I walk 'round with bloody handcuffs in my pocket?' Bowker said in high dudgeon. 'I rely on my DS for that. Meaning you. Don't tell me you've come on a major investigation without a truncheon and a pair of handcuffs!'

Knight thought it best to say nothing to that. Bowker laughed and told him he always kept a pair of cuffs in the glove-box of his car.

From Oxford and Abingdon the eastward-flowing Thames swings in a wide curve south to find a gap in the Chiltern Hills. The way to Long Slaughter was by minor roads, winding, unlit and lonely, hedges and trees on both sides. There were sudden turning climbs up steep hills. Bowker drove the car with the fury he brought to everything, far too fast for the road, peering morosely over the steering-wheel as if expecting a lunatic yokel to drive a herd of squealing pigs across the road at any minute.

'What do you make of Dr Hurst, then?' Bowker asked.

'An easy man to take against on sight,' Knight said, trying to be diplomatic. 'I need to sort out personal feelings from facts before answering your question.'

'You're having a go at me, Knight,' said Bowker, with a sideways grin. 'Stop tiptoeing through the bloody tulips and tell me what you think about him.'

'He made it clear he didn't like his ex-wife, but I can't see much of a motive for murdering her. Not unless he's so hard up that the alimony makes the difference. It's no problem to look into his finances. That what you want me to do?'

'Don't forget about life insurance, while you're looking into the cash considerations. It wouldn't be surprising to find he'd insured her life while they were married; but if it was a lot of money and he kept it on after the divorce, we'd need to ask him why.'

A lone car came at them 'round a bend and passed within inches on the narrow road. Its lights briefly illuminated the interior of Bowker's car, Knight had a glimpse of the Inspector's heavy shoulders hunched over the wheel and the look of outrage on his swarthy face.

'Bloody maniac, driving at that speed on a cart-track! If I had room to turn 'round here, I'd go after him and run him in for dangerous driving!' Bowker shouted.

Thank God we're spared that, Jack Knight thought with a grin. Bowker hauling in a motorist who'd had a couple of pints of ale in a local pub was an experience he would gladly forgo. That was a job for a uniformed bobby. To divert the Inspector's ire from the pursuit and apprehending of delinquent drivers by night, he asked about Hurst.

'You're serious about the Doctor being a possible, are you?'

'I'm always serious. We've got another runner lined up at the starting-gate, that's my view. Make sure he's telling the truth about the telephone call. See if he's been phoning Lynn, and if she's called him recently. Last year was what he said, but to me it sounded bloody unconvincing.'

'His motive would be money, then?'

'How do I know? Money or sex, the usual motives. In his case, it might be both. He still has a lot of feeling for her, though she gave him a hard time. I wouldn't be surprised to find he's seen her on and off ever since the divorce.'

'For what?'

'For a dabble, what do you think for? You said yourself when you read the letters in the cottage that he was besotted by her—sometimes that doesn't wear off, even if the couple concerned hate the sight of each other.'

Knight thought it improbable, but he knew better than say so. In his book, liking, loathing, desiring, hating, did not mix up together. Love-hate was a freakish idea TV dramas liked to play about with. In DS Knight's experience the average person was not so complicated. Love could turn to hate with catastrophic results, but not the two together. It wasn't reasonable.

Not unless you were dealing with a nutter; then anything was possible, however horrible. Nobody could tell what a head case would do, or why. Not even psychiatrists who popped up in Court to get killers off with an eighteen months' suspended sentence.

All the same, phone calls and possible meetings between Hurst and the victim would have to be checked, if Bowker said so.

'We'd better have a word with this Fiona Good,' Bowker added. 'The divorce seems to have been about her, though Hurst wasn't giving much away. See if she's in the local phone directory. He said he hadn't seen her for months, but he came across to me as a slippery customer.'

'Don't like him much, sir, do you?'

'Me? I don't go about liking or disliking people, they're all just suspects to me. Hurst is a possible.'

'Copper's hunch again?'

Bowker paused for a moment before answering. When he did, it was at some length. 'Leave aside heat-of-the-moment killings, where a husband or a wife loses control in a nasty quarrel and sticks the carving-knife into the other. Think for a minute about deliberate cold-blooded murder, which is what we have on our hands. Someone who plans it out and arrives with the weapon up a sleeve or wrapped in brown-paper.'

'I see what you mean—we're not looking for a vicar or a nice old lady. But I never thought we were.'

'Smashing in the back of someone's head is a messy and brutal job, Knight. It takes tough-mindedness, determination, control. We're not talking about one hard blow that dropped her, she was hit six or seven times after she was down, blood and brains and bits of bone all over her head. Not for a squeamish person.'

'It needs someone like a Doctor, you mean, who's used to the sight of blood and guts on the operating table, and carries on regardless?'

'Maybe, but it could just as well be the District Nurse. What I'm telling you as part of your education is not to lose sight of the psychological aspect. From what we know so far about the victim, there's a bloody lot of psychology about this case.'

Hearing Bowker mention psychology came as a surprise to Knight. He was pretty sure the Inspector viewed everyone in the world as criminally inclined: those who hadn't committed an offence already were virtually certain to do so eventually. But it seemed sensible to Knight to keep his mouth shut.

Live and learn, that was the way to go about it.

Bowker parked outside the police house in Long Slaughter. An old lady was coming out. He stood aside for her. She stopped on the doorstep to stare up at his face.

'I saw you this afternoon in School Walk. You're the detective they've sent because of the murder.'

'That's right,' Bowker agreed.

'While you're here, I want you to find my cat,' she said, her voice firm in spite of her age. Bowker put her in her seventies.

'I'm sure PC Whitelock will do that better than I could,' he said, surprising Knight by the sympathy in his voice.

'No, he won't,' she said sharply, 'it's nearly a week now, and he's done nothing. That's why I'm here, to make sure he hasn't forgotten. And all I get for my trouble is to be told he's busy with this wretched murder.'

'Well, he *is* busy,' Bowker said gently. 'We all are. But I'll talk to him myself and find out how far his investigation's got into your case. Tell me your name. Mine's Bowker.'

'Pankhurst,' she said, '*Miss* Pankhurst. And the cat's name is Tiger. He's a ginger tom, nearly four years old.'

'Has he run away before?'

'He hasn't run away, he's been stolen.'

'He's valuable, then?'

Mavis Pankhurst was poorly dressed in a cheap brown coat and a straw hat with imitation cherries round the brim. She didn't look as if she owned anything of value.

'I've been told there's a gang stealing cats,' she answered. 'They want them for the pelts, you see. They skin them and sell the fur to crooked traders who make them up into mink coats for foolish women. Ten shillings a cat they get. If Tiger's dead, I want who did it put in prison.'

'You ever heard of a gang of cat-stealers working this patch, Knight?' Bowker asked.

'No, sir, never,' said Knight, struggling not to laugh.

'Nor have I. You go on home, Miss Pankhurst, and we'll do all we can to find your cat. Where do you live, is it far?'

'I live at number 6 Yatnall's Rents,' she told him. 'It's in Badger Lane. You're very welcome to come in for a cup of tea if you're 'round my end of the village, Mr Bowker. And if you're a good detective and bring Tiger with you, I've got half a bottle of sherry left over from Christmas you can have a glass of.'

Bowker wished her *Goodnight* and took the hand she offered. He shook it very carefully, Miss Pankhurst looked frail enough for her arm to drop off if he was too vigorous. She nodded to Jack Knight and walked off down Bridge Street slowly. Bowker watched her go and shook his head in sympathy. He was muttering under his breath as he went into Whitelock's house.

'What next!' Knight heard him say. 'Lost cats and dotty old women. Colorado beetles and bloody mad cow disease! Who'd ever want to be a country bobby! That Whitelock must be retarded to stay in a place like this.'

4. .... *the black swan*

Outside the Black Swan, by the old stone bridge over the Thames, was a sign announcing *Pub Grub*. It was a description Bowker had learned to distrust over the years as it often meant no more than warmed-up shepherd's pie, mashed potato with bits of gristle. A slab of good cheese with a crusty roll was a better bet in most town pubs.

The landlord of the Black Swan had a belly like a beer barrel and a mottled red complexion that suggested he was his own best customer. He introduced himself to the two policemen as Arthur Cawley, and showed them up to the rooms PC Whitelock had booked for them. He put himself in Bowker's good graces by suggesting steak for dinner.

The Black Swan was neither big enough nor busy enough to run to a separate dining-room. When Bowker and Knight came down to the saloon bar for a pre-dinner pint of ale they found a table set for them at the end furthest from the darts-board. And well set, with a crisp white cloth and shining silverware.

The building was old and the ceilings low, dark brown wooden panelling on the walls, a plastered ceiling once white and now stained dirty yellow by generations of smokers. Bowker ducked his head going through the door into the saloon bar and kept it ducked as he crossed the plain wooden floor to the table.

The windows were small and curtained in chintz, but there was a night-view of the river at the back, beyond a paved area with metal tables and chairs.

It was too early in the year for even the hardiest drinker to sit outside, and much too dark. Even at nine in the evening, not more than eight or nine people were drinking in the saloon bar, two of them playing dominoes at a table, without a word to each other, the rest in two groups at the bar. From time to time one or other would glance furtively across at the plain-clothes men and say something in an undertone.

'Fine bloody lot, the local peasants,' Bowker said to his DS, 'but at least the landlord's got more sense than to have one of those awful bloody Space Invader games. American juke-boxes and beeping Japanese game machines are the death of English pubs.'

'I thought it was the TV that did the pubs in,' said Knight. 'It's Saturday night, and there's less than a dozen people here. And two of them are reluctant coppers who'd rather be somewhere else, given the chance.'

'Now, now, look at the upside. You're on a murder enquiry, and it will look good on your record when we've got it sorted out.'

Knight suppressed a shudder as he thought about what Bowker's record looked like. In the short time they'd been together he'd seen Bowker steam-roller two witnesses and guessed he'd done as much to the other one, the next-door neighbour with the beard.

If by association with Bowker Knight's own record acquired a big black mark or two, that could put the mockers on his chance of promotion.

The trick was to survive this investigation, somehow fend off the flying muck and hope they collared the murderer before many more civilians got the Bowker treatment and started complaining or writing to the newspapers—that really made the top brass furious. Hang on till Bowker's regular DS came back from leave, then slide out from under.

Arthur Cawley served the meal himself, balancing well-loaded plates on each hand. He brought them a large steak apiece with a fried egg on top, and a pound each of crisp golden chips.

'My missus does the cooking,' he said. 'There's apple crumble for afters. Are the rooms all right?'

'They'll do,' said Bowker, too blunt to say much in praise of tiny bedrooms under a steep-sloping roof, iron bedsteads put in sometime during Queen Victoria's reign, bed-linen the years had worn paper-thin.

'Do you get many people staying here in the summer?' he asked.

'A few,' said Cawley, 'not that we try to be a hotel. Bed and breakfast is just a service to the travelling public.'

With that unlikely claim to serving the public, he went to the bar. An ample-bosomed barmaid in a knitted pullover was coping adequately with such trade as there was, the few drinkers there preferring to stare at her rather than at the landlord.

Knight tried not to watch Bowker tackling his food. A hearty appetite was one thing; Bowker's was voracious. He ate with the steady and unstoppable rhythm of a giant mechanical digger at an open-pit coal mine, plying his knife and fork on the steak, jaws chewing ponderously. He had emptied his plate and put down his knife and fork before Knight was halfway through.

Mrs Cawley's apple crumble with thick cream was as plentiful as the steak and chips. It took a determined effort by Jack Knight to finish his, but Bowker sailed through it.

'Good,' he said, 'a faint tang of cinnamon with the apple. I like that. I'll tell Whitelock tomorrow he made a good choice, sending us here. I like to eat well—I was on a fearful bloody investigation once where I had no choice but eat days on end in one of those roadside pull-ups for lorry-drivers.'

'I thought truckies did all right in those places.'

'All right for breakfast, maybe, but fried eggs and bacon and sausages three times a day for nearly a week isn't funny,' said Bowker belligerently.

'Why didn't you drive on somewhere else?'

'I was a DS at the time. My Inspector thought the man we were after would turn up there, and he made me wait for him. We were after a rapist. Offered girls a lift in his truck. Beat them up afterwards, beat them really viciously. He brain-damaged one so badly she was crippled for life, and another was blinded in one eye. There I sat in a dirty shirt and two days without a shave, pretending to be a truckie, eating all that greasy food while I waited for a bloody driver with heart-and-dagger tattoos up his arms. I can't tell you what I suffered from indigestion.'

'Did you get the bastard?'

'He turned up eventually. My Inspector was right about that—the pull-up was on his regular run. Big chap, one gold earring and a beer belly. When I told him he was nicked, he threw a mug of boiling tea at me and tried to kick me in the familiars.'

'Did you have any back-up?'

'Two uniforms in a squad car parked 'round the back. I had time to knock hell out of that evil swine before they came trotting to his rescue. It was to let him know what his victims suffered when he beat them up, that's what I said to myself. But to be honest, some of it was to pay him back for my indigestion.'

'I suppose his lawyer complained about police brutality after that.'

'Not only did he complain, the slimy sod got up a petition to drop me in the clag, and got it signed by a dozen truckers from the pull-in. But there were two who testified in court that it was Chummy who started the fight when I arrested him.'

'What did he get?'

'Seven years. For reasons I never fathomed, they charged him with only three offences, though we put up eight girls he'd done. So with time off for good behavior he'll be out by now and on the rape again.'

When the landlord came back, instead of removing their plates he pulled up a chair and sat down with them.

'Bad business that in School Walk,' he said affably. 'She was a nice enough woman, Mrs Hurst. Not that she came in here much, but she's been once or twice.'

'With who?' Bowker asked. 'Women don't usually go into pubs on their own. Not with leering yokels staring at their chests.'

'Last time was with a flashy-looking chap. He drives a silver Mercedes, I know that because he parked it outside. Her new boyfriend, he'd be, I should think.'

'We've talked to him. Before him who was there?'

'Another man. Not long before Christmastime. Not a local, so I can't tell you who he was. I remember him because he wore a long black leather overcoat, the sort you see Nazis wearing in old war films.'

'Young, old, English, foreign?' Knight asked, producing his notebook.

Cawley puffed out his cheeks in an effort of concentration. 'About the same age as her. If he'd sounded foreign, I'd have remembered it, and as I don't, I think he must be English.'

Bowker grunted, and Knight put away his notebook. There wasn't going to be anything worth writing down in vague memories.

'Why I came over now,' said the landlord, 'was for something else altogether. It's like this. One of my regulars over by the bar, Barry Crick, he thinks he's got something to tell you. He wanted to come and bother you soon as you walked in, but I told him to wait while you had your dinner.'

'Which one is he?' Bowker, turned to stare at the men at the bar.

'Him with the standing-up wavy hair and the brown jacket.

But before he spins his yarn, I'd better warn you he's not all that reliable. He tells tall tales, Barry, particularly where women are concerned. I'll say no more. Shall I send him over?'

'Do that.' Bowker grinned menacingly. 'Give him a pint of whatever he's drinking and put it on my bill.'

'He's drinking Jamaica rum. You want me to give him a pint of that, Mr Bowker?'

'Hellfire! Just give him a double and push him this way.'

After a while, Barry Crick, with a touch of bravado, sauntered across to the policemen's table, a glass in his hand and a grin on his face. He looked to be in his mid-twenties, but Bowker guessed he was younger, a strongly-built man with a weathered outdoor complexion and dark hair standing up like a pan-scourer. He was wearing newish blue jeans, and a brown suede jacket over an open-necked purple shirt. There was a thin gold chain round his burly neck.

'We've got the bloody village Casanova here,' Bowker declared to Knight in a quick aside. 'Thick as a brick and sly with it.'

'Want me to write that down, sir?' Knight asked innocently.

Bowker glowered good-naturedly at him and pushed a chair out with his foot for Barry.

'Sit down, Mr Crick. I understand you've something important to tell me.'

'Might have. Arthur says you're here to see about the murder. Is that right?'

'That's right. We're here to investigate the suspicious death of Mrs Lynn Hurst in School Walk. Did you know her?'

'Not to say *know* her. I mean, not like we were friends, as you could say. But I knew who she was and where she lived.'

Bowker nodded, his expression almost genial. 'Bound to be noticed 'round the village, a good-looking woman like Mrs Hurst, and living on her own.'

Knight could hardly believe what he was hearing. Bowker in a mood of sweet reason, cheerful and friendly. Not even a hint of strong-arm tactics. And addressing a yokel as *Mr*—it had to be a con.

'The trouble was,' said Crick, his leer as subtle as a punch in the ribs, 'she found her friends from outside the village. There were plenty in Long Slaughter as fancied her, but they never got a look-in.'

'That's the way of it with women,' said Bowker. 'Contrary in all they do. Ever been inside her cottage?'

'Not me, no such luck. I used to give her a come-on grin when I saw her around, to let her see I was interested, but it never amounted to anything. More's the pity.'

'When was the last time you saw her?'

'Ah, that's just it, you see. It was last week. She was with somebody I know, and I couldn't believe my eyes.'

Bowker leaned back in his chair, making the wooden back creak under his weight. He looked at Barry Crick with an expression of moderate interest.

'Who?' he asked.

'It was Roy Sibson. I saw him in that white car with her, and I couldn't believe it. He was sitting there bold as brass next to her and talking to her. Roy Sibson, I ask you!'

'Friend of yours, is he?'

'No friend of mine. He was once, but we had a falling-out two summers back over Jilly Ratcliffe. He said I put her in pod, and I knew for certain it was him. I'd been careful, you see.'

'What did Jilly say?' Bowker raised his eyebrows.

'She didn't know. How could she be sure about it, walking out with the two of us? Ever after that I knew Roy was no friend of mine, trying to drop me in it like that. I haven't spoken to him from that day to this.'

'Where was this you saw him with Mrs Hurst?'

'On the road to Wormwold. It was a nice afternoon, and she had the top down on her car. Two miles down the road it was.'

Bowker nodded to Knight to get all this down in his notebook.

His manner was still amiable. Maybe the meal had mellowed him.

'Which way is that? I don't know this area.'

'You go down Church Street, till you're out of Long Slaughter and then you're on the Wormwold road. It follows along by the river. There's not much down that way, only farms and that, till you get to Wormwold itself. That's the best part of seven miles.'

'What were you doing there at the time, Mr Crick? Out for a stroll?'

'It's my work,' he explained, and emptied his glass. 'I'm on the road-mending for the County Council and we were tarring and gravelling. There's six of us in the gang. We've got the lorry and a steam-roller and a tar-boiler.'

'And all the gang saw Mrs Hurst's white Volkswagen go by with Roy in it?'

'We whistled at her,' said Crick with a grin. 'She had to slow down past us where we'd blocked off half the road for tarring. She'd got a scarf round her head, and her hair floated about in the breeze—well, we all fancied her.'

He was sitting sideways to the table, in a graceless posture he considered macho, one elbow on the table, legs sprawled out, thick thighs apart to display the tight fit of his jeans.

'So all the gang will remember the white car with the woman driver they whistled at?' Bowker said. 'But will they remember seeing Roy Sibson with her?'

'I'm the only one who comes from Long Slaughter. I know Roy—he's Long Slaughter like me—the others are from miles 'round. I'm the only one who recognised him, the sly bugger.'

'Didn't you say to your mates on the gang something like *Hey, I know him, that's Roy Sibson, the sly bugger?*'

'What, give him credit for being with her in her car? Not me— if she'd pulled up for a minute, I'd have given him a punch in the face for putting one over on me like that. I didn't know he knew her, let alone get taken for a ride in her car! So I said nothing, but I thought a lot.'

'What's in Wormwold? I mean, why would she take him there? Do you have any ideas?'

'They were never going as far as Wormwold,' said Barry Crick, leering like a gargoyle on a cathedral. 'Down the Wormwold road is where Long Slaughter lads go courting. You can lie down with your girl on the riverbank under the trees and be private together. Other side of the road there's hedges and fields and nobody about. There's broad grass verges where you could park a car.'

'You make it sound bloody poetic,' Bowker said thoughtfully.

'It made me furious when I saw Roy with her, thinking he was off for a rollick and me sweating at putting tar on the bloody road. Why should Roy have the luck, not me? He's never been anything special.'

'How old's this Roy Sibson?' Knight asked, note-book poised.

'Same as me, we were in the same class at school. I'll be twenty-two this year, like him.'

'Say they were off for a rollick together,' said Bowker. 'Why in a car down a country lane? Why not in Mrs Hurst's cottage? They'd be a long sight more comfortable in bed.'

'Don't know,' said Crick. 'She was stuck-up, thought herself better than the rest of us. She mightn't want the neighbours in School Walk to know she'd let Roy have her.'

'What time of day was it?'

'Middle of the afternoon. We'd stopped for a drink of tea out of the flask when the car went by. We were talking, and then we all whistled at her together. About three or half-past, I don't know.'

'Last week, you said. Which day?'

'Tuesday. I know that because what we were talking about was the football on TV the night before—the Monday Match, they call it. Spurs versus Rangers, a right shambles it was from start to finish. Did you watch it?'

'No, I didn't. Just so I've got it clear in my mind, when you say you saw Mrs Hurst and Roy last week, which last week do you mean? Today's Saturday. Do you mean Tuesday just past, or was it the Tuesday last week?'

'He means this week, sir,' said Knight. 'I watched that game. He's right about it being a shambles.'

'The Tuesday four days ago, is that the one you mean?' asked Bowker, sure his DS was right, but wanting to hear it from the witness.

'That's it, Tuesday last week, four days back,' Crick agreed, highly amused that a policeman couldn't understand simple words like *last week*.

Bowker sat in thought for a second or two. He made a rasping noise in his throat that drew Knight's attention to him in time to see his face darkening and the veins stand out like cords on his neck. His shoulders seemed to thicken and bunch, his fists clenched. It was like seeing good-hearted Dr Jekyll change into malevolent Mr Hyde.

Barry Crick was staring open-mouthed at the Inspector. Knight thought as Bowker seemed to grow bigger and bulkier that he was going to grab Crick by the throat and shake him like a rat in a terrier's jaws. *Mad Mangler is about bloody right,* the DS said to himself. *If he goes for the yokel, I'll have to drag him off. And he's three stones heavier than I am!*

'Now listen to me carefully, Barry,' said Bowker, his tone of voice that of a High Court Judge sentencing a wrongdoer to twenty-five or thirty years' hard labour on a bread-and-water diet. 'I'm going to check every little detail of what you've told me. And when I find out what lies you've told, God help you!'

Crick was visibly alarmed.

'I swear I've told you the truth, without the word of a lie,' he said, beads of sweat appearing on his forehead. 'Why would I want to tell you lies?'

'To get your own back on Roy. Nobody but you knows him on the road-mending gang. You said so yourself. It might have been the Kleeneze Brush man with Mrs Hurst, or her bank manager, or her regular boyfriend. But you've got an old score to settle, and so you've put Roy on the spot. Think hard, Barry, before you sink yourself so deep in the clag you'll suffocate.'

'It *was* Roy—my bloody oath it was! If you don't believe me, you can ask him where he was Tuesday afternoon last week.'

'I mean to,' said Bowker. 'Where does he live?'

'Four doors from me in Orchard Row. He's at number 23, we're number 19.'

'What, you're nearly next-door neighbours? Don't tell me you haven't seen him since Tuesday! He must have had a good laugh at you about getting his leg over. Or did you make it all up?'

'I told you I'm not speaking to him. I haven't seen him since then, no reason why I should. I go to work early in the morning, and he goes out later to catch his bus.'

'It's Saturday today, you're both off work. You're bound to have seen him today,' Bowker insisted.

'I slept late. He works Saturday mornings. He'd be gone when I came out of the house.'

Bowker rose to his full imposing height, towering over Barry Crick, who seemed to shrink down in his chair, his arm raised half up to his face as if he expected Bowker to clobber him.

'You stay in this pub till closing-time, Barry,' said Bowker in a throaty growl. 'I'm going 'round to talk to Roy. If he says anything different from what you've told me, I'll come back for you, and you'll find out all about helping the police with their enquiries.'

According to the pub landlord, the distance to Orchard Row was too short to bother with the car. Bowker and Knight set off up Bridge Street, and although it wasn't yet 10:00, there was nobody about.

At the bridge end, by the junction with Church Street, there were a few small shops, a butcher, a chemist, a baker, the Post Office and grocery combined, a newspaper shop. After that Bridge Street was old houses. Bowker's great legs covered the ground at an uncomfortable speed, and Knight found himself almost trotting to stay alongside.

'He's not all there, Barry Crick,' said Knight. 'He can't be, if he thought he had a chance with a woman like Lynn Hurst.'

'Uncouth village charm might play hell with the local girls,' said Bowker, 'but our Lynn aimed upmarket. Is that what you're thinking?'

'Everything we know about her so far indicates that, sir.'

'You never know with women, Knight, some of them fancy a bit of rough. I ran a titled lady in for murder last year, and not that far from here. She'd been having it away with the gardener for ages. Nice-looking woman in her forties, very Radio 3, the way she spoke. There was some talk of her husband being made Lord-Lieutenant of the county. The gardener was a local lad, around Barry Crick's age, all muscle and straw-coloured hair, not much in the upper storey.'

'What did he do, try to blackmail her?'

'Nothing so villainous. One afternoon after a roll on the bed, he told her he was going to get married the next week to a girl he'd put in the family way. Her ladyship fetched one of her old man's shotguns and gave him both barrels, close up. You never saw such a bloody mess. His insides were splattered all around the room.'

'All the same,' said Knight, holding his ground, 'I don't see Lynn Hurst as randy Lady Chatterley. She comes over as a woman with an eye to the main chance. There's no Caribbean trips and pink champagne to be got out of yokels.'

'She got the high-life from boyfriends like Mark Stanhope. It might be to her liking to enjoy a bout of sweat-and-thump with a Long Slaughter thickie now and then.'

'I don't see it myself,' said Knight. 'The men in her photo album were the same sort, smooth and flash. If she had a bit of rough now and again, I'd expect to see a photo or two. Navvies with no shirts and jeans so low they show cleavage behind.'

'Women don't usually do what you expect them to,' Bowker said in a voice fraught with suspicion. 'In your opinion, then, if she was out with Barry's mate on the courting patch on the Wormwold road, it wasn't for a diddle by the Thames?'

'*If* it was him in the car, they were going somewhere else and for a different reason. That's what I think, sir.'

'Time will tell,' said Bowker, sounding amazingly reasonable. 'This must be Orchard Row on the right.'

Perhaps once upon a time Orchard Row was a pleasant backwater of thatched cottages and pretty gardens with tall foxgloves and lupins. If so, then progress had overtaken it. What Bowker and Knight saw when they turned off Bridge Street was a short road of council-built semi-detacheds, put up in the 1950s, ugly and shabby. The front gardens were overgrown grass and bare patches of earth.

At number 23 curtains were drawn over the street-side window, a light was on inside. Bowker rat-tatted at the front door and showed his warrant card to the woman who opened it. In reply to his polite request to speak to Mr Roy Sibson, she said he wasn't in and tried to close the door.

To Knight it seemed that Bowker hardly touched the door, but it flew open hard enough to make the woman step aside quickly.

'You don't want the neighbours knowing your business,' Bowker said as he strode over the door-step. 'We'll come in for just a minute while you tell us where to find Roy.'

Knight followed the Inspector down a short passage cluttered with hanging coats, into a sitting-room. A large TV stood on a sideboard. There was a quiz show in full swing, with shrieks of maniac merriment from a studio audience. A man and a woman sat staring at the screen, both in their late fifties.

The woman who let them in was wearing a shirt and blue jeans. She was under thirty, and wore a wedding ring on her finger. She was pretty, or would be but for her worried and drawn expression.

'Mrs Sibson?' Bowker asked calmly, under the circumstances. He disliked his entrance being barred.

'Harris,' she corrected him. 'Mrs Harris. Roy's sister. This is Mum and Dad.'

Mum and Dad had glanced up briefly at the visitors when they came into the sitting-room, then back to the TV, not interested in whoever it might be come calling at this time of night.

'Where can we find your brother, Mrs Harris? We need to have a word with him.'

'Well, you can't,' she said sharply. 'He's on his holidays.'

'Knight—turn that bloody machine off!' said Bowker, temper rising as he felt himself being thwarted. 'I want everybody to hear me.'

The DS found the switch and turned it off. As the screen went dark, Roy's parents muttered and scowled at him.

'I'm Detective Inspector Bowker,' the Inspector announced at loud-speaking volume to the room at large, to make sure he was heard and understood. 'I want to know where to find Roy Sibson. You, Mrs Sibson, where's your son?'

Mrs Sibson was a plump woman in a home-knitted pink pullover, unsuitable dark-blue stretch-pants and carpet slippers. Vaguely she looked at Bowker, as if he were a quiz-master asking her to answer an impossibly hard question to win a microwave oven.

'Don't know,' she said, after she had thought it over for a few seconds. 'He's away. Ask our Joyce, she'll know.'

'When did he go?' Bowker asked, holding her attention with a beady stare. 'When did you see him last?'

'It was one day in the week,' Mrs Sibson said. 'When was it— Tuesday or Wednesday, Billy, do you remember?'

Mr Sibson shook his head in doubt and hooked his thumbs into his braces. He had a thick grey moustache but had lost most of his hair. A few wisps of streaky-brown clung above his over-size ears.

'Don't ask me,' he said. 'I don't see him from one week's end to the next. Always out somewhere, he is.'

Bowker was beginning to seethe. He was making growling noises as he switched his glare to daughter Joyce. She was standing by the door, arms folded, jaw set, no intention of asking them to sit down.

'Well, Mrs Harris?' Bowker said in a menacing rumble. 'When did your brother go away?'

'Wednesday,' she said, shaky but standing up to him. 'He said he had a few days off from work.'

'What sort of work does he do?'

'He works for the Chalfont Building Society in Reading.'

Bowker and Knight exchanged a look. Lynn Hurst's savings book was from the Chalfont Building Society—the book with a balance of over £42,000 in it.

'Where has he gone on holiday?' Bowker asked.

'He didn't really say. It might be Spain. Or Malta even.'

'Mrs Harris, do you know the reason I'm in Long Slaughter?' Bowker asked in a warning tone.

'Because that woman's been killed, I suppose. It's nothing to do with me, or Roy.'

Knight saw Bowker's face darkening at this obstructionism, and he headed off the imminent outburst. 'The Inspector didn't suggest it was. But the fact is your brother was seen with Mrs Hurst a day or so before she was killed. We want to ask him about that, so we can cross him off our list.'

Joyce Harris stared dumbly at Knight, her face paler now than when they came in.

'How long had your brother known Mrs Hurst?' Knight asked in hope, rather than expectation of a sensible answer.

'Our sort don't know her sort,' said Joyce. 'Anybody who says different is telling you a lie.'

Bowker had been looking 'round the room while Knight asked the questions. On the sideboard by the now-silent TV stood a large framed colour photograph, a wedding scene outside a grey stone church. Joyce, in a long white dress and a veil, was hanging onto the arm of a man in a new suit and a fixed grin. Mum and Dad in Sunday best were to one side, a young man with sleeked-back hair standing with them.

'Nice,' said Bowker, picking up the picture. 'Was that at the local church?'

Joyce nodded. 'St Elfreda's, summer before last, when Reg and I got married.'

'And this is Roy here, is it, standing by Mum and Dad?'

She nodded again.

'I can see the resemblance to you,' Bowker said, genial in a terrifying sort of way. 'Is your husband about, Mrs Harris? Roy might have said something to him about where he was going.'

'He went with a coach-load to watch Reading play Southampton. They'll do a pub-crawl 'round Southampton afterward, there's no saying when he'll be home. He'll be in no state to talk to you—there's no point in waiting.'

'I'll borrow the photo for a few days,' said Bowker. 'You'll get it back. Knight, write Mrs Harris a receipt for it.'

Five minutes later, they were out of the house. They heard the roar of idiot laughter from the TV before they got to the road.

'Roy's done a runner,' said Bowker with hearty cheerfulness. 'His sister's nerves are in shreds and tatters. She suspects he murdered Lynn, and she's covering up for him. Guilty knowledge, Knight.'

'Shouldn't be too hard, finding him.'

'We'll go to the local bobby's house and start the hunt going from there. But with tact, no talk about arresting him. We want to speak to him in connection with our enquiries. Got it?'

'Tact,' said Knight, finding it hard to associate that virtue with Detective Inspector Bowker. 'Kid gloves and delicacy.'

'If we're lucky, he went off in Lynn Hurst's car; and if we're very lucky, the poor silly sod is still driving it 'round.'

'There's enough coppers looking for that car already,' Knight said. 'It's only a question of time before it's spotted.'

'We'll get the Building Society manager to audit his books or whatever they do, to see if any money's missing. Roy might have made those deposits in Mrs Hurst's account by transferring cash from some other account.'

'Doubt it, sir, not over any length of time. They'd be bound to spot it. Even with bloody computers keeping accounts instead of clerks with pens and big books.'

'You're having a go at me, Knight, you insolent devil. I know they'd have spotted it, but it still has to be checked. There's a connection between him and her, that's pretty certain. Money and sex mixed are as good a motive for murder as you'll find.'

5. ⋯⋯⋯⋯⋯⋯⋯⋯⋯⋯⋯⋯⋯⋯⋯⋯⋯⋯ *birley spinney*

On Sunday morning Bowker lent Jack Knight his tired-looking car and sent him to London to find Mrs Myra Barton, the dead woman's sister, and talk to her. They had her phone number from Lynn's book, from which it was easy to get her address in Chiswick.

'Talk her into identifying the body for us,' Bowker told his DS. 'Only take her a minute if you offer to drive her, but make sure that idle doctor's finished his butchery and put her back together again before you take the sister there. We don't want to shock her and be accused of police brutality.'

'No, sir,' said Knight patiently. 'Are you happy with the ex-husband refusing to do the formal identification?'

'Happy?' said Bowker, his gypsy complexion turning black as thunder. 'What bloody silly question is that to ask? *Happy?* I am *not* happy about that slippery bastard Hurst, not by a bloody long chalk! He told me lies—barefaced lies—and that's not the sign of a man with a clean conscience.'

'What lies, sir?' Knight asked, sorry he'd triggered the outburst.

'We shan't know that until we check the little he told us. My instincts tell me he lied to my face. He's hiding something.'

'For instance?' said Knight, greatly daring.

Bowker scowled at him like Frankenstein's monster and did not answer directly.

'Refusing to identify a body is one of the stupid games some people try to play with the police,' he said, his voice full of foreboding. 'We're supposed to conclude from it that he doesn't give a sod about his ex-wife. She's nothing to him; he couldn't be bothered to bash her skull in.'

'Well, it's just possible he's too broken up by the news of her death to go through the ordeal,' Knight suggested, but not very sincerely.

'Or he can't face his own handiwork,' said Bowker. 'You know what they did in the Middle Ages when somebody was done in? It was easier then. They made people touch the body. They believed it started to bleed again when the murderer touched it.'

'Handy for a detective, if it was true, sir. Do you think our Dr Hurst is that superstitious he won't go near the body?'

'I see you grinning, Knight, but don't go thinking I've wiped the Doctor off my little list because we've found a lead on Roy Sibson. I mean to cause that medical person a certain amount of grief before all this is over.'

'Right. I'll be on my way to Chiswick, sir.'

'Wait a minute. I haven't finished briefing you yet. Find out all you can about Lynn Hurst from the sister. What was she like— have we got it right, or are we jumping to conclusions? Have a really good dig and see what you turn up. I'd go myself, only there's too much to get going here in Long Slaughter. I want to look 'round Roy's bedroom for a start, and I don't really want to ask for a Search Warrant at this stage. I'll have to sweet-talk his sister into letting me ferret about.'

It seemed highly unlikely to Knight that Bowker would be able to persuade the defensive Mrs Harris to let him search in Roy's room. Sweet-talk was not an art for which the Inspector had any obvious talent.

'Don't let yourself be sidetracked at Chiswick,' said Bowker with a warning scowl. 'Be firm and keep at it till you get some useful answers.'

'I'll follow your example, sir.'

'Clear off, you cheeky sod. Get back soon as you can—there's plenty to do. And don't wreck my car with careless driving.'

While Knight drove to London the Inspector settled himself in the official part of PC Whitelock's house and made himself busy on the telephone. There had been no sighting yet of the missing white Volkswagen, nor of Roy Sibson. The list of names and addresses to match initials and numbers in Lynn's address book was not yet ready. Exasperation was an emotion Bowker was prone to.

A frogman team was promised for that afternoon, to see what was to be found in the Thames under and near the bridge. It was so obvious a place to dump a weapon that Bowker had great hopes for it. What the blunt instrument had been, he had no idea, but he thought it was probably metal. With a brick or a stone, there were usually bits left in the wound.

He had seen nothing in Lynn Hurst's clotted hair except her own dried blood and bone fragments. That made it likely the assault was with a heavy metal object. Might be a hammer, a weapon easy to get hold of by anyone planning a murder. Forensic might have something to say eventually; Sunday was a bad day to get action out of anybody.

The branch manager of the Chalfont Building Society had to be tracked down at his home. But he wasn't there. He proved to be at church, highly bloody commendable, Bowker snarled, no use to me. 'Have him ring me when he comes in, I've got some really bad news for him.'

Bowker was at Whitelock's old metal desk. Whitelock was up at the counter at the front where members of the public stood and stated their business; lost cats, stolen bicycles, whatever was irking them. He was talking to a woman in a green raincoat and a pony-head scarf round her hair. After a while he came over to speak to Bowker, who was scribbling himself a morose note: *What else does Hurst have to lie about besides doing his wife in?*

'Sir, there's a reporter here from the local paper. She wants a statement to print. What shall I tell her, we're pursuing our enquiries and expect an early result?'

'That's bloody good, Whitelock. You'll make a detective yet.'

'Thank you, sir, very good of you, but I never want to be in the plain-clothes branch. I like it here in Long Slaughter.'

'Girl reporters,' said Bowker. He shook his head as he stared across the room at her. 'Crime reporters used to be hard-bitten old drunks when I was a constable. Bloody famous they were; men who never missed a story, especially if they could sex it up at all. Downright notorious, some of them were. They bought you a double whisky and shoved a tenner in your hand—anything to get a lead they could use.'

'That right?' PC Whitelock was impressed.

'You could tell them any old Mary Ellen, and they'd put it in the paper. The laughs I had out of them! Now the paper sends a girl. I don't know if that's Women's Lib in action, or the red-nosed old drunks all died off. But one way or the other, it's got to be progress.'

'Of a sort,' Whitelock said doubtfully. 'What do you want me to do?'

'Send her across. I'll talk to her. Nobody could tell lies to a nice young lady like that.'

Her name was Sara Thomas. She was from the *County Examiner,* a paper so old-fashioned it was a wonder it was still publishing. She was fair-haired and pretty, not very tall. She smiled up at Bowker warily as he lumbered to his feet to shake hands.

She undid the raincoat when she sat down, revealing a striped red frock. Nothing wrong with her shape, Bowker decided with a gleam of approval. He indulged the usual male speculation about her naked body while he told her who he was. She wrote his name in a thick shorthand notebook.

'What can you tell me, Inspector? For publication, I mean.'

'We are investigating the death of Mrs Lynn Hurst, whose body was discovered yesterday at her home. She was hit on the head sometime on Wednesday, according to medical reports. And that's about all I can tell you.'

'I knew that already. I've talked to the cleaner and tried to talk to the neighbours, but they're not very helpful.'

'Cleaner? Damn it and blast it—why didn't somebody tell me there was a cleaner! Who is she?'

Miss Thomas grinned and flicked back through her book. 'Mrs Ardwick, lives in Cow Lane. Goes in—or rather went in—three times a week to clear up, Mondays, Wednesdays, Fridays.'

'What can she tell us about Wednesday and Friday this week?'

'I'm only the reporter here,' said Sara Thomas with another grin. 'You're the policeman. Shouldn't you have questioned Mrs Ardwick?'

'You've saved me the time, Sara. Tell me what she said, and I'll tell you something for your story in return.'

'Something important?'

Bowker nodded, amused by her eagerness. She would be about twenty-two or twenty-three, he thought, probably not on the paper long and very keen to show the News Editor what she could do. Looking for a career in newspapers, aiming for Fleet Street or whatever they called it now. At least she wasn't likely to turn into a red-faced old drunk of a crime reporter. Or was she? You never knew in these days of equal opportunity for all. Equality to go down as well as up; not many seemed to grasp that.

'Mrs Emma Ardwick,' said the reporter, not bothering with her shorthand book, 'went in on Wednesday to clean, chatted to Mrs Hurst, finished about four-thirty and went home. She says that she saw nothing at all out of the ordinary.'

'We think Mrs Hurst was attacked between six and nine that day, so the cleaner had gone by then. What about Friday, when there was a body lying on the carpet? What does she say about that?'

'Would you believe it? She didn't go in on Friday. Had a bout of her rheumatism, she says. Gets it all down one leg, can't do much except sit by the fire with a drop of whisky in hot water and take two aspirin—that's her story.'

'If she'd gone to clean on Friday, we'd have found the body a day earlier,' Bowker said thoughtfully, 'but I don't suppose it would have made any difference in the long run. Did you talk to Mrs Hurst's neighbour with the beard?'

While he asked the question, he was jotting *Ardwick, Cow Lane* on a notepad. The cleaner might be able to give him some useful tips on Lynn Hurst's boyfriends, past and present.

'Mr Rowley—yes, I did,' said Sara. 'He wasn't in a talkative mood. In fact he told me to "eff off." He said he'd had enough persecution and he'd sue the paper if I didn't leave him alone. Seemed a bit paranoid at the time. You must have upset him.'

'Me? Not a bit of it, we had a pleasant chat. He even showed me his paintings, strapping blondes with death-ray guns, things from Outer Space, all that Science Fiction nonsense.'

'Is he a suspect?'

'You know I can't answer a question like that. All I can tell you is he's no more a suspect at present than anyone else who knew the deceased.'

'That can mean anything,' said Sara. 'Now I've told you all I know. What's the hot item you promised me?'

'Mrs Hurst's car is missing. There's a chance it was taken by whoever killed her. I'll write the registration number down for you and a description of it. We're looking for it, and it might give us vital information when we find it.'

'That's great,' said Sara. 'Thank you, Inspector. Will you be here for a few days? I'm sure they'll send me back again.'

'I'll be here till I catch the murderer—you can rely on it,' said

Bowker, sticking out his jaw in a show of honest pugnacity to impress her with his determination.

She'd do a nice piece about him on the front page. With a bit of luck, Chief Superintendent Maurice Horrocks would go blue in the face when he saw it.

'What's your first name?' Sara asked, still scribbling.

'Denis, with one N. I'll tell you something else you can use— I'll have a diving team here later today to see what's down on the riverbed. Get your editor to send a cameraman, you'll get a picture or two. I'll even let him take my photo.'

Off she went, mission accomplished. Bowker felt pleased he'd made someone happy that day. If only it were always that easy.

'Whitelock,' he called across to the constable, 'do you know somebody called Emma Ardwick? It seems she went cleaning three times a week for the deceased. Lives in Cow Lane—what bloody names you call things 'round here!'

'Cow Lane? That's down the end of Orchard Row where you saw the Sibsons. It runs into Thames Street by the river, where the almshouses stand on the corner.'

'I don't give a bugger where it runs to!' said Bowker, going dark in the face. 'I asked you about somebody called Ardwick!'

'I know Emma Ardwick. She was very nearly in bad trouble, not long back. Goes out scrubbing, does she? I didn't know that.'

'What sort of trouble? Did you run her in, or what?'

'Not trouble with us, sir. It was to do with her Benefits. A man with a briefcase came from the Social Security. The way I heard it, she gets Child Allowance payments, the Social Security and her Widow's Pension. I think she gets something paid by the parish as well—there's an old charity to look after hard-luck cases in the village.'

'On the fiddle, was she? Not our business. I want to talk to her to see if she knows anything interesting about Mrs Hurst's callers. Is she the nosy sort?'

'That I don't know. She's pretty sharp, though. From all they say, she persuaded the chap from the Social Security somebody'd made a mix-up and she had seven kids to claim for.'

'Has she?'

'Never seen more than four myself, but how can you be sure? And as you said, sir, her Social Security money's not our business. They've got Civil Servants to investigate claims. Live and let live is what I say.'

'Spare me your village villainies!' said Bowker. 'You're the good shepherd in Long Slaughter, I'm sure you know everything about your black sheep.'

'Thank you, sir. Do you want me to walk you 'round to Cow Lane and show you where Mrs Ardwick lives?'

'I can find my own way. A walk will do me good after sitting here all morning. I'll have lunch at the Black Swan and call on Mrs Ardwick afterwards.'

It didn't work out so conveniently. Bowker was eating his way through a massive helping of roast beef with Yorkshire pudding when he was interrupted by PC Whitelock in a hurry. The ten or a dozen drinkers in the Black Swan saloon bar went silent and strained their ears to catch what Whitelock was telling Bowker.

'We've found the missing car, sir. It's just down the road a way, not above three miles. There's a dead man in it.'

'Roy Sibson, is it?'

'Can't say for sure. The man who found the car didn't stay to look. He came straight to me to report it.'

Bowker put down his knife and fork, his sigh expressing regret and exasperation. If the car had been found twenty minutes later, he would have had time to finish his lunch. The landlord's missus had promised treacle tart with cream after the roast beef.

'Come on, then,' he said. 'Got your car here? Take me to it. Have you notified your Sergeant and all the other routine?'

'All done, sir. Scene-of-Crime, the Doctor, Coroner's Office, Forensic—all on stand-by on your authority, till you tell them there's a body.'

'Who's in bloody charge here?' said Bowker. 'Me or you? But at least you've saved me some time, I'll concede that.'

Kevin Whitelock's police car was outside the Black Swan, blue light flashing on the roof, looking very official. Bowker pushed the passenger seat as far back as it would go. Even then he had to bend his legs double to fit in.

'Which way are we going?' he asked as Whitelock zipped away from the kerb, foot hard down.

There wasn't much excitement in Whitelock's life, mostly Foot-and-Mouth-Disease regulations, or some bloody fool sicking up and falling down drunk in the street when the pubs closed. Now the chance was his, and he was making the most of it. He'd have put the siren on, but Bowler glared at him and shook his head.

'Over the bridge, sir, out towards Sandy Bottom.'

He turned onto the old grey stone bridge, empty of traffic on a Sunday lunchtime, and accelerated hard down the middle.

'Stood here since 1768, this bridge,' he said. 'The date's on the keystone, with the name of the chap who paid for it. Local squire he was, Sir Peverel Talbot. Seems there was poverty and unemployment about, so he set the village men to work labouring at eightpence a day, carting stone for the bridge. You can read it all there in carved letters.'

'Skip the guide-book chat. Who found Mrs Hurst's car?'

Across the bridge there were two rows of old brick houses, an off-licence on a corner, a tin tabernacle with a sign declaring it to be the Evangelical Church of the Second Coming. That was the end of Long Slaughter.

The police car was speeding along a tree-lined lane, its blue light flashing and no one to see it but an occasional cow with its head over a gate.

'Local farmer, sir, Bobby Liggins. Taking a walk with his dog 'round his land and noticed a car parked in Birley Spinney. Not his land, where the spinney is, but joining it. He went to see who'd be parked off the road on a Sunday morning this time of the year. I expect he thought it was a courting couple.'

'And did he stop to gawp at what he'd found?'

'He says he came away quick without touching anything soon as he saw the pipe. Bit shook up by it.'

'Pipe? What bloody pipe?' Bowker said savagely.

'From the exhaust into a side-window, so he says. And inside there's a man dead on the front seat.'

'Right car, is it?'

'Positive, sir. White Volkswagen. He wrote the number down on a bit of paper. It's the one we're looking for—Mrs Hurst's.'

'This Farmer Giles who found it—anything known?'

The question took Whitelock by surprise. His jaw dropped and the car wobbled on the road.

'You can't think Bobby Liggins had a hand in it,' he said in a tone of astonishment. 'He's well thought of 'round here, gives a lot to the church at Harvest Festival time.'

'I don't care if he pays for the bloody Salvation Army all on his own! When somebody finds a dead body, the question always has to be asked. You should know that. Some silly buggers think we'll be baffled if they kill somebody and then report the body themselves.'

'Not Liggins, sir, he's very respectable. Gives the prizes at the horse show, grows a lot of barley for the brewers.'

'That's no bloody recommendation, I saw something very nasty in a barley field once,' Bowker snarled, his tone so forbidding that Kevin Whitelock daren't ask him what.

'That's the turn to Liggins farm,' he said, about half a mile further on. 'You can see the house from here. He'll be waiting for us by Birley Spinney.'

Bowker was not entirely sure he knew what a spinney was; some sort of small wood, he thought. He decided against exposing his ignorance of country matters to the constable, and in another five minutes he saw he was right. There was a broad gap in the hedge without a gate, and beyond it a rough track to a wood of young trees. He knew they must be young because they had thin trunks.

A mud-spattered Land Rover was parked by the gap, and beside it stood a middle-aged man in a corduroy jacket and a tweed hat with a brim turned down all the way 'round. He had a briar pipe clenched between his teeth, puffing billows of blue smoke into the air. He'd brought his bloody dog, Bowker saw with a scowl, a bloody great shaggy hound of a thing, black and white with a tail like a yard-brush.

'Mr Liggins?' said Bowker, climbing out of the police car. 'Detective Inspector Bowker. Where is it, then?'

'Not far in the trees. Sway sideways and you'll catch just a glimpse of white—that's what caught my attention.'

Bowker had no intention of swaying. He was going to march up to the stolen car and see it properly.

'Have you been back to it since you reported it?' he asked.

'No, only this far. There's my footprints in the soft ground, going in and coming back. One set, that's all. And Blackie's.'

'Blackie's the dog? Right, now you stay here, Mr Liggins, in case anyone turns up and tries to drive in. The constable and I are going into the wood to have a look.'

'Spinney,' said Bobby Liggins, 'not a wood. Not what we call a wood.'

Bowker ignored this rural gem of wisdom and told Whitelock to stay close behind him and not make more tracks than need be. He started for the spinney, watching the ground. Just like bloody Hiawatha, he thought, tracking a buffalo, a fine bloody caper for a grown man. Tyre tracks crisscrossing each other faintly, several sets, some of them made by tractor wheels, to judge by their size.

None of them looked very recent, except one set which were a bit clearer than the rest. And Liggins seemed right; there were footprints here and there going in, and others coming out, both the same.

The track went into the spinney to the middle, curving to the right, and evidently used to haul timber away when trees were cut. At the end, where it opened out for tractors to turn in, a white Volkswagen was parked. Bowker looked for footprints, saw none, and went up to the car, Whitelock behind him.

A length of green garden hose ran from the exhaust-pipe up to the near-side window, which had been wound nearly to the top to grip the pipe and hold it in place.

'Stand still and don't touch anything,' Bowker ordered.

He moved 'round the car slowly and carefully, looking for any sign of getting in or out. The trees sheltered the car and the ground was dry. There were unclear marks that told him nothing much. He put a hand on the bonnet. It was stone cold.

He looked in through the windscreen. He didn't expect to see the inside fume-filled, not after the hours that must have gone by since the engine stopped for lack of fuel, but it was still murky. A man in a grey jacket lay sideways on the front seat, an empty Haig whisky bottle on its side near his head.

'He's dead enough,' he announced to Whitelock. 'Been here for some time, if I'm any judge. There's nothing we can do without the experts, no point in hauling him out. Drive back to Long Slaughter and set the cog-wheels turning, I'll stay and talk to your pal Liggins till the Doctor and assorted others get here.'

Bowker used his handkerchief to grip the door handle and pull it open. He touched the dead man's neck, cold as the grave and stiff as a board. His eyes were closed and his face was pink, a sure sign of carbon monoxide poisoning.

There was no suicide note to be seen, but it might be in his pocket. Bowker decided to wait until photos were taken before moving the body to search.

He thought of leaving the car door open to let residual fumes dispel while he went back to the road to wait, but there might be wild animals about; never sure about those things out in the countryside. If one got in and had a nibble of the body there would be complaints. He strolled back to the road to wait, and he had a long wait, after all it was Sunday lunchtime.

It began to rain hard. Bowker and Bobby Liggins and the dog got into the Land Rover. The farmer had a half-bottle of brandy in the glove-box and offered a drink. Bowker accepted; he was a man never inhibited by rules.

The hairy black-and-white dog snuffled and scratched itself

behind the seats. Bowker stared morosely through the windscreen at a sodden landscape and knew why he hated the countryside.

'Out walking, then, were you?' he asked. 'I'd have thought an upstanding chap like you would be at church on a Sunday morning and not striding 'round the acres.'

'Never go now except at Christmas and Harvest Festival,' said Bobby Liggins. 'I can't stand the new parson—he's a different breed from the old chap. Goes on about social awareness and the deprived. Never a bloody word about religion. Somebody like you not knowing Long Slaughter would think to hear him ranting that we've got barefoot children starving in the streets.'

'I didn't see any myself,' said Bowker. 'Nobody takes bloody parsons seriously these days. Always go for a walk on your own, Sunday morning?'

Liggins gave him a hard look. 'I don't know what you're getting at. Damned if I do. It's plain to see that chap in the car did himself in. That was the first thing came into my mind when I found him. It's to do with the murder of that poor woman in Long Slaughter, got to be. The way I see it, he killed her and then himself. Remorse—there is such a thing, you know.'

'There is,' Bowker agreed sombrely. 'I've seen what people do to themselves because of it. Very nasty, sometimes, poor sods. Did you know the woman who was killed, Mrs Hurst?'

'Met her once, in the Post Office, a very fine-looking woman she was. Elsie Warley who runs the Post Office introduced us to each other; that was the only time. She wasn't Long Slaughter-born. Came from Oxford a year or two back, I think. They were talking about her last night in the pub—not kindly either, I'm sorry to say.'

'In the Black Swan? I didn't see you when I was there.'

'You wouldn't. I drink in the Bull's Head. They keep the beer better there. Other end of Church Street from the Black Swan.'

'I'll remember. What were they saying about Mrs Hurst?'

Bobby Liggins took his terrible tweed hat off and rumpled his thinning brown hair with his hand. 'Usual chatter about a woman living on her own. Guesses and wishes, nothing real.'

'Anybody mention Roy Sibson?'

'He the chap in the car? I don't recall his name coming up.'

'Who could tell me if it did, or should? Who was the leading chatterer in the pub last night?'

'I don't know that I want to mention any names to you. Seems an unneighbourly thing to do, that. What's the point now you've got the chap who killed her, though he's beyond mortal judgement now. Surely you can leave it at that.'

'No, I bloody can't,' said Bowker, reining back his temper in the face of honest scruple. 'I've got to find out why he killed her before we can close the case. *If* he did—that's yet to be decided.'

'Can there be much doubt? Kevin Whitelock told me that it's her car he killed himself in. The motive seems obvious enough.'

'You're thinking it was most likely jealousy,' Bowker agreed gloomily. 'Silly young fool in love with a woman older and more worldly than him and soon out of his depth. But I've got to be sure, Mr Liggins. Someone who knew him saw him with Mrs Hurst in her car, a day or two before she was killed. But his sister denies it outright. What do you say about it?'

'You could try talking to Brian Fox, maybe. You'll find him in the Bull's Head most nights. He's the local scandalmonger.'

The rain was still pelting down hard when the police surgeon turned up, in convoy with a photographer, PC Whitelock bringing Sergeant Dobson, and an ambulance to remove the body.

'Nice weekend?' said Bowker to Dr Pendleton, a malicious grin on his face.

'Saturday and Sunday as well!' said Pendleton. 'Out back of beyond! What the devil are you playing at? Have you set up some sort of rural feud just to break up my family life?'

To Bowker's amazement, Pendleton put up a big red-striped golf umbrella to ward off the rain as he trudged into the spinney. Alongside him Bowker was getting very wet, his rumpled suit was turning even darker grey as it became saturated.

The photographer was sensible. He put on a vivid hooded yellow raincoat before he moved away from his car, a metal box of cameras and spare film hanging on a strap from his shoulder.

Bowker stood beneath dripping trees, shoes muddy and trousers snagging on brambles, pretending he was not getting wet through while the photographer took pictures from every angle he could think of.

Then it was the Doctor's turn. He examined the body where it lay, had the ambulance-men lift it out and set it down on the wet ground for a more extensive look.

Bowker held the Doctor's colourful umbrella over him while he knelt to examine the deceased. Roy was on his side, legs bent, very awkward to examine, his muscles set stiff in the attitude he had died in, slumped sideways across the car seat.

'Carbon monoxide,' pronounced Dr Pendleton, surprising no one at all. 'Rigor mortis fully developed, dead about twenty-four hours.'

'That's what I thought,' said Bowker, sounding impatient. 'It happened yesterday afternoon. Saturday's a nice quiet time in these parts, nobody much about. Has a post-mortem been done yet on the body I gave you yesterday, or is the medical profession pending everything till Monday morning?'

'The pathologist finished before teatime yesterday. I don't know when you'll see a report, I'm not responsible for typists' working-hours. If you'd been there you'd know what was found.'

'So you tell me what he found, in nice simple words, and none of that medical claptrap you try to baffle coppers with.'

'Woman in the prime of life, healthy. She wasn't pregnant and never had been, though she was sexually active. Cause of death was several very hard blows to the back of the skull, at least five, with a heavy metal object.'

'A hammer?'

'Hammers leave round dents. The assailant used something like a tyre-iron.'

Knight had seen a tyre-iron in Stanhope's car parked outside

Lynn Hurst's cottage. A clean new tyre-iron. It could have been washed and dried, to get rid of any blood and hair on it.

'Now we're getting somewhere,' said Bowker, forgetting he was soaked to the skin, his suit clinging 'round him. 'How sure can we be it was a tyre-iron? Not a crowbar, or a golf club or a coal shovel?'

'Humour does not become you, Inspector Bowker,' Dr Pendleton reproached him. 'You can be reasonably certain it was a tyre-iron. After the assailant knocked the woman down, he continued to strike her until he broke her skull open. Then he rammed the flat end of the weapon deep into her brain. The damage caused was extensive.'

'Bloody hell, he must have been certifiably sick in the head to do a thing like that!'

'Not necessarily,' said the Doctor, pleased he had scored one at last over Bowker. 'It was a logical thing to do—logical for a murderer, that is. He was making absolutely sure she died. Do I take it from your use of the past tense that this new cadaver of yours was the man responsible?'

'There's a good chance. I'd be be happier if he'd left a note to say he was doing himself in because of a guilty conscience. *Good-bye, Mum, I never meant to do it.* But there's nothing in the car I could see. Anything in his pockets?'

'That's your job, not mine,' Pendleton said.

He held the umbrella uselessly over Bowker, who could get no wetter, while he turned out the dead man's pockets. There was nothing of any use to him—£80 or £90 in the hip pocket of his jeans, half a packet of cigarettes and half a box of matches in his jacket pocket, a comb in the breast pocket. No suicide note and nothing to identify him.

'Oh, sod it!' Bowker said. 'No note.'

'Perhaps he was illiterate,' Pendleton said unhelpfully. 'The young often are these days, I find.'

'No, he worked in a Building Society office. He'd have to be able to read and count up to ten.'

'Office? Not with those hands,' said the Doctor.

He was right. The hands were rough and hard, nails broken off short, the hands of a manual worker. Bowker cursed himself for not noticing them before.

'You're a cold-hearted bastard,' he told Pendleton. 'An evil and irritating man, but you have your uses. You're right about this joker—he was no office-worker.'

'Whitelock!' Bowker shouted, his voice sending bedraggled birds flapping up from the tree branches about him. 'Where are you!'

'Here, sir,' said the local bobby, ambling to his side.

'Why didn't you tell me this isn't Roy Sibson?'

'Isn't it?' Whitelock said, sounding amazed. 'I didn't get a look at him. You told me to stand back when we saw the car.'

'No excuses!' Bowker growled. 'Who the hell is he?'

'I know him,' Whitelock said with quiet triumph. 'I took him in charge once. His name's Gavin Fowler. Lives in Thames Street just past the almshouses.'

'What did you run him in for?'

'Drunk and disorderly. I found him obstreperous on the foot-path outside the Bull's Head one night after closing time.'

'Can you be absolutely hundred percent bloody sure it's Fowler we've got here stone-dead and not Sibson?'

'Positive, sir. He was a big, strong lad, and he tried to give me trouble taking him in. It took a a good week for the bruises to fade on my chest where he punched me. He was a slaughterman by trade. He worked in the Co-Op abattoir over at Wantage.'

6. ························ *chief superintendent's office*

Ten o'clock Tuesday morning saw Bowker sitting in the office of Detective Chief Superintendent Horrocks, explaining what he had been doing for the past few days. And for once he was not being told off. In fact, Horrocks seemed moderately pleased with him. He was even chatty.

'Still reading Charles Dickens in your spare time, Denis?'

It was a source of wonder and amusement to Bowker's fellow officers that he was a Dickens fan. In fact, Dickens' novels were the only books he ever read. He had a complete set, given to him by his father on his twelfth birthday. They were worn and dog-eared by now but he still read them one after another, then started again at the beginning, taking the titles in alphabetic order. Each complete cycle took him about a year.

'Which one are you on now?' Horrocks asked. He had once taken a personnel course which taught the importance of being interested in subordinates' family life and leisure pursuits.

'*Hard Times*,' said Bowker. 'Have you read it?'

'I can't say I have.' Horrocks' total knowledge of Dickens' novels was limited to *Pickwick Papers* at school and the film of *A Christmas Carol* on television.

'Interesting story for a copper,' said Bowker, enthusiastic. 'It's about serious crime in an awful bloody black-pudding town up North. There's a chap stealing from his employer, who's his brother-in-law. Then a politician on the make fancies his young sister and tries to get his hand up her clothes. Just the sort of thing still happening. You remember the Euro-MP the Brighton police nicked with a thirteen-year-old girl in a hotel room?'

'Are you sure we're talking about the same Charles Dickens?' Horrocks said, astonished. 'The one who wrote that stuff about Christmas turkey and Tiny Tim? He didn't write crime stories.'

'All his books are full of crime. He was a police reporter,' Bowker said. 'There's all sorts of crime and criminals in them. Muggers, murderers, break-and-entry artists, gangleaders, moneylenders, theft, fraud, street riots, arson, kidnapping, sexual relations under duress. Every kind of lawbreaking we're still chasing.'

DCS Horrocks felt himself on unfamiliar territory. He thought he'd done enough in the way of personnel enhancement for one day. Back to the business in hand. The Hurst murder.

'Nice and tidy,' he said, head nodding, fingers tap-tap upon Bowker's report lying on the desk. 'Now you're satisfied Fowler killed Hurst and then himself, write it up and that's it—the coroner won't have any trouble with that.'

Horrocks was a broad and cheerful man, his benevolent manner totally misleading. He could be a bastard to a hapless copper who incurred his displeasure. Bowker had endured his wrath many a time, sometimes in silence, sometimes not. Usually it was for what Horrocks called his cavalier attitude to proper procedure.

But Bowker was well aware that Horrocks shielded him from far worse. Without the DCS to look after him, he would have been out on the pavement years ago. Horrocks liked results; arrests that made sense, evidence to convince a jury, convictions that stuck. While Bowker produced, he was safe.

The protection was unacknowledged on both sides. That made it awkward to cross Horrocks or disagree with him openly. Bowker's natural bluntness made it even more awkward not to, when he was sure he was right.

He stared over the desk with a morose expression at the DCS, who was wearing a nearly-new dark-brown suit. Probably meeting someone important at lunch, someone he was trying to impress, a Very Senior Officer. Why else would he wear a tie patterned in bright-coloured blobs? Not a copper's tie, that.

It was a pity to spoil Horrocks' good humour, but facts were facts. Things had to be said.

'I can't prove Fowler killed her,' Bowker said, mouth turning down at the corners. 'The presumption is that he did, but we've found no evidence at all.'

'We don't often get an eyewitness, Denis,' said Horrocks, a pained expression coming over his round and shining face now he recognised the signs of typical Bowker recalcitrance.

'You've got the car and the weapon,' he went on. 'The method is right for a slaughterman. You've got his suicide. What more do you want, Denis, a signed confession and a photo?'

'We found him dead in Lynn Hurst's car; that doesn't prove he stole it,' Bowker said morosely. 'The killing was done the way a slaughterman knows best; a metal bolt into the brain to stun and kill. It's as if it was planned deliberately to incriminate Gavin Fowler. I wonder he didn't hang her up by the ankles and slit her throat as well.'

There was a pained look on Horrocks' face; it was no longer kindly.

'But none of it's evidence,' Bowker ploughed on. 'A crafty lawyer could make us look fools in Court. The plain fact is, we haven't found even a ghost of a connection between Fowler and Lynn Hurst. Unless you want to think he was a nutter strolling in off the street to commit murder at random.'

'You've got the murder weapon,' the DCS pointed out. 'You

can trace that to him if you try hard enough. We're talking about a small community. How many places sell them?'

'We've got a tyre-iron the divers brought up from the river,' Bowker agreed, though his tone was mulish. 'Traces of blood and tissue on it, right blood group for Mrs Hurst. No prints on it, not a single print.'

Chief Superintendent Maurice Horrocks was starting to fume in a restrained way.

'Why are you being so bloody negative? he asked. 'There's no great mystery here that I can see. Do you seriously doubt that Fowler did it?'

'Other things being equal, though they rarely are, I have to agree, sir, Gavin Fowler killed her,' Bowker allowed, sliding in a most uncommon *sir* to flatter his edgy superior. 'But there's a bloody big *But*.'

'What do you mean, there's a *But*? What *But*?'

The green-wire-mesh In-Tray on Horrocks' desk was stacked six inches high with files and papers. In his Out-Tray were only a letter he'd signed and a memo he was sending back for retyping. He'd planned to give Denis Bowker fifteen minutes; now it looked as if it was going to take all morning.

'The assumption is that Gavin Fowler got his leg over Lynn Hurst,' said Bowker, scowling in concentration. 'In my view, it's bloody unlikely, but let's go with it for a minute. We next have to assume she gave him the Soldier's Farewell. At which Gavin took umbrage and broke her skull.'

'It's not inherently impossible,' Horrocks argued, knowing he would never convince Bowker now.

'It's bloody nonsense when you think about it,' Bowker said. 'She was right out of Gavin's league. She was used to more than a bag of fish and chips and a skinful of ale. That's all she'd have got from him.'

'After that Lady Mary–and-the-labourer case you were on, you can't be ignorant of certain facts of life, Denis.'

'He was a gardener, not a labourer. I said what you just said to my DS. Some women like it rough and sweaty. I didn't believe it much then, and even less since I got a Warrant yesterday and had a look into bank statements and telephone records. A lot of men contributed to Lynn Hurst's upkeep.'

That drew Horrocks' attention, it sounded more like fact than theorising. To Horrocks' pragmatic mind, theories were ten a penny, but facts could be evaluated.

'Blackmail, you mean?' he asked.

'I don't think they call it that any more. Though in one case it looks very much like it. She bought a new car fifteen months ago. The dealer's name is printed on the tax certificate holder on the windscreen, so he was easy enough to find. He took her old car in part exchange, and she wrote him a cheque for the rest, that being something over nine thousand pounds.'

'I don't see the connection.'

'A day or two before that, she paid a cheque for ten thousand quid into her bank account. Her next-door neighbour, a scruffy artist for comic books, wrote her a cheque for that amount. What it comes to is this: he bought her a new car. I bet he didn't mention that to his common-law wife.'

Horrocks was staring hard at Bowker, fingers drumming on his polished desk-top. He didn't want these complications, but they had to be listened to.

'There's no such thing as a common-law wife,' he said. 'It's a misnomer—you ought to know that.'

'Just a handy description,' said Bowker, eyebrows rising stubbornly. 'It sums up an arrangement between a man and a woman. Committed without being committed, you could call it. Relationships like that tend to be edgy. Particularly when there's a child.'

'Generalisations,' said Horrocks. 'Theorising.'

Bowker shrugged his big shoulders like a dray-horse flicking away a fly that was irritating him. 'But apart from that one-off with the car and the neighbour, I don't think she operated like that at all. She had a talent for friendship with well-off men. It wasn't a case of just one after another, the way models and star-lets do. She was able to keep several interested in her at the same time. They helped pay her bills.'

'Stop beating 'round the bush, Denis. Was she on the game?'

'Not if you mean one hundred quid down for a short-time. We've got a list of names and addresses of eleven men from ini-tials and phone numbers in her address book. It's being looked into and I think we'll find they wrote her cheques every now and then, five hundred quid here, a thousand quid there. They got their money's worth, I'm sure. She was a very good-looking woman. They could take her to Switzerland for skiing or to the South of France in the summer. She'd be a credit to them.'

'Talent for friendship!' said Horrocks, a frown creasing his forehead. 'Are you suggesting a connection between her death and these payments? One of her friends decided not to make any more contributions? That it?'

'You've got to admit it's a possibility, sir. So far I've had words with two of the men; it'll take time to get around to them all. They deny anything improper about the payments, as you'd ex-pect them to. Just cash presents from time to time to an old friend. My impression is that Lynn knew enough about them to make it hard to stop giving her presents.'

'Impressions are not evidence,' Horrocks said impatiently. 'I reckon we're talking blackmail here, and I'm surprised to hear you dressing it up as something else.'

'Blackmail, yes, but a genteel form of it,' Bowker said with a wolfish grin. 'The sort the victims enjoy, up to a point.'

'How the bloody hell do you tie this in with the dead man in her car?'

'I can't. There's something else, though. Her ex-husband, Dr Harvey Hurst, told me he'd not seen or heard from her since the divorce, only once, and that was last year.'

'That reminds me,' Horrocks interrupted with a pained look on his face, 'I've had a serious complaint about you from Dr Hurst. He alleges you threatened him with physical violence. What was that all about?'

'He went paranoid when I tried to question him. I did explain that if he continued to refuse, I'd have no choice but take him to the nick. I begged him not to make me arrest him.'

'You begged him!' Horrocks sounded disbelieving.

'I advised him not to make things worse. Being arrested at a dinner-party wouldn't do his reputation any good, and resisting arrest was a serious offence. I explained all that to him, sir, and eventually he calmed down and answered a few questions.'

'You know I've got to ask your Sergeant for his version.'

'Naturally you have to. I made him write it down at the time. Dr Hurst was obviously the sort who moans night and day when he doesn't have his own way. You've only to look at him to know he writes letters to the *Times* twice a week to complain.'

'That's as may be, Denis. But has he got a legitimate reason to complain about you, that's the point.'

'Question DS Knight,' Bowker suggested, his tone mildly hurt. 'His notebook will bear me out.'

'You sure about that? It was the Assistant Chief that Hurst phoned; it seems he knows him. What was it made him go twitchy? Nothing you said or did, I hope?'

'Bad conscience,' Bowker said pugnaciously. 'He decided that attack is the best form of defence. When he finally answered my questions, he told me lies. I knew he wasn't telling the truth, and I can prove it now I've seen copies of his telephone bills and his ex-wife's.'

'He lied about phone calls to her?'

'As soon as he knew she'd been murdered, he tried to distance himself from her. Very twitchy he was, and he had good reason to be—there've been calls from his number to her number, and the other way 'round as well, twice or three times a month for a year or more.'

'Interesting he lied about that. It might not mean much; she could have been nagging about her alimony,' Horrocks suggested. 'A lot of ex-husbands are slow payers.'

'Not Dr Hurst. There's a Standing Order at his bank to pay on the first of the month.'

'Hurst's bank, as well! You've been invading a hell of a lot of privacy,' Horrocks exclaimed in dismay. 'Why wasn't I told you were trampling all over people's rights to secrecy?'

'Well, being stuck out in Long Slaughter, it wasn't practical to get hold of you,' said Bowker. 'You're a very busy man.'

He meant that Horrocks might not have given him permission to proceed if he'd asked, so he didn't ask. Horrocks knew what he meant and groaned silently.

'As you say, the question is,' Bowker continued, awarding the credit to the DCS to ease his dismay, 'why did Dr Hurst and his ex-wife phone each other so regularly? To arrange meetings? I see that as the most likely explanation at present. Whatever it was, he lied to me about the calls.'

'Did he?' Horrocks' voice sounded strangled. 'I shouldn't think there's many bold enough to lie to *you*, Denis.'

'There are, though,' Bowker rumbled, shaking his head more in anger than in sorrow. 'The next-door neighbour with the beard told lies when I asked how well he knew Lynn Hurst. Hardly at all, he said, just to pass the time of day over the garden wall. But the bank accounts say he knew her ten grand worth.'

'It's not technically a crime to lie to a copper,' said the DCS, struck by the menace in Bowker's tone. 'Deplorable, that I grant you, but the public at large often have a tendency to fob us off with untruths for sly reasons of their own.'

'In a murder enquiry, it's a bloody serious matter, sir.'

'Of course it is, but where does that take us? You've turned over a big stone, and there are some nasty things crawling about underneath it. What do you want to do about it?'

'For a start, I want to find Roy Sibson and see what he has to say about his drive along the Wormwold road with Mrs Hurst. And I want to know why he's gone missing.'

'Are you sure he *is* missing? Have his family reported him as a missing person?'

'His sister says he's on holiday somewhere; he didn't bother to tell her where. Dear old Mum and Dad don't know what to say—they let the daughter speak for them. He hasn't been in to work since Monday last week. They thought he must be off sick till I asked the branch manager to see if there's any money missing.'

'Is there?'

'They're still looking. Or the computer is. Who can say when they will come up with an answer? If Sibson went abroad, as his sister claims, he had to buy a ticket. There's no travel agent in Long Slaughter. There are three near his office, and none of them has any record of a booking for him. We've put a query out to the package-holiday companies—no answer yet. What I want to do is have a look in his room to see if his passport's there. Or anything else of interest. I'll get a Search Warrant today.'

'The connection's pretty feeble,' said Horrocks, looking for the relevant bit in Bowker's written report. 'Mrs Hurst had an account in the Building Society branch where Sibson works. That could be a coincidence. If there turns out to be money missing, that's a different story.'

'He was seen with her two days before she was killed. In fact, he's the only man seen with her lately, except her boyfriend.'

'That's if you believe the word of—what's the man's name?' said DCS Horrocks, fumbling with the written report.

'Barry Crick. Not much of an upstanding citizen, but he's the best we've got at the moment.'

Horrocks glanced up at the clock on the office wall. He had a busy morning, but it wasn't working out as planned.

'What it comes to is this,' he said. 'You're satisfied Fowler killed Mrs Hurst, but not about the motive. And now he's killed himself, you can't question him about it. That it?'

'No, sir,' said Bowker.

DCS Horrocks couldn't be steam-rollered.

Bowker tried hard to make what he was going to say sound reasonable. 'Fowler murdered Mrs Hurst, though we don't know why. I don't think he committed suicide.'

'What?' said Horrocks in an anguished voice. He was appalled at this new and unexpected complication. 'What are you telling me, for God's sake? You can't think Fowler was murdered. Where in your report is there any evidence for that?'

'It's all there between the lines, if you look for it,' said Bowker stubbornly. 'Fowler was dead drunk when he died, bloody nearly a bottle of whisky in him, according to the post-mortem. The bottle was beside him, the top off and his prints on it.'

'Yes, yes, I've read all that,' Horrocks' fingers drummed on the desk-top. He had short and thick fingers, a wedding ring on the third.

'He was getting his courage up to kill himself,' he suggested to Bowker. 'Nothing strange in that. Suicides usually have to, it's not an easy thing to do yourself in. Fowler got very drunk to ease the dying.'

'Maybe. Suppose he was sitting in the car talking to someone, sharing swigs from the bottle, and he drank enough to make him nod off. Then the someone connected the hose to the exhaust and turned on the engine.'

'Supposition, nothing more.'

'His prints are all over the bottle except the neck, which is clean as a whistle, as if someone wiped it. Someone careful to hold it by the neck to drink, a someone who wants us to believe Gavin Fowler did himself in.'

'What are you on about, Denis? Is this a fairy tale?'

'Why did Fowler take Mrs Hurst's easily recognisable car when he killed her? It's a ten-minute walk from her cottage to where he lived. It was asking for trouble if he was seen driving it.'

'What's your theory, then? Why did he take it?'

'Because he was told to. The same someone who talked him into killing Mrs Hurst told him to bring the car away with him when he'd done it. Perhaps he was given a reason, of sorts. The real reason was so he could be found stark dead in it, apparently by his own hand. If we accept that, it brings the investigation to a close. The person behind it all can breathe easy again.'

'God love me! We're talking about an English village, not New

York City, Denis! Hired hit-men and double-killers—no, it won't do!'

'If I'm right, sir, what we've got is a double *killing*, not a double-killer. And if someone is to be killed by proxy, a good choice for it is a slaughterman. He kills twenty or more times a day and thinks nothing of it.'

'Cows, not people! There is a *difference*, damn it all. We've agreed he did it, you've said he was drunk when he died. Drunk when he killed her, most likely. There's a link between him and the dead woman, and I don't know why you haven't found it. Fifty-to-one, it's sex, in spite of what you say. She could have led him on; things got out of hand; he lashed out.'

'She was killed Thursday. You think he stayed drunk from then till Saturday afternoon? Then he was overtaken by remorse?'

'It's more likely than your theory.'

'It's not likely Fowler was a sensitive sort—not in his job, up to his knees in blood and guts every day. Not a trade for an intellectual type. After you've slaughtered thousands of great big dumb animals with your own hand, is there such a difference in cracking the skull of a person who means nothing to you? If someone you *do* know is making it worth your while? I can't see remorse in this.'

Horrocks got up from his desk and went to the window to stare out. The view was not likely to restore his mental equilibrium—his office overlooked the car park.

'It won't do,' he said, 'Fowler might not have been a regular *Guardian* reader, but you're pushing things too far. He wasn't a hardened crook, ready with a sawn-off shotgun when a guard gets between him and the money. How old does your report say he was, twenty-five? Lived all his life in Long Slaughter. Was he married?'

'He was twenty-eight, he was married and he had four children. He earned a decent wage, and he liked a drink. I talked to his wife, and she looks fifty, poor woman, squalling kids all over the sitting-room floor, her belly sticking out with another on the way.'

'When he didn't go home Saturday night, didn't she worry?'

'She thought he'd gone off with the coach-load to Southampton to see Reading play. She knew he'd be drunk afterwards. When he didn't get home by bedtime, her guess was he'd passed out. Not a big surprise to her—he'd done it before.'

'And next day?'

'When there was no sign of him Sunday morning, she thought he had spent the night with another woman and was still at it. Not the first time he'd done that, either.'

Horrocks ran his hand over his greying hair and went back to his chair. He stared at Bowker as if willing him to retract all he had said in the past fifteen minutes.

'Not a model family man, Denis,' he said. 'A right bastard, if you like. Beyond that it's only guessing.'

'It won't hurt to make sure,' Bowker said angrily. 'I want to talk to the ex-husband again, Dr bloody Harvey Hurst. I can pin his lies down now. And the next-door neighbour who bought her a new car, him and his monsters from outer space! And I haven't taken my eye off the boyfriend, either.'

'Why him?'

'He drives around in a flashy silver Mercedes and takes Lynn off for a weekend in Paris, first-class seats, expensive hotel, champagne in the bath, for all I know. And Mr Mark Stanhope is broke. His bank manager writes him nasty letters, the overdraft has to be reduced right away. A woman in Esher is after him for overdue child-maintenance payments, threatening to take him to Court and have him jailed.'

'How do you know that? You haven't searched his house, have you, for God's sake?'

'No, no,' Bowker said quickly. 'Information received.'

He was not about to tell the DCS he had his information from letters Jack Knight found in a briefcase in Stanhope's car.

Horrocks knew when he was being bamboozled. He glared

hard at Bowker and asked no more about his sources. 'Are Stanhope's financial troubles relevant?'

'Hard to say. Suppose he'd seen Mrs Hurst's Building Society book; it was in a drawer where anyone might come across it. Her forty-two grand would get him out of his immediate bother, if he could get her to lend it to him. Though from what we know of her, she liked to see money coming in, not going out.'

'Well, murders have been committed for a lot less than that,' said Horrocks, pleased to have a firm and understandable motive offered at last. 'It's a lot of money, forty-two thousand pounds, especially to a man in debt. Was he sure of inheriting it?'

'We shall know for certain when we find her will. It's not at her bank; we're checking with lawyers where she's lived before. It's in my mind that if you had forty-two grand, you could well afford to give a share to whoever you'd got to arrange the convenient demise of your benefactor.'

'A paid killer would insist on a down-payment in advance. Is there any sign that Fowler had more money than his wages?'

'We're looking. He gave his missus an extra fifty quid about a week ago—she's not sure which day. He told her he'd come up on a horse; that had happened before.'

'You've got far too many bloody suspects,' said Horrocks. He sounded disgruntled. 'What the hell am I saying? You've got me tied up in your spiderweb now! I was led to believe we had a straight-forward sex killing and subsequent suicide.'

'Not by me, you weren't,' Bowker put in sharply. 'I knew we'd something nastier than usual on our hands the minute I saw Lynn Hurst's body, a fine-looking woman with her brains on the rug.'

'Be that as it may, you'd better get to work and eliminate as many of your suspects as you can, including the one supposed to be on his holidays.'

'Roy Sibson? He's no more on holiday than I am!'

'Then, if he's hiding, why? Are you seriously suggesting he's the one who put Fowler up to killing Mrs Hurst?'

'It's possible, if he wanted to get out of any funny business with the Building Society she involved him in. But Roy's not my front-runner at the moment. There are two other obvious reasons he might have vanished.'

'Only two?' Horrocks said, quailing inwardly.

'One is he might have had a hand in the arrangements. Suppose Chummy is from outside Long Slaughter, Roy could have been the one who recommended Fowler to whoever it was wanted Mrs Hurst dead. Then it dawned on him he's an accomplice. So he's hiding himself until the investigation is dropped because Fowler is dead. Then he'll be back in Long Slaughter with a cock-and-bull tale about his holidays in sunny Malta.'

'How will he know when it's safe to come back? Read about it in the newspaper?' Horrocks asked, intending to be sarcastic.

Bowker shook his massive head mournfully.

'His sister knows more than she's saying, sir. She wears the trousers in that family—Dad and Mum sit silent. I haven't seen her husband, but I'd bet he jumps to it when he's told. Roy will follow her orders when the time comes, and he'll pop up again.'

'You said you had two reasons. What's the other?'

'Maybe Roy's frightened for his life. When Fowler was killed after the job, Roy would realise late in the day that Chummy is ruthless. Roy's a loose end. Dead men tell no tales. Roy's gone to ground.'

'I've never heard so many mixed bloody metaphors before! If you think Sibson's in danger, you'd better find him quick and see what he can tell us. According to your theory, he knows who Chummy is.'

'I'm working on it, sir,' Bowker said doggedly. 'His photo's been circulated. A lot of coppers are looking for him.'

'A lot of coppers were looking for Mrs Hurst's car,' Horrocks pointed out, 'but it wasn't found until a local Sunday rambler tripped over it by blind chance.'

'Luck of the draw. We'll have Roy sooner or later.'

'Sooner, I hope. I'm glad you explained to me about Dr Hurst.

I can see he was upset by the news of his ex-wife's death, very distressed, it's only natural. Misunderstandings can happen at times like that. I'll explain it to the Assistant Chief.'

'Thank you, sir.'

'So get on with it, Denis. You've been on this case four days and found nothing. We've got two dead bodies, and we don't want any more. This isn't bloody Los Angeles.'

Number 23 Orchard Row looked even more unappetising in daylight than it had in the evening. A dented metal dustbin with the lid half-off stood by the pebble-dash wall close to the front door, and on a scruffy patch of grass which represented a back garden there was a homemade rabbit hutch.

It was a little before three in the afternoon when Bowker arrived with Knight, a Search Warrant and the local bobby in support. He knocked briskly. There was a long wait. He knocked again, this time an insistent thumping.

'Must be somebody in,' said Knight. 'I can hear the TV.'

After a further pause the door opened slowly and Roy's mother put her head 'round it. She stared uncertainly at Bowker, as if she'd never seen him before. His dark suit had been cleaned and pressed after the catastrophe of Birley Spinney, but already it was starting to look rumpled.

'Good afternoon, Mrs Sibson,' he began, striving for courtesy and consideration. 'Remember me? Inspector Bowker. I came here to see you Saturday evening.'

'What do you want? Joyce isn't here—you can't come in.'

Bowker had been wondering how he would handle a confrontation with the protective sister. If need be, she'd be steamrollered, like any other obstructive witness, but he was never happy when it was a woman to be brow-beaten. Her absence spared them both that, but there were questions he wanted answers to. Sooner or later, he was going to interview Joyce Harris.

When he did, it was going to be on his terms, not hers, with no lies from her about Roy sunning himself on the Costa Brava.

'I have to come in, Mrs Sibson,' he said as gently as he could. 'See this paper? It's a Warrant to search your house.'

'You can't come in,' she repeated, seeming not to have heard what he said.

Bowker had his size-12 foot in the door to stop her closing it on him. He was glad he'd brought the local bobby along.

'Tell her, Whitelock,' he said.

'You have to let them in, Mrs Sibson,' Kevin Whitelock said. 'It's the law. The Inspector's got a proper Warrant.'

He eased himself past Bowker to put a hand flat on the door. A moment of uneasiness all 'round; then Mrs Sibson surrendered to the authority of the blue uniform and stood back. She wore the same navy-blue stretch-pants as when they saw her on Saturday, unflattering to her flabbiness, bereft of any style, probably mail-order. And the same carpet slippers.

They followed her into the sitting-room. Bowker was surprised to see her husband in front of the TV with a cup of tea in his hand. He wasn't old enough to be retired.

'Billy, it's them two men again,' Mrs Sibson informed him. 'I told them Joyce is out, but they won't listen. They've brought the policeman with them.'

Mr Sibson wiped tea from his thick grey moustache and looked up in wonder from the TV game-show, hardly knowing what to make of the unexpected information. His glance travelled slowly from his wife to Bowker, whose presence filled the small room.

'Day off, Mr Sibson?' Bowker asked with as much geniality as he could muster. He was containing himself, but his patience was being stretched out very thin.

'I haven't worked since I got made redundant six years back,' said Dad. He was on familiar territory now, a question he could grapple with. 'Eighteen years I worked at the tannery, not late once for work in all that time, never a day off sick. They went and closed it down. Wicked, really. There's no jobs for men over fifty if you get made redundant. The Government never ought to allow it. You work for the Government, do you? So what do you want—have you come about the TV licence?'

'I'm a policeman,' said Bowker.

He'd had enough chitchat and more than enough yokelry to be going on with. He wanted to get on and find Roy Sibson before Chummy got to him and closed his mouth nastily and permanently.

'I don't give a tinker's damn whether you've got a TV licence or not. This is a Search Warrant; read it if you like. I'm here to look at your son's room.'

'Our Roy? What's he done?' Mrs Sibson exclaimed.

'A policeman, are you?' said Mr Sibson. 'Not 'round here.'

Bowker ignored him from then on. 'Can we get on, Mrs Sibson? I want you to show me Roy's room.'

'What's he done?' she said again, apprehension and defiance mixed in her voice.

Bowker had heard the selfsame words many times from aggrieved mothers. Their next statement was usually *my boy's never been in any trouble with the police*. He could remember being told by the mother of a thug who'd gone on a rampage with an axe and killed another teenager and wounded five others that her Melvyn was a good boy, wouldn't hurt a fly.

'Whitelock, you stay here and help Mr Sibson watch TV,' said

Bowker. 'If Mrs Harris gets back, keep her down here till we've finished upstairs. Now, Mrs Sibson, lead the way to Roy's room.'

She led them ponderously up the narrow staircase.

'He's not here; you needn't think that,' she grumbled over an ample shoulder. 'He's on his holidays. You ask our Joyce.'

'I did,' Bowker said with a grin intended to be cheerful, but which was daunting.

It daunted Mrs Sibson. She said no more till she pushed open the door to a small bedroom at the back of the house. There was a single bed in dark-varnished wood, a wardrobe with a mirrored door and panels of smooth grey plastic, a dressing-table with three drawers.

The low spindly-legged bedside table was once a coffee table. On it was a lamp with a mock-parchment shade, three dog-eared paperbacks, and a comic book. The view from the window was of the empty rabbit hutch in the back garden.

'A bit bloody basic,' said Bowker, glaring 'round. 'Don't they pay a decent wage at Building Societies?'

'Five people living on two wage-packets,' Knight said, 'and the old man's dole money. We don't know how Joyce's husband earns a living, but he's not likely to be a stock-broker, is he, sir?'

'Make a start on the dressing-table,' Bowker said, he had no intention of being drawn into a discussion of living standards and the plight of the deserving poor. It led nowhere and proved nothing.

'What does Roy read himself to sleep with?' he said, sitting on the bed.

He picked up the paperbacks while Jack Knight turned out the dressing-table drawers.

'*Elvis Is Alive,*' he read aloud. 'Did you know that, Knight? Elvis Presley didn't drop dead, like a big blubbery whale going belly-up. He felt hemmed in by all that fame and money and did a runner. He's working as a petrol-pump attendant in Nebraska and never been happier in his life, it says here. Who the hell did they bury in his coffin, I wonder?'

'You want me to contact the Tennessee police and advise them to get an Exhumation Order, sir?'

'Ho bloody ho! Have you found anything yet?'

'There's no passport here, but his sister could have taken it to keep up the pretence. It might be in her room. And if he has a savings account with the Building Society where he works, the book's not here. He must have taken it with him.'

'I suppose you didn't think to ask the branch manager if Roy had taken any money out legitimately?' Bower grumbled. 'Phone him when we leave here and find out. If we know what money he's got on him, it might give us a lead how far he's gone.'

'There's a packet of condoms here,' said Knight. 'At least he took an interest in girls.'

'That all you've found?'

'Nothing else, just shirts and socks. A few photos taken at a party, could be an office Christmas party. Got his arm 'round a girl with a big chest.'

Bowker held out his hand for the picture and studied it.

'Not much else to recommend her,' he said. 'Those glasses are terrible. If she's Roy's regular, he'd be bloody bowled over by Lynn Hurst showing an interest.'

'*If* she did,' Knight said, thinking a note of caution mightn't come amiss. 'We've only Barry Crick's statement, and I'd trust him as far as I can throw him.'

'We'll take the photo,' Bowker decided. 'That branch manager can tell us who she is. If she turns out to be Roy's girlfriend, he might have said something to her. Have a look what's in the wardrobe.'

Another of the paperbacks had a grisly picture on the front, a black-hooded man holding a knife with a curving blade a foot long. The title was *Secret Blood-Rites of the Freemasons*.

'Bloody hell!' said Bowker, riffling through the book with a grin. 'I wonder if DCS Horrocks has read this; he's one of the secret-sign-and-apron brigade, they reckon.'

The third paperback was *The Truth About Nostradamus.*

'We've learned something today about Roy,' said Bowker. 'He's a conspiracy fan, it's his nighttime reading. That and Science Fiction. Roy goes in for the sort of fantasy our Mr Rowley with the beard in School Walk draws.'

'Nothing in the wardrobe,' Knight reported. 'One suit and two jackets, one denim, one leather. Two pairs of shoes. This lad doesn't seem to own much. I'll just have a look on top.'

'Conspiracies,' said Bowker. 'I wonder if Roy's one of those loonies who think the entire world's run by a secret committee of International Jewish Communist Freemason Bankers.'

'Isn't it?' Knight asked, straight-faced.

'Loonies like that are easily drawn into little plots, nearly always criminal. If all the world's a big plot against you, why not grab a share?'

'There's a biggish gap between world domination and straight-forward thieving,' Knight suggested.

'All conspiracies are criminal,' Bowker stated firmly. 'That stands to reason. Joining one makes simple-minded loonies think they're striking a blow for liberty and equality and all that.'

Knight was not convinced, but thought it wiser not to say so.

'Can you see Lynn Hurst as leader of a conspiracy to defraud, and Roy as a member?' Bowker asked, more or less of himself.

'If you listen to her sister in Chiswick, Lynn was practically a nun,' said Knight. 'Devoted wife, good housekeeper, all that, certainly not the type to embezzle from Building Societies.'

'Waste of time sending you to interview her,' Bowker said in a suspicious voice. 'Perhaps I should have gone myself.'

Knight gave a noncommittal grunt and moved the only chair in the room close to the wardrobe. He stepped up and looked on the dusty top.

'Here's something—a cash-box.'

He put his handkerchief over it before he lifted it down, not to get his own fingerprints on it, just in case. He set it down on the bed beside Bowker.

'Feels light, can't be much in it,' he said.

It wasn't even locked. Inside they found £30 in new fivers.

'Funny he didn't take that with him when he scooted,' Knight said, 'unless he didn't come back here after he decided to go.'

'That seems the most likely reason,' Bowker agreed, a look of furious concentration on his face. 'We've no reliable sighting of him after Tuesday afternoon in Lynn Hurst's car going along the Wormwold road. We can't believe any contrary statement made by Joyce. She'd lie herself black in the face to shield him.'

'And dear old Mum and Dad are useless as witnesses,' Knight added. 'All we've got is Barry Crick's word to go on.'

'Let's assume for a minute we can trust that shifty sod. Then it looks as if something was said on Roy's drive with Lynn that decided him. And it was so urgent he didn't even come back here first.'

'That can't be right, sir,' Knight said, chancing his luck by contradicting the Inspector. 'Mrs Hurst couldn't have known she was going to be murdered, could she, now?'

'No, and if she'd suspected it, she'd have moved out of Long Slaughter, to her boyfriend or somewhere else she thought safe. I think we can be sure she didn't feel herself in danger.'

'So what could she say to our Roy to scare him that much?'

'How the hell do I know!' Bowker growled. 'I'm even starting to ask myself if we've got the story the wrong way 'round.'

'You mean, did Roy murder Lynn, not Gavin Fowler?'

'That would be a bloody good reason to make himself scarce,' Bowker said with a malignant scowl.

'And then he'd have to be the one who killed Fowler as well,' Knight concluded. 'The question then is, where was Roy between Tuesday and Saturday?'

'No, it won't do,' Bowker said irritably. 'If he was anywhere 'round Long Slaughter between Tuesday and Saturday, somebody would have seen him. There's only half a dozen streets; no one could move without being spotted. It was Fowler killed Lynn—few have the guts to do it that way, a bloody great steel spike into the brain. Roy's little mystery has to be about something different.'

They searched the other bedrooms, but found nothing useful, certainly not Roy's passport. They searched downstairs, working 'round Mum and Dad, who kept their eyes on the TV screen. In the sideboard was a biscuit-tin with a picture of Windsor Castle on the lid; inside was a TV licence two years out of date and a rent book with a fortnight's arrears owing. But nothing of interest.

'When Joyce gets back, tell her I want to speak to her,' said Bowker. 'She can reach me through PC Whitelock.'

He wondered if his message would ever get through.

'Where is she, anyway?', he asked.

'Didn't say,' Dad Sibson offered. 'Might have gone on the bus to Oxford. Did she say anything to you, Hazel?'

Mrs Sibson shook her head. 'Might have gone to Reading,' she suggested, 'or was that last week, Billy?'

And she might have gone to see Roy, thought Bowker. If anyone knows where our wandering boy is tonight, it's bloody Joyce.

'You tell her the Inspector wants to talk to her,' Whitelock said slowly and with deliberation.

'Nothing for us there,' said Knight when they were out of the house and walking along Orchard Row to Bridge Street. 'I wonder the married daughter is still living at home, or Roy either. It must be like living with a couple of zombies.'

'Housing,' said PC Whitelock, shaking his helmeted head in a gloomy manner. 'I expect Joyce and her husband have been on the Council Waiting List since the day they were married. Roy could find himself a bedsitter near where he works if he tried, only he'd have to do his own washing and cooking. I'm surprised that Joyce hasn't got a babe-in-arms by now; that pushes you up the Waiting List a bit.'

'You sound like bloody Thomas Hardy,' said Bowker, a scowl on his face. 'Roy will go and hang himself in a barn in his shirt-sleeves because he's in love with Lynn Hurst, and now she's gone, he can't live without her. Sister Joyce had a bastard child by the vicar before she was married to Harris, and it was adopted. Lynn was murdered by a passing tinker when she found him trying to steal her gold locket.'

'I saw that film, sir,' said Knight, 'at the Walsall Roxy, it was. The girl I took liked it, but I didn't think much of it.'

'He's completely anonymous, this Roy,' Bowker said, ignoring the film critique. 'A twenty-two-year-old blank with some damnfool ideas in his head. Lynn couldn't have been interested in him, unless she saw a way of adding him to the list of friends contributing to her savings.'

'And as he had no money except his wages, contributions would have to be the Chalfont Building Society's money,' said Knight. 'I'll give the dozy manager a ring and see if anything's turned up yet on the computer.'

He started to laugh uproariously.

'What's so bloody funny?' Bowker demanded.

'It just struck me—Roy and that old lady's cat went missing about the same time. I had this sudden thought of him doing a flit with a ginger tom under his arm.'

'According to the owner, it's worth only ten shillings,' said Bowker with a grin. 'Roy can't be that hard up. So what are you doing to find Miss Pankhurst's cat, Whitelock? What's the normal routine?'

'Doing, sir? We don't actually do anything about missing pets except make a note of the owner's name and address. We wait for somebody to report they found the missing animal, if they ever do. I keep my eyes open when I do my twice-daily walk round the village, but I've seen no ginger cat, dead or alive.'

'Many cats go missing 'round here?'

'Don't rightly know, sir. This is the first one that's been reported.'

'Miss Pankhurst—what do you know about her?' Bowker asked, surprising Knight by the way he was pursuing his enquiries into the missing cat.

'Nice old soul,' said Whitelock. 'Born and bred here in Long Slaughter, getting on for eighty, I'd say. She never married; lived with her parents and looked after them till they died. Left on her own now. Lives on about fourpence a week Social Security.'

'Poor old duck,' Bowker said thoughtfully. 'A pity about her cat.'

'Where are we going now, sir?' Knight asked, wanting to hear no more about missing ginger toms and sorry he'd ever mentioned the creature.

'To talk to Mr Empson Rowley, the best-known Fantasy Artist this side of the Atlantic. According to him. There was a lot of fantasy in the tale he told me on Saturday, I want to have the truth from him now.'

At the police house on the corner, PC Whitelock left them and went inside to get on with his routine. He would relay anything that arrived from DCS Horrocks or Forensic. Bowker strode down Long Street, Knight stretching his legs to keep up, heading for Badger Lane and School Walk.

Long Street lived up to its name. It was the long way 'round, a street of faded red-brick houses from the early years of the century, with here and there in gaps between a more recent but equally ugly bungalow or two.

'Not a bloody thatched roof anywhere in sight,' Bowker said in irritation. 'What's wrong with this village?'

'Nothing much,' said Knight with a grin. 'There's a murderer on the prowl, done two in for no reason we can see. Apart from that, everything's fine, and the Parish Council is doing a grand job.'

Empson Rowley's motorbike stood in his front garden, a huge dangerous matte black and chrome machine, a crash helmet in Day-Glo orange slung from the handlebars.

'That bike cost him, not a lot less than the new car he bought for Lynn Hurst,' Knight said. 'You said he wasn't hard up.'

Rowley opened the cottage door himself when Bowker rapped. He was still wearing his washed-out jeans, but he'd changed his T-shirt. This one was black, with SURVIVAL RESEARCH LABORATORIES printed on it in white. When he saw

Bowker at his door, he stuck his chin and black beard out pugnaciously.

'You again?' He sounded very hostile. 'What do you want this time?'

'To ask you a few more questions,' said Bowker, matching the nervous hostility with his own glowering version.

Rowley didn't invite the two detectives to come in. He turned his back to them and marched into the cottage, leaving the door wide open. Bowker took that to be as good as an invitation and went in, Knight a step or two behind.

In the sitting-room, Judy Holbooth in a pink cotton dress had the little boy on her lap, she was turning the pages of an oversized picture book for him. She glanced up at the policemen with wary eyes and made no move.

Rowley threw himself into an armchair and hung his legs over the side of it. In a disgruntled snarl, he said '*Well?*' Obviously he knew Fowler's body had been found in the car. He felt safe, and he meant to be defiant.

'Mr Rowley,' said Bowker, looming over him and ominously calm, 'there are questions to be asked, answers to be given. It would be better if the interview was in private.'

'I'd better take Kris upstairs out of your way,' Judy offered at once, confirming Bowker's theory about the boy's name.

She went out of the room and left the door half-open behind her. Another of Bowker's theories was confirmed.

'It would be better if we went into your studio to talk,' he said to Rowley in an undertone, glancing at the half-open door to make his point. 'Detective Sergeant Knight will enjoy seeing your drawings. And there are questions about the purchasing of a certain white car.'

Rowley sat still, fists clenched and eyes stony. For a moment Bowker thought he was going to refuse. The questions were going to be asked, either here or there, whether Judy eavesdropped or not. It meant nothing to Bowker if Rowley dropped himself right in the clag with her, but it seemed a pity to upset her.

Antagonism to the police was nothing new, all sorts of people thought the law didn't apply to them. Lifetime crooks making a living out of thieving, big or small. Well-off middle class who believed upstanding citizens were allowed to bend the rules now and then. Loons like Empson Rowley who thought they hated and despised the Establishment and wanted to prove it by being rude to a copper.

After Rowley thought it through, he stood up and nodded toward the studio. He was shaking. Jack Knight glanced 'round the walls of the windowless room, taking in the colourful cut-outs pinned to the cork boards. Bowker was far more interested in the work in progress on the drawing-board, not the big-bosomed blonde with the dragon, but a new example of Rowley's fantasy.

The landscape was volcanic, jagged rocks sticking up toward a black sky, in the middle two chromium-plated metal posts a yard apart. A woman was hanging upside down between them, her ankles chained to big hooks on top of the posts, her legs pulled wide apart, her wrists tied behind her back.

Her only covering was something that looked like a strapless bathing suit made of steel scales. What caught Bowker's eye was that she did not conform to the pattern of over-endowed blondes beloved of Science Fiction illustrators. She was a brunette, and she resembled the late Lynn Hurst.

On the stony ground stood a semi-human in silver briefs, face masked, a ridge of bone spikes down the middle of his back, his feet like a dragon's, with four toes and curving claws. He was swinging a long iridescent metal bar. Another second and it was going to crack open the hanging woman's head.

'Nice,' said Bowker, his tone brutal. 'Very tasteful. Look at this, Knight, Mr Rowley's been inspired by the murder.'

Knight stood beside Bowker, he stared at the nearly-finished picture and made tutting noises.

'I'm an artist,' Rowley protested. 'I make use of everything, no matter how shocking other people think it.'

'*Shocking* is not the word that comes to mind,' Bowker said, a black scowl on his face. '*Disrespectful* is more like it.'

'It's therapeutic,' Rowley insisted. 'You police are used to brutality and violence and think nothing of it, but the rest of us aren't hardened to sudden death. It's a shock to the psyche, finding a woman murdered. I have to work the terror and agony out of my system. The only way I know is to turn it into art.'

'SURVIVAL RESEARCH LABORATORIES,' said Bowker, pointing at Rowley's T-shirt with a long hard finger. 'That what it means, making comic-book pictures out of somebody's tragedy?'

Rowley made no reply. Knight did his tutting again.

'I think we'll take it with us as evidence,' Bowker said with a grin so intimidating that Rowley took a step backward. 'What is it supposed to be, so we can give you a proper receipt?'

The possible loss of his picture stung Rowley into protest.

'You can't have it!' he said. 'It's evidence of nothing. The man who murdered Mrs Hurst committed suicide. He was frightened of being interrogated by you lot—that's my guess. Anyway, this picture's got nothing to do with it. I'm doing illustrations for a book, and this is one of them.'

'What sort of book has pictures like this, horror-comics?'

'Certainly not!' Rowley sounded as if he was offended by the Inspector's suggestion. 'It's for a new illustrated edition of Nostradamus. I'm planning a series of twenty illustrations for it.'

'That's the Frenchman who foretold everything that's happened since the Middle Ages?' Bowker said before Rowley demonstrated his superiority over secret policemen by telling him. 'Bloody Adolf Hitler and the Common Market and the San Francisco earthquake and UFOs from outer space? It's funny you're interested in Nostradamus. Do you know Roy Sibson, lives in Orchard Row?'

'No, I don't.'

'Did you know Gavin Fowler?'

'That's the one who killed himself in the car?' Rowley said, starting to sound truculent again. 'It's all 'round the village that he killed Mrs Hurst. I didn't know him either. Come to the point, if there is one.'

'Right,' said Bowker, seeming to grow an inch or two above his six foot six, and half a yard broader across the chest. 'When I was here before, you told me you knew Mrs Hurst only casually. A *good morning* over the garden fence and a glass of sherry before Christmas. Very bloody casual. You didn't tell me the truth. In fact, you paid for a new car for her.'

He made the statement and stopped. Rowley had to decide whether he should deny it or admit it, knowing both led him into trouble. Bowker and Knight had turned to face him, silently waiting for his response, their eyes accusing. There was a long and awkward pause before Rowley took a decision.

'I didn't want to tell you about that,' he said.

He was trying to sound less shaky than he was, but not doing a very good job.

'I mean, after what happened, you were bound to think I'd had something to do with her death,' he said feebly.

'Why should I think that?' Bowker asked, gesturing to Knight to get this down in his notebook.

'Well, she asked me to lend her the money for the car.'

'Where was this, over the garden fence?'

'She asked me 'round for a cup of coffee one day. Judy was out with Kris to buy him clothes or shoes or something. We chatted, and she eventually asked me to lend her the money.'

'For your own good, Mr Rowley, I'd better warn you every word is getting you in deeper. You're right up to your neck in clag now; you'll go under in a minute.'

'What do you mean?' Rowley tried to bluster.

'How will it sound in Court when your words are read out and shown to be a lie? There was no question of lending Lynn Hurst money, it was an outright gift. A forced donation, if you like, bordering on bloody extortion, if you wanted to be candid.'

Rowley closed his eyes. He was imagining himself in the dock, accused of God-knows-what, his words being read back by Knight from his notebook, prosecuting counsel like a vulture hovering above, ready to flap down and rip him open.

'We know how Mrs Hurst persuaded men to give her money,' said Bowker, his tone brutal. 'Don't imagine you're the only one.'

'Look, Inspector, does Judy have to know about this?'

'I've no reason to tell her, as long as you tell me the truth,' Bowker growled. 'If you lie to me again, I shall have to put a few questions to Judy to get at the facts.'

The words *you evil vicious bastard* were trembling on Rowley's tongue but he didn't say them. He looked down at the floor and asked Bowker what he wanted to know.

'You were having an affair with Lynn Hurst—we know all about that,' Bowker said savagely. 'When did it start?'

'A long time ago, a few weeks after we moved in here. I never meant it to happen, believe me. Somehow it did; she knew how to make herself irresistible. Every time Judy went out, there Lynn was, in the garden or at the door. She looked stunning, and she bubbled over with life and happiness. You said it yourself; I'm not the only one.'

'First the fun, then she asked you for the ten thousand pounds?'

'Not for a long time. Looking back now, I see she wanted the time to find out how much I could afford without screaming. I was a bloody fool—I don't need you to tell me that.'

'The affair went on after that, I've no doubt,' said Bowker. 'She'd want to keep you cosy; you were valuable to her. Did she ask for more money later?'

He'd seen Rowley's bank statement for the past two years and he knew there was only one payment. But there might well have been a second request, and that could be the reason for her death.

Rowley shook his head; his black beard wagged.

'She was saving you for a rainy day,' said Bowker, letting it go for the moment. 'Sooner or later she'd have touched you for another five grand, or even ten again, if she thought you were hard enough on the hook. Were you?'

For once in his life Empson Rowley acted prudently; he heard the question and kept his mouth shut.

'My assumption is Judy knew nothing about the money,' Bowker said slowly, 'but did she suspect you of getting your leg over, next door?'

The deliberate brutality of his phrasing stung Rowley; he was sharp in his response.

'What's the point of these questions? The man who killed her is dead; everybody knows that. You're just harassing me, asking about things that don't concern you.'

He also sounded uneasy about what Judy might know.

It was Knight's turn, to save Bowker the need to give a reply to Rowley's counter-question.

'Where were you on Saturday afternoon, Mr Rowley?' he asked.

'What's that got to do with anything?'

'It's a simple enough question, sir, and I shall be grateful for an answer. Where were you after lunch on Saturday? Here at home with Miss Holbooth and your little boy? At the cinema on your own again? Watching Reading play away at Southampton?'

'You know damn well where I was,' Rowley said indignantly. 'I was here being interrogated by your Inspector.'

'Don't be a bloody fool all your life,' said Bowker, resuming the attack himself. 'That was before lunch, I was here about noon and stayed half an hour. What did you do after that?'

Rowley licked his lips and stared at the floor. When he spoke, he sounded very worried.

'I was upset by all that happened, finding Lynn on the floor in her own blood. Then you more-or-less accused me of murdering her. It was bad for Judy, too; she was as upset as I was. After you'd gone, we had a row—that's the truth. When it got too much for me, I stormed out.'

'What time was that, sir?' Knight asked, his voice tight.

'How do I know? About two o'clock, maybe. I went for a ride on my bike to cool off.'

'Where to?' Bowker asked in a disbelieving growl.

'Nowhere, I just kept going. When I hit the motorway, I opened up and went like a bat out of Hell. A police car tried to catch me, and I outran it easily. I suppose you'll arrest me for that, now I've told you.'

'Traffic violations are nothing to do with me,' said Bowker. 'Where did you get to eventually?'

'Bristol. I had a sandwich and a cup of tea and mooched 'round till I felt better. Then I came back.'

'What time?'

'It must have been getting on for eight by the time I got home.'

'What it comes to is, you've no way of proving where you were on Saturday afternoon, and you don't know where Judy was,' said Bowker in a voice cold enough to have come over the Arctic ice pack.

'What the bloody hell does it matter where we were?'

Knight told him why. 'Saturday afternoon was when Gavin Fowler died in Mrs Hurst's white car, the one you bought for her. He parked off the road in Birley Spinney, only a mile or two from here.'

'He killed himself with the exhaust. I read it in the paper.'

'He died of carbon monoxide poisoning,' said Bowker, his tone malign. 'He died alone, but someone else was with him before he passed out. The signs are all there. It could have been you, Mr Rowley. Or it could even have been Judy.'

'She was here all afternoon. She didn't know the man any more than I did.'

'For which I have your word, of course. You'd better hope the officers in the police car you ran from remember the incident. That might put you in the clear.'

'You're going to question Judy,' said Rowley. He sounded sick, and his words were more statement than question.

'No,' said Bowker, showing his executioner's grin. 'Not yet.'

8.   *princess margaret rose clinic*

Walking back from Empson Rowley's home to the police house on the corner of Bridge Street, Bowker damned the Fantasy Artist with words of heartfelt annoyance.

'That silly bastard's determined to get himself arrested,' he said in a growl that could be heard a hundred yards off.

'I'd pretty well eliminated him from our enquiries; now he comes up with a rigmarole about speeding on the M4 on Saturday afternoon. There's got to be something wrong with his brain, if he's telling the truth.'

'The traffic patrol will have a record if they chased a biker and didn't catch him, sir,' Knight said consolingly.

'I bet you'll find they chase two or three every day without catching them. Unless they got close enough to see the license plate, we can never be sure it was Rowley.'

'What made you sure he could be eliminated?' Knight asked.

'I think it was that picture of his. To me it didn't fit with the nasty cold hate Chummy had to feel to get the slaughterman to crack Lynn Hurst's head. Rowley's picture *looks* violent, but it's mushy.'

Knight thought about it for a minute and gave up. In his book, the grisly fantasy painting showed an obsession with the death of Lynn Hurst which pointed the finger straight at the artist.

'How do you mean?' he asked.

'Haven't you got eyes in your head?' Bowker said, exasperated, 'and a mind to understand what you see? His bloody picture is about sex, not death. He still fancies Lynn in his thoughts.'

'Sex and death go together very often,' Knight said, sounding slightly aggrieved. 'There's been sex-murderers by the dozen in the past few years, caught and put away.'

'Put away for a few years,' Bowker said bitterly. 'Then they get let out to do it again. You want me to quote you cases?'

'What would you do, sir, hang them?'

'No, that's bloody barbarous, hanging people,' Bowker said in outrage. 'I'd have a surgeon slice their particulars off before they were let out. That'd deter them. It would make rape a once-only crime.'

Knight thought it best not to continue in that direction. For all he knew, Bowker could be serious.

'Apart from putting the wind up Rowley,' he said, 'why did you let him know we're not happy about Fowler's death in Lynn's car—you must have had something in mind.'

'So he can tell Judy.'

'I don't understand that,' Knight said.

He glanced sideways at Bowker, taking in the heavy set of his jaw and his prize-fighter shoulders. When he was enraged, the resemblance to the Mad Mangler on TV was unmistakable.

'Why did you say you don't want to interview her, if she's a suspect?'

'Wasting our time,' said Bowker. 'She'll say she was there at home with the boy Saturday afternoon when Fowler died in Birley Spinney and the loon with the beard was out on his bike. Maybe she was. We have nothing to show she wasn't.'

'You hinted she might know about the affair—that made Rowley sweat. Do you think *she* might have put Fowler up to getting rid of Lynn for her? If she'd found out Rowley gave her ten grand, besides having a romp on her bed, that could be her motive. Not much use leaving him and taking the little boy if he's going to keep on forking out the cash to Lynn instead of her.'

'That's the general idea,' Bowker agreed, though he pulled a long face. 'But it's no use tackling her until we find a crevice to stick a fingernail in. If she *is* involved, when Rowley tells her we're not disposed to let Fowler's death rest easy, she'll start worrying. People do silly things when they're worried. I'm hoping we can start a rabbit running out in the open so we can get a clear shot at it.'

What was passing through Jack Knight's mind was that Bowker's methods of detection were as subtle as a punch in the face. Was it true he solved his cases by glaring at people till they broke down and confessed? Could he be as aggressively insensitive as he appeared, or was it a front he put on?

'We've got rooms at the Black Swan again tonight,' he said. 'PC Whitelock fixed us up. I told him we wanted to move across to the Bull's Head, but it seems they don't do rooms.'

'The food's good at the Swan,' said Bowker. 'We'll be back in time for dinner, I hope. We'll stroll 'round later to the Bull's Head for a word with this character Farmer Giles told me about. His name's Fox, and he's supposed to be the local gossip-monger.'

'Back? Where from? Where are we going?'

'To call on Dr Hurst,' Bowker said, astounded that Knight had to ask him anything so obvious. 'We're eliminating them, one by one, like knocking down skittles. The one left standing at the end, that's the one we run in.'

'We haven't eliminated anybody yet,' Knight pointed out.

Bowker's face turned very dark and bellicose. 'I was certain we'd done with that silly bugger of an artist and his girl. Now they're both back on the list. We'll let them stew for a bit and see if we can knock anyone else out.'

When they stopped in at Whitelock's, he told them Joyce Harris had been in, as requested. She hadn't waited; she said she had to go over to Wallingford because her Auntie Madge wasn't well. She'd be home tomorrow morning if the Inspector wanted to call, but only till about noon.

'Hell's bloody bells!' said Bowker. 'The woman's like a yo-yo the way she flits about. We'll go 'round to Orchard Row tomorrow morning to see if she's ready to tell us yet where bloody Roy's hiding himself. I suppose she didn't mention where she went to today?'

'No, sir,' said Whitelock. 'She didn't say, and I didn't think to ask her. Her husband came with her. I realised who he was when I saw him, Reg Harris. He got Third Prize for the Best Marrow when I took the First at the Flower Show last year.'

'What's he like?' asked Bowker, rolling his eyes upwards in disbelief at the unexpected horticultural information.

'Quiet sort of chap. He's a gas-fitter, I believe, no trouble to anybody. Somebody else was asking for you as well—the young lady from the newspaper, the one you were chatting up when she came 'round on Sunday. Sara Thomas. She seemed very keen to see you, sir.'

Knight looked at Bowker with new interest. He'd been off on a wild-goose chase talking to Lynn Hurst's sister at Chiswick the first time the reporter turned up.

'Pretty, is she?' he asked.

'Nice-looking girl,' said Bowker, sounding human. 'She found the cleaning-woman we ought to have looked for. She might have come across something else we've missed. If she's found Roy for us, I'll kiss her! Is she coming back, Whitelock?'

There was a pause, as the constable and DS Knight tried hard to imagine Bowker in a show of affection, or even gratitude. It was a very daunting thought. In fact some women would regard an embrace by him as tantamount to rape.

'Said she was being overworked as usual, sir,' Whitelock said at last. 'She's going to telephone later to see if you're back. You can't phone her because she's out and about, and the *County Examiner* editor is a mean old sod who won't give her a portable phone. That's what she said, sir. Her words.'

'When she calls in, tell her she can get me at the Black Swan sometime tonight.'

While they were getting into his car parked outside, he gave Knight a foreboding grin and explained about the reporter.

'She's crafty,' he said, with grudging respect. 'She made out she was helping me with information, and she told me nothing of any use whatsoever. I said she could take photos of the divers bringing up that tyre-iron out of the Thames. I've already had DCS Horrocks shouting in my ear about that. You saw the picture in the paper; it was harmless enough.'

'Perhaps I'd better talk to her next time, if she can wheedle you,' said Knight, his audacity breathtaking.

'Don't be silly, I've got her believing she can drop in for a story to put in the *Examiner*. Assuming Chummy reads it, we've a direct line. We can get Sara to print what suits us, so long as she thinks it's true. That could come in very useful.'

Mercifully, he let Knight drive the Honda. The ride was less hazardous this time, by the winding lane from Long Slaughter to the main road, then on toward Abingdon.

It was not yet five when they reached Hawthorne Lodge. Bowker stayed in the car while Knight went to see if Dr Hurst was in. He thought it best to avoid another complaint about his conduct for the time being, and there was no point in getting embroiled with the housekeeper. She might have useful information. It was sensible to let Knight approach her this time.

Jack Knight was a fine-looking man, well-set, clear-eyed, and a look of complete honesty about him, a neat dresser, his brown hair cut tidily and yet dashing at the same time. In Bowker's estimation Knight should be able to charm information out of a middle-aged housekeeper.

For instance, had the late Mrs Lynn Hurst been here to visit the Doctor in the last six, twelve months? If so, did she stay long? What did they talk about? Had the housekeeper by chance over-heard them? Not with her ear to the door—no one suggested that—but a word or two caught inadvertently?

Not today though; the first thing was to tackle Dr Hurst. For that Bowker wanted the DS with him as a witness that he didn't beat Hurst up or kick him unconscious, whatever the slippery bugger might claim afterwards to his friend the Assistant Chief.

Knight came back to the car.

'Not home yet. The housekeeper says he hardly ever leaves the Clinic before six.'

'We'll talk to him there. Drive a bit faster this time so we arrive before midnight. Coming here it was like having my dear old granny behind the wheel!'

Knight stabbed his foot down on the accelerator and took off in a hail of flying gravel from Dr Hurst's drive.

'Do you mind telling me, sir,' he said, 'when you interview a suspect, have you got the questions all worked out in your mind before you start?'

'The real question I want to ask any suspect isn't worth the asking,' said Bowker with a heavy frown. '*Did you do it?* That's all we really want to know. But all you get by asking that is a pack of lies and a reputation for being simple.'

'Yes, but as a general rule, how do you go about it, sir?'

'I don't like general rules. Anyway, you should know by now; you've heard me interviewing suspects. You have to use a bit of subtlety with most of them.'

Knight struggled not to laugh when he heard the claim to sub-tlety. Was Bowker serious, or was he having him on?

'Take this slippery bastard we're on our way to see,' Bowker said. 'A real clever dick, if ever I saw one. He thinks himself a cut above the rest of us. What we have to do with him is push him off balance, not let him get the better of us, keep him on the bounce.'

Well, Knight thought, *it's going to be an interesting sort of interview, if the DI is going to insult Hurst in the interests of justice.*

The Princess Margaret Rose Clinic was in North Oxford. Knight took the ring road to avoid the cluttered town centre, earning himself a look of complete incredulity from Bowker, he favoured ramming through any obstacle between him and his goal. Past the Ashmolean Museum they drove north on the Woodstock road, an eye open for the Clinic.

It was a long two-storey building in red brick, with a lot of windows. The concrete car park was at the side, not very large. The handiest slots, nearest the Clinic entrance, were reserved and labelled DR C F DAWLISH, DR H A HURST, DR M KHAN, DR AILEEN DODINGTON, DR P SETH-CHALMERS.

The cars parked in them were well up in the executive league. Dawlish had treated himself to a sleek blue Daimler. There was a Mercedes 500 in Aileen Dodington's slot.

The Clinic's reception area was designed and furnished with a view to persuading patients it was a country-house drawing-room and had sofas and armchairs. The current issues of *Country Life* and *Harpers Bazaar* were arranged on low tables.

Behind an expensive-looking writing-table with a white phone sat a youngish receptionist with an over-elaborate hair-do and an over-helpful voice. Her smile faded when Knight explained who they were and why they were there. She glanced anxiously at the two or three people waiting. She was nervous that policemen in her reception area could sully the Clinic's reputation.

She consulted Dr Hurst's secretary by telephone and announced with mild relief that Dr Hurst had departed for the day.

'That be damned for a tale,' said Bowker furiously.

His tone was so menacing that the receptionist almost dropped her sleek white telephone.

'His car's in the car park,' Bowker went on, glowering at the shaking woman. 'You tell that secretary she'll be charged with obstructing the police in a murder enquiry, if she lies to me.'

Everyone in the reception area was staring at him by now, his heavy-weight stance, his rumpled dark suit. They dropped their eyes and pretended to be reading magazines when he stared 'round with a look that told them to mind their own bloody business.

Definitely not their sort of person, they were thinking; not the type who should be allowed into this genteel medical oasis. Heaven spare them from the attentions of plain-clothes police who didn't know their place.

The receptionist dialled again and spoke very urgently to the secretary, who now said she had just caught Dr Hurst as he was leaving; please send the police gentlemen to his office.

'Through there and the second on the right,' the receptionist directed them, flustered and trying not to show it.

The secretary's office had two filing cabinets, a desk and a word-processor and was carpeted in thick-pile maroon. She was a bossy woman with bleached-out blonde hair and a pearl necklace. She tried to hold them in her office while she announced their arrival to Dr Hurst. Bowker merely nodded a greeting at her and swept through to the door of the inner office.

Dr Hurst was dressed more formally than when the officers saw him at his dinner-party. He was wearing a nicely-cut plain grey suit and a red paisley-pattern silk tie. Lots of white cuff and solid gold links. His walnut desk was reproduction-antique, his black leather chair swivelled, and was a buttoned Chesterfield design. To have him diagnose your ailments obviously cost a lot of money.

The corners of Bowker's mouth turned down at the sight of the abstracts hanging on the walls. But he spoke very cheerfully to Hurst and waited until he was asked before sitting down on the patient's side of the desk. Knight perched himself on the other patient's chair and ostentatiously got out his notebook.

The mildness of Bowker's manner perhaps deluded Dr Hurst into thinking his complaint about him had subdued the Inspector. And Bowker let him think this for a little while.

'Dr Hurst, I'm sorry we couldn't make a proper appointment

to see you,' he started, 'but I'm sure you understand in a murder enquiry there's not a minute to waste. We daren't let the trail go cold.'

Knight's jaw almost dropped at this conciliatory approach. He clenched his teeth to stop his amazement showing.

'Hot pursuit, Inspector?' said Hurst, having a private laugh at Bowker's expense. 'Have you solved the mystery of who killed my ex-wife?'

'You could say so,' Bowker agreed, still polite.

'Really?' said Hurst, his eyebrows riding up his forehead exaggeratedly. 'I've a patient waiting outside to see me, but I'll do everything I can to help you clear up this dreadful business with poor Lynn. Unless it's me you've come to arrest.'

He was still not taking Bowker seriously.

'Good of you, Doctor. When DS Knight and I were at your house on Saturday, you were distressed by the news we brought, I know that. In the shock, things might have slipped your memory.'

'What sort of things?' Hurst asked, his tone suddenly wary.

'You said that after the divorce there was no contact between you and your ex-wife, no need for any. But you remembered she'd phoned you once. It was last year, Knight, wasn't it?'

DS Knight thought he'd got the hang of Bowker's dialogues. He knew the answer to his question; he wanted Knight to confirm it just to make the suspect twitch.

'Last year, sir,' he said gravely, turning over a page in his notebook. 'Dr Hurst thought it was in the spring, but he wasn't certain about it.'

Bowker's voice remained polite and reasonable.

'As an actual matter of recorded fact, how many times has Mrs Hurst phoned the Doctor this year alone, Knight?'

'Seven altogether, sir. The dates were January 11, February 3 and 22, March 8, March 13, April 12, May 2.'

A pained look flitted over Hurst's long face. He ran his hand forward over his Roman Emperor haircut as if to smooth it down.

'Seven, yes,' Bowker said, almost casually. 'And what dates *this* year did the Doctor phone his ex-wife at Long Slaughter?'

Knight made another show of consulting his notebook, flipping pages over as if searching for the facts, but in fact to build suspense.

'January 30, February 16, April 22. Three in all.'

'So we're saying there were ten separate occasions the Doctor and his ex-wife talked to each other, this year alone?' Bowker said, carrying on the chat with Knight as if Hurst wasn't in the room at all. 'What do you make of it, Sergeant?'

'They had something of importance to both of them which they needed to discuss,' said Knight. 'Something not settled between them, perhaps couldn't be settled. I've got the dates for last year as well, if you want them.'

'Look here!' said Hurst, but both policemen ignored him.

'What was so urgent they needed to talk regularly about it, I wonder,' said Bowker. 'Usually with divorced people it turns out to be a wrangle about money, but we know the Doctor paid on the nail by Standing Order. Take a guess what they were up to, Knight.'

'I will not tolerate this impertinence!' Hurst exclaimed.

He was out of his buttoned chair like a jack-in-the-box and halfway across the room toward the door, his face set and teeth clenched. Knight was on his feet instantly and inserted himself neatly between the Doctor and the door, a meaninglessly polite smile on his face.

'Can't go yet, sir,' he said mildly. 'The Inspector wants to ask you about your telephone calls with Mrs Hurst. I'm sorry to say you haven't been straight with him.'

'Get out of my way!' Hurst demanded.

There was a pause while he tried to stare Knight down. Bowker said nothing, waiting for Hurst to decide whether he was going to assault Knight to get out of the room. Eventually the Doctor gave a long loud sigh, like a balloon deflating, then went back to his seat behind the desk.

Knight stayed by the door. Bowker leaned forward to rest his huge clenched fist on the Doctor's desk, as if measuring it for a karate chop that would break it in half. A hangman's grin was on his face as he addressed Hurst.

'You misled us, Doctor,' he said. His voice was not loud, but bone-chilling as a winter blizzard.

Hurst avoided eye contact; he ran his hand over his skull in the nervous gesture he had.

'I should have told you,' he said, feeling his way. 'I almost did, but there are personal things which none of us will readily talk about.'

'How many lots of alimony are you paying?' Bowker broke in, not letting Hurst continue his explanation.

'Two, but that's irrelevant!'

'It's for me to decide what's relevant,' Bowker informed him, his teeth bared in a snarl. 'The first Mrs Hurst hasn't married again, she lives in Worthing, you pay her a thousand pounds a month, and have been doing now for seven years. Your second cost you more—that's inflation, I suppose. A thousand and a half a month. Two and a half grand monthly together, thirty grand a year.'

He left it like that, drawing no conclusion. With Hurst there was no need; he was bright enough to work out the implications for himself.

'Look here!' he said. 'This is complete nonsense, you can't possibly think I murdered Lynn for the sake of the alimony. God almighty, I've heard of stupid policemen but that beats all!'

'Is there a third Mrs Hurst pending?' Bowker asked, ignoring the insult. 'Be careful, Doctor, I've been making enquiries.'

'You've been spying on me,' Hurst said, his self-possession wilting under Bowker's relentless glare. 'In that case you know I'm interested in Tania Walker. But that's got nothing at all to do with Lynn's death.'

'A wife costs money,' said Bowker. 'It would help you if your two ex-wives weren't around to draw their alimony every month.'

'But you told me yourself Lynn had become engaged. My support would have stopped anyway on her remarriage.'

'Or on her death,' said Bowker, 'whichever is the earlier.'

He eyed Hurst over the desk as if he were a dangerous animal and the only real question were how to put him down quickly and humanely before he attacked someone else.

'Lynn's marriage to Mark Stanhope was a very on-off affair,' the Inspector said morosely. 'You knew that. You pretended you didn't know about him, but it's a racing certainty she told you during one of your regular meetings. That's what all the phone calls were for, to arrange to meet.'

Several interesting points were established in Bowker's mind. Hurst gave no sign of knowing about Gavin Fowler's death. Maybe he hadn't seen the brief news item in the newspaper, and if he had, no connection had been suggested between it and the murder of Lynn Hurst. Village gossip had made the connection at once, but the Doctor did not live in Long Slaughter.

By assuming that Bowker suspected him of Lynn's murder, Hurst, in a strange way, was testifying to his own innocence.

'Yes, we met often,' the Doctor admitted, staring down at his desk-top and almost mumbling. 'Do I have to spell out why?'

'Yes,' Bowker said. He was by no means disposed to let Hurst off the hook. 'We've read your Pooh-Bear letters—did you know Lynn kept them? But I want to hear your explanation.'

Dr Hurst flushed, what man wants to hear his intimate letters have been read by policemen? It was a low punch, but he'd laid himself wide open to it by his untruths about the phone calls.

'She fascinated me sexually,' he said, 'obsessed me, in fact. I was bitter and I hated her after the divorce because she had deliberately set me up. She was greedy for her independence. It wouldn't have mattered who she was married to; it wouldn't have lasted for long. She wanted to get rid of me; she also wanted to be awarded as much alimony as possible. So she engineered it so I was caught with my secretary. I had very good reasons for hating Lynn, but I couldn't stop myself wanting her. And that's what we met for, to go to bed together.'

'What did she want in return?'

'Sometimes money, sometimes she handed me an overdue bill she wanted paying, sometimes she asked for air tickets abroad. Once or twice she even did it for fun. She was a complicated woman.'

'So I understand. Did you pay for two First-Class air tickets to Paris this last Saturday?'

'No.'

Bowker believed him: that didn't soften his approach.

'She had the upper hand,' he said, his tone a flat statement. 'You must have resented being exploited.'

'I hated her, and I hated myself for being weak. On Saturday, when you told me she was dead, I didn't know whether to laugh or cry. I was free of her, but I'd never see her again.'

Hearts and flowers are all very well, Knight was thinking as he scribbled in his notebook, *but the silly bugger's just given us an even better motive for having Lynn done in than saving on his alimony. But if he's that open about it, maybe he's in the clear—what's the Inspector going to make of it?*

'You were having casual relations with your ex-wife three or four times a month, and at the same time you were interested in Miss Tania Walker—is that right?' Bowker asked. 'I suppose by *interested* you mean you were sleeping with her as well.'

'Maybe you find it complicated and hard to understand,' Hurst said, 'but my relations with Lynn had nothing of regard or even affection in them. It was physical attraction and nothing more. She was an exceptionally attractive woman. It's different with Miss Walker. We've more-or-less agreed to marry.'

'If by some mischief it came to the ears of Miss Tania Walker that you and the former Mrs Hurst the Second got together for a rollick regularly, would she still be likely to marry you?'

Bloody hell, he's given us another motive now, Knight thought at Bowker's question and saw the strained look on Hurst's face.

'No, no, no,' the Doctor said softly, keeping a tight control of himself. 'This won't do, Inspector, it really won't. You may think my relations with women are to some extent unconventional, but I am incapable of the violence of murder—surely that must be obvious to a man with your experience of human nature.'

'My experience of human nature!' said Bowker with a snarl of unconcealed fury. 'Since you raise the question, I'll tell you. My experience has taught me people are capable of every kind of cruelty and viciousness. It's only a question of circumstances and motives. You had more than one reason to want Lynn dead and out of your way, however keen you were to have her clothes off. Or so you say.'

'I've told you the truth,' Hurst protested.

'Have you? For all I know, these get-togethers might easily have been to plan some swindle the pair of you were cooking up. The Chalfont Building Society's counting its millions right now to see if any's gone missing. Does that send a shiver down your back, Doctor?'

'Building Society? I don't know what you're talking about! Are you accusing me of stealing money?'

Bowker didn't bother to explain.

'Where were you last Saturday afternoon, from midday to about six in the evening?'

Right, thought Jack Knight. *If he can establish where he was when Gavin Fowler was drinking whisky and dying of car exhaust, he's in the clear, and we can rub one suspect off the list. With a bit of luck he was here in the Clinic, surrounded by operating-theatre nurses, seeing to somebody's piles.*

Knight had a quick check in his notebook, but there had been no reason to write down what was said on the phone on Saturday evening when they were tracing the Doctor. As he remembered it, the housekeeper simply said he was out, and the Clinic said the same when they tried there. Perhaps he'd taken his wife-to-be, Miss Tania Walker, to the pictures, or for a drink. Something nice and simple that would scratch him off the suspect list.

'Saturday afternoon?' Hurst said, sounding puzzled. 'What is the point of that? I was here in the Clinic for an hour or so in the morning, I had lunch at home, and drove over to Lambourn. I went for a long tramp on the Downs. I often do that. I find it clears the brain as well as the lungs.'

Bowker's face turned dark with frustrated rage. Knight could almost hear his silent howl of fury. Another suspect had blown his chance of being eliminated from the enquiry. It was bloody maddening.

9. ⋯⋯⋯⋯⋯⋯⋯⋯⋯⋯⋯⋯⋯⋯⋯ *the bull's head inn*

The pub-keeper's wife at the Black Swan served up a tremendous dinner when Bowker and Knight got back from Oxford. There were lamb chops first, four each, done to a turn, with new potatoes and broccoli in a thick cream sauce.

As Bowker tackled his plateful of food with all the tireless energy of a bulldozer demolishing a row of houses, he explained to Knight between mouthfuls that he was fairly sure they could take Harvey Hurst off the list of suspects.

'What?' said Knight, his fork clattering on his plate as he dropped it in surprise. 'But he's given us a perfect motive for having her killed. They may have been divorced by law, but they were still married emotionally. At least, he was. While he felt like that about her, nobody was ever going to put them asunder, as the parsons say.'

'So?'

'If you ask me, Dr Hurst's a sort of sex-killer. Lynn married him and then dumped him for money, but she made sure she kept a chain round his neck with the other end in her hand, by letting him have a leg-over from time to time. If you look at that list of telephone calls, sir, there were seven by her to him, as against only three from him to her. Lynn was making the running.'

'Agreed,' Bowker said with a scowl of concentration. 'So you think Hurst is our man? He put Fowler up to splitting her head open and paid him for it? Even though we can't find the money. That what you think?'

'I'm saying we can't take him off the list, sir. He's still a prime suspect. And the best he can come up with for the time of Fowler's death is bloody pathetic. He was having a long hike on the Downs, all by himself!'

'Establishing an alibi is always the tricky part for any sort of criminal,' said Bowker, 'especially for a murderer. You might get your wife or your girlfriend to say you were in bed for the usual with them if you've been out doing the Post Office or the wages-van. But when it comes to the question of a nasty murder, even your nearest and dearest start going a bit paranoid about backing up your lies. Which is not to say they won't alibi you, I've known it to happen. But given time you can break them down by keeping on at them. Once they crack, the lie is exposed, and Chummy's done for.'

'What you're saying is—better no alibi at all than one that can be broken?'

'Right. There's no bloody way on God's earth of proving Hurst *wasn't* striding about on the bloody Downs singing hymns ancient and modern all Saturday afternoon. Unless we find somebody who saw him here in Long Slaughter. And we haven't found a solitary soul. We had PC Whitelock trampling round asking questions, and a lot of bloody good it did us! Nobody saw anyone looking like Hurst or a car anything like his, all last week.'

'Doesn't mean he wasn't here,' Knight maintained. 'I was on a sex-murder case in Walsall only last year, a very ordinary sort of chap who strangled his wife because he found she was having it off with one of his friends. Only about twenty-five, him and her, and married not more than a year or two.'

'A crime of passion, as the French say?'

'That's what his lawyer claimed at the trial,' Knight agreed. 'Said he'd lost control in a blind fit of rage, not responsible for his actions—the usual rubbish lawyers come out with. Only the thing was; this Anson—that was his name—he was bloody well in control of his actions when he dumped his wife's dead body.'

'I remember reading about that case,' said Bowker, his plate empty. 'He stripped her naked and threw her body on the rubbish dump—that the one you mean?'

'That's him. After he'd strangled her, he waited until it was dark before he put her in the boot of his car and drove her all the way to the Municipal tip. His lawyer tried to get him off by claiming temporary insanity, diminished responsibility, more sinned against than sinning, all that old Mary Ellen.'

'Symbolic, I suppose, heaving her on the tip naked. Showed he regarded her as rubbish.'

'No other way of looking at it,' said Knight, 'but in his own weird way, Anson was in love with that woman. In the witness-box he wept and cried when he was asked why he'd done it. I've seen enough fakers to know real grief when I hear it.'

'As I remember the newspaper, his lawyer got him off,' Bowker said, his tone indicating stark incredulity.

'You know what juries are like these days, sir. Layabouts and no-hopers hauled in from the high-rise slum estates, anti-law, anti-police, anti–bloody everything except bigger hand-outs.'

'Who was it called us bigots and racists just the other day? It was Rowley the Fantasy Artist with the motorbike. And if he could hear what you just said, Knight, he'd write to his bloody MP or the *Guardian* or Channel 4, even. What was the verdict?'

'Involuntary manslaughter. He got eighteen months suspended.'

'It was a bad day when they stopped handing out hard labour; that used to keep them out of mischief. I wonder sometimes now if it's even worth catching them,' Bowker said thoughtfully. He shook his head in wonder. 'Still, somebody has to clear up the mess. All the same, you can't compare Hurst with your domestic strangler. He might have strangled Lynn in a fit of rage in one of their frolics; I'm sure he'd be capable of that. But that's not how it was.'

'Not so very different,' said Knight stubbornly.

'Chalk and bloody cheese!' Bowker sounded exasperated at his Sergeant. 'Some wicked sod suborned, paid or otherwise procured Fowler to do Lynn in. I can't see Hurst being up that degree of nastiness, unsatisfactory though he may be as a human being.'

'You're the boss. Do we scratch him off the list?'

'Not quite. There's still a loose end or two there. It won't do any harm to have a chat with the secretary he says Lynn set him up with to get a divorce. He told us her name when we first saw him. I've forgotten it, but it's in your notebook.'

'Fiona Good,' Knight said instantly.

'She can probably tell us some hair-raising tales of the late Mrs Hurst, which may or may not be useful. At least the episode taught the Doctor a lesson. He's got a new secretary who's the wrong type to tempt him; that blonde in the cultured pearls who tried to stop us getting in to see him.'

'Looked all right to me,' said Knight. 'You're sure she's not his type?'

'I've met idiots like Dr Hurst before. The latest love of his life is Miss Tania Walker, he told us. I can tell you now what she's like.'

Jack Knight had finished eating. He whipped out his notebook and pen.

'Go on, then,' he said. 'Let's have a fiver on it, sir. What's she like?'

'A fiver it is,' Bowker agreed, his smile like a shark about to bite off a swimmer's leg. 'When we track down Tania, she will be about nineteen, very pretty, with big eyes, a nice big chest, and legs up to her armpits. Her Daddy is very well-off and lives in a house bigger than Hurst's. Tania's dead keen on horse-riding, skiing. That's enough to be going on with.'

'Right,' said DS Knight with a grin, 'you're on. How shall we settle the bet, send somebody round to have a look at her?'

'No need,' said Bowker, he held his hand out over the table. 'There's photos of her on the mantelpiece in Hurst's sitting-room. That's how I know. It's a shame to take your money.'

The landlord of the Black Swan brought them vast platefuls of Mrs Cawley's next offering, Spotted Dick dowsed in custard. He asked if they wanted cheese afterward; he'd a nice half-Stilton they could dig into. Bowker hesitated over it, he said sadly if they had more time he'd certainly have a go at the cheese. But bloody duty called; they had to go across to the Bull's Head to interview somebody.

Long Slaughter's other pub, the Bull's Head, was down past St Elfreda's church, where Badger Lane ran into Church Street. It was smaller than the Black Swan, there was only the Saloon Bar and a box-like Snug at the back for old village biddies wanting to get away from the men.

There were five men in the Saloon Bar when Bowker and Knight arrived. Two of them were playing a noisy game of bar-skittles. A wooden ball the size of an apple, on the end of a string tied to an upright post, was swung at nine skittles in an oblong box.

'I haven't seen that played for years,' said Knight. 'It went out after the Japanese invented the Space Invader machines. Bet you they even play shove-ha'penny here!'

Bowker glared balefully round the bar. The farmer who had found the white car with Gavin Fowler's body in it wasn't to be seen.

'Two pints of best bitter, please,' he said to the barmaid, an over-endowed woman of forty-something. He didn't know it, but she was the landlord's wife. Her amplitude was contained in a gypsy-style blouse with short sleeves and a drawstring neckline.

'Has Mr Liggins been in tonight?'

'Bobby Liggins? No, not all night,' she told him, the shake of her head causing her protuberant parts to shake in sympathy.

'How about Mr Brian Fox? Is he in?'

'You'll be the detective come about the murder,' Mrs Johnson said; she didn't answer his question. She pulled two pints very expertly—not too much froth, not too little—and set them upon the bar in front of him.

'Bowker's my name. Detective Inspector. It can't be more than five minutes' walk from where Mrs Hurst lived. Did she ever come in for a drink?'

'Not that I remember. I knew her by sight, that's all. Maybe when she first came to Long Slaughter and was looking 'round. I couldn't say. Now you tell me something, Mr Bowker. Why ever did that young chap kill her and then himself? Was there a bit of hanky-panky going on between them nobody knew about?'

'I wish I knew what's been going on,' Bowker said morosely. 'It's as big a mystery to me as it is to you.'

'Brian Fox doesn't know either,' she went on, trying to sound helpful, her elbows on the bar and her bosom resting solidly on her arms. 'That's why you asked for him, because you were told he knows everything that goes on in Long Slaughter. We've all asked him already, and he's in the dark as much as the rest of us. That's him in the corner talking to Freddy Boulter.'

Two men were chatting over a small round table with cast-iron legs, a pattern of interlaced foliage and old-fashioned-looking nymphs with bare breasts. Both men were in their forties. One wore a black beret and a checkered tweed jacket, the other a greyish raincoat and a flat cap.

Bowker made for their corner, Knight close behind him.

'Evening, gentlemen,' he said politely. 'I'd like a word with Mr Brian Fox.'

'That's me,' said the man in the beret. 'I know who you are. Clear off, Freddy, the Inspector wants me to help him with his enquiries.'

'I'll be off, then,' Freddy announced to no one in particular. He slid out from the three-legged table and away. Bowker sat on a stool that put him opposite Fox. Knight took the vacated seat on the wall-bench where Freddy had sat.

'So help me with my enquiries, Mr Fox,' said Bowker, studying his new witness, though witness to what, God alone knew.

Fox was a thin, angular man, long jaw and long nose, bifocal glasses, a tie with stripes that could be some dim regiment now merged into anonymity. Sharp-eyed as a magpie, missing nothing, beady and fast to pounce. A schoolmaster, most likely, was the thought in Bowker's mind.

'I thought you were supposed to ask me questions,' said Fox. 'Then I tell you the answer, if I know it, and I usually do.'

Knight realised Bowker was playing it canny when he said, 'I don't even know what questions to ask, Mr Fox. So you tell me the right answers, and I'll guess the questions.'

'Seems a bloody funny way of going about things,' said Fox, a sly grin on his long face. 'My first answer won't help you much at all—I've never seen Mrs Hurst with young Fowler, and never heard of anything going on between them.'

Bowker saw his DS reaching into his inside pocket to get the notebook. He shook his head, Fox might go tight-mouthed when he saw his words being written down.

'I'd be bloody surprised if you had,' Bowker said, approval in his tone. 'It never looked a starter to me. What about Roy Sibson's baby?'

What the hell's he on about? Knight wondered. *What baby?* He racked his brain and came up with Barry Crick's tale of a girl named Jilly Something being turned into a one-parent family by either Roy Sibson or himself. Roy did it, according to Barry, though Roy was sure to tell a different tale. A connection with the murder of Lynn Hurst seemed utterly unlikely. It would have to wait for the Inspector to explain, Knight was baffled.

'You mean the baby Jilly Ratcliffe had two years ago?' Fox said. 'That wasn't Roy's doing, from what I heard. He and Barry Crick had a shouting-match over it right outside here one night after they'd had one too many. Barry's never set foot in this pub since; he goes to the Black Swan to do his drinking now.'

'So the poor mite's fatherless; neither of them ready to take responsibility?'

'Interesting thing,' said Fox, his eyes glinting behind his glasses. 'Jilly never had either of them up in Court over it. A few pounds a week for paternity payment was a certainty—you'd think a girl in her position would be after that, with only her wage part-time at the Post Office to keep her.'

'What's the answer, then?'

'What's the question, Mr Bowker?'

'Roy or Barry?'

'Neither of them. That's why she never went to Court.'

'You know more than you're saying,' Bowker said. His grin was surprisingly encouraging.

'Jilly's getting her few pounds a week to keep her mouth shut tight. And she's getting it from a married man who drinks here sometimes. He's got four kids of his own and doesn't want his wife to find out he plays Away matches.'

'So Roy's off the hook for that one,' said Bowker, pulling a long face. 'I don't suppose he knows that; it's not in Jilly's interest to tell him. I wondered whether he had a sudden need for more money than his wages, but obviously he didn't.'

Knight thought he saw the relevance at last. Bowker had ruled out a possible motive. It wasn't much, but eliminating anything at all was a help.

'What about Roy and Mrs Hurst?' Bowker asked, raising one of his thick black eyebrows in humorous interrogation. In someone else it might have been humorous, but on his gypsy-complexioned face it was distinctly threatening.

Jack Knight was thinking the Inspector had taken the long way 'round, but he'd got there now.

'Ah!' said Fox. 'More to that than meets the eye. She was a fine figure of a woman, absolutely made for it. With the right temperament for it, too. She picked her men-friends from outside Long Slaughter, as a rule; well-off chaps with big cars. I've seen her with three or four since she moved into the village.'

Bowker waved at the barmaid as if he were directing traffic, and pointed to the three empty glasses on the table.

'Roy was a come-down for her?' he suggested.

'If you knew him, you wouldn't need to ask. He's a bit weedy, Roy, not much of a personality. He's got a weak chest, suffers from bad colds a lot in the winter.'

'I've only seen a photo of him,' said Bowker. 'He didn't look to me like a scrum-half. Nor did he look the sort of chap that Mrs Hurst would find attractive. But the fact is they were seen together only last week, in her car.'

'Going along the Wormwold road,' said Fox with a leer. 'Yes, I heard about that, Inspector. There's only one reason I know why young couples go out there.'

'I can't see it,' said Bowker, his scowl black as thunder.

Fox did not shrink away. Either he had a clean conscience, or he felt he had nothing to fear because he had information.

'They tried to keep it secret,' he said. He dropped his voice to avoid being overheard, though the clatter of wooden skittles and imprecations from the players was cover enough. 'I know for a fact they've been getting together since before Christmas.'

'What for?'

Fox said nothing while Mrs Johnson came from the bar, bringing them three pints on a tin tray. Bowker thanked her. Fox touched his black beret and grinned lecherously at her superstructure.

'What for?' he repeated after she'd gone away. 'What do you mean, what for? Bloody hell, Inspector, there's only one thing a couple get together for in secret.'

'No,' said Bowker, 'I can give you ten reasons straight off, none of them requiring the removal of clothing.'

'What, for instance?'

'Conspiracy, for instance.'

'Conspiracy to do bloody what?'

'Now you're asking *me* the questions, Mr Fox; that's the wrong way 'round. Leaving aside this bloody notorious Wormwold road of yours, where else did Mrs Hurst meet Roy?'

'He was seen going into her cottage in School Walk, and by a person I trust to tell the truth. But only the once, as far as I know. They were seen together in Reading, in the big pub near the bus station. And someone else I know swears she saw them in Oxford in a tea-shop.'

'Dates?'

'Spread out, from about last November till recently.'

'Very bloody recently,' Bowker said with a grimace that would have scared the average murderer into instant confession. 'Last bloody Tuesday, in fact, a week ago, he was in her white car on the way to God-knows-where. Since when Roy's not been seen and she's dead.'

'The silly bugger's run away,' said Fox, with sly relish. 'He heard she'd been killed and thought he'd be arrested for it, on the strength of him having a rollick with her. So he's buggered off. When he gets to know it was young Fowler killed her, he'll come trailing home.'

'Ah, but I think his sister Joyce knows where he is,' Bowker said, making it sound confidential. 'So if she's told him about Fowler found dead in Mrs Hurst's car and strongly suspected for her murder, why hasn't he come back? The story's all over the village that Fowler's our man. But still no bloody Roy. There's got to be more to it.'

Fox looked pleased with this new item of information for his scrapbook of gossip.

'A strong-minded woman, Joyce,' he said, approval evident in his tone, 'and very good-looking, you can't deny it. I wouldn't mind having Joyce looking after me, if I was the marrying kind. She's had Reg Harris under her thumb since the day she wed him. The only time he's ever let off the leash is when Reading play an Away game, Joyce lets him travel with the supporters and get drunk after the match. Even then he has to be home by eleven.'

'She sounds an interesting woman,' said Bowker, astonishing Knight. 'I haven't seen her at her best, of course. I'm pleased to meet an admirer of hers.'

'Nothing goes on in that family without Joyce says so,' said Fox cheerfully. 'You're absolutely right, Mr Bowker, Joyce must know where Roy is. Why not ask her?'

'I have, and she told me a fairy tale about going away on his holidays.'

'There's always the chance Roy's been warned off by somebody else who had an interest in Mrs Hurst,' said Fox. 'Maybe he was scared and made himself scarce a while to let the dust settle.'

Bowker's jaws ground together, there was a short pause before he asked the question.

'Now who could have seen Roy off?'

'I make no accusations, Inspector,' said Fox, his tone loaded with enough heavy innuendo to warrant instant arrest of whoever he named. 'There is one local person who was taking an interest in Mrs Hurst not long back. For anything I know, he might still have been interested till the day she died.'

'Who?' said Bowker, his teeth gritted.

'Somebody who kept it very quiet. I was walking my dog late one night, and I saw him with my own eyes leave her cottage.'

Knight could practically measure the pressure building up in Bowker. He was afraid for Fox if he tantalised the Inspector any longer. Bowker might leap to his feet and send the bereted berk cartwheeling across the bar.

'Stephen Fenwick.' Fox spoke the name almost in a whisper.

'And who's he?' Bowker growled, the sinews on his neck jumping dangerously.

'He's an important chap, Fenwick,' Fox confided. 'He came to live in Long Slaughter seven or eight years ago. Commutes up to London. He's some sort of posh lawyer in the City.'

'Married?'

'Oh, yes, nice-looking woman, always very well dressed. There are children you see out riding at weekends.'

'You saw him leaving Mrs Hurst's cottage. When was that?'

'About three months ago.'

'He might have been advising her on investments,' said Bowker with a frown, 'or perhaps he was dropping in socially.'

'It's definitely social if you stay till eleven-thirty at night,' Fox agreed with a leer, 'but the sort of sociability best kept away from his own home and family. Her upstairs lights were all on; it was that sort of social gathering.'

'Where is his home?'

'Just across the road from here. He bought the Old Rectory.'

'That little book we found,' Bowker said to Knight. 'Is there an SF in it that you remember?'

'Not offhand. It's at Whitelock's house for safekeeping. Do you want me to go 'round and look?'

'We'll check it tomorrow first thing and arrange a chat with Mr Fenwick.'

Bowker saw Knight look up and smile pleasantly. Then he heard a woman's voice behind him.

'Hello, Inspector, may I sit with you?' Sara Thomas asked.

Bowker stood up courteously and introduced Jack Knight. Sara said she knew Brian Fox, who nodded to her. She was trying the businesslike look tonight in a navy-blue jacket and skirt, with a white shirt but no tie. She took a seat on the bench next to Fox, on his other side from Knight.

'Get Sara a drink, Jack,' said Bowker. 'What's it to be?'

'Large vodka and tonic,' she said at once, making him wonder if he'd been wrong about reporters changing. Maybe this slender fair-haired girl would turn herself into a red-nosed old drunk of a harridan in the interests of the newspaper. Pity, really.

'Kevin Whitelock said you'd be at the Black Swan,' she said, 'but Arthur Cawley said you were here. When I heard that I knew I'd find you with Brian.'

'He's your local correspondent, so to speak—your insider, is he?' Bowker asked. 'He certainly knows his way around the dark secrets of Long Slaughter. But one question he hasn't got the answer to is, where's Roy Sibson?'

'If he's anywhere in the *Examiner*'s circulation area, it won't be long before you'll have your answer,' Sara told him. 'We've had his picture circulated by your HQ, and it'll be on page one tomorrow.'

'What sort of words did they give you to go with it?'

'The usual guff your lot put out,' she said. 'It's believed he can help the police in their enquiries. Anyone with information on his whereabouts or movements is kindly requested to tell any handy bobby. What do you suspect him of, Mr Bowker?'

'The name is Denis,' he said, so massively pleasant that Knight's hand shook as he set Sara's drink down on the table and spilled a drop or two.

'Denis with one N,' she said, smiling and wrinkling her nose. 'What's Roy Sibson done? Off the record.'

'There's no such thing as *off the record*,' he told her. 'With me everything's out in the open. I don't know what Roy's done, maybe nothing. But he's been away from home for a week with no good explanation. His family say he's gone on holiday, but they don't know where. Maybe he has. For all I know he could well be blind drunk on rotgut wine in a bar on the Costa Brava, singing *Viva España* at the top of his lungs.'

'Can I quote you on that?'

'Please yourself, he'll only sue me for defamation. I need to talk to Roy Sibson because he may be able to shed some light on the last few days of the murdered woman.'

'Particularly what they got up to on the Wormwold road,' Fox said with a sly grin.

'He was her lover—is that what you're saying?' Sara asked.

'Mr Fox might be saying it, but I'm bloody not,' Bowker said very firmly. 'Finish your drink and stroll with us to the Black Swan for another one. And maybe one of Mrs Cawley's cheese-and-pickle sandwiches? Very nice as a late-night snack.'

Five minutes later, they were walking up Church Street.

Bowker and Sara in the lead, Knight bringing up the rear, the pavement not wide enough for three of them. And for once Knight found he wasn't having to trot to keep up, Bowker had slowed his mighty pace to accommodate the girl.

'If you didn't want Brian in on the conversation, you only had to tell him to push off,' she said.

'Can't do that,' said Bowker. 'I'm not allowed to be rude to people. Besides, it's not in my nature.'

'Bloody hell!' said Knight, utterly amazed.

'What?' Bowker demanded, swinging 'round to face him.

'I was thinking how little use Fox was to us, after everybody cracked him up to know it all,' Knight was improvising to cover his exclamation. 'All we got was some piffling stuff about who put Jilly Ratcliffe in the plum-pudding club.'

'Always the trouble with self-appointed bloody experts,' said Bowker, wanting no mention of the mysterious Stephen Fenwick in front of a reporter. 'They turn out to know no more than anybody else with a pair of eyes to see and a pair of ears to hear. Has Fox ever been any use to you, Sara?'

'He put me on to a story about a big brewery company wanting to buy the Bull's Head and modernise it. But they changed their mind after we'd run the story in the *Examiner* and lots of local residents wrote in to object.'

'Human nature,' said Bowker. 'I expect half of them had never set foot inside the place. I don't think anybody should try to modernise it—I think they should keep it exactly as it is, as a memorial to this miserable bloody village.'

'Apart from that one time, Brian's always been pretty useless to me,' said Sara with a giggle that made Jack Knight decide he was instantly in love with her. 'He specialises in who's having it off with whose wife—we can't print that sort of thing.'

'PC Whitelock said you wanted to talk to me, and here you are in Long Slaughter at this time of night,' said Bowker, and his voice rumbled like a mastiff tickled behind the ears. 'What did you want to talk about, Sara?'

'It's nothing much, really, but it might interest you, Denis.

Worth mentioning, anyway, I thought. My evil old editor sent me to do an interview with the murdered woman's boyfriend. Well, fiancé, I should say. He said we had all the makings of a *love-triangle tragedy* story, my idiot editor that is, two men madly in love with the same woman, passions raging, Lynn torn between her two hot-blooded men and unable to make her mind up. I told him it was bilge, but he wouldn't listen to me, silly old sod.'

'You interviewed Mark Stanhope? When was that?'

'Yesterday afternoon. The idea was for him to open his heart to me, talk about the nights of passion and days of despair, or maybe the other way round. My editor's idea, that is, not mine. But I have to do what I'm told, so I went to talk to him to see if anything could be salvaged from the wreck.'

'What wreck?' Knight asked, eliciting an angry *shush* from his superior officer.

'The wreck of my editor's aspiration to print a sex-story and pretend it's human interest. As you can imagine, I expected to find a broken man grieving over Lynn's death. I was going to be very sympathetic and let him have a cry on my shoulder. I even put this suit on, to make myself look serious.'

'Well, well,' said Bowker, sounding like a tiger purring in the bass register after eating a Bengali peasant, and mightily pleased with itself. 'And how did you find our Mr Stanhope?'

'He was defensive, shifty, unfriendly and furtive. I was with him no more than five minutes before he threw me out.'

'Did he now!'

'I know what you both must be thinking—pushy reporters who intrude on personal grief—but it wasn't that.'

'Your lot do have a reputation for asking mutilated accident victims how they feel, instead of hauling them to safety,' said Knight.

'Not me,' said Sara Thomas. She sounded almost convincing. 'I am known throughout the county for my softness of heart. There were practically tears in my eyes when I asked Stanhope what he thought had happened in Long Slaughter that fateful day.'

'*Defensive, shifty,* and *furtive,*' said Bowker. 'Make a note of those words, Jack.'

'Too bloody dark to see what I'm doing. Have to wait till we get to the Black Swan.'

Bowker ignored him. 'Do you understand what I mean by guilty knowledge, Sara?' He clasped her arm gently above the elbow in his giant hand. 'Tell me your impression: did Stanhope act as if he had guilty knowledge?'

'If you put it like that, yes, he did.'

'Thank you. We'll drive over and talk to him, Knight,' Bowker dropped the first name now it was business again. 'To be honest with you, I've never felt comfortable about Mark Stanhope. He's a wrong'un, though I can't see how.'

'If you arrest him, Denis, I'd really appreciate being given the inside story,' said Sara, her voice very little-girlish. In fact she sounded so oncoming that Jack Knight thought he might ask her for a date—if Denis Bowker ever gave him any time off from the investigation.

10. ··· *the old rectory*

Modern-day parsons at Long Slaughter do not have the pleasure of living in the large and handsome Queen Anne rectory erected for their predecessors. It stands right on the corner of Badger Lane, near St Elfreda's church, almost facing the Bull's Head public house. The fine old rectory became much too grand for a parson of the Church of England in terminal decline, and it was sold off, like many another, to bump up Church funds.

Stephen Fenwick had bought the Old Rectory some years ago and lived there with his family, according to the information given to Inspector Bowker by Nosey Parker Brian Fox, later confirmed, after Sara Thomas left, by the landlord of the Black Swan.

It occurred to Bowker that Fenwick had to make an early start if he commuted up to London to work. And it would be a shame to miss him and have to wait all day till he got back.

Late as it was, after eleven, Bowker had Knight phone Fenwick and arrange for him to be available for interview the next day at nine. Fenwick protested vehemently at the appalling waste of his time, he had early appointments in London, he insisted, he normally left home at 7:30 at the latest. It would be far more convenient if the police saw him at his office in the City.

For all his pleasant manner, Jack Knight was no pushover. He reminded Fenwick sharply that this was a murder enquiry. In fact, it was a double murder enquiry. Two Long Slaughter inhabitants had died by foul means, Long Slaughter was the scene of the crime, and the location of Mr Fenwick's own domicile. Inspector Bowker would be calling on him at 9:00 A.M. sharp, and expected him to be there.

'How did he sound?' Bowker asked when Knight came back from the telephone. 'Upset, I hope.'

The pub was closed, Bowker was in his room, sitting on a hard single bed and scribbling on a large pad of ruled paper. He had taken off the jacket of his rumpled suit and hung it on a hook on the back of the door. Comforts for travellers were sparse at the Black Swan. The WC was at the end of the passage; for night emergencies there was a white china utensil to be found in the bedside cabinet.

'He sounded peeved,' said Knight, striving for the right word to convey his impressions. 'He thinks his time is too valuable to waste on coppers.'

'I expect it is. He probably charges £500 an hour to talk to financiers in trouble,' said Bowker, with a grin. 'We're a dead loss to him, Jack, no fee and every chance of grief. He can be as peeved as he likes. Did he sound as if he's going to suffer through a sleepless night because he's seeing us tomorrow?'

'Not exactly. He's a lawyer; they're far too crafty to let on what's in their minds. He sounded a bit fidgety when I mentioned Mrs Hurst to him.'

'What did you say?'

'Only that you are investigating her death and have reason to believe he can help with your enquiries.'

'I love that phrase.' Bowker's smile was as cheerless as the

Eiger North Face. 'I've had people helping me with my enquiries down on their knees begging to be allowed to confess. The trick is not to let them, when they get like that—sneer at them and sling them back in the cell. Leave them stewing for another two or three hours. You get a better class of confession that way, more detail that can be used at the trial.'

Knight stared hard at Bowker, wondering whether to take him seriously when he said things like that. Or was it his twisted sense of humour?

'It won't be easy getting a lawyer to confess, if he did it,' said Knight. 'They mostly get off, even when they swindle their own clients out of money they've been fool enough to hand over to them.'

'Lawyers, I abominate them!' said Bowker. 'They get paid for making up lies so criminals can get off scot-free. It's a nasty profession to be in; I respect a brothel-keeper more. If either of my children grew up wanting to be lawyers, I'd know for sure I'd failed as a parent.'

It was difficult for Knight to envisage Bowker as a parent of any kind—good, bad, possessive, caring, or tough. But then, it was next to impossible for the puzzled DS to imagine what woman would want to marry him in the first place.

Of one thing Knight was sure; Bowker might be extremely good or impossibly bad as family man, but he'd never be indifferent.

'Have you ever managed to put a lawyer away?' Knight asked. A black scowl warned him he'd touched an uneasy topic.

Being a newcomer, he couldn't know he'd asked about the only murder case Bowker had investigated where the man he arrested escaped conviction, a case that still shot his blood pressure up into the high numbers when he thought about it.

'There was a rich old lady died in mysterious circumstances a year or two back,' said Bowker, so ominously that he sounded like the Ancient Mariner collaring a reluctant wedding-guest. 'She'd been a widow twenty years or so. She was well into her eighties and getting vague in her mind. She owned a big house on the Thames near Wargrave, beautiful place. She had a house-keeper companion type of woman living in.'

'A victim in the making,' said Knight, shaking his head sadly and making tutting noises. 'Poor old soul.'

'She was found dead one morning at the foot of the stairs in her dressing-gown and nightie. Broken neck, nobody thought much of it. The housekeeper said the old lady was shaky on her pins, her doctor confirmed it.'

'The housekeeper heard nothing, of course,' Knight suggested.

'Slept like a log, she said. There was no direct family. Just as you said, she was a victim waiting for a crime to happen. A sort of distant nephew nine times removed crawled out of some hole in Sussex, a bald-headed coot in his fifties, and he was all bloody indignant because he wasn't in the will.'

'The old lady knew about him, did she?'

'According to him, she sent him a card every Christmas and he sent her one on her birthday. Anyway, he made a big fuss and so we took a look, which means DCS Horrocks sent me round to prod about a bit and see what I could stir up. Damn me if her lawyer hadn't bloody well put himself in the will for the entire bloody bundle! Over a million and half in property and invest-ments.'

'How about the housekeeper? Did she get anything?'

'She'd been left ten thousand pounds, and I got a strong im-pression she'd expected more. The nearly-nephew chap claimed the will had been made under duress or undue influence or what-ever. Or forged. It was dated twelve months before the old lady went arse-over-tip down the stairs.'

'Very, very suspicious,' said Knight, shaking his head.

'Yes, well, whether the lawyer had influenced a client in his own favour or not, that was something for the nephew to take to a civil Court and argue out. But apart from that, it looked to me there was a good chance the lawyer had bloody well heaved an old lady down the stairs to get at her money sooner.'

'But could he get into the house after dark?' Knight asked, his forehead wrinkled in concentration. 'The lawyers I've met are a long sight better at twisting the truth than at breaking and entering. Were you looking for collusion between him and the housekeeper?'

'It had to be that. But to admit it would put her in the dock with him as accomplice to murder. He had no alibi for the night it happened, but with a million and half quid, he had a perfect motive. I got nowhere with the housekeeper—my guess is she put the grab on the lawyer for a bonus when the pressure built up.'

Knight didn't dare ask whether Bowker had nailed the wicked lawyer for his crime. The furious look he was given earlier had told him the answer.

'You were certain he did it?'

'It was never in doubt for a second,' said Bowker, his voice a bearlike rumble. 'I knew it in my bones the first time I set eyes on him, and I bloody nearly had him for it. Then the evil bastard played a trump card. At the last moment he produced an alibi he'd bought.'

'How did he do that?'

'He paid a tart to say he was with her all night and claimed he'd been too ashamed before to come forward with the truth. I tried to shake the tart's story, but she stuck fast. I was nice to her, I was nasty to her, I promised her immunity, I promised her seven years in the clink for perverting the course of justice. Nothing shifted her an inch. She was on a promise of big money to get him off—that was bloody obvious.'

'I can guess how you felt,' Knight said.

'A miscarriage of justice to make you spit tacks! The bloody nephew did better than I did. It took him a couple of years, but he got that lawyer struck off for unprofessional conduct, or whatever happy name they call stealing in the legal business.'

'Well, that's something.'

'No good came of it,' Bowker said gloomily. 'By that time the murdering swine was long gone—he slipped off abroad and took the money with him.'

'Where'd he go, Spain?'

'He's got a fancy villa with a swimming-pool at Marbella with the rest of the criminal fraternity. Inspector Turnbull was out there last year on holiday with his wife and kids. He stopped by to see how Chummy was getting on.'

'Funny thing to do,' said Knight.

'That's what I said. It's like picking off a scab to see what infection is underneath. But there it is, Ronny Turnbull is the sort of copper who broods, not like me. He hates and loathes it when criminals get off.'

That statement made Knight stare in amazement at Bowker. He'd never before met a copper who took things so personally as did Denis Bowker.

'He was torturing himself, visiting like that,' said Bowker. 'Chummy had put about two stones on and found himself a seventeen-year-old Spanish bird with a big chest.'

'It's bloody criminal,' said Knight, wishing he'd never asked about lawyers. 'There ought to be a law against it. I'll be off to bed then, if we've finished for the day.'

There was a worn-looking book on Bowker's bedside table.

'Not one of Roy's you borrowed, is it?' he asked as a joke. 'The inside story of the International Freemason conspiracy?'

Knight was a newcomer; he didn't know about the Inspector's reading habits.

'It's Charles Dickens,' said Bowker, looking very interested. 'One of my own books. I've got all of his. I've read them over twenty times. This one's called *Hard Times*—have you read it?'

'Don't get much time for reading,' said Knight, wishing he'd never asked. 'The last book I read was one of Jackie Collins a girlfriend lent me.'

'You'll rot your brain, reading stuff like that,' said Bowker in an appalled tone of voice. 'Now this book's all about a mean and miserable bastard named Thomas Gradgrind who forces his under-age daughter to marry a middle-aged millionaire who's been drooling to get his hands on her young body. A young politician tries to get a leg over, which makes her so confused she leaves her husband. It gets more complicated when her brother frames somebody else for thieving he's been up to himself.'

'Sounds a lot like Jackie Collins to me,' said Knight. 'You sure it's Charles Dickens?'

The Old Rectory was a pleasant-looking building. In 200 years the brick had mellowed to a dark rose, the window frames gleamed creamy-white, the low box-hedge in front was cut geometrically square.

The brass lion-head knocker was as old as the house and if it was on a door in anywhere less law-abiding than Long Slaughter, it would have been stolen by now and sold to an antique dealer. On the worn-down doorstep, a cat with a blue-grey coat dozed in the morning sun.

'Wrong colour,' said Bowker thoughtfully. 'Otherwise I might be tempted to take it for Miss Pankhurst. I doubt if Whitelock will find hers now; it's been gone too long. And one ginger tom looks like another when you're her age. But blue's too bloody different; she'd spot it right away.'

'Steal the cat? You've got a real down on lawyers!' Knight said with a grin as he banged with the lion-head knocker.

Stephen Fenwick was a man of forty or thereabouts, his wavy hair had a touch of silver over each ear, very old-style film-star. He wore glasses and was not very tall. And he was charming.

With the benefit of knowing Bowker's general views on lawyers, Knight had been wondering how the Inspector would approach this one. Lawyers were slippery creatures. Steamrollering them was tricky; they slid sideways out of harm's way.

Evidently Fenwick had given some thought overnight to his own response to the police visit. On the phone he had been brusque and supercilious to DS Knight, maybe because he'd been taken by surprise late at night and in his own home. This morning he was charm itself, smiling as he said, 'Come in, my dear Inspector,' to Bowker, giving Knight a friendly nod, offering them coffee.

The room he took them to was furnished in period, pleasingly done with genuine or repro Queen Anne. Knight couldn't tell the difference and was sure it was expensive, whichever it was. For his taste it was heavy and dark, walnut, maybe, too old-fashioned to appeal to him.

'I've cancelled all my appointments this morning, Inspector,' said Fenwick. 'How can I help you in this ghastly business?'

'I take it you knew Mrs Hurst socially,' said Bowker, keeping his hatred of lawyers well in check.

Fenwick took an armchair that put his back to the window. Bowker had to sit down facing him.

'Oh, yes, she and my wife got on very well. She's been here to dinner more than once. Sometimes she went riding with my un-ruly brood.'

Knight had his notebook out. To his surprise, Bowker shook his head and told him to put it away.

'There's no need to write down what Mr Fenwick tells us,' he said, sounding almost genial. 'In his line of work, he's used to thinking before he speaks and giving clear answers.'

'I'm flattered,' Fenwick said. He looked closely at Bowker to see how he should take his words. 'I imagine you come mostly in contact with practitioners of criminal law . . .'

Knight smiled at the way Fenwick had avoided saying *criminal lawyers*; the phrase that never failed to recall the policeman's joke: *Criminal lawyer—what other sort is there?*

' . . . I know very little about that; my speciality is corporate law. You'd find it very dull.'

'Advising on big-money deals,' said Bowker, a broad smile on his face, not unlike a man-eating crocodile showing its rows of teeth. 'You don't make your living by defending bank robbers in ski masks and that sort of low-life. Very sensible.'

There was nothing Fenwick could pick on in the words, it was the tone that was offensive. He frowned, his charm dimmed down to 40 watts from its original 150.

'What exactly do you want to know, Inspector?' he said.

'Just a few routine questions. When was the last time you saw Mrs Hurst?'

'I'm not sure I can remember that precisely,' Fenwick said, a note of sincere desire to help in his voice. 'Several weeks ago, it must have been. My wife has probably seen her more recently than I have. Shall I ask her to come in?'

'Not yet,' said Bowker, still moderately pleasant. 'I suppose you can remember if it was here or at her place, the last time you saw her?'

'Oh, here of course,' Fenwick said without any hesitation. 'I seem to remember coming home one evening to find her here having a drink with my wife. They'd been shopping together, I think.'

'In the book she put her friends' phone numbers in; yours is listed under SF,' said Bowker. 'I take it to stand for Stephen Fenwick, unless your wife's first name begins with an S.'

'My wife's name is Melanie.'

The flatness of the reply told Knight that Bowker was moving along a useful line.

'From what you said, I got the impression Mrs Hurst was more a friend of your wife than of you. It's odd she listed the phone number under your name—SF, and not MF.'

Fenwick said nothing; he hadn't been asked a question.

'Have you been to Mrs Hurst's cottage in School Walk?' asked Bowker, aware that Fenwick was too bright to volunteer information.

'A couple of times,' he answered. 'My wife asked me to drop off a book that she'd borrowed. I stayed for a cup of tea on that occasion, I think. I walked 'round there with my wife once, something to do with the children and riding, I think it was.'

'In the daytime or late at night, would that be?'

Fenwick uncrossed his legs and crossed them the other way. He stared at Bowker thoughtfully. 'I must assume there is a point to these questions,' he said. 'It would be regrettable to think you were taking advantage of my desire to be of assistance.'

'I knew I could rely on you to assist me with my enquiries,' said Bowker, his voice even. Knight suppressed a guffaw when he remembered how the Inspector had used those words the evening before.

'Yes, there is a point, Mr Fenwick. You were seen coming out of Mrs Hurst's cottage late one evening recently. On your own, unaccompanied by Mrs Fenwick. At nearly midnight.'

There was a pause while Fenwick absorbed the implications. He had again been asked no question, but this time he decided that he should supply an answer.

'From this you have deduced that I was having an affair with her.' He didn't sound at all worried, he turned up the charm to 100 watts. 'You're right about that, Inspector. I need hardly remind you it is not against the law, but I do appeal to your sense of fair play not to divulge what you have learned to my wife.'

'I've no reason to do that,' Bowker responded, 'so long as it has no bearing on my investigation. When was the last time you saw Mrs Hurst?'

'The simple answer is the Sunday before last when she was out on a horse and I waved to her in passing. But what you want to know is when I last went to her cottage. That was Friday of the week before, almost a week before she was killed, according to what I've heard and read.'

'Time of day?'

'Late. I never went into School Walk alone in daylight.'

'There are lots of payments into Mrs Hurst's savings account—tokens of esteem you could call them, from men friends. Some of them came from you, I should imagine.'

Fenwick nodded but said nothing.

'Was there a regular payment?' Bowker asked.

'It wasn't like that. Lynn was a marvellous person, vivacious and charming, sensual, beautiful, fascinating. In money matters, she was somewhat scatterbrained. She had her alimony payments, hardly enough to live on, and from time to time she asked me to help her, when the bills were accumulating. I was glad to help; it was a friendly act. Or as you put it, a token of esteem.'

Bowker was thinking that the crafty lawyer had been manipulated by Lynn Hurst as easily as the bearded artist who lived next door. Or her ex-husband. Or her fiancé, the bankrupt architect.

And a half-dozen others with initials in her book he hadn't got 'round to interviewing yet.

By all accounts, she had been a remarkable woman. Bowker was sorry he had seen her only as a dead body in a black and white dress, her hair clotted with dried blood.

'Did you ever meet her ex-husband, Dr Hurst?' he asked.

'No, never. There was no contact between them after they were divorced.'

That's all you know, Jack Knight thought. *She took you for a fool, just like the others.*

'Did you know Gavin Fowler?'

'The man who killed her? No, I understand he lived here in the village, but I wouldn't know him if I saw him.'

'The only place you can see him now is in the mortuary,' said Bowker, 'but there's no need for that. It's quaint how the idea has spread through the village that Fowler murdered Mrs Hurst, I suppose because we found him dead in her car. The local paper jumped to that conclusion and printed some heavy hinting.'

'What? You don't think he killed her?' Suddenly Fenwick was alert and cautious, no longer into his man-of-the-world act about how these things happen between men and women, we chaps understand each other.

'Where were you last Thursday evening, Mr Fenwick?'

'Thursday. The day she was killed. But why should you suspect me? I've been completely open with you. I very much enjoyed her company; her death was a dreadful shock. I shall miss her.'

'Routine question,' said Bowker, his tone noncommittal, or as near it as he could manage. 'Everybody who knew the deceased is asked to account for their movements. Where were you?'

'Thursday. Yes, I had dinner in London with four directors of a company I am doing some work for. At the Savoy. I'll give you their names, of course, though I would ask you to be tactful in your enquiries. It will not enhance my professional reputation to be associated with a murder enquiry.'

'We're always tactful,' said Bowker, sounding like a headsman claiming to be painless.

It didn't matter whether Fenwick had an alibi for Thursday or not, Knight was thinking, it wasn't the key time. Going on the assumption that Fowler had killed Lynn on somebody else's behalf, it became a question of who was available on Saturday afternoon to shut Fowler's mouth. And that was Bowker's next question.

'Saturday afternoon,' he said, coming at it sideways, 'a man named Empson Rowley raced through the village on his motorbike. He lives in the next cottage to Mrs Hurst's. Did you see him?'

'The man with the black beard—I've seen him about. He's some sort of artist, I believe.'

'Do you know him?'

'Only by sight. He's an unconventional figure.'

'Did you see him Saturday? School Walk is only two minutes from here; there's every chance he came past your house at high speed, and that would be very noisy. About two o'clock, he told me.'

'I wasn't here on Saturday afternoon,' said Fenwick, fingers tapping on the chair arm. 'I was in Oxford until about five.'

'Visiting someone?'

'What is your interest?' Fenwick asked sharply, waking up to where he was being led.

'Routine,' Bowker assured him with a savage grin. 'There was someone with Fowler in Lynn Hurst's car on Saturday afternoon.'

'Well, it wasn't me,' said Fenwick, stiffening his back as if to resist further encroachment on his privacy. 'You've already asked me if I knew the man, and I told you I did not.'

'So you did,' Bowker agreed. 'Then you won't mind telling me what you were doing on Saturday afternoon in Oxford. You don't know Dr Hurst, you said, so you didn't go to the Clinic to see him.'

It became clear now to Stephen Fenwick that Bowker distrusted him and disbelieved his story. This disconcerted him; he'd been of the opinion that utter frankness about his affair with Lynn had been enough. But with irritation he concealed he recognised that this over-sized bruiser with the hunched shoulders and the dark gypsy look entertained unpleasant suspicions of him.

As Fenwick had explained, he had nothing to do with criminals or criminal law, not in the sense that Bowker probably thought of criminals. Bank robbers in ski masks, Bowker had said. Low-life, he had called them. The men with whom Fenwick associated did not hit others on the head with iron bars or point sawn-off shotguns at security guards.

In the ordinary way of things Fenwick had nothing much to do with policemen. He saw them as men in uniform standing about at tube stations in case a Provo strolled past and left a bomb in a Tesco carrier-bag. Bowker didn't seem to fit into this scheme and Fenwick felt he was on dangerous ground.

It would be sensible to take advice. But it sounded silly for a lawyer to say he wanted to consult a lawyer. Worse even than that, it sounded highly suspicious.

Suspicion was like a stain; it attracted attention. And left untreated, it spread bigger and bigger. Policemen wouldn't leave it alone; to get rid of them, it was urgently necessary to rinse the stain out. A semblance of honesty was the best policy.

'Look here,' said Fenwick, switching on the charm. 'I've got this awful feeling you don't entirely believe me. Naturally, I understand that. You don't really know me, and it's your job to be suspicious. But I want to do anything I can to help you find the madman who brutally murdered poor lovely Lynn.'

'Two minutes ago, you were sure Gavin Fowler killed her,' said Bowker. 'What makes you think it was a madman now?'

'You gave me to understand Fowler was *not* the murderer,' said Fenwick, sounding very puzzled.

'I expressed no opinion,' Bowker corrected him. 'What I said was the newspaper had decided it was Fowler. What did you do in Oxford last Saturday afternoon?'

'Nothing much. I didn't go to meet anyone. I'd had a bad week at the office—business problems, to be candid—and I was upset and depressed. If I'd known about Lynn's death, that would have affected me badly, but I didn't hear about it until later that day, when I came home. For the life of me, I cannot understand why anyone should want to harm her.'

'Oxford,' said Bowker insistently, bringing him back to the point.

'I was up at Balliol College years ago; Oxford is a place I know pretty well. I don't know if I can reconstruct my thinking clearly, but I suppose I thought it would be a peaceful retreat for an hour or two while I thought through my business problem. Or even forgot about it altogether, for a while.'

I, I, I, seven bloody times in one sentence, Knight counted. No doubt where Mr Fenwick's main affections lay, and it wasn't the late Mrs Hurst.

'Where did you go looking for this peace?' Bowker asked.

'Nowhere in particular,' Fenwick said, the boyish charm now a trifle strained, but he was determined to keep it up. 'I walked along the river by Osney Lock and down to Folly Bridge. I had a cup of tea and a Chelsea bun in the town somewhere.'

'Did you meet anyone you know?'

'Not a soul,' said Fenwick, honesty radiating from him. 'I'm afraid that makes things look bad for me, doesn't it? But it's the simple truth, and I can't change it.'

Knight could see Bowker's face darkening dangerously; perhaps Fenwick's words had reminded him of the lawyer who hired a tart to give him an alibi. Knight was in no doubt that Fenwick was easily capable of protecting himself similarly, if it came to it.

'Thank you for being open with me,' said Bowker, restraining his natural instinct for mayhem with commendable effort.

'There is another acquaintance of Mrs Hurst who lives in the village—you could have met him. Roy Sibson.'

'Sibson? No, the name means nothing to me. Who is he?'

'A young man who lives in Orchard Row. He's been missing for some days.'

'I'm sorry, Inspector, I know nothing about him.'

When they left the Old Rectory, Bowker and Knight walked 'round to the police house by the other route, up Badger Lane and past School Walk to Long Street. They walked in silence for a while, each thinking over the interview and making up his mind.

Knight spoke first. 'He wasn't telling the truth, not the whole truth.'

'He's a lawyer,' said Bowker. 'It goes without saying he lied— that's not the question at all. We have to decide whether he was lying out of habit, which doesn't necessarily mean anything at all, or whether he was lying to cover up guilty knowledge. Allowing for prejudice and knowledge aforethought of the legal trade on my part, I got a feeling he's covering up something.'

'Right,' Knight agreed. 'Anybody who comes across sounding as honest and unbesmirched as him has got to be on the fiddle.'

'He simply dumped the affair with Mrs Hurst in my lap as soon as I got anywhere near the subject,' said Bowker. 'That was to convince us he's a decent chap. *A bit of a frolic with a pretty woman, chaps do that sort of thing, wink, wink, nudge, I'm only human, you know. But murder a mistress, good Lord, no, never.* He set that bloody scenario up for us, Knight. He'd given it some thought after you phoned him.'

'His attitude today was so different from last night, it had to be fake,' Knight said.

'At least we've given him some inconvenience,' Bowker said, a malignant grin on his face. 'He'll have to explain to his wife why we wanted to talk to him about Lynn Hurst, when Mrs Fenwick is supposed to be the one she was friendly with.'

'He's bloody glib,' said Knight. 'He'll worm out of it. Have you put him down as a serious suspect for the murder, sir?'

'What's your view?' Bowker bounced it back.

'By no means impossible for him to make contact with Fowler, to arrange a deal to kill Lynn,' Knight said, anxious to sound intelligent. 'At the time Fowler died in the spinney, Fenwick was meandering 'round Oxford, he'd have us believe. Opportunity he had, but did he have the motive?'

'Same as Rowley next door with the beard,' Bowker suggested.

'Yes, Lynn was taking money from Fenwick, maybe threatening to let Mrs Fenwick in on their little secret if he tried to cut back on her. But where the hell does Roy Sibson fit in?'

'Ask me another,' Bowker said. 'The motive's not good enough for Fenwick. He could afford to give Lynn a few thousand quid a year and not even notice it. By his own account, he was getting value for money. I can't see him arranging for her to be done in for that reason. But there's something bloody wrong about this Mr Lawyer Fenwick.'

'Right,' the DS agreed.

'I'm going to ask DCS Horrocks to get on to Scotland Yard in a hurry,' Bowker said with grisly determination. '*And* the City of London police. *And* the Serious Fraud Office, if they'll talk to a humble copper. I need to know if Fenwick's in their files for anything, and if so, what.'

'Long way from our crime, sir, even if he's involved in some financial swindle.'

'Maybe. I don't see him having Lynn Hurst done in for a grand or two. But if we started talking hundreds of thousands or even millions, maybe, I wouldn't put it past him to arrange something very nasty. For all his chat about *poor lovely Lynn,* Fenwick's a conceited cold-blooded bastard. Say she'd stumbled accidentally on some sort of big-money swindle he's into. And then she tried to pressure him into giving her a share of it. He'd pay for her to be done in and never lose a night's sleep over it. I'd bet a year's pay on that.'

'No takers,' Knight said quickly. 'You rig your bets, sir.'

11. ············· *the thames at pangbourne*

Denis Bowker had assured DCS Horrocks that Roy Sibson would pop up when the time came. The time came on Thursday morning, very early. Roy popped up out of the Thames and drifted face-up into the lock at Pangbourne.

Bowker and Knight were having breakfast at the Black Swan or, to get it accurate, Knight was eating breakfast and Bowker was devouring a plate of four fried eggs, a good half-pound of best streaky bacon, fried mushrooms, bubble-and-squeak, and the better part of a cottage loaf sliced and toasted and spread thick with English butter.

Kevin Whitelock was the bearer of the news. He raced into the smoky Saloon Bar, where the two detectives sat at their table. Bowker glared at him ferociously, knowing his appearance meant bad news.

'Morning, sir,' said Whitelock with irritating cheerfulness.

'They've fished Roy Sibson out of the river, I've just had word on the telephone. And DCS Horrocks wants you to call him when you've had a look.'

'Sit down, Constable,' said Bowker, restraining himself, 'and you, Knight! If Roy's drowned, then he's drowned. He can bloody well wait till I've finished my breakfast.'

Knight sank back into his chair. He'd been up on his feet at Whitelock's announcement, like an Olympic sprinter sweating on the blocks for the starting gun to go off.

'Where is he? Who fished him out?' Bowker asked.

'The lockkeeper got him out with his boathook, sir, the way they do with drowning accidents. Downstream at Pangbourne.'

'You've made your mind up it's an accident, have you? Do you know more than you told us so far?'

'No sir, the message was only what I've reported.'

'There's one deduction we can make, Knight.'

'What's that, sir?'

'The body has some form of identification on it. Otherwise it would be a week before anybody told us they'd found a dead 'un, and please, sir, could it be the man you're looking for?'

'That's right—I hadn't thought of that.'

'It spoils our plan to drop in on Mark Stanhope this morning and bounce him about. A pleasure delayed but not forgone—we might get round to him after lunch.'

As the rook flies, from Long Slaughter to Pangbourne is not more than 10 or 11 miles, but further by boat along the winding river and further still by road. When Bowker decided he'd eaten enough of a fresh supply of toast and thick Oxford marmalade to keep him going until his next meal, he said he was ready to go. Whitelock drove the police car at breakneck speed.

'You're enjoying all this,' Bowker accused him.

He was in the front passenger seat, alongside the uniformed constable, a look of intense gloom on his swarthy face. Knight sat in the back, thinking about the implications of what they were on their way to see.

'We don't get much excitement in Long Slaughter as a rule,' Whitelock answered the Inspector, unabashed. 'Three people dead in a week. There's been nothing that interesting since the time when Tommy Barstock shoved his brother head-first in the beet-slicing machine.'

'Rural bloody shenanigans!' said Bowker, much disapproving. 'Say Roy went into the river at Long Slaughter or nearby. Then how long does it take to float downstream to where he is now? A day, two days? As long as a week?'

'That I can't say, sir. To tell the truth, I was surprised to hear he'd got that far, when there's two locks between to get through. I'd have expected a floating body to be seen before it got that far. But I'm not expert on these things; the river police will be able to tell you.'

'Alive or dead, bloody Roy is trouble,' said Bowker, his tone ominous. 'Now we've got a bloody guessing game where he went in the water, apart from did he fall or was he pushed? Or did the silly bugger jump?'

'That's something for Forensic to tell us, sir.' Knight gave his opinion, rashly as it turned out.

'Unless there's a bloody great bullet-hole in his head or his throat's been cut or he's full of arsenic, bloody Forensic will tell us nothing that's any use to us,' Bowker said in complete and utter disgust. 'They'll tell us he's drowned. Or he died of natural causes, you'll see. I've told you before and I'll tell you again—if you start putting your trust in Forensic, you'll never get a criminal behind bars in your life.'

Knight thought it better to say nothing.

'So when was this yokel murder of yours, Whitelock?' Bowker enquired. 'Recently?'

'No, it must have been four or five years back. They sent Inspector Turnbull over to take charge. Do you know him, sir?'

'I've worked with him. So what was it all about?'

'Hard to say, sir. As far as I could make out, Tommy Barstock wanted his old Dad to leave the farm to him and Arnold jointly and equally, if you follow me, though Arnold was the eldest by a couple of years. Old Barstock was a mean sort. He never gave anything away in his life, not even his potato parings.'

'What did he do with them?'

'He fed 'em to the pigs, of course. The main trouble was that the old devil never could bring himself to make a will. In his mind, that was giving the farm away. So if he died intestate, as seemed most likely, Arnold stood to inherit, or so both of the sons believed.'

'You'd think this Tommy would have bloody sense enough to see a lawyer about his position,' Bowker said.

'The Barstock brothers were brought up to grudge every penny spent. They'd never pay out to a lawyer, not even if their life depended on it.'

'It sounds as if Tommy's life did depend on it after he'd done the other one in, at least his life outside jail.'

'Tommy maintained high and low that he was entitled to legal aid when the case came into Court. He wasn't going to pay good money to a lawyer. Then, when he was turned down for legal aid, he insisted on defending himself.'

'He said it was an accident, did he? Arnold's foot slipped on a cow-pat and he nose-dived into the bacon-slicer?'

'Beet-slicer, sir, thing with big heavy blades. They use it for chopping up beets and turnips to make cow-feed. You're dead right about the plea. Tommy said it had been an accident. There was something else, though. Both were after the same woman, you see. Arnold even had a daughter by her, but she got fed up with him and went with Tommy.'

'God save us all from idiots!' said Bowker. 'This Tommy ought to have got life for being such a clown.'

They were at Pangbourne before nine o'clock. The body recovered from the Thames had been moved from public view, 'round the side of the lockkeeper's house, laid out flat and covered over with a boat tarpaulin. A youngish Sergeant and an older Constable of the river police were there, their launch moored neatly above the lock.

There was another Sergeant and a Constable to represent the

local force, both wearing helmets, nothing to do now they'd got a statement from the lockkeeper except drink cups of tea that his wife made for them. A police surgeon had arrived. It wasn't Kenneth Pendleton this time, a younger man altogether, wearing a beige suit with the sleeves pushed up to his elbows, buttoned shirt and no tie, pop-star style.

'Who are you?' Bowker asked, astonishment and displeasure in his voice. 'Where's the miserable old bastard they usually send me to look at dead bodies?'

'Dr Pendleton's off sick. My name is Truscombe. And you must be Inspector Bowker—he warned me about you.'

'Cheeky old devil, him! Let's have a look at what you've got under the cover.'

Harry Truscombe nodded to the two constables standing nearby, and they peeled back the tarpaulin. It was a man—young or old was hard to say. His face and the rest of him was bloated from long immersion in the river, his flesh softer and paler than seemed possible. At least he had hair on his head, and he wore a suit, too sodden to guess what the colour was. He'd lost one shoe.

'Identification?' Bowker asked. He took shallow breaths to spare himself the smell of death coming from the body.

'Drying out on the window-sill there, sir,' said one of the river police. 'Driver's licence, bankbook, video library card, all in the name of Roy Sibson.'

Bowker nodded. The mortal remains of Roy were a sorry sight, he thought. He was only twenty-two, poor little bastard, what life had he ever had? Not much of a home, a boring job at the other end of his daily bus-ride. Some sort of intimacy with Lynn Hurst for a few weeks, maybe a leg-over a time or two, God alone knew what that was about. Now he was just a sodden bundle.

Knight was standing beside the Inspector, staring down at the body on the concrete path.

'Look at his ear, sir,' he said. 'There's a wound.'

'It's only his earlobe gnawed off, nothing important,' said the river police Sergeant. 'The voles do it, or the water rats. There are often marks like that when we find them.'

'I'm the doctor here!' Truscombe sounded outraged. 'Do you bloody well mind!'

'Well?' said Bowker.

'The lobe is ragged, not been cut with a knife or other sharp instrument. Teeth marks, I would say. The probability is that a water creature has fed on it.'

'How long's he been dead?'

'Several days,' Truscombe said judicially. 'Decomposition has begun and is well established.'

'That I can smell for myself,' said Bowker, beginning to sound aggrieved. 'How bloody long?'

'It's impossible for me to be more precise at this point, not after a cadaver's been in the water for some time.'

'Apart from a rat nibble, I can't see any wounds on him,' said Bowker, giving up in disgust. 'Have you had a look at his back yet? Anything there?'

'I've examined the body as closely as is practical at present and in these circumstances. I've seen no marks of violence.'

'Then what did he die of? Did he drown?'

'I can't possibly tell, I'm only here to certify he's dead.'

'You're prepared to certify that, are you?' Bowker said with dangerous calm. 'You're sure he's not shamming?'

'The post-mortem will determine whether he died of drowning,' said the Doctor. He had caught the menace in Bowker's tone and was edging away from him. 'Other things being equal, I'd risk a guess that he might have drowned.'

'Take him away and get the bloody pathologist to cut him up,' said Bowker, his voice expressing loathing of Truscombe for his inability to offer any useful information. 'And I want it done bloody quick. This is the third dead body we've had in the case, and I'm getting to the end of my bloody patience.'

He turned away from the Doctor to the river police Sergeant.

Knight heard him muttering to himself, *other things being bloody equal!*

'What's your name?' he demanded. From where he was standing, he could look across the weir to the far bank of the Thames and see a nice-looking pub by the riverside. He wished he was over there with a pint of ale in his hand, not stuck here on the towpath with the rotting remains of Roy Sibson.

"Wilton, sir,' the Sergeant answered. 'The lockkeeper called us, and we gave a hand to shift the corpse out of public sight. I had a look for anything to identify him by, and when I saw the name, I knew it was the man you put out a circular for.'

'Good, good. So how long do you think it's taken him to float down from Long Slaughter, assuming that's where he went in?'

'There's no way of telling that, sir. You say floating, as if he was on the top all the time, but he could have been bumping along on the bottom, and only have risen to the top when he began to swell up a bit. There's always the chance he got caught on tree roots sticking out under the bank and stayed stuck in one place for hours at a time, even days.'

'Could he have got through the locks between Long Slaughter and here, do you think?'

'That's why I said he was most likely to be bumping along on the bottom. It's early in the year yet, but there's quite a few pleasure boats going up and down. The locks are in use all day till about six. After that boaters work them themselves if they want to go through. A body could drift through unnoticed if it was below the surface.'

'You're the expert, Sergeant. Is it likely?'

'No sir, it's not. Not through two locks. Mind you, he's been in the water a long time, this one. He could have come a pretty long way from where he went under.'

'You're sure of that? The Doctor only says *some days.* I take that to mean anything from twenty-four hours to a long weekend. What do you say?'

'I've been pulling them out of the Thames dead for getting on seven years. I know what they look like and what they smell like—I'd give this one a week in the water.'

'Thank you, Sergeant. This identification, you said there was a bankbook. Can you see what his balance was?'

'No, it's too soaked for that. If you try to open the pages, it'll fall to pieces. His name's on the front in block letters. Strictly speaking it's not a bankbook, it's a Building Society paying-in book.'

'The Chalfont?'

The Sergeant nodded.

'Right, we'll let Forensic have it to play with. I can get a reading of his account from where he worked.'

Knight had been listening closely. 'The Chalfont Building Society,' he said, grinning. 'It keeps coming back like a song.'

'So far it's a song without words,' said Bowker. 'We'll drive to Reading now we're this close and see if their branch manager is ready to tell us anything. I thought bloody computers were supposed to be lightning-fast; otherwise there's no point. This one's had three days already, and we're still waiting. The Chalfont would be better off with an abacus and a Chinaman to work it.'

On the drive to Reading, he had Knight write down the sequence in his ever-ready notebook, in case seeing it in writing jogged their brains into supplying any connection.

'According to the medic, Lynn died on Thursday last week, the twenty-first that was, but wasn't found until Saturday, the day Fowler died in Lynn's car, and he wasn't found till Sunday. Our river bobby thinks Roy's been in the water about a week. We'll accept his view for now until a pathologist tells us different.'

'Today is Thursday. Shall I put Roy down for last Wednesday then, sir?'

'Let's say last Wednesday, for now, or maybe last Tuesday, as the day Roy took his dip in the river. The last sighting of him was last Tuesday, on the Wormwold road, which runs along by the Thames, as everybody keeps on telling us. Perhaps he never came back from his trip down Lovers' Lane with Lynn.'

'You think *she* did him in?' A careful listener would have heard the unsounded raspberry in Knight's tone.

'How the hell do I know?' Bowker said morosely. 'Let me see what you've written down.'

Knight reached over from where he sat in the rear seat of the car and handed him the notebook.

Timetable of events

Tuesday 19th—Roy Sibson drowned?
Thursday 21st—Lynn Hurst head cracked
Saturday 23rd—Gavin Fowler asphyxiated

'Very nice,' said Bowker. 'The question we'd better start to ask ourselves is are all three deaths connected? Answer; maybe. Truthful answer; we don't bloody know.'

'Surely we've established Fowler did Mrs Hurst in. He had her car. Her blood-group was on the tyre-iron we recovered from the river.'

'Pointers, not proof. He died in her car; that much we can be sure of. It doesn't mean he took it. There was blood and brains on the tyre-iron, no prints, and no way of proving it belonged to Gavin. But if for the sake of argument we allow that Gavin did in Mrs Hurst, we've got this nasty question of who did him and Roy in.'

'The basic problem is why any of them were murdered,' Knight said. 'If we had a motive, we'd have a murderer.'

'Or two murderers.' Bowker sounded exasperated. 'Maybe even three! It's a bastard, this case.'

'Three murderers—that's overdoing it, sir.'

'I know. I expect we're only looking for one, when it comes down to it. With any luck, we'll get some hint of a motive from the Building Society when their computer finishes all its sums. Money plays some part in this; of that I'm fairly sure.'

'Why, sir? Copper's hunch again?'

'No, I base that on what we know of the people involved, or some of them. Lynn was greedy for money. She extracted it from Hurst and Rowley and at least half a dozen other men listed in her address book. Mark Stanhope is in urgent need of large sums of cash; we know that from the letters you had a look at in his briefcase. Roy might have access to money where he worked, if he knew enough to trick the computer. There was a link between Roy and Lynn, and another between Lynn and Mark Stanhope.'

'Bit thin,' said Knight.

'My idea of a nice afternoon is to drop in on Mark and arrest him for two murders,' said Bowker, his tone vibrant with gloomy relish. 'Have you brought the handcuffs with you this time?'

Before Knight could bring acid scorn on himself by confessing that he hadn't, PC Whitelock spoke up.

'I always have mine with me, sir,' he said enthusiastically. 'Haven't had a chance to use them for years.'

'Good man,' said Bowker. 'Trouble is, I don't think we've got a cat in hell's chance of running Mark in today.'

The Chalfont Building Society branch was all green and white, the organisation's colours, white Formica and green carpeting, the effect more bilious than impressive. There were two clerks behind the bullet-proof glass, and a third position unstaffed. Roy's place, Bowker assumed.

One of the clerks was the plain-looking girl in the Christmas-party photo Knight had found among Roy's meagre possessions in the search of his room. She had a nice smile, Bowker thought, and a word or two with her might yield some useful bit of information about Roy.

At mid-morning, two or three people were busy paying money in or drawing it out. They huddled so close to the glass barrier it was impossible to make out what they were doing. The manager had a small office with a desk and a computer terminal, a phone, and a square safe in the corner with a big brass handle. Bowker hoped it wasn't used for keeping real money overnight; any half-competent crook would have it open in five minutes.

Mr Henshawe looked at the two detectives over the top of his glasses and asked them to sit down. He was a man of forty-five or so, a cautious-looking man in a sombre suit and a plain dark red tie. He was not the manager of the branch, he explained; he was from Head Office, sent to take charge temporarily.

'Ah!' said Bowker, his dark eyes glowing. 'So there's money missing, is there?'

'Your deduction is correct, Inspector,' Henshawe said. He had been trained in the money-lending tradition to be as tight with information as cash.

'How much?'

'A considerable sum.'

Bowker's fleeting unaccustomed cheerfulness faded like clouds drifting across the sun. 'Stop fiddling about,' he said ominously. 'We're not here for a mortgage, we're police investigating very serious offences. I can tell you we've come straight here from seeing the dead body of an employee of yours, Roy Sibson. He worked in this branch, but he's been in the Thames for a week. He's dead, Mr Henshawe, very dead. And if he went in by accident, I'm a Dutchman.'

'Good God!' said Henshawe. 'What a terrible thing!'

'Sudden death is always terrible,' Bowker told him. 'It's the worst and most terrible crime in the bloody book. It's snuffing somebody's life out. So how much is missing?'

'This is confidential information, of course. It would be bad for the Society's reputation if it got out that we'd lost money belonging to depositors.'

'How much?' Bowker raised his voice to a roar. Although he was sitting down, he seemed to be seven feet tall.

Leonard Henshawe cowered back in his chair. "A little over eight thousand pounds, as near as we can tell at this stage,' he said nervously.

'Not enough,' Bowker said malignly, and Henshawe was staring at him anxiously. 'Write it down, Knight. Eight bloody thousand pounds. It's not nearly enough to explain three murders.'

'May have been a trial run, to see if it was spotted,' Knight suggested. 'If not, next time could be the jackpot.'

'That makes sense,' Bowker agreed. 'And they hadn't missed it before we asked. And it's taken the best part of a week since, for them to find out it's missing.'

He addressed himself again to Henshawe. 'Did Roy Sibson take your money?'

'That is probably our first tentative inference, bearing in mind that Sibson has been absent for a week without permission or explanation. As to the method by which money was transferred without authorisation, that is still being traced. On the other hand, it is difficult to credit an ordinary counter clerk like Sibson with the degree of expertise required to bypass all the security systems written into the computer programmes we use.'

'Don't you believe it, sir,' said Knight helpfully. 'There's paperback books you can buy for a couple of quid that tell you how to do it—American hackers write them. How to break into any system to cancel your electricity bill, give yourself nine O-levels, change your pension entitlement.'

'You can even get books by bloody insane back-street teenage revolutionaries telling you how to make bombs to lob at coppers going about their duty,' Bowker added morosely. 'What you are really saying is you don't know how Roy diddled you.'

'Computer systems are complex, Inspector,' Henshawe said with a note of misplaced pride in his voice. 'A considerable degree of ingenuity has been applied to the embezzlement of funds, for as such we must regard it for the present.'

'Sibson had all he needed,' said Knight. 'A computer terminal linked to your mainframe machine. He carried out his fiddle in normal working hours, sitting behind your counter and in broad daylight—in full view of the branch manager.'

'Where was this money transferred to?' Bowker asked. Henshawe looked wan and shocked. 'Another account in your system? It's too much to hope Roy slipped it in his own account—police work is never that easy.'

'As you say, it wasn't transferred into Sibson's own account. His balance stands at £146, and there have been no transactions in or out for over a month. The most he ever had in it was £273 towards the end of last year, of which £100 was drawn out just before Christmas, presumably for seasonal presents.'

'Or a booze-up with his mates,' said Bowker, irritated by the man's mealymouthed way of putting things. 'So the question is, where's your money gone?'

'This is where the problem lies. Simple logic demands it was transferred to another account, within or without the Society. There's no record of such a transfer. When we knew the amount of the difference, we naturally looked for an account showing a similar increase.'

'And was there one?'

'I must emphasise that this is extremely confidential, as it concerns depositors. Four accounts showed increases of between eight and nine thousand pounds in the period concerned. Only one is a personal account; the others are corporate accounts. It's taken time to contact all four, but this has been done, and they have accounted satisfactorily for the increases.'

'You're sure about that? None of them could be an accomplice in the fraud?'

'We are satisfied of their *bona fides*. Simultaneously we have looked for combinations of two, three, or four accounts showing balances up in the same time period by the total amount unaccounted for. Again, I regret to say, nothing significant has come to light.'

'He's been too clever for you—is that what you're saying?'

'No, you may rest assured, Inspector, the discrepancy will be traced. Further computer runs are proceeding even as we speak; more sophisticated combinations are being tried. We shall find where the money has gone, never fear.'

Bowker shook his head in massive doubt. 'You're sure the money is missing?' he asked.

'Sadly, that is one fact we can be certain of.'

'There were people when we came in just now sliding handfuls of tenners across the counter to your clerks, to shove in their savings accounts. I suppose the answer couldn't be as simple as Roy stuffing his pockets with money when he went home?'

'Out of the question! Each clerk must account for cash taken in before the branch closes. On this screen in front of me the manager can monitor every transaction, in and out. He knows how much there is in cash and how much there should be.'

'So why are you here, Mr Henshawe, instead of the real branch manager? Does your Head Office suspect he's an accomplice in Roy Sibson's crookery?'

'It's a matter of policy. When a serious discrepancy shows up, the manager of the branch is automatically suspended from duty until the figures are reconciled. This is in no possible way or manner an aspersion on the integrity or competence of Mr Bonner who manages this branch. He is at home, on full pay, I may add, until such time as the problem is resolved satisfactorily.'

'You must get the odd bent manager from time to time,' Bowker said ruminatively. 'I'd better have Bonner's address.'

'Speaking on behalf of the Chalfont Building Society, I refute that slur most emphatically,' said Henshawe. He spoke strongly, but his cheeks were pale as putty at this monumental affront to the uprightness of the business.

'We pride ourselves on the calibre of our employees, on their loyalty and devotion, their sense of duty. The Chalfont may be a smaller Society, Inspector, and not one of the Big Forty with branches throughout the United Kingdom, but we are second to none in our ethical practices.'

'With eight thousand quid short and an employee at the bottom of the Thames? Very bloody ethical!' Bowker said ferociously. 'If it turns out the manager was in on the fraud with Sibson, a very serious view is going to be taken of your coyness. Give DS Knight the address of the branch manager while I make a phone call.'

Leonard Henshawe was reluctant to leave Bowker alone in the

office to make his call. Perhaps he thought he might steal the paper clips, or kick the brass-handled safe open. Knight urged him along, leaving Bowker in peace to confer with DCS Horrocks.

Horrocks sounded remarkably unhappy when Bowker got through to him.

'Three bodies, Denis!' he trumpeted down the wire. 'What the bloody hell's going on there? I sent you to Long Slaughter to tidy up a simple little domestic, thinking you'd be back in two days at most, everything wrapped up tidily. But you've been the best part of a week and you've turned it into a bloodbath! Do you know you're front-page in the local rag? When the fish-and-chip papers pick it up, they'll go bloody berserk and invent the usual *Village of Doom* tale!'

'Maybe the Paddies will chuck a bomb over the railings at the House of Commons to keep the newspapers busy, sir.'

'I'll pretend the line went bad and I didn't hear that,' said Horrocks in a strained voice. 'We don't want half a hundred of the press photographing and interviewing and bribing everybody in Long Slaughter. They make us look as if we don't know our job.'

'Crime-solving doesn't run to newspaper deadlines. You know that as well as I do, sir.'

'We need a fast result, Denis, understand? I'm being pushed from above. You've got about two days to feel the collar of the killer or killers. If you can't do it, I shall be told to send a Chief Inspector to take over from you.'

'Sod that!' said Bowker. 'Things are just beginning to make sense. There's over eight grand missing at the Building Society where Sibson worked—that's the lad we pulled out of the river. He was last seen in the company of Mrs Hurst, the first of them to be found dead.'

'Yes, I've read the report, I know who she is,' Horrocks said grumpily. 'It was her car the other body was found in. Reading your report's like a bloody guessing-game. Where in the hell is the motive for any of it?'

'It's all to do with the money—I'm sure of that.'

'Eight thousand—doesn't seem right,' the DCS echoed Bowker's own earlier thought. 'Sure it's not eighty thousand?'

'I'm in the manager's office. They claim it's eight, but they don't know how Sibson did it. From what I can make out they're ordering the bloody computer to explain how it could be fiddled by a counter clerk. I expect they'll make it apologise to their board of bloody directors before they've finished.'

'It's a motive, of a sort,' said Horrocks, very unhappily. 'I don't think much of it though.'

'It gives me a new and very useful line of enquiry. I want to get back to Long Slaughter fast and talk to Sibson's family to see why they've been lying to me.'

'I've complete faith in you, Denis. You know that. But I'd be misleading you if I told you everybody here shares my faith in you, especially the Assistant Chief. I explained to him in the Senior Officers' dining-room, how your misunderstanding with Dr Hurst came about. And the unreliability of the Doctor, when it comes to matters of fact, like telephone calls. But he's a hard and disbelieving sort of man, the AC.'

'I think I'd better get on,' said Bowker. 'I'll ring you from Long Slaughter as soon as I've anything to report.'

With that he put the phone down and made for the door in long strides. If the Chief Superintendent had any more to say, it would have to wait for another time. Three strides took Bowker out of the office and into the public area where punters queued at the glassed-in counter.

'Just like a bloody betting-shop,' he said to himself, gazing round for Knight and Henshawe, 'though I never knew till today a jockey can bolt with the stake-money.'

'You'll be hearing from me,' he said to Henshawe, sounding a lot like a giant grizzly bear looking for something to kill and devour, 'and I expect to hear from you the minute your computer comes up with anything. If I can find where your money went to, I've got my killer.'

Henshawe shuddered and promised faithfully to keep in touch, a promise Bowker regarded as worth the paper it was written on.

'Have you spoken to Roy's girlfriend?' Bowker asked Knight, nodding towards her through the glass.

'Yes, sir, Eileen Speke's her name. She's got nothing useful to tell us. She and Roy were good friends at one time, but it's all faded out lately. I expect he dumped her in easy stages as he got involved with Lynn Hurst.'

'When did she see him last, apart from work?'

'She says they haven't been out together for over a month, and I believe her. She had a bit of a weep when she said it, poor girl.'

'Then we won't waste any more time here, Knight.'

PC Whitelock was parked outside, on a double yellow line. He was chatting in friendly style to a well-shaped Traffic Warden with her elbow on his door.

'Back to Long Slaughter,' said Bowker, fastening his seat-belt tight. 'I want to be at your house twenty minutes from now, Whitelock. No excuses. I don't care if you break every traffic regulation in the book.'

Whitelock switched on his blue flashing light and pulled out from the kerb.

'Put the siren on, let's do it in style,' Bowker said.

'Sit tight, sir,' said Whitelock, all agog. 'Twenty minutes, you said? That can't be done, not if you had a World Champion racing driver behind the wheel, but I'll see just how close we can get.'

'DCS Horrocks is not exactly joyful,' Bowker informed Knight, sitting in the back of the car. 'He says we've had long enough by now to feel Chummy's collar. He's threatening hell-fire and brimstone if we don't put somebody behind bars double quick. It seems somebody up above is starting to twitch in case the fried-fish wrappers accuse us of being slow.'

'We could run Empson Rowley in on spec, sir,' Knight offered hopefully. 'Now that we know the M4 patrol can't confirm his story, he's got no alibi for when Gavin Fowler was done in.'

'Pity about that,' said Bowker. 'I knew they'd turn out to be useless, the traffic Gestapo. They logged two bikers and a red Ferrari that ran away from them. They called in the helicopter to get the Ferrari, and one biker ran out of petrol and gave up. But it wasn't bloody Rowley—it's never that easy.'

'It makes you wonder if it's safe to be out in a car,' Knight observed. 'All these bloody fools on the motorway thinking it's a racetrack.'

A sudden thought came into the Inspector's mind. 'Whitelock, you never told me the end of that horrible bloody tale, the Barstocks and the beet-slicing machine. You left it at Tommy defending himself at the trial. How did it come out?'

Whitelock was racing the car across the bridge over the river Thames at upwards of 70 miles an hour. He was heading for the Wallingford road, terrifying other motorists by his weaving and overtaking. He rammed his foot down harder and grinned sourly at Bowker's question.

'He got off, sir. The jury brought in Not Guilty. The old man died soon after—of grief, some said, but plain miserliness, some others thought. There was no will, and Tommy got the farm.'

'You said he shoved his brother into the slicer,' Bowker said accusingly, 'but if a yokel like him could convince twelve good men and true, maybe it *was* an accident after all.'

'He gets drunk now and then in the Barley Mow, that's over at Sandy Bottom, where he does his drinking,' said Whitelock, 'and when he's got a skinfull he talks about how he did for brother Arnold and got clean away with it. He's a crafty devil, is Tommy Barstock. He knows he can't be tried again for the same crime. He brags about it.'

'He ought to be in that Dickens book you're reading,' Knight told Bowker, 'a villain like that.'

12. ⋯⋯⋯⋯⋯⋯⋯⋯⋯⋯⋯⋯⋯⋯⋯⋯ *orchard row*

Where the sign-post pointed left for Long Slaughter and Sandy Bottom, Kevin Whitelock drifted the police car 'round the corner in a controlled skid and floored the accelerator again. Bowker lurched in his seat-belt and snorted, but said nothing. He could hardly complain after he'd ordered Whitelock to break the world speed record.

The car barrelled along 6 1/2 miles of winding country lane from the main road to Long Slaughter, sliding through blind turns in a very stomach-wrenching way. Jack Knight braced himself on the back seat, his fingers clenched hard on the seat-edge. He was speculating what Whitelock would do if a tractor chugged out of a field in front of them, hauling a trailer-load of something heavy right across the road—like turnips, for instance.

He was dragged from his gruesome speculation by an unexpected burst of admiration from Inspector Bowker, addressed to nobody in particular.

'All that greenery!' he rhapsodised. 'The trees and hedges, flowers growing wild on the verge! I can think of nowhere to beat the English countryside. I understand why you said you want to stay in Long Slaughter, Whitelock. It beats the shabby streets where we have to go chasing after evil bloody child-rapists and wife-killers and jewellery-shop shotgun artists.'

Whitelock was too engrossed in the heady pleasure of driving without due care and attention to say much in reply. Knight was too amazed by the glimpse of Bowker as a nature lover to offer any suggestion at all.

'Do you get much time for trout-tickling and hare-coursing?' Bowker asked. He knew no more about the countryside than he had gleaned from a Sunday-afternoon farming programme on TV.

'Trout?' said Whitelock, his attention caught briefly. 'This is the bloody Thames, sir, not a trout stream. Lucky to catch a skinny little roach in it. I wouldn't want to eat anything that came out of the river below Oxford.'

'Not after what we've seen come out of it at Pangbourne this morning,' said Knight, trying to pull himself together.

'You've no soul, either of you,' Bowker announced. 'Forget I ever mentioned it. Change of plan: when we reach Long Slaughter drop us off at Orchard Row. I'll inform the Sibsons officially we've found their son, poor old devils. And Joyce is going to answer some questions. I'm not standing for any more Mary Ellen about holidays down the Costa Brava. Not now that Roy's gone on a permanent holiday in parts unknown.'

'Didn't have his passport on him,' said Knight. He was trying to sound on the ball though his attention was greatly concerned with the chance of surviving Whitelock's driving. 'It wasn't in his room when we searched. There's every chance Joyce hid it to back up her holiday story.'

'Don't need a passport where he's gone,' Bowker said grimly.

'I suppose Joyce took it. What we want to know is why it seemed important to her to lie to us about her brother's whereabouts. What did she hope to gain by it?'

'That's not difficult, sir,' said Knight, closing his eyes in fear as Whitelock took the brow of a low hill on the wrong side of the road and accelerated hard down the long winding slope to Long Slaughter. 'She knew he'd stolen money and was covering up for him while he made his getaway. She didn't know he was dead and drifting downstream, or there'd be no need to cover up.'

'Makes sense,' Bowker agreed. 'And the money not being on him when he was found suggests it was taken off him before he went in. That's if he had it in the first place.'

'Somebody's had it,' said Knight. 'Roy's the most likely. And maybe he gave it to Joyce to look after for him, as nobody else seems to have it.'

'My own thoughts precisely,' said Bowker, sounding displeased with the conclusion. 'We might be able to get her for that. You park outside the house and wait, Whitelock. Turn the car 'round and stand by to move off at once if we decide to run her in. I don't like scenes in the street, crying and carrying on.'

'Do you think Joyce might have pushed Roy into the river and drowned him?' Knight asked, holding on to the back of Bowker's seat with both hands to lean forward and confer without having to shout over the roaring engine noise. 'They could have fallen out over splitting the loot.'

'Possible,' said Bowker, 'but not very. The money's not much to kill for, especially not between brother and sister. But you can never be sure. There was a shopkeeper coshed in Cowley only a fortnight ago and died of a fractured skull. I think his ribs were kicked in as well. All that for less than seventy quid in the till.'

'We're talking about a village,' Knight added, 'not the West End of London. Eight thousand might only be a morning shopping-trip up Bond Street for some, but in Long Slaughter it could be seen as a lot of money.'

'What do *you* say, Whitelock?' Bowker asked. 'You're the one with the gory tales about sliced-up farmers. What did Tommy get out of doing his brother in? How much is a farm worth?'

'Lot more than eight thousand pounds, sir. The Barstock farm was valued for probate after Tommy got off scot-free, and it was well over five hundred thousand pounds then. Might be more now, with all these hand-outs they get from the Common Market people.'

'Changed his life, did it?'

'Tommy was nobody when old Barstock was alive. And he's still nobody now, only the bank manager shakes his hand when he sees him. He still lives in muck and old clothes he gets second-hand, so I don't know whether he did himself a good turn or not with the beet-slicer back of the cowshed.'

'It's a bloody disgrace!' Bowker said blackly.

For a horrible minute, Knight had the distinct impression the Inspector was thinking of going to the Barstock farm to balance things up by throwing Tommy into some handy piece of machinery. Something with big slashing blades, like a combine-harvester.

'We're talking here about eight grand,' Bowker added, 'not half a bloody million.'

'Eight thousand pounds may not be a lot of money to Detective Inspectors,' Whitelock said with great foolhardiness, 'but it might be enough to tempt Joyce Harris into doing something silly.'

'The trouble is,' said Bowker, sounding unusually moody, 'if Joyce did her brother in over the money, who did the others in, and why? Where's the bloody point of it?'

'Not easy to see anybody as a mass murderer,' said Whitelock, who had included himself in the discussion now that his opinion had been sought, 'but there are such people—we all know that, sir. Not in Long Slaughter, maybe; we're too slow and sleepy in our ways. But down the road only a few miles there was that chap at Hungerford who went 'round the village with a high-powered rifle and shot every blessed soul he met. Ten or twelve of them, as I think it was.'

'Not the same thing,' Knight said sharply, finding himself on a level with a uniformed bobby and not liking it much. 'He was a genuine head case, that one; no reason at all for what he did. There's rhyme and reason in the Long Slaughter murders, even if we don't understand it. You can see real cunning in how each of the jobs was planned and carried out. Dear old Chummy was long gone every time a body was found, and there were no traces.'

'I thought Mrs Hurst was killed by young Gavin Fowler,' said Whitelock. 'The Inspector said so himself. In that case, what's wrong with supposing he killed Roy Sibson as well? Then he got the chop himself from whomever it was that put him up to it in the first place. That's if it wasn't his own idea.'

'Stop gabbling like a pair of old aunties and let me think,' said Bowker. 'Did Gavin kick Roy into the Thames to drown? It's possible. We don't know where Gavin went after he left work any day last week. His wife told us he got home about nine most nights for his meal, and she thinks he passed the time in a pub, though he never said.'

'Lot of public houses between here and Wantage,' Knight said. 'Hell of a lot.'

'We're going to need a squad to check 'round and see which of them Gavin used, and try to pin down his movements. Not that it will prove anything useful if nobody can remember seeing him in a boozer any evening last week. But going with the flow, so to speak, let's assume that somebody put him up to disposing of Roy and Lynn. And then shut his mouth for safety's sake.'

'Roy Sibson and Lynn Hurst,' said Knight. 'Accomplices to rip off the Building Society? They had the trial run, and it worked out a treat. Then something happened that made them a danger to a third party. Third party hires Gavin to hush them up.'

'That gives you a third party in on the fraud,' said Bowker. 'It's getting too complicated. We're dealing with a village, as DCS Horrocks keeps reminding me, we're not dealing with insider trading for bloody millions on the Stock Exchange where they get let off with six months suspended and a forty-pound fine.'

Knight thought he'd got the hang of Bowker's way of playing devil's advocate. He wanted to be argued against to see if the theory stood up.

'Stephen Fenwick might be involved in a rip-off for hundreds of thousands, even millions—you said that yourself yesterday, sir. But why he should be involved in a strictly local fraud on a Building Society, I do not pretend to understand.'

The car swept down the long slope into the village. Whitelock braked hard for the turn into Orchard Row.

'No, it's not that bloody lawyer's handwriting,' said Bowker. He sounded very morose. 'When he chances his arm, it's for a lot more than Roy was after.'

'So the Building Society is a separate issue, and Fenwick had Lynn done in for different reasons?' Knight suggested.

'I'd prefer that,' said Bowker, 'but my preference is neither here nor there. Concentrate on Lynn and Roy for a minute. What about this: for reasons we don't yet know, Lynn offers Roy the run of her amenities, to put it politely. Dr Hurst gets to hear about it; she didn't seem to hide much from him. He gets blind jealous of a peasant handling what he still regards as his own property, so he pays Gavin to do them both in.'

'Then arranges to meet him in the wood to give him his money, gets him drunk, and leaves him with the engine running,' Knight said. 'Yes, I think I could go for that, sir.'

'We'd need to trace a link between the Doctor and Gavin to go anywhere with that theory,' Bowker said ruminatively. 'Somebody might have seen them together. In fact, we need to trace a lot of links and movements if we're ever going to make sense of it. I'll get on to DCS Horrocks after we've seen Joyce and ask him to organise some help for us.'

The car had been stopped outside the Sibson home for several minutes, Whitelock sitting silent behind the wheel, nodding his head as he listened to the two detectives arguing.

'Come on, Knight,' Bowker said. 'I think this is going to be a very interesting chat with Joyce.'

'We ought to have a woman PC with us if we're going to run her in,' Knight said. 'Proper procedure, sir.'

'Take bloody hours to get one.' Bowker shook his head fiercely. 'Besides, we're here for the sad duty of informing Mr and Mrs Sibson of the demise of their son, something I hate and detest doing. Who said anything about running Joyce in?'

Knight almost said *'You did,'* but thought better of it.

The time was coming up towards midday, an overcast day with a stiff breeze from the northeast. A disappointing day for early spring, Bowker thought, and 23 Orchard Row was still far from being a desirable residence. He side-kicked the dented dustbin by the front door in a moody sort of way as he passed it, then beat a brisk tattoo with his knuckles.

Joyce Harris opened the door. She had a white apron on over a pink gingham dress. Her hair was tied in a scarf and looked in need of attention. Her drawn look was unchanged and unrelieved, her prettiness was turning to plainness from worry.

And you've got a lot to worry about, Bowker thought. *Lying to me all week about Roy, covering up because you knew he'd stolen money. And there was no need for covering up because Roy was in the Thames.*

'Well?' said Joyce, her mouth turning down when she saw who was on the doorstep. 'What do you want this time?'

'I'd like to come in, Mrs Harris. There are things I have to tell you, and your parents.'

'Is it about Roy?'

'Yes.' Bowker's voice gave nothing away.

'You'd better come in, then.' And she led them to the sitting-room, where her mother was busy setting the table for the mid-day meal.

The TV was on, the sound turned down. Nobody was watching it. Dad Sibson sat in a corner smoking his pipe and reading one of the raucous dailies DCS Horrocks on the phone had referred to as fish-and-chips papers.

The room was not large. With Bowker standing in the middle of it, his head seeming almost to touch the ceiling and DS Knight crowding in behind him, the space was very confined.

'Mr and Mrs Sibson,' said the Inspector, 'I'm sorry to be the one to bring bad news. Your son Roy is dead; he drowned in the river.'

Roy might not have drowned. He could have been coshed on the head or stabbed or poisoned or whatever. The state his body was in, only a pathologist could tell, when he'd opened him up. But Bowker felt it kinder to give the Sibsons something they could easily understand, not leave them dangling until after a post-mortem. If it turned out he was wrong, no real harm was done.

Joyce burst into tears and sat down, her face in her hands. A few seconds passed while Mrs Sibson took in the news, her face turning pale. Then she began to sob. Billy Sibson took his pipe from between his teeth and stared open-mouthed at Bowker, as if not believing him.

But he was the first to recover. The women were still weeping in shock and sorrow when he asked, 'Where?' He suddenly looked a lot older than his years.

'His body was found at Pangbourne Lock this morning,' Bowker answered. There was more sympathy in his tone than Knight would have thought possible.

'He's been gone over a week,' said Sibson dully. 'We thought he was on his holidays—Joyce said he was. I can't make out how he could be drowned in the Thames.'

'Nor can I,' said Bowker. 'It's a mystery, but I mean to get to the bottom of it. You can be sure of that.'

He explained why formal identification of the body was needed for legal purposes, and where it had been taken. He offered the use of a police car and driver to take Mr Sibson there.

'Joyce had better go,' said Sibson, his face very pale.

Bowker took a step nearer. 'I don't think so,' he said, dropping his voice. 'Roy's been in the water a week; he's not a sight for a woman.'

The Libbers would gnaw his particulars off if they ever heard him saying a thing like that, Bowker thought, but there was no point in pretending. It was bad enough asking a man to look at Roy, especially his father.

Billy Sibson turned whiter. Even his oversize ears seemed to be drained of colour. 'All right, then,' he said. 'I'll go and do what's necessary.'

'I'll let you know when,' Bowker promised, 'and send the car for you. This is not the best of times, I know that, but I have to ask Joyce a few questions. Why not take Mrs Sibson upstairs? She's taking it hard. She needs a cup of tea and a lie-down. It won't take me long to talk to Joyce.'

'No,' Sibson said, surprisingly vigorous, 'I won't leave her alone to be got at. I've heard how the police make people say things they don't want to and twist their words to get them in trouble.'

The daft old bugger's been watching too much television. He's done his brain in, thought Bowker, he's seen all that cobblers about the Nuneaton Nine, the Sunderland Seven, the Formby Five, the Farringdon Four, the Thornbury Three, the Taunton Two and the Wanstead One. He thinks we run people in at random off the streets and torture them till they sign a confession to any big crime we've got outstanding. Poor old sod's been brain-damaged by clever-dick TV presenters.

The mental recital of the litany of numbers calmed Bowker to some degree, like counting up to ten after trapping a thumb in the car door.

'Please yourself, Mr Sibson,' he said mildly. 'You stay here and see fair play, if that's what you're worried about.'

Joyce was sitting at one end of a sag-backed sofa, misery in her slumped attitude. Bowker took a wooden chair from the table and sat down facing her, close enough for their knees to nearly touch. She raised her head. Her eyes were swollen from weeping; her face was red.

'Let's get this over with,' said Bowker, trying not to sound intimidating. 'Why did you tell me Roy had gone on holiday?'

'I thought he was,' she said hesitantly. 'He told me he was.'

'No, he didn't. You made that up to stop me looking for him.'

'That's a lie,' Joyce said, but her heart wasn't in it.

'Roy took eight thousand pounds from where he works,' said Bowker patiently. 'I was there this morning; they've tracked the loss through the computer. If Roy was alive, I'd have to run him in.'

Joyce sniffled and wiped her eyes with her apron. She looked very forlorn.

Bowker asked gently, 'Was he killed for the money, or have you got it? He could have given it to you for safekeeping.'

Joyce twisted her fingers together, nervous of the direction the questioning was taking. 'He never really told me what he was up to, but I guessed he was taking money that didn't belong to him.'

'You stop that now, Joyce,' her father broke in sharply. 'Let the dead rest, I won't have you slandering Roy now he's gone.'

Bowker turned to glare ferociously at Billy Sibson. 'Stay out of this.' His voice grated enough to take a thin layer off a block of marble. 'I let you stay only out of goodwill. If you're going to interrupt, I'll have no choice but take your daughter to the police station for questioning.'

'It's not right,' Billy said weakly. 'Not right.'

'You were saying?' Bowker prompted Joyce.

'I didn't know for sure what Roy was doing. You can't hold it against me.'

'There are two things I'm looking for, Mrs Harris. The money that's missing and the truth about Roy's death. The two things might be connected—I don't know yet. For a start, you can tell me if Roy could swim.'

'No.' She shook her head sorrowfully. 'He hated the water and wouldn't go near it, not even in a rowing-boat.'

'When was the last time you saw him? Exactly, I mean.'

'Tuesday last week. He got up late that day, though I called him at seven for his breakfast, in time to catch the bus, as I did every morning. He said he'd been given a day off. They did that when he'd worked two Saturdays in a row.'

'The manager didn't know anything about a day off last week,' said Bowker. 'He thought Roy might be off sick, and he wasn't pleased no one rang up to tell him. What time did Roy go out?'

'He stayed in bed all morning, I took his breakfast up to him about nine. Then after his lunch he got dressed up and went out, I guessed he was meeting a girl. He's got a girlfriend where he works. Eileen Speke.'

'Didn't you ask him?'

'I tried pulling his leg about it, but he just grinned back.'

'We have a witness who saw him with Mrs Hurst in her car that afternoon,' said Bowker.

'Mid-afternoon,' Knight added, 'about three, three-thirty.'

'It's a lie,' Joyce said angrily. 'I know where you got that from—you've been talking to Barry Crick. Well, let me tell you something: Barry Crick is a born liar. It was him tried to get Roy in trouble when Jilly Ratcliffe clicked for a baby, to save himself. He went 'round telling everybody it was Roy's, and when that didn't come off, he's always on the lookout for some way of getting at Roy.'

'You don't believe Roy was with Lynn Hurst Tuesday afternoon last week—that's what you're saying?'

'How could Roy know somebody like her, with her fancy clothes and the rest of it? Where was this car supposed to be going?'

'Along the Wormwold road.'

'That proves it's a lie,' Joyce said. 'It's Lovers' Lane, the Wormwold road. Courting couples go down there.'

'Why are you so sure your brother wasn't on those terms with Mrs Hurst?'

'I ask you!' Joyce sighed in exasperation. 'Roy and her—is it likely? She was years older than him. And besides, we're Long Slaughter born and bred, she wasn't our sort.'

'Not our sort,' Dad Sibson echoed feebly from his chair.

Bowker tried a different angle of approach. 'We found a driving licence on Roy. Did he have a car?'

'No,' said Joyce. 'He took driving lessons last year. He was saving up to buy a car.'

'Funny sort of saving he was doing,' Bowker growled, his lack of any progress was starting to make him impatient. 'How much is in his account, Knight? Less than a hundred and fifty quid, as I recall, well down on last year. Negative saving, you could call it.'

Knight flipped over a page in his notebook. He was recording Joyce's answers.

'As of now, sir, it's £146. Before Christmas it was £273.'

'So there you are,' Bowker said to Joyce. 'He wanted money to buy himself a car. He took eight thousand that wasn't his. It's not been found. Did he give it to you to look after for him?'

'You've searched the house,' she said bitterly. 'You know if there's any money here.'

Mrs Sibson, forgotten in her corner, stood up unsteadily.

'I won't sit here and listen to you insult my boy,' she said. 'Leave him alone now he's dead.'

She went out of the room, dabbing at her eyes. They heard her footsteps going heavily up the stairs.

'It's how he came to be dead that's bothering me,' said Denis Bowker, a black scowl on his face as he left the vexed question of the money. 'An accident, maybe? Did he take a walk along the riverbank and fall in? Did he jump because he was worried he'd be found out as a thief? Or was he pushed? What do you think, Mrs Harris? Which is the likeliest?'

'Roy would never harm himself,' said Joyce.

'An accident, then, or a nastier explanation?'

'You ask yourself why Barry Crick told you lies about seeing Roy with Mrs Hurst,' she retorted.

Days ago Bowker had asked for all the road-mending gang to be questioned separately if they remembered a white car going past them, and if they did, who was in it. Two remembered a white car with a pretty woman driving.

Only one of them recalled seeing a man with her, no idea what he looked like, if he was young, old, middle-aged, black, white, or a Chinaman. The identification of Roy Sibson in Lynn's car rested on Barry Crick's word alone—very unsatisfactory, that, in Bowker's opinion.

'I've asked myself why Barry should tell lies,' he answered Joyce. 'But why do *you* think he did?'

'He took the money from Roy and then pushed him in the river. It stands to reason,' she said immediately.

'That's a very serious allegation, Mrs Harris. What proof do you have for saying a thing like that?'

Bowker was listening intently, trying to analyse the emotions driving her. Grief, that was certain—and resentment, a lot of that. He was used to people resenting the police, especially if they came with bad news.

The accusation had startled Dad Sibson. He ran a shaking hand over his bald pate and told Joyce to watch out what she said.

'I'll say what I like,' she flared at him. 'You don't know anything about it, Dad, so shut up.'

'But *you* know something about it,' said Bowker. He sounded as chilling as the Judgement Day trumpet summoning sinners. 'Tell me why you think Barry Crick killed your brother.'

'I don't say he meant to,' said Joyce, 'but he's always been a bully. Maybe he pushed Roy in while he ran off with the money and thought he'd scramble up the bank. He's malicious, but not a murderer, not deliberate. But you find out where Barry was last week on Tuesday, after he finished work.'

'Did you see him yourself, somewhere about the village?'

'I saw him go past on his way home. The Cricks are only a few doors away, at Number 19.'

'What time was that?'

'Getting on for seven; it was nearly dark. Working for the

County Council they stop soon after four most days, and Fridays they stop at midday. But it was near on seven when he came past.'

'Were you expecting Roy home?' Bowker slid the question in to unsettle her.

'I didn't know what to think. He went out dressed up as if he was going to meet his Eileen, but I knew something was going on, and he hadn't really got a day off. It was the way he said it. I wondered if he'd been given the sack, but he'd have told me if it was that. He was agitated—not exactly worried, but there was something on his mind.'

'Was he usually like that when he went to meet his girl?'

'No, that's what made me think of the money. For weeks he'd been dropping hints—they didn't realise how clever he was, all that sort of thing. When I asked him straight out what he meant by it, he only grinned and said nothing.'

'You've already said that.' Bowker was very unsympathetic. 'If you suspected he was planning to commit a criminal offence, didn't it strike you that you ought to do something about it?'

'Do what? Report my own brother for something I wasn't sure of, is that what you mean? Get him the sack from the only good job he ever had since he left school?'

Bowker growled and let it go; there was nothing to be gained.

'When he didn't come home that night, what did you think?' he asked. He sounded very prone to instant disbelief of anything she said now.

There was a long pause before Joyce answered. When she did, it was to clarify her own position. 'Shall I get into trouble if I tell you the truth?'

'If you were an accomplice in Roy's dishonesty, yes, I shall bloody well arrest you,' he said. 'If it was only guessing and not actual knowledge of what he was doing, I'll forget about it if you tell the simple truth and help me clear up the mystery surrounding his death.'

'There's no mystery about it. Barry Crick pushed him in,' she said. 'When Roy didn't come home, I thought he'd taken the money and run away with it. I said he was on holiday to give him time to think better of it and put the money back.'

She sounded sincere, but Bowker had trouble believing her. He thought it more likely that she lied to give Roy more time to vanish with the loot. Eight thousand quid—pathetic!

'Was your husband at home, Mrs Harris?' he asked. 'Did he see Barry Crick going past?'

'They were having a union meeting that night after work,' she said. 'He wasn't home until nearly ten o'clock.'

'Were he and Roy very friendly?'

'They always got on very well. They used to go bowling together. Why?'

'I need to talk to Mr Harris, in case he knew anything about Roy's tickle with the Building Society's computer. If they were as friendly as you suggest, Roy could have given him the money to look after.'

'Leave my husband out of this!' Joyce said sharply. 'He's a good, hardworking man. He's not involved in anything.'

'Time will tell,' said Bowker with cheerful ferocity. 'In the meantime, I must ask you to come with me to the station and make a proper statement about the events of that Tuesday.'

'No!' Dad Sibson protested. 'You can't arrest our Joyce!'

'Yes, I bloody can. But, as it happens, I don't mean to. All I want from her is a written statement. Come on, Mrs Harris.'

'I've told you all I know,' she said stubbornly. 'Barry Crick killed Roy. Why don't you go after him and leave me alone?'

Bowker rose to his feet, looming over her, his executioner's smile on his face.

'Come along,' he said softly. 'No use making a fuss. We'll go to PC Whitelock's house and write it all down on paper and have it typed for you to sign. You'll be back home again in a couple of hours, and then I'll look for Barry Crick.'

B‌y arrangement with the vicar, Bowker took over the Church Hall as Incident Room for his new team to work from. Detective Chief Superintendent Horrocks had promised to send him ten Detective Constables and two more Detective Sergeants, and begged him to get a bloody move on as he'd been on the case long enough.

The hall was a single-storey building in Victorian flint. It had a low slate roof and a down-in-the-mouth appearance and was located 'round the back of St Elfreda's Church.

There was no shortcut to the hall through the churchyard. A row of iron railings with spikes on top ran right 'round to keep the resurrection-men away from new graves back in the days when a fresh corpse was worth two or three guineas to anatomy teachers.

The way to the hall was up School Walk, the dead-end running off Badger Lane. The members of the Murder Squad would walk by Lynn Hurst's cottage every day they were there and also past Empson Rowley's home, the silly-named Karma Kottage.

Arranging to have the use of the hall for the squad proved to be more ticklish than Bowker guessed. Since the Old Rectory had been sold off, Long Slaughter parsons had an easily forgettable semi-detached further along Church Street, roughly at the point where it turned itself into the Wormwold road.

Bloody ironic, Bowker said to himself as he stood outside and knocked at the door; the vicar's well-placed to see the sinners going past for an hour of the carnal by the river. If he was at home Tuesday afternoon last week, he might even have glanced out of his front window and seen Lynn go past with Roy in her car.

The Reverend Andy Gibbs answered the door himself. He looked to be in his late thirties, thin, with a short scrubby ginger beard, making Bowker instantly suspicious.

He had on a clerical collar, but he wore it over a lumberjack shirt. And he was wearing blue jeans. It would have been bloody sacrilege, dressing like that in the Old Rectory, but it looked about right for the semi.

Bowker explained who he was and what he was there for. The parson looked doubtful, but asked him in. They sat in the front room overlooking the road, a room furnished as if for meetings with twelve uncomfortable tubular metal chairs, DIY book-shelves along one wall, a small desk littered with pamphlets.

The Reverend Gibbs was evidently not married, if that was his home style, Bowker decided. No woman yet born would put up with her front parlour being turned into a committee-room.

Nor did the vicar express himself as happy to co-operate with the police—a sad admission for a man of the cloth.

'Not at all sure I can let you have the Church Hall,' he said unhelpfully. 'It's in constant use, very much a part of village community life. The Mothers' Union has it on the first Tuesday of each month. The Christian Farmers Green Ecological Movement have it the second Thursday. The Brownies meet once a week in it. The Long Slaughter Young Socialist Guitar Club have it on alternate Wednesdays, to say nothing of the once-a-month jumble sale, and the Men's Christian Fellowship AIDS Awareness Group.'

Bowker could hardly believe he was hearing this flimflam from a parson. If anybody else tried to stall him he would have gone into a cataclysmic rage. It took a huge effort to restrain his emotions. Co-operation beats coercion, he told himself.

'I'm glad you mentioned the community,' he said, keeping his voice reasonable. 'In the past week or so, three members of your community have come to violent ends, Vicar. Two of them done in very brutally, the third very probably murdered as well, though the post-mortem will settle that. Murder is a serious offence. It's my duty to find out who's doing it and put a stop to it.'

'I am not comfortable with the thought that any decision of mine, however peripheral, could result in the imprisonment of a fellow human-being,' said the Reverend Gibbs very earnestly. 'It's a question of conscience.'

'How comfortable are you with the thought a local human being had her head smashed in, another killed with car-exhaust fumes, and a third human being shoved in the river to drown?' Bowker asked.

'Two wrongs never make a right, Inspector.'

Bowker was wondering whether it was possible to find a good reason to run a parson in. He couldn't recall a case of a vicar tried for murder, not even for aggravated assault. The only notorious parson he'd ever heard of was the Rector of Stiffkey, and all he did to get himself into the Sunday newspapers was get a leg over a tart or two while he was calling them to repentance.

On second thought, one of Scotland Yard's suspects when Jack the Ripper murdered his half-dozen tarts was a Bible student in Finsbury Park. And they never caught the Ripper, thought Bowker morosely; not all they're cracked up to be, Scotland Yard. Hope they bloody know something about Stephen Fenwick.

'There's a dangerous killer loose in this village,' he said, trying not to stare at the ginger beard. 'I'd have thought it would be on your conscience if we've got another dead body on our hands tomorrow?'

'Yes,' said the Reverend, looking excessively worried at the suggestion. 'We are all responsible for each other. Every death diminishes me.'

Bowker remembered what Bobby Liggins had told him, the farmer who found the body of Gavin Fowler in Lynn Hurst's white car in Birley Spinney. All bloody social awareness, the new vicar, and never a word about religion. That or something like it was what Liggins said.

'What sort of person do you suppose can take three lives and go home to his dinner and a good night's sleep?' Bowker asked. 'I'm interested in your professional opinion as a clergyman and theology expert.'

He was stretching the facts a mite. He had no good proof that one person had done the three of them in, but he was trying to make a point. 'If we're all responsible, do you feel personally responsible yourself for somebody that wicked?' he added.

'We live in a sick and corrupt society, Inspector, warped and unloving. It is only to be expected that some will necessarily be crushed beneath the monstrous pressures we live under. But I shall give you a straight answer to your question. You deserve that from me, at least. *Yes,* I can feel sorrow and sympathy for a poor soul driven to these dreadful acts.'

Bowker was embarrassed, not for himself but for the vicar. No wonder the Church of England was dying of leukaemia. If bloody Adolf Hitler turned up in Long Slaughter, the vicar would treat him to a cup of instant coffee and tell him he was a victim of bloody society, and the gas chambers weren't his fault.

'Very properly Christian,' Bowker said through gritted teeth, 'but I've got to find this *poor soul* before any more dreadful acts are committed. I need the use of your Church Hall.'

He was coming to an understanding of why religious persecutions used to happen in the good old days, how they justified burning dissidents at the stake, not a good feeling at all for a copper to have. He glowered at the Reverend Gibbs.

'Very well then,' said the parson. 'I hope I never regret it. I shall say a prayer for you, Inspector.'

Bowker was struggling to force himself to say *thank you* when the parson's next words erased his gratitude.

'And I shall pray for the person you are seeking out,' said the Reverend Andy Gibbs, 'that he or she may find peace of mind and understanding in God's eternal mercy.'

'Amen,' said Bowker. It came out like a snarl.

By teatime, he had his Incident Room operational. Better than his word, DCS Horrocks had sent him twelve Detective Constables, two Detective Sergeants, two uniformed Women Police Constables, and a truckload of gear.

It was a big truck, the sort used for house-removals, loaded up with trestle-tables, metal filing-cabinets, folding chairs, computer terminals, blackboards with easels, wire filing trays, typewriters, pin-up boards, glue, pencil sharpeners and paper clips, staplers, fifty reams of paper, a Japanese copying machine, twelve copies of the Area phone directory, two gross message-pads and various other essential paraphernalia of murderer-catching.

The truck couldn't get to the Church Hall. It was stopped in Badger Lane by the iron posts at the end of School Walk. Teams of cursing detectives carried the gear in and deployed it about the hall under the supervision of Jimmy Payne and Jason Roper, Bowker's newly acquired Detective Sergeants.

Jack Knight was out. Bowker had sent him to find Barry Crick and bring him in to answer a few more questions. It wasn't that Bowker took Joyce Harris's accusation at face value. She didn't like Crick and was trying to make trouble for him. It might be useful to find out why Joyce thought Crick could be set up. Her tale about seeing him arrive home seemed pointless, only there might be more than met the eye in this village feud.

His thoughts were interrupted by Miss Pankhurst in her

shabby brown coat and imitation-fruit hat. She stared about the Church Hall, bewildered by the bustle of detectives lugging equipment from the truck and setting it up.

My first caller, thought Bowker, getting to his feet, *and it's nothing to do with the murders. It's about her bloody tomcat.*

Mavis Pankhurst had never been very tall; old age had shrunk her to a bit less than five feet. Bowker towered above her like a giant, an uncomfortable thought for him, and perhaps for her. He settled her on a folding chair and sat down again to reduce the discrepancy between their sizes.

Her hair was snowy-white under the unbelievably old-fashioned hat, her face lined and thin, but her eyes were still alive and her expression vigorous.

'We used to have Whist Drives here years ago,' she said, 'in the old vicar's day. But the new vicar's very down on gambling; he put a stop to it. Not that anybody ever won more than a home-made fruitcake. I used to enjoy the Whist Drive.'

Bowker nodded in sympathy. His view of the Rev Andy Gibbs as a prize muttonhead was reinforced by Miss Pankhurst's dismal news item. No wonder there was a tin tabernacle just across the river for those who couldn't put up with the man and his trendy obsessions. Before long, the village would be swamped by loony Jehovah's Witnesses and smarmy Mormons.

'You haven't found my cat, then.' Miss Pankhurst pursed her lips in displeasure. 'Even with all these men to search for him. Somebody told me you'd taken over the Church Hall, and so I thought I'd come round and see what was going on. In case you'd forgotten about my Tiger.'

'I hadn't forgotten about him.'

'Don't suppose I'll ever see him alive again,' she said with a sniff. 'He's been gone too long.'

'I don't know a lot about cats,' Bowker confessed. 'Can they find their way home from a long way off, like dogs are supposed to?'

'That I couldn't say, but Tiger would find his way home from anywhere 'round the village, if he was still alive. Will you be able to catch the men who took him, Mr Bowker?'

She'd remembered his name; nothing wrong with her memory, old as she was.

'I'll have a very good try,' he promised her, feeling guilty.

He walked her slowly to the door, holding her arm lightly to keep her from falling over equipment boxes dumped carelessly on the floor. When he saw her safely on her way down School Walk, he closed the door and stood in the middle of the room to face his new Squad.

'Right, listen to me!' he bellowed. They'd had long enough to sort themselves out. Time to put them to work.

His voice rattled the Church Hall windows, putting DS Payne in mind of a very hostile gorilla he had seen on a TV wildlife programme.

'Sit still and listen,' Bowker ordered. 'I'll lay it out for you as best I can and tell you what we're going to do.'

There was instant attention. Bowker was a legend.

'To date we've got three dead bodies,' he said, 'and enough bloody suspects to start a football team. Motives are as clear as ink, but it looks as if all this drama revolves around Lynn Hurst, the first deceased to be found though not the first one to die. What we haven't got is even a whiff of Chummy yet.'

He handed a sheet torn from an exercise book to DS Payne and nodded at the blackboard standing behind him.

'DS Payne is copying the names of our suspects so far on the board for you. We've got Dr Harvey Hurst, the ex-husband of our dead woman, and now more or less engaged to a nineteen-year-old with a big chest. We've got Mark Stanhope, an architect of sorts. He claims he was engaged to Lynn, though she hadn't got a ring on her finger. He's the one who found her body. Next we've got a comic-book artist, Empson Rowley, her next-door neighbour. Now he was having a rollick with her and he's worried in case his live-in girlfriend finds out.'

He paused while his audience scribbled notes for themselves.

'In the past twenty-four hours Stephen Fenwick has been added to the list,' he continued. 'He's a lawyer, business not criminal, but he might be that as well. He's another one who got his leg over the dead woman.'

'Before she was dead,' he added quickly, quelling the ribald guffaw of his squad with a look capable of turning living flesh into stone.

'Our prime suspect for Lynn's murder is a roughneck of this parish, Gavin Fowler. But he turned up dead in her car, maybe a suicide except I don't believe it, so we can't very well ask him to account for his movements.'

'There's two murderers, then?' a Detective Constable asked.

'In this bloody case, there might even be three,' Bowker said with a ferocious scowl. 'I said we've got three bodies; there's precious little evidence to link them. And what there is could have been faked to throw us off the trail. Nothing can be ruled out. It's taken till today to establish the order in which the three were done in, but we've got that much straightened out.'

'Bloody hell!' said the Detective Constable who had asked the question.

'You may well say,' said Bowker, giving him a look as dark as night. 'We've been lied to consistently, DS Knight and me, ever since we started this enquiry. None of these buggers with their names on the blackboard has an alibi worth mentioning.'

The twelve Detective Constables looked at each other with a wild surmise. They had heard about Denis Bowker, and they weren't sure what they were in for.

'I want to know what the victims and the suspects were doing, and when and if they were seen in the village. You're going to find out for me. That means asking every living person in this miserable bloody village, including the bloody vicar. DS Payne will assign streets to you from the map; there aren't all that many. Everybody over the age of four who lives in the village is to be asked if they saw any of the victims or suspects. Half of them will be out at work, so go back when they're at home.'

'Are we on overtime, sir?' asked a greatly daring copper.

Bowker was instantly enraged. His hands clawed at the air and he looked so much like the Mad Mangler that his new Sergeants feared he would seize the stupid detective by ankle and throat and hurl him across the Church Hall.

'Till I say different, you're on duty twenty-four hours a day,' he said in a voice like a tidal wave wiping out a coastal town. 'And by this time tomorrow, I want a piece of paper for everybody living in Long Slaughter, on which it says whether they saw any of the suspects since Monday last week. And if they didn't, the paper is to be a Nil-Return. Understand me? This time tomorrow.'

'Yes, sir,' said the detective in a small voice.

'The same for the victims,' said Bowker, ignoring him. 'We've got photos of them for you, looking as well as can be expected in the circumstances. The Lynn Hurst photo is from her album of happy-holiday snaps; the post-mortem picture with her skull bashed in is too bloody gruesome to show people. So be careful you don't frighten children or any nervous old ladies with the others.'

Then, as an afterthought, he added, 'The man who questions the vicar, make sure he takes a bloody good look at the Lynn Hurst scene-of-crime photo with her brain hanging out. Tell him the gory details. There's a commendation for the man who makes the Reverend sick up on the lino.'

There was a nervous titter from his listeners, not certain if he was serious or not.

'Bit of a berk, is he, sir?' DS Roper asked with a grin.

'It's high time he found out about wickedness,' Bowker said, 'that's by the way. The important thing I want to know is where each of the victims was, day and night, from breakfast-time on Monday last week till the minute they were killed.'

'Lot of work for twenty-four hours, sir,' said DS Payne. 'Might take a bit longer than that.'

'It won't,' Bowker corrected him harshly. 'I want this bloody case wrapped up so I can have Sunday off. This squad may all be illegitimate orphans. I've got a wife and kids to go home to.'

A chorus of disbelief rose from the squad. Bowker glowered.

'Listen to me, you idle and unloved coppers,' he said. 'I've an eight-year-old daughter so pretty they pay her to be in the shampoo ads on television. And a ten-year-old boy who plays the piano better than Richard Claydermann. And I've got a wife who understands me and pines for me when I'm away. So get off your backsides and get this case bloody well wrapped up. I'm missing my home comforts.'

'Right, sir,' said Payne, wishing now he'd said nothing.

'Before you go,' Bowker said to the silenced squad, 'I'll say it once more: this investigation has gone on long enough. Out there in the village, some yokel's laughing his head off because he thinks he's got away with it. We're here to prove he bloody hasn't. So DS Payne will be out with you controlling the house-to-house and making sure you don't slope off into a pub and get drunk. DS Roper will stay here and co-ordinate what you bring in. A team from Telecom will turn up any minute now to put in a switchboard and phones. Not that you need them today—I want you out and about on your flat feet 'round the village, knocking on doors.'

One of the trestle-tables was set up alone at the far end of the hall for Bowker. He sat down behind it and scowled blackly at the empty wire trays.

Lynn Hurst, Gavin Fowler, Roy Sibson, choose any two out of three, he thought. *It looks easy enough, but it comes out wrong every time.*

We've been assuming Gavin Fowler the slaughterman killed Lynn and Roy on behalf of somebody else and was then dumped himself. Suppose he didn't. Say Chummy did in Roy and Lynn *and* Gavin for reasons that are so bloody baffling they make no sense at all. Who the bloody hell in Long Slaughter was even remotely capable of a massacre on that scale?

Nobody he'd talked to so far; he was reasonably sure of that.

On the other hand, there were three dead bodies in the mortuary and that was an undeniable fact. The only thing all three had in common, as far as Bowker could make out, was that they lived at Long Slaughter. A miserable bloody place though it might be, living there seemed grossly inadequate as a reason for murder.

What it came to in the end, he thought, was that looking for motives made it impossible to see the trees for the wood. Today was Friday. He'd been here with Knight since last Saturday and accomplished nothing worthwhile. Asking why had led nowhere.

We'll try the other way now, he told himself gloomily. *Do the routine bit to find out who could have done it, irrespective of who wanted it done. Motives can be sorted out later after we've got the bracelets on somebody.*

The commonsense plan had little appeal for Bowker. It was not his way of catching killers. Leaving out domestic, where it was all too obvious, your average murder was not a random event. Find out the motive, and you'd found the killer. The evil bloody lawyer who pushed an old lady down her own stairs—there were a million and a half reasons to run him in when the will came to light.

Bowker's face darkened and veins stood out on his neck at the memory of how the villain he arrested had skidded off to Spain, a free man, taking the loot with him. If ever a ghost cried out for vengeance, it was old Mrs Diamond's. Her broken-necked body lay mouldering in her grave.

Bowker glared around the gloomy hall where the Mothers' Union discussed damson-jam recipes, where little girls in brown sang *Dib-dib-dib* and the Young Socialists twanged their guitars, and where the Green Ecological Farmers, if there were any such loonies in these parts, got together for a talk about muck-spreading.

All very normal, he thought, *what you expect in a village.* If the Men's Christian Fellowship sounded a right bunch of tulips, there was no law against it.

Long Slaughter wasn't the sort of place you expected to find motives for mass murder. Chief Superintendent Horrocks was bang on right about that; this wasn't bloody New York. What it came in the end was that the only rule was there weren't any rules. The most harmless-looking people were capable of atrocities.

Take the Lassiter case. Very nasty that one—a motive pointed straight to the killer. Sharon Lassiter's husband was having an affair with his secretary, a marvellous-looking young woman who wanted the wife out of the way so she could marry Lassiter.

Lassiter was a bloody fool who more-or-less promised he'd get a divorce from Sharon and marry the secretary—Mandy Griggs, her name was. Then he changed his mind when Sharon became pregnant. The upshot was that Mandy paid a visit when Lassiter was out playing golf one Sunday. Sharon opened the front door, unsuspecting, and Mandy stabbed her fourteen times.

It took Bowker less than forty-eight hours to clear up that one. Mandy hadn't even got rid of the raincoat she wore for the murder. It was in the boot of her car, rolled up and heavily blood-stained.

At the trial Mandy paid a woman psychiatrist to tell the jury she had been temporarily off her trolley at the time because of PMT and various other female inconveniences. She got off with a three-year sentence for manslaughter, astounding Bowker who'd never seen a more open-and-shut a case of wilful murder.

With good behaviour, Mandy would be out in no time, but Sharon Lassiter and her unborn baby were dead and forgotten. Sometimes Bowker asked himself why he bothered to catch murderers.

He was still sunk in gloomy contemplation when DS Knight came in, looking discontented. He glanced round the uninhabited rows of trestle-tables loaded with new equipment, at the blackboard where names of victims and dates were chalked up. He recognised DS Roper and nodded to him. All this without stopping a moment as he walked quickly the length of the hall and sat down across the table from the Inspector.

'So where the bloody hell's Barry Crick?' Bowker demanded.

'He's done a disappearing trick, sir.'

'I don't bloody believe it! Where've you looked?'

'At the Council depot. The foreman said Crick clocked on this morning and his gang were out on the road between Sandy Bottom and Little Wittenham, mending pot-holes. I found the gang easy enough, sitting by the side of the road drinking bottled beer, but Crick isn't with them.'

Bowker's jet-black eyebrows came down and moved together in a scowl of titanic proportions.

'They're a pretty thick lot,' said Knight. 'Not all there, if you ask me. I waved my warrant-card at them and threatened blue murder and thirty-year sentences for obstructing the police if they didn't speak up. It came out that Crick didn't turn up for work this morning; one of his mates clocked on for him.'

'Bloody funny we had Joyce Harris yesterday accusing Barry of doing Roy in, and today he's missing,' Bowker rumbled.

'I thought that myself, sir, but it seems it's not unknown if one of the gang wants a day off for one of the others to punch his clock-card for him. They won't admit it, but I'd not be at all surprised to find they had a day a week off each.'

'You tried his home?'

'Straight away, nobody in. The neighbour says Pa and Ma Crick went off on the Church charabanc trip early this morning. It's an outing to Weston-super-Mare.'

'Hell of a day they've got for it,' said Bowker. 'It's been drizzling all bloody morning. You ever seen Weston-super-Mare in the rain, Knight?'

'No, sir, not even in the dry. The neighbour didn't see Barry leave for work today, but his car's gone from where he leaves it parked outside the house.'

'Got a car, has he? What sort?'

'A red one—that's all the neighbour could tell me. It might be a Ford, but she doesn't really know anything about cars.'

'That bloody vicar never mentioned a Church outing to me

when I talked to him,' Bowker said. He sounded like a large and very destructive bomb about to explode.

'No reason to,' said Knight. 'He may be dim, but I don't think you can blame him for not expecting a mass murderer amongst his congregation. What do you want to do about Barry?'

'Might just be having a day off. We'll give him until tonight before we mark him missing and start looking for him seriously. He's a clown. You said it yourself: a lot of them are not right in the head in Long Slaughter. Crafty they are, and bloody sly some of them, but definitely not all there.'

'Yes, but you have to admit it's a bit like Roy Sibson going missing,' said Knight. 'You don't think Chummy could have done Barry in as well, do you? It would look very bad for us to be sitting here doing nothing while Barry went floating down the Thames belly-up.'

'We're not doing bloody nothing,' Bowker said loudly. He was outraged by the suggestion. 'This is the first time you've been on a case with me. You don't understand how I go about things.'

'No, sir. Perhaps you'll explain to me what we're doing.'

Bowker scowled blackly at him. A lesser man would have backed off halfway across the Church Hall, but Knight stood his ground.

'We're bloody well analysing information as it comes in,' said Bowker threateningly. 'After DS Roper has co-ordinated it first for us. I fully expect to make an arrest by teatime tomorrow.'

'Yes, but what are we really doing?' Knight persisted.

'We're going to call on Mark Stanhope, hard-up architect and heartbroken fiancé of the late Mrs Lynn Hurst,' Bowker said, a grin on his broad face. 'That nice girl reporter said Stanhope has stopped grieving and turned devious. We were going to find out why when Roy surfaced in the bloody river and changed our plans for us.'

'Miss Thomas never used the word "devious," ' Knight said, and he reached for his notebook. 'I wrote it down when you told me to. She said Stanhope was defensive and shifty and furtive. In her opinion, that is. It might be he just hates reporters, even when they're pretty girls.'

'I can understand that, Knight, and even sympathise with the feeling. By and large, reporters are the pain in the proverbial. But sometimes you come across one sober enough to notice things that can be useful. So we shall judge for ourselves if Sara got a true impression of Stanhope being shifty and devious.'

'Defensive, sir, not devious. And furtive.'

The telephone team arrived, consulted with Detective Sergeant Roper and brought in the portable exchange, cursing because the van couldn't drive right up to the Church Hall door. This was a good time to leave, while the engineers fiddled about making it work and trailing wires across the floor for unwary coppers to trip on, clattering about spreading phones 'round the tables.

Down at the bottom end of School Walk two more overalls and a BT van were parked by a manhole cover in the pavement of Badger Lane. They were doing technical things to the cables below.

'I hope they've sent us a Fax machine,' Bowker said. 'Then we can send the confession over the wire to DCS Horrocks. Complete with Chummy's own signature. He'll like that.'

'What confession?' Knight asked in amazement. 'All we've got is more suspects than we know what to do with. Nobody is going to bloody well confess.'

The two of them climbed into Bowker's disreputable car, Knight at the wheel.

'They nearly always do confess,' Bowker said glumly. 'It gets them off at the trial.'

'How do you make that out, sir?'

'If the jury's told the accused refused to say anything when charged, it's a hint even the stupidest can't miss. They know they're dealing with a guilty person, and they listen harder.'

'Stands to reason,' Knight commented as he pulled smartly out from the kerb.

'When Chummy gives us a full confession, his lawyer tells the jury we forced it out of his innocent client by ill treatment, physical abuse, threats and sleep deprivation. Not content with that, we changed the wording to suit ourselves, as can be shown by some blind-'em-with science foolery they've devised. Then the defence lawyer trots out another bloody expert on phonetics and linguistics and breathing patterns, to prove we're a rabid gang of frame-up artists. With all that, it's ten-to-one Chummy gets off—which is why they're so bloody anxious to confess when we run them in.'

'I hadn't thought of it that way,' Knight said.

Mark Stanhope lived in the penthouse of a small block of flats in landscaped gardens on the better side of Reading. It was not very likely Stanhope designed the block himself, Bowker thought glumly, just as well for his reputation as an architect. It was a concrete cube with a lot of tinted glass windows.

'He likes to live well, our Mr Stanhope,' said Jack Knight as he parked right next to the silver Mercedes that he'd rummaged through a few days before. He slid Bowker's tired-looking Honda into a space clearly marked RESIDENTS ONLY.

'That letter from his Bank Manager you read was dated about a week before Lynn Hurst was killed,' said Bowker. 'That right?'

'Near enough. It was written on the twelfth.'

'It would be interesting to know what Mark wrote back,' said Bowker, staring maliciously at the Mercedes alongside.

'Can't be done,' Knight answered hastily. 'Not here in bloody broad daylight, in a car park. Besides, there's no guarantee he leaves his briefcase in the car when he arrives home.'

'True, but we know it's the sort of letter he doesn't keep in his office. My guess is he doesn't want his secretary to see it and spread the bad news.'

The Inspector uncoiled himself out of the confines of his car and stretched. He looked about eight feet tall and broad-shouldered as a buffalo.

'It's stopped raining,' he observed. 'There's no briefcase on the back seat, it might be in the boot.'

He placed a hand the size of a dinner plate on Stanhope's car and pushed gently. The car rocked sideways and began to squeal loudly as the alarm was triggered.

'Dear me,' said Bowker, his teeth showing in a crocodile grin that lacked the least trace of humour, 'I seem to have set off the alarm—very careless of me. Stanhope will have to run down and stop it.'

As with all car alarms screaming blue murder, it was ignored. Bowker and Knight made their way to the entrance to the block, a door of thick glass with Art Deco curlicues etched in it.

A series of push buttons on the wall had small printed names beside them.

It took some time after the Stanhope button was pushed before the entry-phone squawked *Who is it?* Long enough for suspicious thoughts to stir in Bowker's mind. There was something Stanhope was nervous about. Maybe someone he didn't want seen.

'Inspector Bowker,' he said. 'Let me in, Mr Stanhope, I have questions to ask you.'

There was another long pause, as if the person at the other end was thinking it over.

'Open the door, Mr Stanhope.' Bowker's tone conveyed a threat of indescribable consequences.

After a delay of another ten or fifteen seconds, the lock buzzed and clicked open.

'Stay down here, Knight,' said Bowker. 'See who comes down in the next few minutes. Get the car registration number. Then you can follow me up.'

The penthouse was the sixth floor. The lift had mirrors on all sides and was carpeted in greenish-blue to match the entrance hall. Bowker stared at his gypsy-faced reflection on the way up and thought about Mark James Stanhope.

He was a chancer, Stanhope. He knew the world owed him a good living and he cut corners to make certain he got it. Flash car, paralysing overdraft, bills overdue all 'round, business sagging and income doubtful. Didn't stop him flying Lynn Hurst to Paris for a weekend of fun and frolic.

None of that was a crime, of course, but it illustrated Mark James Stanhope's character. Bowker read it as meaning the sort of irresponsibility that would not jib at any kind of financial fraud if the opportunity showed up. As, for instance, bilking the Chalfont Building Society.

To prove that needed a link between Stanhope and the late Roy Sibson—a better link than both of them being friends of Lynn Hurst. If Roy *was* a friend—there was only Barry Crick's word for it. And Barry was the sort not to be trusted, unless he had a sworn statement witnessed by three clergymen and a Justice of the Peace. And even then it would be dodgy.

For a while Bowker had wondered if Stanhope had murdered Lynn for her savings. Not that £42,000 would last long at the pace he went. But it would tide him over his sticky patch. His type were blissful optimists, true descendants of Mr Micawber, a Charles Dickens character Bowker had met more than once under different names. They were certain-sure something would turn up: all they need do was hold on long enough.

Marry Lynn and then take the money from her as a loan; that seemed the sensible thing to do. But maybe Lynn didn't want to marry him. Going to Paris and the Caribbean with him was a long cry from any permanent arrangement. There was only Mark's word for it that they were going to be married—only one engagement ring had been found on Lynn's dead hand, alongside her wedding ring from Dr Harvey Hurst.

Hard-up or not, Stanhope would have insisted on giving her an impressively expensive diamond ring. Bought on tick, probably. Common sense said there ought to be two engagement rings on her hand. Now she was dead and silent, nobody could contradict Mark when he said they were to be married.

So bash her head in and claim to be the heir as her intended—was that the plan? No guarantee that would work; the sister in Chiswick was the next-of-kin. She had the better claim, in the absence of a will.

No will was to be found—they'd searched for it. They didn't find it at Lynn's bank, nor with the lawyer who had handled the divorce from Dr Hurst. Her sister hadn't got it; she said that she knew nothing about it. Nor did her ex-husband Hurst.

It was a racing certainty that if a will existed and if Stanhope's name was in it, he'd be waving it about and claiming the money to get a nagging bank manager off his back.

Stanhope stood to gain more if Lynn was alive, in money terms, maybe, if he could talk her into lending him her oddly acquired savings. And if she was as fascinating a woman as her bitterly infatuated ex-husband insisted, Stanhope had lost a great deal emotionally by her death.

Which was all very well as far as it went. Stanhope was not a good prospect as First Murderer, but Bowker was sure there was something crooked about him.

The lift doors opened and Bowker stepped out into a tiny hall with a black-and-white marble floor. It looked like marble, at least, but very likely wasn't.

Opposite the lift was a white-painted door with a spy hole. When Bowker rang the bell he found it didn't sound the usual *Dingdong*. Muffled through the woodwork came the first few notes of Beethoven's Fifth Symphony: *Ding-ding-ding DONG!*

Stanhope opened the door. His blondish bouffant hair-style had been carefully brushed, he was in a crimson silk shirt under a baby-blue cashmere pullover. Silvery-grey linen trousers. Gucci slip-on shoes with tassels, a picture of delight, Bowker in his rumpled dark suit thought sourly.

Stanhope raised his arm casually, elbow bent, to consult the massive gold Rolex on his wrist.

'Come in, Inspector, I'm pushed for time. I hope this isn't going to take long.'

Bowker followed him into a sitting-room furnished in gold and black, something he'd never imagined existed outside the pages of men's magazines. Miss Universe in a lurex dress slit to the thigh ought to have been draped sensually on the settee but she wasn't. Nobody was, though there was a trace of expensive scent in the air. Not Stanhope's after-shave—that was different.

'Sit down,' said Stanhope, gesturing loosely at the furniture. 'Have you got time for a drink?'

No wonder his Bank Manager is agitating, Bowker thought as he sank into a matte black leather armchair with golden piping. The bedroom must be like a bloody Sultan's harem!

'No, thank you,' he said, treating Stanhope to an evil grin to let him know this was no social occasion. "My Sergeant is with me. I left him outside trying to stop the alarm on your car. We recognized it because we saw it in Long Slaughter the other day at the bottom end of School Walk.'

'Damn the thing! Sometimes I wish I'd never had it installed. The least little thing sets it off,' Stanhope said, annoyed.

'Officially all car owners are recommended to fit them,' said Bowker, trying to sound genial and not succeeding. 'I never yet heard of a car thief being put off by one. They buy a gadget to switch them off instantly, you know.'

'You can't hear it up here, with the double-glazing,' Stanhope said, very irritated. 'I never know unless somebody from below comes up to tell me. Your colleague won't be able to stop it—I'll have to go down.'

Off he dashed. Bowker was on his feet the moment he heard the lift whine. The thin black briefcase lay on a matte black wooden desk by the wall, beside a personal computer with an elaborate-looking keyboard and a letter from the Institute of Architects regretting that Stanhope's annual subscription was overdue.

By the side of the computer stood a plastic filing-box filled with floppy discs. Bowker wondered briefly if he could persuade a magistrate to give him a Search Warrant. He was certain that everything he ever wanted to know about Mark James Stanhope was to be found on those discs.

The expensive briefcase was unlocked. The dunning letter from the Bank Manager was in it. So was a second letter demanding an answer within twenty-four hours to the first.

Also in it were two Court Summons for debt, one for £780, the other for £43. And a letter written on pastel green paper from somebody signing herself Rachel, informing Stanhope that he was a cold-hearted bastard. She also told him she was applying for a Court Order for child maintenance.

There was a letter from someone who signed himself Howard, who sounded like a relation, begging Stanhope to pay back a loan of £10,000. It was only going to be for six months, Howard wrote in anguish, and it was already over a year.

None of the desk drawers was locked, Bowker went through them like a hungry stoat down a rabbit hole. He found a large bundle of bills, most of them stamped OVERDUE by aggrieved senders.

A brown manila envelope held eleven unpaid Parking Fine tickets. Perhaps Stanhope was starting a collection. There was a letter from the Chalfont Building Society drawing Stanhope's attention firmly to the fact that he was three months behind in his mortgage payments, and inviting his suggestions as to what could be done to regularise the position.

There was a plastic ring-binder with bank statements for two years past. Mark James Stanhope's financial viability had been deteriorating month by month, from a bearable overdraft to one that made Bowker flinch. The economic recession seemed to have tipped Stanhope's business into the waste-bin. But on the other hand, maybe he wasn't a very good architect.

In the middle drawer of the desk was a thick address book. It had hundreds of entries. There wasn't time to go through them. Bowker flicked over the pages quickly, looking for names that meant something to him.

No entry for *Sibson*—common sense said there wouldn't be. The Sibson family had no telephone at home, and Stanhope was hardly likely to ring Roy at work if they were partners in a swindle.

Fenwick wasn't listed either, nor *Dr Hurst*. The only relevant name entered was *Hurst, Lynn, School Walk, Long Slaughter,* with a phone number.

The lift was whining upwards. Bowker tidied up very rapidly. He was sitting on the black and gold chair consulting his note-book when Stanhope came in with DS Knight close behind him.

'You were right, sir,' said Knight, bogus cheerfulness in his voice. 'It *was* Mr Stanhope's car alarm that was going off. Good thing you recognised the car, or he'd be in danger of creating a public nuisance.'

Mark Stanhope was curiously ungrateful. He said nothing.

'Unfortunately,' said Knight, cheerier than ever, 'I happened to notice Mr Stanhope's Road Tax ran out six weeks ago. Busy men like him sometimes overlook these things, but he's promised to walk 'round to the Post Office first thing tomorrow morning and renew it.'

'Very sensible,' said Bowker. His savage frown suggested the penalty for unpaid Road Tax was deportation to a Russian labour camp, at the very least. 'Sit down, Mr Stanhope. There are a few points I want to clear up with you.'

It was the first time Stanhope had been offered a seat in his own home. He grunted with annoyance and flung himself on to the black leather settee, trying to look proprietorial.

'When I saw you at Long Slaughter last Saturday,' said Bowker to set the scene, 'you had discovered Mrs Hurst dead and were in a shocked and distressed state. Odd little details may have slipped your mind, understandable in the circumstances. Now you are calmer and more yourself, you have had time to reflect and I hope you are going to assist me with my enquiries.'

'Why haven't you found out who did it?' Stanhope demanded, a rate-payer irritated by obvious police incompetence, or perhaps a man with troubles trying to sound like one.

'Have no fear, we're very close to an arrest,' said Bowker, a general air of doom and dread about him, like a headsman honing his axe blade. Knight stared at his notebook. He felt sure the Inspector wasn't serious, he was saying that just to intimidate Stanhope.

'Tell me if I've got it right,' said Bowker, more ominous yet as he proceeded with the questioning. 'You were in Edinburgh on business and you flew back on Wednesday last week. That evening you talked to Mrs Hurst on the phone, to arrange to take her to Paris for the weekend.'

'Yes, that's right, Inspector.'

'How did she sound when you talked to her? Depressed, happy, fearful, content?'

'She seemed perfectly all right.' Stanhope was suddenly alert and cautious. 'Why do you ask that?'

'Someone she knew at Long Slaughter went missing only one day before you phoned her, someone she was with on the same day. If she knew he was missing, she would have sounded worried on the phone. Did she say anything to you at all about a local friend when you rang her?'

'What *is* all this?' Stanhope asked. 'What friend?'

'His name is Roy Sibson. Did she mention him?'

'I've never heard of him. Who is he?'

'Write that down in your book, Knight. Mr Stanhope states he has never heard of Roy Sibson. We have to get these things very clear.'

Stanhope's demeanour was beginning to resemble the impression Sara Thomas got when she tried to interview him: shifty. He was fidgeting with his heavy wristwatch, as if to convey to thick-witted policemen that urgent business matters were awaiting his indispensable incisive executive decision-making touch.

Bowker could see that a few hours in solitary in a cell was all that would be needed to reduce Mark Stanhope to a gibbering jelly who'd tell all. Whatever *all* might be: fraud, conspiracy, embezzlement, murder.

The only really tricky bit was to think of a reason to sling him into a lock-up and keep a lawyer from rescuing him too soon before he melted like a choc-ice on a hot day.

'If Mrs Hurst knew Sibson was missing,' he said, his voice a bass growl of pure malevolence, 'she would be worried.'

He paid no heed to Stanhope's fidgeting. He knew in his bones that the architect was being devious and evasive.

'How could she have known?' Stanhope countered, starting to use his mind at last. 'You said she saw him the day before. How could anyone know he was missing that soon?'

'His family knew.'

'That's different. His family would expect him home at din-nertime, I imagine. Look here, Inspector, I hope you're not trying to suggest anything improper about Mrs Hurst and this chap, are you? We were going to be married, I trusted her absolutely.'

'To say Roy Sibson went missing isn't exactly accurate,' said Bowker, ignoring the question. 'He drowned.'

Stanhope tried to return Bowker's glare, but he wasn't up to it. He looked down and said nothing. He was very wary now.

'If Mrs Hurst was with him when he drowned in the Thames, she would have sounded very worried on the phone,' said Bowker. 'In fact, she may have sounded distraught.'

'This is arrant bloody nonsense,' Stanhope said. 'What in the hell are you suggesting?'

'I'm trying to clear up a point.' Bowker was unstoppable as an earthquake now, the ground splitting and dropping away under Stanhope's feet.

'Don't come it with me!' Stanhope said, hoping to get into a safer position. 'I can see what you're hinting—you're trying to make out Lynn was somehow responsible for the death of this chap, whatever-his-name-was.'

"Well, was she?' Bowker demanded.

The blunt question startled DS Knight as much as Stanhope. It never occurred to him before that Mrs Hurst might have been the one who pushed Roy into the river. There was no motive, if they were planning to steal from his employers. Accomplices fell out after the crime, not before. Eight thousand quid wasn't enough for Lynn Hurst to commit murder for.

'If you'd ever known her you would understand how ridiculous that question is!' said Stanhope, sounding outraged. 'Lynn was a warm, loving, generous person. She'd never hurt anyone.'

Bowker made no comment on that. Evidently Stanhope didn't see Lynn's calculating ways with men as hurtful.

'Last Saturday afternoon, Mr Stanhope,' he said forebodingly, 'at PC Whitelock's house, you and I talked and then I told you to go home. That was about three o'clock, or twenty minutes after, I didn't note the time exactly. Did you go straight home?'

'Yes.'

The answer was too curt to pass over unexamined.

'Which way did you go?' Bowker asked.

'What do you mean? There's only one way.'

'I can think of several ways. You could have gone across the bridge at Long Slaughter and driven to Sandy Bottom, then on to the main road between Wantage and Reading.'

'Well I didn't. I went my usual way through the village up to the main Oxford road.'

Bowker sounded as if he didn't believe one word of Stanhope's story. 'If you'd gone the other way, you would have gone past Birley Spinney, a couple of miles outside Long Slaughter.'

'What of it?'

'You must know that another Long Slaughter resident came to a mysterious and bloody unfortunate end in Birley Spinney on that afternoon. Gavin Fowler was his name. Did you know him?'

'Good God, no! The only person I ever knew at Long Slaughter was Lynn Hurst.'

'We think Gavin Fowler knew her, too.' Bowker's voice was like a surgeon's scalpel slicing through subcutaneous fat. 'He died in her car. You must have read about it in the newspaper.'

'I never bother with local papers. What was this man doing in Lynn's car?'

'It wasn't far off the road; being white, it's distinctive. I don't see how you could fail to spot it if you drove along that road to Sandy Bottom last Saturday afternoon.'

Bowker was relentless. Stanhope was becoming desperate.

'I tell you I didn't go that way!'

'You would have recognised the car and pulled up to find out who was in it and why it was parked there. Only a few hours had gone by since you discovered Mrs Hurst dead in her cottage. Why would her car be out here, half-hidden?'

'No.' Stanhope sounded frightened.

'Are you sure you never met Gavin Fowler? He was sitting in Mrs Hurst's car. And he stayed there all afternoon. All day, in fact. And all night as well. He was found sitting in it Sunday afternoon, and he was very dead.'

'You're making this up!' Stanhope said shakily. 'I told you I didn't go that way.'

'What time did you get home that afternoon?' Bowker asked, a chill in his voice that would turn boiling water to solid ice.

'I don't know—I was too upset to notice. I couldn't get the scene in the cottage out of my mind, Lynn lying on the rug with her head covered in dried blood.'

'There's every chance Gavin Fowler did that,' Bowker said.

'What? But you said you were going to arrest somebody! You can't if he's dead! Nobody told me about him, whoever he was. Why wasn't I told?'

'If you'd driven home by way of Sandy Bottom and seen the car and stopped to find out what it was doing there, you might have reached a conclusion that the man sitting in it was responsible for the death of Mrs Hurst.'

'For the last time, I didn't go that way!' Stanhope sounded almost hysterical.

'Sergeant Knight has made a note of that. Did anyone see you arrive home, anyone who could vouch for the time?'

'I don't know. I was too upset to notice.'

'If we ask the other residents of this block of flats if they saw you arriving home on Saturday, will any of them be able to support your statement?' Bowker asked.

'Ask and find out.' Stanhope was lapsing into sullenness now. 'Why are you badgering me like this? If this man killed Lynn, that's the end of it. Your investigation's finished. So why are you here?'

'We'd like to know *why* Fowler killed her, to make sense of it all. And it might not mean much to you, Mr Stanhope, but in our funny way, we'd also like to know who killed Fowler. And we take an interest in how Roy Sibson came to be drowned in the Thames. I hope you can assist me in sorting out these mysteries.'

When Bowker said *hope*, he didn't mean it. There wasn't a hope in hell he'd get a straight answer out of Stanhope.

He kept up the pressure for another twenty minutes, then gave up. He and Knight rode down in the lift together, leaving Stanhope with a menacing promise to be back with more questions.

Knight waited until he and Bowker were clear of the building before he voiced his feelings.

'I thought you were going to run him in,' Knight said. He was disappointed they hadn't got a prisoner to take back to Long Slaughter with them. 'It stands to reason it happened the way you said—he did Fowler in when he found him in Lynn's car and guessed he'd killed her.'

'No, it was planned in advance, the Fowler murder. It didn't happen by chance. Fowler was waiting for somebody, hidden away in the spinney. The bottle of whisky suggests that.'

'He might have been a solitary drinker,' Knight said without much conviction.

'Not Fowler. He was a very public drinker, from what we know about him. There's a glimmer starting to show through the murk at long last, but don't quote me on that.'

'On what, sir?'

'I'm pretty sure Stanhope somehow started it all off, all the death and disaster that's been happening in Long Slaughter. It was his scheme to swindle the Building Society, and not Lynn's—she was in it only for the ride. Stanhope's so deep in debt, he'd sell his own mother for spare-part surgery if someone made him a cash offer.'

'He got the scheme going, then somehow it went wrong,' Knight said. 'That what you're saying, sir? And we wind up with three dead bodies.'

'Right. For some reason things got out of hand. He's a crook, all right, Mark James Stanhope, but he's as much in the dark as we are. He's scared because he can't understand what happened. I bounced him 'round the walls to see if he let anything useful drop.'

'Did he? I didn't spot anything.'

'No. All I got came from his briefcase and desk was confirmation of what we knew before. I'm surprised he hasn't pawned his gold watch by now. What did you find out in the car park, anything?'

'I'm not sure, sir. When you went up in the lift, a woman came down the stairs. A well-dressed woman of about forty, dark haired, full figure. She was wearing black sunglasses.'

'In the bloody rain?'

The drizzle had set in again, Bowker and Knight sprinted for the car.

'That's what made me think she was worth watching. She got in a tan Renault and drove off. I wrote the number down.'

'Odds on she came down from Stanhope's playpen,' Bowker said as he crammed himself into the passenger seat of his car. 'When he knew who was ringing his bell, he sneaked her out. He doesn't want us to know about her. I caught just a trace of perfume in his sitting-room.'

'Would you say he was dressed for company?' Knight asked. He switched on the car engine and started the wipers going.

'He wasn't dressed for jogging,' Bowker said. 'Pullovers like that cost a hundred and fifty quid and more. I don't know what fancy brand of gent's silk knickers he wears, but I reckon that he had at least five hundred quid worth of clothes on his body without counting the gold watch, just for a quiet afternoon at home.'

'Nice!' said Knight.

'I found more bills and more threatening letters about money than I'd ever want to get, if I was him. There wasn't time for a look at the bedroom, but I'd put a tenner on it that the smell of high-class perfume would be thick there. And another tenner that it looks like something out of the Arabian bloody Nights.'

'Shame!' Jack Knight said. 'Did we interrupt his fun?'

'From what you said, she doesn't sound to me like a customer dropping in to talk about building a building. Is that what you thought when you saw her?'

'Never crossed my mind, sir. I was thinking she'd be nice to have an hour's frolic with. She's got the build for it. But not young, more the mature sophisticated lady sort. Where to now?'

'Find a telephone. I want to run that car number through the computer and find out Lady Dedlock's real name so we can have a chat with her.'

'Lady Dedlock? Is that her professional alias? Do you think she's on the game?'

'No, you unread copper. Lady Dedlock's a mystery woman with a guilty secret in one of Charles Dickens' stories.'

'That one you're reading in bed, you mean.'

'No, another one—*Bleak House*. Lady Dedlock is a woman with a secret past. She sets up a midnight meeting and arrives with a veil over her face—dark glasses hadn't been invented then. She has a murder done, to suppress incriminating evidence. The case is cracked by a detective called Bucket, and she decides to do herself in rather than face the shame.'

'Bucket? Bloody strange name for a detective,' said Knight. 'He must have been undercover and using an alias himself.'

While the computer at Swansea was looking for the registration number Jack Knight had written in his notebook, he asked for an update from DS Roper at Long Slaughter. Bowker sat in the car, out of the rain, brooding over the facts such as they were.

It was tempting to do what Knight suggested—run Stanhope in and charge him with fraud. They were £8,000 short at the Chalfont. If that useless bloody head-office manager would get a move on and find the hole it leaked out through, a charge against Stanhope would be all the stronger.

On the other hand, Bowker's job was to find a murderer, not a thief. He was sure Stanhope was of no use to him at all in that direction; the man was baffled and afraid.

Naturally, Bowker meant to arrest him eventually, and it was useful to have him in hand, so to speak. If Chummy hadn't been collared by teatime Saturday, as Bowker had announced he would be, and if DCS Horrocks began to howl for forceful action, he'd run Stanhope in as a diversion.

Of course, proving Stanhope was an accomplice with Roy Sibson to rip off the Building Society was bloody nearly impossible to do with Roy dead and Lynn dead, unless the loot was traceable directly to him but he was too bloody crafty for that. There would be a bank account somewhere in a bogus name, eight thousand quid in it, waiting to receive the big money that wasn't ever going to arrive now Roy Sibson was dead and drowned.

Or unless Stanhope confessed. There was a chance of that. He looked the sort to fall apart if he was in a cell for a day or two. But only if bail could be objected to, and of that Bowker was far from confident. Better leave Stanhope for now and make use of him as a life raft if the ship looked like going down.

Knight ran back through the drizzle and got into the car.

'They've found Barry Crick," he said, all agog.

'Not bloody dead?' Bowker exclaimed wildly. 'Don't you tell me the bugger's dead—he can't be, I won't have it!'

'No, he's not dead, sir. They've got him in a police cell at Abingdon. He was picked up drunk and disorderly, breach of the peace, causing an affray, wounding with intent, actual bodily harm, aggravated assault, damage of property, attempted murder. He's dropped himself in deep trouble, and they're chucking the book at him. I think he must have punched a uniform or two.'

'Let's go there,' said Bowker. 'How'd you get to know?'

'Abingdon checked with PC Whitelock at Long Slaughter after they got Barry bedded down to see what he knew about him. And Whitelock passed it on to Roper at the Incident Room, he felt sure you'd be interested.'

'I am! Abingdon—that makes you think, doesn't it? We know somebody who lives there.'

'Dr Hurst,' Knight said cheerfully. 'I know the way your mind is working."

'No, you bloody don't!' Bowker snarled. "Nobody knows the

way my mind works. I don't know myself half the bloody time how my mind works!'

Knight was sorry he'd spoken. He tried again. 'There's a logical chain. Hurst knows Barry, don't ask me how. Barry puts him onto Gavin Fowler. Gavin is paid to do Hurst's ex-wife in for him. Barry is paid to do Gavin in for Hurst, to tidy things up. Barry goes back to Hurst for ask for extra money. They fall out, Barry gets drunk, and winds up in a cell.'

'I'd give a month's pay for the chance to run Dr Hurst in for conspiracy to murder,' said Bowker with savage glee. 'He's a slippery bastard. He reported me to the AC. But sad to say, I'm positive your theory is piffle.'

'No, it's not,' Knight protested, trying to slide through the traffic. 'Hurst is a sex-murderer, I said that days ago. He got raving-mad jealous when he found out Lynn was obliging a yokel from Long Slaughter. So he hired Gavin Fowler to do them both in, nasty and messily. Barry's the go-between.'

'When you were at school, did you read *The Three Musketeers*?'

'Not that I remember, sir. Why?'

'There's a woman in that. They call her Milady for a reason I can't recall. She's very sexy, this woman. The men go crazy for her, and she leads them a dance. Betrays most of them. She's out for herself—nobody's little woman.'

'Just like Lynn Hurst, you mean?'

'The husband she's dumped finally goes mental years later and pays somebody to chop her head off with a sword.'

'Just like Dr Harvey Hurst,' said Knight, sounding victorious at this evident justification of his theory. 'I remember now—I saw the film, that fat Oliver Reed was in it.'

'It won't bloody do,' Bowker said with a sour grin and Knight realised the Inspector had been leading him on. 'Barry came to us voluntary with his tale about Roy and Lynn driving along the Wormwold road in her car. If he'd really been in on the murder, he'd have kept his head down and his mouth shut.'

'So you think it's only coincidence he's been picked up over in Abingdon?'

'Not for a second. Barry knows more than he's told us; that's for certain. But I doubt if it's the big break we need. Barry's low-level. Nobody in their right mind's going to trust him with any secrets of importance.'

Knight wasn't going to give up so easily.

'What if Barry did the murders?' he asked. 'The targets were Mrs Hurst and Roy. Gavin was thrown in for luck, to bamboozle us. He's a big strong lad, Barry, shovelling tar all day on the roads. He'd have no trouble punching Roy on the jaw to stun him while he dropped him in the Thames to drown.'

'What punch on the jaw? Who said anything about punching Roy on the jaw?'

'Sorry, sir. DS Roper said the post-mortem result had come in, and they found a bruise on Roy's chin consistent with a blow. I forgot that in the excitement of telling you about Barry.'

'Barry instead of Gavin as First Murderer,' Bowker growled ruminatively. 'No, it won't wash, Knight, Barry's too thick for any serious crime.'

'Then it's back to Gavin, is it?'

'I'm buggered if I know. But one thing I'll tell you for sure—if Barry can convince me Dr Hurst had his wife murdered, I'll personally stand bail for him, with my own money. And if God is very good and Barry's got any proof of Hurst's complicity, then I'll give him a character reference when he's up for trial.'

'If you don't mind me asking, sir,' said Knight, not sure of his ground but curious, 'as this is the first time I've been on a case with you, I'm feeling my way. The thing is, are they all as bloody complicated as this one?'

'They only give me the complicated ones,' said Bowker, but he wasn't being serious about it. Or so Jack Knight thought.

'What else have you forgotten to tell?' Bowker asked. 'What about that car registration and Stanhope's new girlfriend?'

'Take about half an hour, they said. They're having a union

meeting, or they're on a tea break, or maybe they're oiling the computer or it's shift change-over time. They've always got a bloody reason.'

'Ring from Abingdon when we get there and tell them to bloody hurry up—this is a murder enquiry.'

The Interview Room they let Bowker use at Abingdon was small, windowless, and smelled of old cigarette smoke and sweat, as if the sheer strain of suspects lying had somehow in-grained itself into the beige-painted walls.

When Barry Crick was brought in by a wary-looking uniform, it was all too clear he had been in a monumental fight. His or-ange shirt was ripped from collar to halfway down his left side, one eye was swollen and closed, his cheek was bruised, and a stitch or two had been put in his right ear before they locked him up.

'Sit down, Barry,' said Bowker, ferociously genial. 'Sit down before you bloody fall down.'

Barry winced as he sat down on the opposite side of the table—he'd limped slightly when he came in, and evidently a leg hurt him. Knight remembered what Bowker said about him in the Black Swan, that first time they laid eyes on him: *thick as a brick and sly with it.*

'You're in bad trouble now, Barry,' said the Inspector with a smile like a heavyweight torturer turning the crank on the rack to tighten the ropes. 'I had a word with the Sergeant outside and he says they've got you on nineteen different charges. It must be a bloody record for a place like this. Have you been in prison before?'

Bowker knew very well he hadn't; he'd checked Crick's record after meeting him at the Black Swan. It was routine with him to check everybody he talked to in a murder enquiry, including the victims, their nearest and dearest, Mr Stephen Fenwick the big-time lawyer, even the vicar with the scraggy ginger beard.

Barry shook his head and said *No, never!* through split lips.

'Then it'll come as a very nasty shock to you,' said Bowker, a look of sympathy on his face, or the nearest he could manage to sympathy. 'What happened to you?'

'Had a few drinks, Mr Bowker, that's all. I was a bit fed up, you see. Then this chap slops beer on me and I punch him one in the face. Next thing you know there's five or six of them beating me up in the street outside the pub. Well, I had to defend my-self—you can see that.'

'And you defended yourself very well, Barry, no doubt about that. There's two been kept in hospital for treatment and three more sent home in bandages. I like a chap who can use his fists to look after himself.'

'Wasn't my fault,' Barry muttered. 'They started it."

'Not what they'll say in Court. They'll make out you started it on purpose. And the uniforms here have a thing or two to say about it. You've broken one's wrist and blacked another's eye. Lucky you didn't clobber either of *them* with the rum bottle, as you did one of the civilians. They're still X-raying his head.'

'What do you think's going to happen to me, Mr Bowker?' said Crick, beginning to sound alarmed.

'It's stir for you, Barry, there's no way 'round it. Not after the damage you did to the pub, four shops and five parked cars, police equipment including two torn uniforms, a dented helmet and a smashed walkie-talkie—all on the charge-sheet. Besides the personal damage you did to five chaps in the pub and two constables who tried to run you in. How much did you have to drink?'

'Only about a bottle, no more than that.' Barry was surly.

'A bottle of dark rum, that would be? The very same bottle you clobbered them with? What do you think Barry will get when all this is read out in Court, Knight, eighteen months?'

'More. Two years I'd say, sir.'

'So there you are, Barry,' said Bowker, cheerful and friendly of manner. 'I'm glad we had this chat, though I'm sorry to find you in such bad trouble. The Sergeant and I will be on our way. I don't suppose we'll meet again, so I'll wish you luck. You're going to need it.'

'Wait a minute!' Crick was amazed to see Bowker and Knight making for the door. "Aren't you going to help me?'

'Help you? What gave you a bloody comic idea like that? We just popped in to wish you good luck, as you were helpful to us before with information about Roy Sibson.'

'Listen, Mr Bowker, if you'll put in a good word for me, I'll tell you everything I know.'

'You don't know anything worth knowing, Barry. The Law has to take its course now you've dropped yourself in the clag. You're bloody lucky Dr Hurst isn't prosecuting you for demanding money with menaces.'

Bowker was guessing, but he thought he knew Barry Crick well enough to bluff with success.

'He's not, is he?' Barry said, very alarmed now.

'You came to Abingdon to put the black on the Doctor. We know that,' Bowker said, his tone changing instantly from amiable to brutal. 'How much did the silly bugger give you to go away and leave him alone?'

'Twenty bloody quid, that's all I got,' said Barry, outraged by the paltriness of the amount. 'It's worth thousands, what I know, but he wouldn't pay up. He laughed in my face and told me to go to the coppers.'

'But he gave you twenty pounds?' Bowker said viciously. 'Put that down in your notebook, Sergeant, we can tell the locals to add attempted blackmail to the charge-sheet now.'

'Worth another five years, blackmail,' Knight said lugubriously, 'on top of what he'll get for starting the fight and resisting arrest. And if that poor sod he cracked on the head dies, it's going to be manslaughter and a long stretch.'

Barry knew when he was beaten. He gave up the struggle.

'I'll tell you everything I know, Mr Bowker, and hope you'll put in a good word for me. This is between you and me, mind. I don't want to say anything that'll drop me in any deeper.'

'Agreed.'

'It's like this: when I told you I'd seen Roy with Mrs Hurst that day, it wasn't the first time I'd spotted them together. A week before that I'd seen them standing talking under a tree by the almshouses at the bottom of Cow Lane. I knew straight off what was going on. It wasn't right Roy was rollicking her, when I fancied her myself. Not after the way he tried to do me down over Jilly Ratcliffe's baby. I wanted to pay him back—it's only natural.'

'How did you do that, pay him back?'

'I stopped Roy in the street one day and told him I knew what was going on. I said I was going to ring up her boyfriend about him, the one with the big silver car. That put the wind up Roy, I can tell you.'

'Am I hearing right?' Bowker demanded, his face thunderous. 'Are we talking about the same Roy Sibson you haven't spoken to for two years, since Jilly Ratcliffe got in the family way?'

'Well, I didn't exactly tell you everything, Mr Bowker, but I will now, you see.'

Knight stared at Crick in mild astonishment. Was it after all going to turn out to be a case of ordinary jealousy? Could it possibly be Stanhope who murdered Lynn after all, then tried to put himself in the clear by discovering her body with a witness present?

Mark with the bouffant hair-do didn't seem right for the job, though you never knew. Lizzie Borden was a well-brought-up young woman, and she fatally vandalised her Dad and Stepmum with an axe.

Was the Long Slaughter bloodbath only the result of a village roughneck telling Mark his girlfriend was on closer terms with silly Roy Sibson than was necessary for the swindle they were working?

'Did you tell him, Mrs Hurst's boyfriend?' Bowker demanded, his fists clenching and unclenching violently as if he meant to complete the pounding Barry had got in the pub fight.

'I would have, but then she was found dead. So instead I told *you* I'd seen her with Roy, just to get my own back on him. It was the truth I told you, I did see him with her.'

'You saw them by the almshouses the week before you saw them on the Wormwold road, is that right?'

Barry nodded.

'You threatened Roy after the first time?'

'I never threatened him, I just said I'd tell on him. Just to make him squirm a bit.'

'Leave that for now and tell me: what made you think Dr Hurst would want to give you thousands of pounds? Why would he do a thing like that? How did you know about him, anyway?'

'It was all 'round the village she was divorced from a doctor. I got Jilly Ratcliffe to go through the phone books for me, she works part-time in the Post Office. There's only one Dr Hurst for miles round here.'

'The Jilly Ratcliffe who couldn't decide if it was you or Roy who put her in the club?' Bowker asked, utter disbelief in his voice at this fresh instance of moral turpitude in rural Long Slaughter. 'I thought she wasn't speaking to either you or Roy after she became a one-parent family.'

'I never said that, Mr Bowker. We've always been friends, her and me, even after the misunderstanding.'

'Why did you want to speak to Dr Hurst? If he'd divorced his wife, he wasn't likely to care who she was seen with, was he?' Bowker asked, knowing differently.

'Wasn't that. After the news came out that she'd been killed, I got to thinking Roy maybe did it. That's why I told you about seeing him. And then when he was found drowned, I knew it wasn't him. And then I remembered I'd seen a car parked in Badger Lane more than once, a big car with a doctor's sticker on the windscreen, that one that lets them park anywhere they like.'

Bowker glared at Barry with a new respect. He was certain the yokel Romeo wasn't all there, but he knew how to use the brains he'd got, such as they were.

Barry leaned back in his chair with a crooked grin, aiming at nonchalance. He started to cross his legs, winced and swore and thought better of it when his strained thigh-muscle hurt him.

'And so you thought the car belonged to somebody visiting Mrs Hurst, did you?' said Bowker, steely-eyed. 'Why was that?'

'It was a doctor's car, see, because of the sticker. I knew it never belonged to Dr Merrydew in the village, miserable old sod he is. And Lynn had been married to a doctor—stood to reason he was calling on her.'

'When was the last time you saw the car there?'

'Not long ago,' said Barry, going vague.

Bowker drew the obvious conclusion from that. His impression had been that meetings between the divorced Hursts had been at the Doctor's house. It was slightly surprising to hear some had been in Long Slaughter. But why not? There were no rules for former spouses wanting to frolic with each other again.

'So you went to Dr Hurst's house to tell him that you'd seen his car near Mrs Hurst's cottage the night before the murder—is that it, Barry? You told him you'd keep your mouth shut if he made it worth your while. Otherwise it was your bounden duty to report what you knew to the police, right?'

'I don't know if it was the night before or not, but I didn't want the Doctor to get into trouble.'

'Why should you care about him? Is he a friend of yours?'

'No, I never met him before today. But I thought he'd see me right if I helped him stay out of trouble. That's only fair.'

'You turned up on his doorstep with this rigmarole,' Bowker said in utter disbelief and dudgeon. 'If it had been me, Barry, I'd have set the dogs on you! What did he say?'

'He listened and then laughed in my face. Then he threw a twenty-pound note at me and said *Clear off*! He shut the door on me, I gave it a kick and he shouted he was sending for the police if I was still there in thirty seconds. I heaved a big stone off the rockery through his car windscreen and walked back into the town.'

'Where you found a public house and drank the Doctor's twenty pounds in Jamaican rum and started a riot? You've had a busy little day, Barry; you must be worn out. You go on back to your cell for a lie-down.'

'You promised to put in a good word for me, Mr Bowker.'

'It's not going to do you any good, after your rampage 'round Abingdon, but I'll do it on one condition. Have you told me all you know about Mrs Hurst and Dr Hurst?'

'I swear I have. One thing—last time I saw his car standing in Badger Lane, I waited to see how long he'd stay. The cottage was dark downstairs, but the lights were on in the bedroom, so I knew what was going on.'

'He might have been there in his capacity as a medical man,' Bowker suggested straight-faced, 'examining her for symptoms.'

'That he was!' Barry winced as he grinned through his assorted contusions. 'He kept on examining her till gone two in the morning. I'd bloody near fallen asleep when he came out and drove off.'

'The fact is,' said Bowker—he sounded like a hanging judge—'we know all about Dr Hurst's hanky-panky with his ex-wife. He doesn't even deny it, I know because I've asked him. There's no way you could blackmail him—except over which day you saw his car parked there the last time. What's the last date we've got, Knight?'

Jack Knight flipped back through his notebook.

'Mrs Hurst phoned Dr Hurst on second May from her home. If she phoned on a later date from a box, we wouldn't have a record.'

'Well, Barry, when was the last time you saw the Doctor's car near School Walk—was it after second May or before?'

No sensible answer was forthcoming. However hard Barry Crick tried, his perception of dates was hazy. Only to be expected in a clown who wasn't sure whether *last week* meant the week before last or the part of this week now past.

'The truth of it is that you were trying it on with Dr Hurst, just seeing what you could get out of him by threatening to lie about when you saw his car in Long Slaughter,' Bowker said in mounting fury.

'It was worth a try,' Barry said, unabashed.

'You've been wasting my time—if I had my way I'd put you on

bread and water and hard labour from now till you go on trial! Come on, Knight, we've got a murderer to catch. Let's get back to some serious work and leave this village idiot to reflect on his offences.'

By then DS Roper on the phone had the car registration number of the visitor Mark Stanhope had smuggled out of his penthouse. The car was registered to Mrs Laureen Willet-Jones. Her address was in Henley-on-Thames.

'Oh, bugger it!' Bowker said when Knight told him. 'That means traipsing all the way back again, we were practically outside her door when we left Reading. What did you say her name was?'

'Laureen Willet-Jones, sir.'

'Must be a mistake. Nobody's called Laureen. Fifty-to-one the computer's buggered up something simple like Maureen.'

'There's something else, sir.'’

'What?' Bowker asked suspiciously.

'Detective Chief Superintendent Horrocks,' Knight used the full rank for effect. 'He's on his way to Long Slaughter now and DS Roper sounds worried. He wants to know how he should handle him until you get there.'

'Bloody hell! Move over and let me drive. We haven't got time to dither 'round half the county like an old granny out shopping if the DCS is on his way!'

They changed places in the car. Bowker hunched over the wheel with a defiant glare on his face and his foot hard down. It was a drive not to be forgotten—the Ride of the Valkyries without the music. Knight could never make his mind up afterwards which had terrified him the most: Bowker's drive from Abingdon or PC Whitelock's from Pangbourne.

DCS Horrocks had a good start on them and arrived first. When Bowker strode into St Elfreda's Church Hall, Knight one pace to the rear, Horrocks was sitting at a trestle-table with a cup of instant coffee and reading through a sheaf of papers in a brown cardboard folder.

'There you are, Denis. This your desk? Your Sergeant's been showing me the house-to-house reports he's got in so far.'

'Sorry to keep you waiting, sir. I didn't expect you here.'

'I'm sure you didn't,' Horrocks said amiably. 'And this is DS Knight, I suppose, on his first murder investigation with us.'

'Sir,' Knight acknowledged his name.

'Good. Well, don't let me keep you from your work, Knight. An investigation like this keeps us all busy. I want a word or two in private with the Inspector.'

Jack Knight nodded and moved away smartly. He went across to the table where Roper and a WPC were shuffling papers about. He noticed that Roper had selected the prettiest of the two women to assist him co-ordinate, a brunette with a well-filled shirt.

'Sit down, Denis,' said Horrocks, a serious look on his face. 'You look like bloody King Kong, standing there with your fists clenched and your eyebrows pulled down.'

Bowker pulled a folding chair up to the opposite side of the table and sat.

'You were in Abingdon, according to the log,' Horrocks began. 'You weren't harassing that bloody Doctor again, were you? The one who put in the complaint about you?'

Bowker explained about Barry Crick and the major disturbance he'd created after Dr Hurst had turned him away.

'Well, well,' said the DCS with an oily smile. 'That seems to me highly significant. How high up your list of suspects is Dr Hurst? It would be poetic justice if you could charge him with murder. He'd have a job complaining about that.'

Bowker was wondering what could be important enough to bring Horrocks over to Long Slaughter on a Friday afternoon. Idle and wicked tongues said the DCS went off after lunch on Fridays to play a round of golf. With a bogus cover-story about going to a regular liaison meeting of the Citizens' Community Police Monitoring Committee, a grisly gang of *Guardian*-reading Marxist trouble-making anarchists, in Bowker's view, their main purpose in life was to stop coppers running in criminals.

'He's not my prime suspect, Hurst,' he said. 'More's the pity—not unless this turns out to be a sex-murder. Then he is. The bloody fool I went to see at Abingdon just might have been able to bolster that theory, but Barry's so bloody thick he doesn't know himself when he's lying. You can't trust a word he says.'

'Who are you left with, then, if Hurst is out?'

'Out for now, sir. Not out altogether, I didn't say that.'

'Don't let your feelings run away with your judgement, Denis. Because you can't stand the man, it doesn't automatically make him a murderer. Your witness in custody at Abingdon may come up with something else you can use, if he gets desperate for help when he comes to trial.'

Bowker shook his head doubtfully and stared over the table at the DCS, a morose look on his gypsy face. Horrocks was wearing a grey suit and a green tie, with a sort of insignia on it, too small to make sense of. He had a worried expression; he brought bad news: that was Bowker's deduction.

'How's your team working out, Denis?' he asked. 'Good bunch I sent you, hand-picked. I wanted you to have the best we could find, so you can get this nasty crime-wave cleared up quickly. If these things drag on, the public lose confidence.'

'They look all right,' Bowker was very noncommittal. 'Early to say if they'll find the evidence I'm looking for. I've still got three on the suspect list.'

'Same three as the last time we talked?'

'There's Stanhope the alleged fiancé and Rowley the next-door neighbour. And the new one, Fenwick the lawyer.'

'Ah yes, Stephen Fenwick,' said Horrocks uneasily. 'You asked me to make enquiries about him in London. This is confidential, Denis, strictly between me and you, understand?'

Bowker gave him the cold eye and said nothing.

'It turns out that the Serious Fraud Office is interested in Fenwick,' said Horrocks. 'He's a trustee of a big pension fund, and they think the money's not all properly accounted for.'

'Ha!' Bowker snorted, a brief expression of vindication.

'The question is,' said Horrocks, a pained look on his face, 'have you got anything concrete against Fenwick for the murders here? Or is he only a general suspect because he was a contact of the dead woman?'

'Motive *and* opportunity,' said Bowker, pugnacious as a police dog after a bag-snatcher. He'd already guessed what the DCS was leading up to, and he didn't like it.

'Fenwick had his leg over Mrs Hurst regularly,' he said, 'and it is entirely possible she was on to his swindle and wanted a share. He lives here in the village and could have found Gavin Fowler to do the crime for him. He hasn't got an alibi for the Saturday afternoon Fowler died in the white Volkswagen. He said he was out walking on the Thames towpath up at Oxford.'

'That's what I thought,' said Horrocks. 'You've got nothing. If you can't make a concrete case against him, London wants him to be left alone. They're not ready to move yet, and there's a chance Fenwick might do a moonlight flit if you scare him unnecessarily. He has his passport and a lot of somebody else's money in foreign bank accounts. Or so they suspect.'

'Is that an order, sir, leave Fenwick alone?'

'No, it's bloody not! You know better than that. If you come across any real hard evidence that Fenwick's your murderer, haul him in fast. You're investigating the more serious crime—London's only investigating theft. You have priority. But if there's nothing beyond vague suspicion, leave the bugger alone.'

'Understood.' Bowker tried not to be surly.

'This Stanhope, you've interviewed him today,' said Horrocks. 'What's the form on him?'

'He's involved, sir. I'm certain it was his plan to steal the Building Society's money with Roy Sibson as his catspaw. If we still had debtor's prisons, Stanhope would be in for life. Both his accomplices are dead, Roy and Lynn Hurst, and that points a finger straight at him.'

Not for a moment did Bowker believe that Mark James Stanhope was up to organising three murders, but he was preparing the ground for running Stanhope in, if worst came to worst.

'I've got a new lead on him, in fact,' he added hopefully, 'a woman named Willet-Jones. She's down for a visit before the day is out.'

'Good,' said DCS Horrocks, getting to his feet. 'I won't take any more of your time, Denis, I know you want to close the book on this one. Is it true you told the Sergeant over there you'd finish it by teatime tomorrow?'

Sod that man Roper, thought Bowker, *that wasn't to be passed on to a senior officer, it was just for the murder team.*

'Trust me,' he said aloud, treating Horrocks to a rare smile of reassurance.

'I'm off, then. Stay away from Fenwick unless something really incriminating turns up.'

'Off to the Citizens' Community Police Monitoring Committee, are you?' Bowker asked him with cheerful malice. 'Do *they* want us to catch the Long Slaughter killer, or are they too busy for catching criminals? Got their knife into some harassed copper not being polite enough to a protester causing a traffic jam in the High Street, have they?'

'It might be your back that gets stabbed, Denis, if you don't handle Fenwick with kid gloves.'

That's all he came here to tell me, Bowker thought.

He stared at Horrocks' broad back as the DCS walked smoothly down between the unmanned tables towards the door.

He didn't want to say it over the telephone, so he drove here to tell me in person. Bloody cheek!

16. .... *henley-on-thames*

On Saturday morning Arthur Cawley had a satisfied smirk on his face when he brought Bowker and Knight their breakfast. Kippers were Mrs Cawley's offering for the day, two pairs each, golden melted butter over them, and tastily smoked in the traditional Scotch way, not some namby-bloody-pamby pallid Euro-substitute.

'What's pleased you?' Bowker asked.

At 7:30 in the morning, the landlord of the Black Swan was in shirtsleeves and without collar or tie, a large grey waistcoat un-buttoned over his beer-barrel belly.

'You're good for trade, Mr Bowker,' he said, nodding his head like a clockwork dog. 'Every room in the house is booked right through till next weekend.'

'What?' Bowker exclaimed, his temper rising dangerously. 'Is it the bloody London newspapers onto us already?'

'Story in the paper about you this morning, half a page of it there is! The other papers have rung up to book rooms already, at this hour of the morning! I'll have to get another barmaid in to help out tonight. You know what reporters are like, drink like fish. The bar takings will be well up.'

'Which paper? Let me see it!'

Knight stared apprehensively at the Inspector. His complexion had turned darker than his normal swarthy Southern European.

A tabloid had picked up the murders, probably from the *County Examiner*, although Sara Thomas might have phoned it in herself.

SEX SLAYER STALKS VILLAGE OF FEAR the headline announced. Not on the front page—that was entirely about a famous thick-head football player falling down drunk in a London disco.

The hack who wrote up the Long Slaughter story for an inside page had concentrated on Lynn Hurst, presented as the beautiful divorced wife of a top surgeon, a raging nymphomaniac, a woman who never said no.

She had been brutally slain, it said breathlessly, and so had two of her lovers. A fiend stalked the sleepy village of Long Slaughter, bent on destroying every man who ever loved Lynn.

There was a bad photo of a woman who looked more like Vanessa Redgrave than the late Lynn Hurst. Bowker wondered where it had come from. It wasn't the photo-album picture his own team were using to jog memories with.

They'd had to reduce the album photo to head and shoulders. It would cause comment if coppers on the doorstep showed photos of Lynn topless.

A top Scotland Yard team is investigating the murders, said the report, which was news to Bowker. He'd never seen even the outside of Scotland Yard. Except on TV news bulletins, with an important-looking reporter in front of the rotating triangular sign. And solemnly reciting to viewers the verbiage of a police hand-out, pretending it was his own shrewd investigation.

The dire wrongheadedness of the newspaper story made Bowker laugh aloud, which startled Knight.

The murders were the work of a homicidal maniac, claimed the Leading Harley Street Psychiatrist consulted by the newspaper, in the interest of keeping the public informed. The story went on to divulge that the police had a book of names and addresses found in the home of the tragic Jezebel. They were grilling every man listed in the *secret book of shame.*

It is believed these included a prominent City solicitor and an internationally-acclaimed artist, Bowker read in wonder.

'Yesterday you had the bloody nerve to ask me what we were doing,' he said, passing the paper to Knight. 'Now it's in the paper—we're interrogating every bloody name in Lynn Hurst's address book, that's what we're doing. It says so here.'

'But we're not Scotland Yard,' Knight objected.

'It's the same thing to the hairy yobs who read bloody papers like this. Scotland Yard, Interpol, FBI, they think we're all branches of Crime-Busters Inc. Get a move on—you've fifteen seconds to finish your breakfast.'

'What's the burning rush suddenly?'

'I'll tell you,' Bowker said grimly. 'DCS Horrocks might read this drivel with his cornflakes, instead of the *Times*. And if he does, he'll be on the phone right away to blame me for it—I won't be here. But you will be, if you don't get a move on, and then it'll be *your* ear that's chewed off.'

'Where shall we be, then?'

'Talking to that woman with the funny name at Henley. We were going to do that yesterday, before the DCS turned up. You can't have forgotten.'

'Mrs Laureen Willet-Jones,' said Knight, not even looking at his notebook. 'Bit early to go calling, sir.'

'We'll find a lorry-driver's pull-up somewhere on the way and have the breakfast we haven't got time for here. Pity about the kippers. Come on.'

'Will you be in for dinner tonight, Mr Bowker?' the landlord enquired as the two policemen swept past him on their way out. 'Mrs Cawley's doing a lovely big roast, prime beef it is, as we expect a full house tonight and they've got to eat somewhere.'

Bowker scowled ferociously and said nothing. He wanted to be away from Long Slaughter before evening. He had hopes of eating dinner at home with his wife.

'Hard to say, Mr Cawley,' Knight told the landlord. 'Busy day we've got today; you've read the paper. I can't say where we'll be even an hour from now, let alone this evening.'

'We'll be harassed by mongrel reporters from now on,' Bowker said, getting into the passenger seat of his weary-looking car. 'It's a bloody miracle they've left us alone as long as this. I say thank God for the Church of England.'

Knight knew he meant the story of a randy vicar that had been holding the attention of the tabloids for days. No less than seven married women parishioners said the Reverend Ken Toplow had affairs with them; three claimed some of their children were his, not their husbands'.

The Reverend denied the allegations. A tissue of lies by demented women, he said, part of an evil plot to get rid of him from the parish. He believed Satanists were behind it, because he always spoke out fearlessly against ritual child abuse.

'People like reading a bit of scandal,' Knight said, 'long as it's somebody else in trouble, not themselves. You can't blame the papers for serving up what people want. Sometimes they can even be useful. Give them a photo of a wanted criminal, and they bang it on the front page for you.'

'Then you get phone calls from ten thousand prats up and down the country who spotted him two days before in a supermarket,' Bowker retorted. 'Or he was riding on a number 19 bus away from Milton Keynes. Or he was down on the beach at Skegness with his shirt off and his tattoo showing. It takes millions of hours of police time following up leads like that—you know you're on a wild-goose chase before you start.'

Bowker sounded more annoyed than usual. Knight guessed it was the memory of some previous run-in with a newspaper irking him. He drove the car up Bridge Street, past PC Whitelock's house on the corner, and on towards the main road. A mile or two before they reached their destination they saw a truck-drivers' diner and pulled in for breakfast.

Knight grinned to see Bowker glare round the place, taking in the eighteen-stone customers in string vests and broad leather belts, six days' growth of ugly bristle on their faces, shovelling down their greasy breakfast, fork in one hand, cigarette smoking in the other.

The truckers stared back pugnaciously at the two policemen in suits, quailed before Bowker's glower, and went back to eating. Knight wondered what size the rapist was that Bowker waited for in a diner like this. He was sorry he hadn't seen the fight, it would have outclassed the real Mad Mangler's performance in the wrestling ring—the forearm smashes, karate chops, knee to the kidneys that Bowker and the trucker landed on each other wouldn't be faked.

'Why do you think Stanhope wanted to hide the woman from us?' he asked when they settled to gargantuan plates of fried eggs, baked beans, chips, grilled pig's liver, black pudding, streaky bacon, mushrooms, and bubble-and-squeak, with stacks of thick toast and strong tea in mugs.

'Because he's up to something criminal with her,' Bowker said gloomily. 'He's a chancer who's gone bad because his architect business has folded. If we'd found a will made by Lynn Hurst to leave her money and cottage to him, I'd have run him in without a second thought.'

'Bloody hard up he may be, but would he kill for money?' Knight asked. His appetite for food was less than the Inspector's, who seemed to regard eating as his hobby.

'No way of telling. He didn't kill any of the three at Long Slaughter because there's nothing in it for him as far as I can see. Though it was his scheme to swindle the Building Society.'

'You near as damn-it accused him of doing Gavin Fowler in. He went so paranoid, I thought we'd have to call an ambulance and the men in white coats,' Knight said.

'All I did was hold his head under water to scare him,' said

Bowker, with a shrug of his yard-wide shoulders. 'He's a crook, I don't have to like him.'

They delayed their arrival at the address they had been given for Mrs Willet-Jones till just after nine. They saw a big white house overlooking the Thames, impressive and well looked-after, the sort of house that estate agents compose sick-making prose-poetry about for their advertisements.

It didn't take the special talents of an estate agent to see that Laureen Willet-Jones was generously-proportioned and well-maintained as her house. She was about forty, dark-blonde hair in plaits round her head, cream silk blouse and plain dark skirt, both expensively simple. She wasn't wearing her black glasses today, and her eyes were dark blue.

She received the detectives in her drawing-room, where french windows gave a view of the river, hardly a boat on it so early in the day. She spoke with an American accent, which explained her first name.

Americans had curious names. Bowker's view was their mothers made them up, just to be different. Joleen, Monabelle, Marylou, Laureen. And for the boys, you could take your pick from Shane, Kane, Wayne, Duane, or Zane.

This Laureen must have married a Brit to acquire a name like Willet-Jones, Bowker thought, looking at her appreciatively. At least, she was wearing a wedding ring. He asked her bluntly and learned she was a widow.

Bowker and Knight sat in elegant armchairs while he explained who they were. He was aiming at charm, Jack Knight noticed with silent amusement, though his massiveness and his dark suit that looked as if he's slept in it didn't help. Eventually the point was reached where direct questions were needed.

'You know Mr Mark James Stanhope,' said Knight. He spoke the name as neutrally as he could manage, but to Knight's ear there was a silent curse on it. Mrs Willet-Jones picked it up, too, and stared at the Inspector with a small frown on her face.

'What of it?' she said. 'What's it to the police? I think you'd better explain your interest to me, if you expect me to answer questions.'

'We're making a routine enquiry into Mr Stanhope's movements. It has to be done in investigations of serious crimes.' Bowker was stretching the truth slightly, feeling his way.

'Murder is a very serious crime,' Knight added in support.

'What murder? What are you talking about?' Mrs Willet-Jones sounded alarmed now.

'Surely you are aware Mr Stanhope's fiancée was murdered ten days ago,' Bowker said, his thick black eyebrows rising.

The smooth Laureen Willet-Jones was nonplussed.

'Fiancée? This is the first I've heard of a fiancée. Are you sure you've got the right Mark Stanhope?'

'The one you visited yesterday at his penthouse in Reading,' Bowker assured her, his voice starting to betray impatience.

'You're saying Mark has a fiancée?' Her tone was disbelieving. 'Someone he's going to marry, you mean?'

'Not any more he isn't,' Knight said. He thought it sensible to prevent Bowker losing his temper. 'Her head was smashed in a week last Thursday. Didn't Mr Stanhope mention it?'

Laureen's face had turned very red. She was losing her temper as fast as Bowker, though for different reasons.

'You walked down six flights of stairs to avoid being seen,' Bowker accused her. 'I was in the lift going up. What was that all about—why were you hiding from the police?'

'I didn't know it was police,' she said. 'I'd been discussing business with Mr Stanhope, very confidential business. When the buzzer sounded, he said it was the person we were talking about, and the deal would fall through if he saw me there and guessed I was Mark's partner. So I slid out down the stairs.'

'Hmm,' said Bowker, a throaty rumble expressing incredulity. 'Let that go for now. I'll come back to it later. Have you made a note of what Mrs Willet-Jones said, Knight?'

'Yes, sir, highly confidential business deal. The other party mustn't find out who's putting up the cash for Mr Stanhope.'

He exchanged a quick glance with Bowker. Both had come to the same view: Laureen Willet-Jones was a victim, not an accomplice in Stanhope's swindling. A wealthy widow about to be fleeced.

The situation was tricky, Bowker considered; a delicate touch was needed here. She ought to be protected, but to say too much about Stanhope without proof could lead to nasty accusations of defamation. Laureen and Stanhope were lovers—that was obvious enough—and that was Stanhope's strong card in the game of grab for her money. On the other hand, it could be turned 'round to make it a loser for Mark.

Bowker blinked twice and applied his delicate touch. Knight was reminded of a rhino dancing on tiptoe, a scene stuck in his mind from seeing Walt Disney's *Fantasia* as a schoolboy. Or was it a hippo? Bowker was definitely a rhino, not a hippo.

'Was Mr Stanhope with you, on the evening of Thursday the twenty-first?' Bowker asked, approaching his destination sideways.

'Is that what he told you?'

Bowker said nothing. His question hung in the air.

'His account of his movements that day are unsatisfactory as they stand,' Knight said, knowing full well that he had written in his notebook Stanhope's claim to be at home the evening Lynn Hurst died, at home and all on his own.

'He wasn't with me,' Mrs Willet-Jones said sharply. 'What was this woman like?'

'Very pretty,' said Bowker, 'charming, attractive.'

This was where he drove the wedge between her and Stanhope: a woman scorned would tell whatever most damaged the scorner, and he piled on the pressure.

'Divorced, twenty-seven years old,' he said, his voice melancholy. 'Had a cottage at Long Slaughter, very pretty frisky lady.'

The look on Laureen Willet-Jones' face said that Stanhope was in for a very rough ride. Jack Knight opened his notebook to a clean page, his pen poised.

'Where were *you* on Thursday last week, between six and nine in the evening, Mrs Willet-Jones?' he asked.

'I sure as hell wasn't out killing anybody!' she flared. 'I didn't know the damn woman existed!'

'We know you didn't kill Mrs Hurst,' Bowker said gently. 'The Sergeant is only asking a routine question. Were you at home?'

'Thursdays I play bridge,' she said very angrily. 'I can give you the names of witnesses for last Thursday and every Thursday this year. Did Mark kill her?'

'He was first on the scene when the body was found, two days after the murder,' Bowker said.

It was proving easier than he expected to drop Mark Stanhope in the clag. This could turn out very useful.

'He arrived at her cottage early last Saturday to take her to Paris for the weekend,' he said. 'And there she was, dead.'

'The cheap slimy snake!' Laureen's eyes filled with hate and contempt.

'Do you mind telling me the nature of your relationship with Mr Stanhope?' Bowker asked, his voice very sympathetic.

'Look, Inspector, do I have to talk about that?'

'Depends what *that* is,' he said, trying to sound human.

'You know what I'm talking about.'

'I'm interested only in crime,' Bowker told her. 'Any private amusements are no concern of mine. If they're not linked in any way to an offence.'

'If you think Mark killed the woman because he's in love with me, you're crazy,' she said. 'We've been good friends, why not? It's not exactly what you said, just an amusement, but there's never been a whole lot more. Mark's not in love with me, and I'm not with him.'

That may be true, Bowker thought, *but it doesn't stop you being jealous of another woman in his life.*

'Do I understand from what you said before that you intend to hand money over to Mr Stanhope for a business deal?' he asked.

'We've talked about investments,' she said noncommittally.

'How long has this intimate friendship been going on?' asked Bowker, trying to sound understanding.

'Since last fall. Why?'

'And how long has he been discussing money and investments?'

'That started earlier on this year, maybe two months ago. You said you were investigating a homicide. Now it sounds more like a fraud.'

'Sometimes the two are connected,' Bowker said darkly. 'Don't tell me you've never heard of women being murdered for money in America.'

'Did Mark kill his so-called fiancée for her money?'

'Please, Mrs Willet-Jones, just answer the questions.' Bowker's voice sounded strained as he struggled to keep calm.

'You see, Inspector, as a leading architect Mark comes across some interesting real estate investment possibilities.'

Very bloody interesting, Bowker thought wryly. He could guess what was coming next.

'The slump in property values means commercial buildings can be bought up for rock-bottom prices,' said Laureen, repeating a sales-talk Stanhope had obviously treated her to. 'Mark snapped up a block of six flats for peanuts last year. When prices rise again, he'll make a killing.'

'A bad choice of words,' said Bowker with a scowl.

'I didn't mean it that way. You know I didn't!' Laureen said with a grimace that wrinkled her nose. Bowker gave her a smile of encouragement which would have terrified any woman less sure of herself.

'Anyway,' she went on, 'this new opportunity came up. This is the confidential part, the apartment building Mark lives in. He has a chance to acquire it. Only his funds are tied up with the block he's already bought.'

'I've got the picture,' said Bowker, shaking his head at the duplicity of mankind. 'He's offered you a block of flats that he owns at a knock-down price, so he can buy the block he lives in. That it?'

'That's right, Inspector.'

'Has any money changed hands yet, Mrs Willet-Jones?'

'The papers are being drawn up right now. But I'm starting to change my mind since your visit.'

'Just as well,' Bowker said with a wolfish grin. 'If Stanhope is the owner of a building anywhere, I'm a drunken Dutchman. He owes money all over, and he's broke and worse.'

'God, he spends money as if he hasn't a care in the world!'

'That I've noticed, what with weekends in Paris and trips to the Caribbean with Mrs Hurst.'

'Just wait till I see that creepy rat!' Laureen fumed.

Bowker tried to look impassive; inwardly he was very pleased.

'Yesterday, when you were in his flat, how did he get you to sneak out like that in sunglasses?'

'He answered the buzzer and said it was the man who owns the building. He'd been half-expecting him to stop by to talk about the deal. He's an Asian named Patel. I haven't met him, but Mark explained how they're very strongly against women in business. It's not allowed in their culture. Or maybe their religion—I'm not really sure.'

'I'm sure that can't be true,' said Bowker, shaking his great head, 'but I can see why he told you that.'

'I've been a damn fool,' said Laureen. She blushed at last.

'Not your fault,' Knight said sympathetically. 'He's a smooth operator.

'Are you going to arrest him for fraud?' she asked. 'Will he get a long sentence?'

'Attempted fraud—you haven't actually handed any money over to him yet,' said Knight. 'He'll be put on probation for twelve months, I should think.'

'That all?' She began to sound vicious. 'How about homicide—can you get him for that?'

Bowker shook his head mournfully. 'We're still investigating that. There's hope. Do you mind if I use your phone while DS Knight makes a few notes of what you've told us?'

'Use the one in the hall. That way your police business will stay private.'

Bowker went into the hall to phone the Incident Room. He was put through to Jason Roper, who sounded frayed.

'DCS Horrocks has been on all morning asking for you, sir. He wants to talk to you as soon as possible.'

'I'm sure he bloody does,' Bowker grumbled into the phone. 'I shall be back in an hour or so. I'm over at Henley with Knight interviewing Mrs Willet-Jones—write that in the Log. Anything else?'

'There's a mob of reporters and cameramen outside, been there since about eight this morning. I've had to put two uniforms on the door to stop them forcing their way in here. Never seen such a rabble. They all want you, sir.'

On the way back to Long Slaughter, with Knight driving faster than he should, Bowker sat making growling noises for a while, evidently thinking hard.

'All the evidence points to Stanhope gearing himself up to do a flit,' he said eventually. 'The Building Society rip-off and now Mrs Willet-Jones' cash for a bogus building. Architecting's gone down the plug-hole and he's got a plan to take off for the sunshine with enough money to set up in style. Bank robbers and drug runners go to Spain to live; that's not Mark's cup of tea. Might be Australia he's aiming for—they need architects there, judging by what you see on TV.'

'He won't go now, though,' Knight said. 'Roy buggered that up by getting himself drowned. The Building Society plot went down with him. You've just put the mockers on him cheating the merry widow out of her stack.'

'Maybe.' Bowker sounded ominous. 'But if he's up to running two swindles at the same time, he might have a third. We'd look a right pair of damn fools if he slid away now on an airplane.'

'You want to run him in?'

'We've enough suspicion on the Building Society job to charge him and get his passport taken away. So when we're ready to go ahead with the charges he'll be where we can get at him and not drinking ice-cold beer in bloody Australia or California.'

'Pick him up now?'

'No, I can't spare the time today. The Long Slaughter murders have to be cleared up. Tomorrow I mean to have a day off. You go round to Stanhope's flat about eight tomorrow morning, when he's drinking coffee and reading the Sunday *Times,* and run him in. Give him an anxious day sitting in a cell, and I'll take over on Monday morning.'

'What do you want me to arrest him for, sir? Murder?'

'Bloody hell, no! Suspicion of fraud, conspiracy to commit a felony, theft of eight thousand pounds from the Chalfont Building Society.'

'We don't know he's got it. You said it hadn't been paid into his bank account. Maybe Roy had it on him in twenty-pound notes and Barry Crick drowned him for it.'

'If Barry Crick got his hands on that much money, he'd be on a monumental blinder, and we'd have a call from hospital somewhere to let us know he was dying of alcohol poisoning,' Bowker said.

Knight was not pleased by his assignment for Sunday morning. To be on Stanhope's door-step at eight, he'd have to be up before seven, and he'd been hoping for a day off himself.

'Take a couple of uniforms with you,' Bowker said, 'just in case he bolts down the stairs when he hears you on the buzzer.'

'I'll go in a car with flashing bloody blue light and siren,' Knight said, highly sarcastic.

'Yes!' Bowker was enthusiastic. 'Let the neighbours see what a crook Mark is. Drive up at seventy miles an hour with the siren on and the hooter going full blast. Rouse the entire neighbourhood and get them all staring out of the windows, I like the idea.'

'Are you serious?'

'Of course I'm bloody serious! Did you get some details down from Mrs Willet-Jones about the attempted con on her?'

'Oh, yes,' said Knight, suddenly cheerful. 'Laureen was fully co-operative. She'll go into the witness-box for us and get him convicted.'

'Laureen?' Bowker's thick black eyebrows twitched. 'Laureen?'

'She asked me my first name when you went out into the hall to phone Long Slaughter and she said I should call her Laureen. Americans are like that, very friendly. She wants me to advise her on security.'

'What bloody security?'

'The house. It's big and noticeable, a target for thieves.'

'There's a red burglar-alarm box on the front, put where any break-in artist can't help seeing it. It's very likely wired to the local police station,' Bowker commented sourly.

'Householders can't be too careful, sir, not now there's this crime-wave going on. Bloody teenagers breaking into big houses to steal anything they can sell for crack money. A young widow living on her own naturally feels at risk.'

'She's not all that young, Jack. She's older than you are. My sort of age.'

'Not the point, sir. She's entitled to our protection.'

'And when do you propose to give her this protection? You're tied up tomorrow with Stanhope, then back with me on Monday.'

'One day next week. She's asked me to ring her when I can get some time off and go 'round for lunch with her and a look at her windows and doors.'

'You'll be a toy-boy, Jack!' Bowker said, stark amazement in his voice.

Knight grinned and said nothing.

Bowker and Knight arrived back in Long Slaughter in mid-morning to find cars parked down both sides of Badger Lane. Nearest the corner of School Walk was a TV outside broadcasting van, with a dish on the roof to bounce the reporter's excitable words off a satellite to the distant London studio.

'Oh, sod it!' Bowker sounded extremely irate. 'We need another way into the Church Hall, and there isn't one short of scrambling over six-foot railings with spikes on top.'

'The press are here full strength,' said Knight. 'You'll be a celebrity by tomorrow morning, sir.'

'Let me out here. You find a space to park the car somewhere, I'll make a run for it through the mob.'

Representatives of the tabloids stood about in School Walk, a dozen photographers, news-agency men, TV personnel. Bowker made his run, head well down and shoulders hunched, youthful prowess on the rugger field coming into play. He went through the line-up just like the old days, to score a try between the posts.

There was a time when newspaper reporters wore scruffy raincoats and carried notebooks; now it was short leather jackets with zippers, and scuffed running-shoes. They had cheap Taiwanese tape recorders, microphones on long handles to hold out towards Bowker's face, hoping to catch a few words to quote, never mind how garbled.

'Have you arrested Lynn Hurst's boyfriend why wasn't Sibson's body found before why is this case taking the police so long to solve what drugs showed up in Sibson's body at the post-mortem did he get them from Dr Hurst who paid the slaughterman to kill Lynn Hurst when were you told you're off the case for taking so long to make an arrest was Stephen Fenwick Lynn's lover did the police beat Barry Crick up because he knows too much where have you been this morning?'

Bowker shouldered his way through the pack, ignoring all the provocation. He said several times *Statement later* loud enough to make his voice heard over the baying. Not that he planned to make a statement that day or any other. But any old promise of verbiage might keep them quiet while he got on with his job.

A uniformed policeman stood either side of the Church Hall door. They recognised Bowker from his height as he came through toward them, he loomed head and shoulders over the ruck. One uniform reached warily back to turn the door-handle without taking his eye off the mob in full cry, like hounds after a stag.

The PC pushed the door open. Bowker hurled himself inside with a curse of thanks. The uniforms moved together and barred the way to his pursuers.

'I thought you were exaggerating on the phone,' the Inspector growled at DS Roper. 'It's a bloody siege!'

'It's got worse since you phoned, sir. There's seven or eight more of them now, and that's only the ones wanting a statement from you. The rest are out 'round the village handing out money like sweeties to get silly buggers to talk about something they know nothing about. You can't beat a good sex-murder to attract public interest, especially when it's a triple murder.'

'Sex-murder!' Bowker exploded. 'Of all the bloody silly theories we've had in this case, that takes the biscuit. I'm buggered if I know where newspaper writers get their ideas from. They used to get blind drunk on whisky, but they must be on hallucination drugs nowadays. How's my house-to-house going?'

He gazed 'round the room as he spoke. About half his team were back, sitting at the long tables, scribbling reports, swapping thoughts, drinking instant coffee from plastic beakers, making phone calls to wives, girlfriends, and bookmakers.

'Not a lot more to do, sir. DS Payne phoned in not twenty minutes ago to say they'd be finished by noon.'

'Good. Bring me what you've got so far.'

Bowker sat at the table reserved for him and stared gloomily at the folders Roper gave him. Sightings were co-ordinated by victim, separate folders for HURST Lynn, FOWLER Gavin, SIBSON Roy. There was still more to come when the team had finished the entire village.

Roper had chosen different-coloured folders for the suspects: ROWLEY Empson, HURST Harvey Dr, STANHOPE Mark James, FENWICK Stephen. Their movements charted for the days of the murders in so far as they could be established, from their own statements, and any corroboration that could be found.

Good solid police-work, thought Bowker, though not with much enthusiasm. When you'd no proper motive, no obvious suspect, no logical succession of events, it came down to routine to solve the puzzle. Not the way he liked to do things, but the only way open to him now.

He shuffled the folders, deciding which one to start on. *Any minute now, DS Roper will have this stuff typed into the bloody computer,* he thought. *Then he'll expect it to come up with the answer, as if we'd got a bloody Speak Your Weight machine.*

The forensic had proved bloody useless, laboratory testing of scrapings, probings, swabs, stomach contents, DNA—they'd done it all thoroughly. The experts could tell Bowker not much more than the police surgeon on the spot.

Which added up to not much more than his own observation. The victims were dead and had been dead for some time—one brained, one drowned, one poisoned by car-exhaust fumes.

Depressing, Bowker thought, *bloody depressing*. A week gone by asking questions and trying to make sense of what had happened, and it was bloody nearly as obscure as the day he first arrived in Long Slaughter. All he'd established was that Stanhope had a plot to get rich quick from the Chalfont Building Society, with Roy Sibson doing the actual computer fiddling and with Lynn Hurst as bait for him.

To say he'd established that much was going beyond the facts. He'd settled it in his own mind, he hadn't evidence to prove it in a Court of Law.

Before he could start on any of the folders, a commotion over by the door drew his attention. It was the village bobby, Kevin Whitelock, coming in through the pack outside looking harassed and displeased.

Since the arrival of the team of detectives to assist Bowker, Whitelock was back to his normal duties, missing push-bikes and foot-and-mouth-disease precautions. He was huffy at losing what he thought of as the thrill of a murder hunt. He pretended not to see DS Roper beckoning him and came straight over to Bowker.

'Have a word, sir?'

'Well?' Bowker growled, but in truth he was not unwilling to postpone the boring job of reading Roper's neat folders.

'I'm getting a lot of complaints, sir. The people in the big houses are annoyed about these reporters on their door-steps and stopping them in the street with damnfool questions. They think I should put a stop to it, but I don't see how I can. Not until there's actual trespass or damage to property.'

'You're right, Whitelock. There's not a lot you can do. It's not an offence to make yourself a bloody nuisance.'

'What do you think I ought to do, sir?'

'Stay away from your telephone. Get your missus to say you're out harrying London reporters.'

'Can I refer the complaints here, sir? You've got people who can cope with them.'

'No, you bloody can't! The lines here have to be kept free for official business. I'm not having your village nobs getting in the way of my investigation. What's stopping them turning a garden hose on intruders? Haven't they got any big nasty dogs that bite?'

PC Whitelock saw he was on a loser and let it go.

'Something else, sir. That story in the paper this morning. I don't want you to think I had anything to do with it. I blushed when I read it, never seen anything that wrong before.'

'It made me laugh,' Bowker said glumly. 'A bloody travesty it was! And if you want my opinion, I think that girl was behind it, trying to make her name in Fleet Street or whatever dismal bloody slum-clearance area the papers have moved to.'

'That was my thought too when I read it. Sara Thomas, though I'm sorry to think a nice young lady like her could do a thing like that, especially after you treated her politely.'

'Bloody contrary creatures, women,' said Bowker with a fierce grin. 'I thought everybody knew that. But have no fear, there's always another day. They'll put her on other murder stories, and I'll be there to steer her up a blind alley and have a laugh at what she writes. Anything else?'

'No, sir. I'll get back to patrolling the village in case of any outbreak of violence caused by the invaders.'

'No, don't do that. Stay here, I've got these bloody folders to read from the house-to-house, and I need your local knowledge when things don't make sense. Tell DS Roper over there that you are helping me and ask him if he's got the sandwiches organised for lunch.'

'Right, sir!' Whitelock's face beamed.

Jack Knight arrived at last. He'd walked from the Black Swan, finding nowhere nearer to leave Bowker's dusty old car.

'Sit down,' said Bowker. 'Let's make a start on this lot. We'll both read each folder in turn, looking for anything that might have a bearing. Get somebody to bring me half a pint of that awful bloody imitation coffee.'

He took the folder marked SIBSON ROY and looked into it. His order to produce a return for everyone in the village had been duly carried out. Hundreds and hundreds of sheets of paper had been handed in by the team, each one headed with a name and an address, and below was written either NIL or a brief report of a sighting, a place, a day and a time. Cumbersome it was, but very comprehensive.

Roper had filed the NIL returns by street and household after taking out reports of sightings for the folders he'd presented to Bowker.

Several people had seen Roy Sibson on the day he drowned, not just Barry Crick. Jilly Ratcliffe at the Post Office, friend of Roy and Barry until the dispute over the baby, said she saw Roy in the phone box outside making a call about one-thirty.

She waved at him through the Post Office window. She was very friendly by nature but he turned his back and pretended not to see her. He used the box for a long time, she said. She'd seen him dialling more than once. He might have made several calls.

Who was he talking to, Bowker wondered. Lynn Hurst, to say he had to see her urgently? Barry Crick had threatened to tell on him. Roy would want to see Lynn and let her know that. Perhaps he'd even phoned Mark Stanhope to forestall Barry. He couldn't have reached him; Stanhope was in Edinburgh.

Edgar Rudd, family butcher and licensed purveyor of game. His shop was in Bridge Street, a few doors up from the Post Office. He'd seen Roy walk past a bit before two o'clock. Or somebody who looked like the photo of Roy he'd been shown.

There were very few people about at that time of day. Mr

Rudd had been staring out of his shop window and happened to notice a young chap in a grey suit go by.

Makes sense, Bowker thought. *Lynn would tell him to walk that way 'round the village and she'd pick him up in her car on Long Street somewhere. She'd be anxious not to be seen with him by anyone who recognised her.*

Roper had included in the Sibson file a report on which he'd scrawled a question-mark. William Spence had been walking his dog and came out of the Bull's Head public house, he thought it might be about two o'clock. Funny bloody place to walk your dog, thought Bowker. Why couldn't the prat just say he'd gone for a pint of ale? Mr Spence was nearly knocked down and killed as he crossed the road, he stated, by a damnation big white car going past like a bloody skyrocket.

He hadn't seen who was in the car; he'd been too moithered by his near-escape from instant death. And shocked because the car killed the cat and didn't even bother to stop. At the bottom of the report the detective who'd talked to Spence had scribbled a warning—*This one's at least 90 and probably can't see all the way across the road. He took me for the rent-collector when I knocked on his door.*

It made sense, Bowker thought. Lynn had arranged to pick Roy up somewhere in Long Street and then drove down Badger Lane and headed for the Wormwold road, driving as fast as she dared, to reduce the exposure time in the village.

Jack Knight took the SIBSON ROY folder while Bowker was deep in thought and went through it to see if he could find anything the Inspector had missed.

'We can pretty well trace Roy's movements from the time when he left home to when he disappeared,' Knight said. 'He went out to meet Lynn Hurst. Barry Crick was telling us the truth about that. And if it wasn't a totally silly bloody idea, I'd say it was Lynn who did Roy in.'

'Exactly the conclusion I came to myself,' Bowker agreed in a disgruntled rumble, 'silly or not.'

'But why should she?'

'That's the mystery,' Bowker said. 'She had no reason to, far as I can see. But we know something about Roy's state of mind when he went to meet her—Barry Crick had put the wind up him after he saw him and Lynn in what old-fashioned newspapers once upon a time called a compromising position.'

'Meaning a knee-trembler under a tree in Cow Lane down by the almshouses,' Knight said with a grin.

He didn't need his notebook to remember what Barry told them. 'Barry said that was about a week before.'

'Maybe and maybe not,' Bowker said slowly. 'Barry's grasp of the calendar is a bit chancy. A week before might mean two days or a fortnight, for all he knows.'

'That's true enough, sir.'

'Besides, the important day is not when he saw Roy and Lynn together, it's when he stopped Roy to have a gloat and tell him he was going to inform Mark Stanhope that his intended was not as lily-white as he expected her to be.'

'Lynn was careful to keep Roy away from School Walk,' Knight said. 'Her other boyfriends could drop in for a frolic, but not Roy. She made him meet her away from the cottage. That ought to mean something.'

'Barry gave us the answer to that one: Lynn Hurst was a snob. Roy was a peasant, Long Slaughter born and bred. His own sister said so. Not the same class as her other boyfriends. Even they had to be careful, having wives to worry about. And Roy wasn't even a boyfriend, as such—Lynn was stringing him along as part of Stanhope's plot to diddle the Building Society.'

'There's every reason Lynn wouldn't want Roy dead and none at all why she should push him in the Thames,' Knight said slowly, his brow creased in concentration.

'But suppose Roy had the wind up so bad he wanted to call off the Chalfont swindle altogether,' Bowker suggested. 'Even after they knew it worked because they'd got away with eight thousand quid on the trial run. Lynn would be distinctly peeved. She was keen on money, Lynn was, very keen. And she knew she could get 'round Stanhope, whatever Barry told him—if Barry bothered to carry out his threat. With big money coming their way, Stanhope wouldn't have caused trouble over a quickie with Roy.'

'Roy wouldn't know that,' said Knight. 'He'd have the wind up for sure, after Barry dropped his little bombshell.'

'So maybe Roy and Lynn had a nasty row by the riverside that day,' said Bowker. 'Angry words, rude things said, arms waving about, shouting and abuse, face smacking, pushing and shoving.'

'An accident?' said Knight, in unison now with Bowker's line of thought. 'It makes sense, damn me it does! Lynn could have hit out in a blind rage. The post-mortem found a bruise on his jaw.'

'He wasn't sturdy, like Barry Crick,' said Bowker, nodding. 'A bit weedy in fact, that chap in the Bull's Head told us, what's his name, the chap with that bloody silly beret—Fox. One hard smack to the chin could knock Roy off balance, and in the river he goes, arse over elbow.'

'He couldn't swim, and he hated the water—his sister told us that,' Knight said triumphantly.

'The river's running fast this time of the year,' Bowker said with a scowl. 'Lot of winter rain coming down. Roy's swept away, and there's nothing Lynn can do except watch him go under while she has hysterics on the riverbank.'

'Not murder at all,' said Knight. 'It was manslaughter, if it happened like that. Then there's every chance Stanhope murdered Lynn for buggering up his plan to get rich quick. His alibi of being in Edinburgh has to be a fake.'

'Never mind Lynn for a minute; at least we've found out what happened to the bloody cat. Lynn ran it over.'

'What, you think it was Miss Pankhurst's cat?'

'That's the only cat we're looking for.'

It was news to Knight that they were looking for a cat at all—dead or alive, it didn't seem to him a suitable investigation for two plain-clothes coppers of rank.

'You're taking some old codger's word for it there was a cat, and it was run over,' he said. 'The copper who interviewed him very nearly says he's senile and blind as a bat.'

'Badger Lane's only a narrow little road,' Bowker countered. 'Why would any daft old sod make up a tale about a cat if there wasn't one? He's not too senile to get himself to the pub.'

'Even so, it couldn't be Miss Pankhurst's cat,' said Knight, with a shake of his head, his brain working on the new problem. 'She's put little hand-written notes on all the lamp-posts along Badger Lane, I've seen them, asking for anyone with news of her ginger tomcat to get in touch with her. If there'd been a squashed cat lying on the road, somebody would have told her.'

'You're right,' Bowker admitted glumly. 'Let's have a look at the map.'

On the blackboard DS Roper had pinned up a large-scale map of Long Slaughter and half a mile 'round it. It showed every house, every alley and footpath, every vacant plot.

'We're here in the Church Hall,' said Bowker, stabbing at the map with a forefinger the size of a banana, 'and there's School Walk down to Badger Lane, the Bull's Head pub on the corner. Old Spence and his dog must have been crossing about here when Lynn came racing along in her car and nearly flattened him.'

'So *if* he's right that she ran over a cat,' said Knight, very disbelieving, 'there would have been a body in the road for someone to get rid of.'

'That's something we can easily find out,' Bowker said. 'It's no big problem asking the people living that end of Badger Lane if they disposed of a dead cat.'

'I'll send somebody to ask, if you think it's worthwhile,' Knight said.

His tone of voice made it very obvious he thought it a waste of time to worry about the disposal arrangements of a deceased cat. Bowker wasn't listening to him. He was staring at the map and muttering to himself.

'If the cat wasn't killed outright—just hurt—it would crawl

away and hide,' he said. 'That's why there was no squashed body in the road.'

'You could be right,' Jack Knight agreed, 'but it's dead now. If there was a cat in the first place, it was hit ten days ago.'

'I know where it is,' said Bowker, staring at the map of the village. 'Only one place it can be.'

'Where?'

'Never you mind that. You carry on reading those bloody files while I nip out for five minutes to see if I'm right.'

Off he went, collecting PC Whitelock on the way. Once outside the Church Hall, they were surrounded by reporters howling for a statement.

'Stand off!' Bowker ordered them in a voice that quelled the riot instantly. It would have stopped a Wild West stampede. 'A statement is being prepared and will be handed out to you after I get back.'

With that he ploughed through the mob, Whitelock close beside him, down School Walk. The curtains were drawn over the windows of Lynn Hurst's house to keep cameramen away, the doors locked and police scene-of-crime tape strung along the garden fence to keep out prying newsmen. Fat chance of that, thought Bowker as he went by at his lolloping pace, as soon as it's dark they'll be through the gate and in the house, locked or unlocked.

Next door, outside Karma Kottage, Empson Rowley was fiddling with the engine of his motorbike. His T-shirt, which was an unpleasant shade of purple, said WITTGENSTEIN LIVES. Bowker wondered who Wittgenstein was; another bloody rock-star, most likely. He gave an evil grin. Rowley pretended not to see him.

'Where are we going to, sir?' Kevin Whitelock asked as they turned into Badger Lane. 'My car's parked further along if you want me to drive you somewhere.'

'Only across the road to the Bull's Head. I've got a theory.'

'Ah!' Whitelock said and asked no more.

At the side of the Bull's Head was a double gate into a yard. The gates stood permanently open. The pub yard was stacked with empty beer barrels and metal crates of empty bottles waiting to be collected by the brewer's truck.

'We're looking for Miss Pankhurst's cat,' Bowker said. 'Prod about under all this rubbish and see what you find. It was hit by a car in the lane outside. There's nowhere but here it could have crawled without being noticed by now.'

Whitelock set to work very reluctantly. Looking for dead cats was not the sort of task the Constabulary should concern itself with. In his opinion, it was undignified. Bowker was not at all well informed about the psychology of cats but he looked around for other hiding places. Never ask your men to do anything that you wouldn't do yourself, a simple guideline he worked by.

On one side of the yard was a single-storey extension housing the lavatories. And across the back of the yard was another low building, as old as the pub, early Victorian in Bowker's guess. It would have been the stable, of course, in the days when pub-keepers went about by horse and trap, before there were cars.

The stable had been allowed to become derelict, the glass was broken in both windows, slates were missing from the roof. The wooden door was half off its hinges. Mostly the old stable was used as a dump, Bowker saw, inside there was a push-bike with a wheel gone and a broken washing machine, rusty where the white enamel had peeled off. And other less easily identified junk.

There were pools of water on the earth floor, where rain came in through the roof. And by one of the pools lay the body of a ginger cat.

'Found it!' Bowker called over his shoulder to Whitelock.

He squatted down beside the cat and he saw why Miss Pankhurst was grieved over losing it. Tiger had been well-named; he was a fine big tomcat, his fur still bright ginger.

'Well damn me!' said Whitelock, pushing his helmet up on his forehead. 'How did you know it would be here?'

Before Bowker could answer, the cat opened one eye and made a faint sound of complaint.

'And it's alive!' Whitelock said in astonishment.

'Only just,' Bowker said. 'You can see that back leg's broken as well as ripped open. There's a couple of inches gone off the end of his tail. And he's lost a lot of blood—it's soaked into the ground. He wasn't run over, the car just clipped him as he jumped clear. He's a bloody marvel this tom, he's survived all this time on rainwater—ten days! Where's the nearest vet?'

'There's only one. Mr Webber, lives on the Thames road. He looks after all the livestock in these parts.'

'Right. Get one of those big cardboard boxes from over there by the wall and we'll put Tiger in it. You take him to this vet and see if he can be patched up.'

'The cat's a goner, if you ask me,' said Whitelock, examining the extent of the cat's injuries doubtfully.

'Maybe,' said Bowker, 'maybe not. He's a fighter. He deserves a chance. But if the vet thinks he's too far gone to save, tell the bloody man to put him out of his misery straight away. Have you got that?'

'He'll want paying, Mr Webber,' said Whitelock, shaking his head sententiously. 'From what I've been told he's not cheap. I don't know if Miss Pankhurst could afford him. A lot of farmers 'round here doctor their own cows because they say he charges so much.'

'Tell him I'll stand the bill,' said Bowker. 'Just get a move on before the bloody cat breathes its last while you're arguing with me.'

They were lifting the cat very carefully into a cardboard box for transport to the vet's surgery when a dazzling flash lit up the stable.

'Got it!' crowed a voice from the doorway. A reporter with a cameraman in tow had followed the two policemen from the Church Hall in the hope of getting an exclusive scoop. They'd snatched a shot of Bowker and the local bobby stooped over a dirty old cardboard box, not much of a front-page picture for a tabloid.

'On your way, Whitelock,' Bowker growled. 'I'll see these two clowns off. Report straight back to me in the Incident Room as soon as you can.'

'What are you doing with the cat, Mr Bowker?' the reporter demanded. 'Is it part of the case?'

He was a tall thin man of about thirty, with two days' growth of stubble on his chin, very rock-star. His short and shiny black leather coat had rows of chrome studs. Bowker distrusted him on sight. Meanwhile the cameraman was taking more useless shots of Whitelock with the cardboard box in his arms leaving the yard.

'That cat,' said Bowker, keeping a straight face while he led the reporter right up the garden path, 'is a vital clue in the investigation of multiple murders. If it survives its injuries, it will lead us straight to the killer.'

18. denis bowker makes an arrest

When Bowker forced his way back into the Incident Room through the clamouring reporters, he looked so very nearly pleased that Jack Knight was amazed. He'd never seen Bowker look happy—not that his expression now could be called *happy*, but it was close to it.

'Well?' Knight asked. 'Have you cracked the case?'

'Found the old woman's cat.'

Before there was time to explain, the telephone at his elbow rang. Knight answered it for him.

'For you, sir,' he said. 'It's DCS Horrocks, not too happy by the sound of it.'

The unusually benign look disappeared instantly from Bowker's face, to be replaced by a black scowl as he took the phone.

'I do not begin to understand this refusal to return my phone calls, Denis,' the Chief Superintendent began ominously.

To Bowker's ear, he sounded pompous rather than angry.

'They told me you were in Henley,' he went on. "You must have received a message to ring me urgently.'

'It must have got garbled,' said Bowker, trying hard to sound convincing, but failing. 'I was told you rang through to see if anything was moving. I didn't want to disturb you at home on a Saturday till I'd got something worthwhile to tell you. After interviewing Mrs Willet-Jones at Henley this morning I decided to pull Stanhope in and charge him with attempted fraud.'

'I don't care if it's Saturday or bloody Whit Tuesday. I want to be kept in touch all the time. And I'm not at home, I'm here at my desk! Is Stanhope our murderer, Denis?'

'Not unless he's a bloody good actor. He doesn't come over to me as being up to anything as physical as drowning anybody.'

'But you can get him on the Building Society fraud, can you?'

'Attempted fraud on Mrs Willet-Jones, to start with. He's been giving her a long farrago about investment property and gearing up to take her money for a building he doesn't own. He might do a flit on us, so I want him charged and his passport taken away from him. Knight is picking him up first thing tomorrow morning to let him stew in the cells for a bit. I'll charge him for the Building Society job on Monday, just to keep him reeling.'

'Good, good,' said Horrocks, sounding slightly more cheerful now he knew someone was going to be run in, even though attempted fraud was not much of a charge, and certainly a long way off from murder.

'Let me know what's happening about him, Denis. Why I rang you earlier on is because I had a call from the Serious Fraud squad at eight this morning, as soon as they saw the newspaper story that mentions Fenwick.'

'Not by name,' Bowker countered.

'It didn't need to, did it? There aren't that many prominent City solicitors living in Long Slaughter. Did you tip the press off?'

'Me?' Bowker was genuinely outraged. 'You know I didn't!

And before you ask, nobody has seen the Hurst address book except me and Knight. Nobody else has even been told there *is* a book, apart from the local bobby. There's a reporter from the *County Examiner* been ferreting about. My guess is she was told there's a book of names by Mrs Hurst's cleaner. It wouldn't take more than a few quid to get the cleaner to tell all she knows. She's a petty fraudster called Emma Ardwick.'

'*Sex slayer stalks village of fear*—it won't do, Denis, it's like something out of a penny dreadful. The Serious Fraud have turned twitchy because they think the story will panic Fenwick into instant emigration. Just think what the Sunday papers are going to be like tomorrow!'

'I'm looking forward to a good laugh,' Bowker said.

'There's nothing to laugh about! Any chance at all you might arrest Fenwick today for the murders?'

'Bloody tricky, running a lawyer in if you haven't got a cast-iron case,' said Bowker. He could hear the faint desperation in Horrocks' tone and guessed there was heavy pressure on him from higher up. 'We've nothing on Fenwick except he was having a leg-over with Lynn Hurst and he's a thumping crook. The two things don't have to be connected.'

'There are times,' said the DCS heaving a sigh, 'when I wish I'd listened to my late and sainted mother and trained to be a dentist instead of a bloody policeman.'

'They make more money than we do,' Bowker pointed out glumly. 'They all drive new BMWs, every bloody one. And if the Serious Fraud are so worried about Fenwick doing a flit, why don't they send a team 'round now and run him in themselves? They want the bugger a lot more than we do. It's not up to us to do the heavy work for them.'

'We're all on the same side, Denis.'

'I'm glad to hear that, sir. That wasn't the impression I got yesterday, when you asked me to lay off Fenwick.'

'*Tcha!*' said Horrocks, or something like it. He slammed down the phone and left Bowker to get on with his job.

PC Whitelock was soon back. He marched straight past DS Roper with a self-important air, knowing full well all officers were supposed to report to him on arrival. The village bobby wasn't under Roper's command and didn't care if he annoyed him. He was making the most of his direct contact with Bowker.

'Well?' Bowker asked, all goodwill dissipated by the nagging from DCS Horrocks.

'The vet says the cat will pull through, sir. Found it in the nick of time, he reckons. Another twenty-four hours and it would be done for. I left him setting its leg and stitching it up. He says a day or two of pick-me-up shots and a steady diet of warm milk with a drop of whisky in it and it will be ready to go home.'

'I told you he's a fighter, that cat,' said Bowker, grinning again in approval. 'When we get a minute, I'll get you to stroll 'round to Miss Pankhurst and tell her the news. Stick around for now until I need you—see if you can give DS Roper a hand with anything.'

Whitelock saluted, astonishing Bowker who thought constables had given that up years ago. He couldn't remember the last time he'd been saluted. And he was sure he'd never saluted a senior officer himself when he'd been a uniform.

He turned back to Knight to continue the argument they were having before Whitelock interrupted.

'It's open-and-shut,' Knight said. 'It stands to reason Lynn pushed Roy in the river by mistake while they were having a bit of a barney and the silly sod drowned because he couldn't swim. She rings up Stanhope to tell him what's happened, and naturally he's furious because that's put paid to his scheme to embezzle from the Chalfont Building Society. He drives to Long Slaughter in a blind rage and does her in.'

'Takes her car and kills Gavin Fowler in it, so we'll imagine he did it and look no further?' said Bowker. 'Is that what you think? It won't bloody wash. Gavin killed Lynn.'

'So who killed Gavin?' Knight demanded heatedly.

'It's bloody obvious. One more shred of evidence, and we'll go 'round there and make the arrest,' said Bowker, his thick black eyebrows drawn down in a massive glare.

'What do you mean, obvious? It's not bloody obvious to me.'

'Think about it. Ask yourself what Lynn did after she saw Roy go under for the third time.'

'She didn't report it—we know that,' Knight said, trying to see where Bowker was leading him, 'and for obvious reasons. Her association with Roy was criminal. They'd diddled the Chalfont out of eight grand and were planning much more. She'd have too much explaining to do if she reported Roy in the river. So she went home and phoned Stanhope to tell him their rip-off was floating down the Swanee.'

'But Mark James Stanhope was in Edinburgh trying to drum up a bit of architecting business,' Bowker pointed out. 'No bloody use at all to her in her panic and distress. She had to wait to see him when he flew back.'

'Which wasn't until the next day. Even then he didn't exactly rush over to Long Slaughter to comfort her,' said Knight, well into the swing of it. 'He talked to her on the telephone and he promised to take her away for the weekend to get over it. That was what the Paris trip was about, not the usual.'

'Now you're starting to make sense,' Bowker said, nodding.

'He made her wait till the weekend because if the swindle was off, he had other things on his mind, including Laureen Willet-Jones and her money,' Knight suggested.

'He's a slimy sort of crook, our Mark,' said Bowker, with a look on his face that would have fended off an assailant with a cosh in his hand. 'With any luck at all, we'll put him away for a few years on the fraud charges.'

While they were talking DS Roper brought more pieces of paper for the folders, the last few co-ordinated reports now that the house-to-house was finished and all the squad had come back to the Incident Room. There was a lot more to put into one of the victim files. When he'd finished, he handed it to Bowker.

'Plenty to read in this one, sir,' he said. 'None of it very inter-esting though.'

The folder was labelled FOWLER, GAVIN. Bowker skimmed through it quickly. Gavin moved about a lot. A pregnant wife and house full of squalling children seemingly had little attrac-tion for him. A dozen or more sightings of the slaughterman were noted, in the bar of the Black Swan, the Bull's Head, the off-licence over the bridge, going to work early in the morning, going home unsteadily, late at night.

The off-licence across the river, Thos. Thornton and Son, was where Gavin bought a bottle of whisky on the day of his death. They'd known that before, from PC Whitelock's enquiries. It was not particularly useful information. Thos. Thornton said there was no one with Gavin at the time. And if there was a white car parked outside, Thos. hadn't noticed it.

But there was one report in the folder that drew a long howl of triumph from Bowker—a noise that reminded some of those in the Incident Room of Tarzan roaring defiance through the jungle after wrestling a huge lion and snapping its neck with his bare hands. Detectives seated at the tables stopped work to turn and stare round-eyed.

'What?' Knight asked. 'What have you found?'

He took the folder Bowker handed him.

The page at which it was open was headed with the infor-mant's name and address, Miss Annie Burton, 16 Cow Lane. Below it were a few scribbled lines by the detective who had interviewed her:

Wednesday 20th, Fowler seen in Cow Lane, time approx 23.45 or not much later. Informant on way home from friend's. Saw Fowler standing in alley with a woman. Dark at the time but informant almost sure it was Mrs Joyce Harris.

'Roy's sister talking to Gavin?" Knight said, puzzled. 'What of it?'

'Whitelock!' Bowker called out. 'Over here!'

Kevin Whitelock left his chair next to WPC Avice Morley, the proud brunette owner of the well-filled police shirt, and came across the room to stand in front of Bowker's table.

'Joyce Harris, Joyce Sibson that was,' Bowker said with brisk geniality.

'Sir?'

'Joyce and Gavin Fowler, slaughterman deceased. Both of them Long Slaughter born, both the same age, late twenties. What do you think, Whitelock? Would they know each other?'

'Certain to,' said Whitelock, not even stopping to consider. 'They'd have been at school together in the village, and in the same class, I should think. The Comprehensive the kids go to on the school bus nowadays, that wasn't built until about fifteen years ago. When Joyce Sibson and Gavin Fowler were school kids, there was still the village school.'

'They'd grow up knowing each other?'

'That's right. In a place like Long Slaughter everybody grows up knowing each other. The locals, that is, not the people who buy a house and settle here from outside.'

'They knew each other from when they were children, but Joyce never bothered to mention it to me,' Bowker said.

'Doesn't mean they were friends,' Whitelock pointed out, 'but they couldn't have been strangers to each other. Not possible.'

'So when somebody tells us they saw Joyce and Gavin Fowler in a dark alley in Cow Lane, what do you make of it?'

'I know the place you mean,' Whitelock said in some surprise. 'There's a row of houses with entries through between each two, so you can get to the back door. The street lighting's not much in Cow Lane, and the entries are dark. They get used for immoral purposes after dark by teenagers. I often get complaints in the winter from the tenants.'

'Joyce and Gavin having one of your immoral purposes together there—what do you think, fact or fairy tale?' Bowker asked.

This time Kevin Whitelock thought for some little time before he answered the question.

'I'm sorry to hear Joyce has been straying,' he said. 'Only a couple of years, if that, since she wed Reg Harris. But there's no gainsaying she's always been a spirited woman. She does what she wants, and everybody else has to fall in with her wishes.'

'Leave that for a minute while DS Knight ponders a different question for me. Who had reason to hate Lynn Hurst badly enough to want her dead? Would Roy's possessive sister spring to mind—if she knew Roy was drowned? Cast your mind back to when we first saw Joyce, after Barry Crick told us he'd seen Roy in the car with Lynn on the Wormwold Road.'

'Joyce was drawn and strained, when we called 'round hoping to find Roy,' said Knight, thinking back. 'I remember you said to me at the time her nerves were all in shreds. We thought it was because Roy had disappeared and she suspected he'd fiddled the Building Society. She tried to impede our enquiry with all that Mary Ellen about him going on his holidays.'

'We'll ask her how she knew Roy was dead in the Thames before his body was found,' Bowker said malignly. 'That's the start of it all, an eye for an eye and a life for a life. That's what's been staring us in the face all week, and we never spotted it.'

'My God,' said Knight. 'It makes sense.'

'Joyce wanted revenge and she went to the man she knew could help her,' Bowker growled. 'Someone she'd known since they were both kids. He knew how to hurt Lynn for Joyce, hurt her bloody permanently. Gavin the slaughterman.'

'Joyce didn't give him money,' Knight said. 'We couldn't find any in his effects because there never was any. Joyce persuaded him another way.'

'In a dark entry in Cow Lane!' said PC Whitelock. 'Well, that beats all!'

'And she promised Gavin more of the same after he'd done the job,' said Bowker. His voice was like a church bell tolling for a funeral. 'That Saturday afternoon, while we were rummaging in Lynn's cottage and getting nowhere with that prat of an artist, Joyce was meeting Gavin for a drink of whisky and you-know-what in a quiet place where they wouldn't be seen. Birley Spinney.'

'In Lynn's car,' said Knight. 'Sly touch, that.'

'They went there in Lynn's car, which Gavin took and hid till Saturday on Joyce's say-so,' Bowker agreed. 'Joyce got him dead drunk on his own whisky and left him snoring with the engine on and a pipe in through the window from the exhaust.'

'Bloody hell!' said Knight. 'She's a black-hearted bitch if that's how it happened!'

'I've no doubt she is,' Bowker said gloomily, 'though there's always a reason, not a good reason, the way we see things, but a reason of a sort.'

'Revenge the first time, having Gavin kill Lynn for her, then covering her tracks the second time by doing away with Gavin,' said Knight. 'It's nasty.'

'Murder's always nasty. But look at it like this. Two women— different in most ways, one of them living in style in her own home, with well-to-do boyfriends, glamorous holidays, we saw it all in her photo album. And then the other woman Joyce, married to a decent nobody sort of chap and sharing a miserable rented house with her clapped-out Dad and Mum.'

'You're saying there was envy and resentment behind it?'

'You remember when I asked Joyce about Lynn, she said, *"Our sort don't know her sort."* To me it sounded very resentful. The point is that Joyce didn't have much compared to Lynn, but Lynn took something away from her, and Joyce decided to get her own back.'

'We'll never be able to prove any of this, sir.'

'Yes we bloody will!' Bowker said loudly. 'Come on. And you, Whitelock.'

He stopped by DS Roper's table and glared at the folders and stacks of reports.

'I'm taking both WPCs with me, Roper,' he said with a grin so fierce the Detective Sergeant almost flinched. 'I don't want to have the press on my tail, so I shall tell them you're going to make a statement in five minutes' time. That ought to keep them here while I slip away.'

'Right, sir,' said Roper, blinking like a surprised owl. 'But what sort of statement do you want me to make?'

'How the hell should I know! Think of something, man!'

Roper looked extraordinarily blank.

'I've got an idea.' Jack Knight came to the rescue. 'You can tell them every house, barn, pub and dovecot in Long Slaughter has been visited as part of the investigation and every single person has been questioned. That has produced 4,746 statements which are now being processed and fed into the computer, where they will be cross-referenced and all that.'

'We haven't finished counting the statements yet,' said Roper with an offended look. 'It's not right to guess at the total.'

'Estimate it,' said Bowker, pleased with Knight's idea. 'Then spin your bloody statement out, tell the riffraff outside about the marvels of modern science used in criminal detection. Talk for twenty minutes at the least, give them a load of Mary Ellen for their tape recorders. Good man!'

Roper was so overcome by the intricacies of the job he'd been given that he forgot to ask Bowker where he was going, to enter in the Log in case DCS Horrocks wanted to know.

Bowker pushed his way out into the instantly ravening horde of newsmen with Jack Knight, the policewomen and PC White-lock following him.

'Quiet!' he bellowed. The sheer ferocity in his voice would have stopped a charging buffalo. The press clamour died away.

'In about five minutes from now Detective Sergeant Roper will be making an official statement on our progress to date.'

'Where are you going?' demanded half a dozen voices.

'These officers and I are taking a short refreshment break at the Black Swan,' he said, with total disregard for truth.

The reporters leered at WPC Avice Morley and WPC Sue Hut-chins and drew the wrong conclusion, as Bowker intended. There were a few wolf whistles and then the mob parted like the

Red Sea before Moses for Bowker to lead his little group down School Walk.

He waved cheerily to Sara Thomas in the throng and gave her his bare-knuckle grin.

'Has your pal in the studs told you about that clue we found in the old stable, or is he keeping it for himself?' he asked loudly, pointing at the reporter who'd seen him find the ginger cat.

'What clue?' she said, turning on the man in the shiny black leather jacket. 'We agreed to pool all our information, Trevor. What's the Inspector on about? Tell me, you evil creep!'

Bowker pressed on down School Walk, chuckling malignly at the fuss he'd stirred up. Behind him he could hear a dozen newsmen shouting at the one he'd singled out. Others were hammering on the Church Hall door, bawling for the promised statement.

Whitelock had taken full advantage of his official status and double-parked his police car in Badger Lane, so blocking half a dozen press cars. The three men and two women squeezed into the police car and Bowker told Whitelock to go 'round by the Black Swan, in case any idiot decided to follow them. And drop Knight off there so he could collect the car he'd left.

Ten minutes later they were outside 23 Orchard Row without a press retinue. The official statement ploy had worked, although DS Roper was in for a bad time when it became obvious that what he was saying was time-wasting trivia.

The dented dustbin by the front door had been emptied since he was here last, Bowker noted. The dustmen had left a trail of garbage to the street. He looked at his steel wristwatch. He'd have to note the time of arrest in his report: 12:20 P.M.

He raised a clenched fist the size of a iron cannonball and knocked loudly.

He could hear the drone of a vacuum cleaner inside the house. He knocked again, even louder, and after a minute or two Joyce Harris came to the door. She wore an old grey skirt and a blue pullover and was obviously doing the housework.

'Mrs Harris,' said Bowker, trying not to sound intimidating, though he had automatically drawn himself up to his full height and looked more like the Mad Mangler in the ring than even the TV wrestler did himself.

'I must ask you to come with me for questioning,' he said to her, 'and I think it's only fair to warn you I expect to charge you with murder.'

Joyce stared at him, her face suddenly pale.

'You can't prove anything!' she burst out. 'Gavin killed her and nobody's ever going to prove different. The bitch only got what she deserved!'

'Who are you talking about?' Bowker asked, fascinated by her ferocious reaction.

Joyce's face was a flaming red now, she was spiralling up out of control.

'You know who I mean—that whore Lynn Hurst!' she shouted.

'It wasn't her I had in mind,' Bowker said mildly. 'It's the murder of Gavin Fowler I've come to arrest you for.'

In a single burst of movement, Joyce slammed the door, turned, and ran. But Bowker had his foot over the step in readiness and sent the door hurtling open again, to smash against the wall.

He stood back and waved the two policewomen into the house.

'Bring her out,' he said.

Kevin Whitelock was looking on aghast, not so pleased now to be involved in a murder investigation when it meant using force to arrest a woman he'd known for years and thought well of.

'Get your car started and ready to take off the second we've got her,' Bowker told him sharply.

'Where do you want to take her, sir?'

'Not back to the Incident Room—that mob outside will eat her alive. I want you to take her to HQ. I'll question her there in due course and then charge her. Knight will ride with you, and

278

the two WPCs. I'll go back to School Walk and let the team know we've got a suspect in custody.'

Knight suggested, 'I can do that for you, if you want to go with her and start the questioning.'

'No, I want to explain to the squad what evidence they should be looking for now. I'll give the press a statement, they'll go raving paranoid when they hear I've taken someone into custody and they weren't there to see it. After that bloody silly SEX SLAYER STALKS VILLAGE headline this morning I'm looking forward to having a laugh at the rabble outside the Church Hall.'

They could hear shouting in the house, screams and the sound of feet running up stairs, doors being slammed, furniture being dragged across a wooden floor. Joyce didn't mean to go quietly. But she was in a trap, and there was no way out.

It took about ten minutes. The uniformed policewomen brought her out, each holding her by an arm to control her struggling. By then the neighbours on both sides and across the street had heard the noise and were at their windows to watch.

Joyce's Mum and Dad followed their daughter out as far as the doorstep. They stood there and stared white-faced and trembling at what was happening. There were tears trickling down poor old Dad's cheeks.

They got her into the back seat of Whitelock's car, a WPC on either side of her. Knight jumped in the front beside Whitelock and the car accelerated noisily away, blue light flashing.

Mrs Sibson came to where Bowker stood on the pavement beside his own car. Dad Sibson was sagging against the door-jamb, not taking much in now.

'What are you going to do to our Joyce?' Mrs Sibson asked.

It wasn't easy to know what to say to a woman who had lost both her children, one dead and one facing life imprisonment.

'She'll be charged with murder. I'm sorry, Mrs Sibson.'

'He wouldn't listen to her, Roy,' she said distractedly. 'She told him a dozen times no good would come of hanging 'round that woman in School Walk. But he was young and silly, and she turned his head. He wouldn't listen to Joyce.'

Standing there on the pavement, feeling unsettled at the way things had gone, Bowker took a chance and got the missing piece of the puzzle.

'Did Joyce go to see Mrs Hurst when Roy didn't come home?'

'She thought he'd stayed the night with her,' said Mrs Sibson in high disapproval. 'She went 'round there the next morning to drag him home and give that woman the rough edge of her tongue. Only Roy wasn't there after all. There was a row, and Joyce got it out of her that Roy was dead. She swore it was an accident, but Joyce never believed her. It was done on purpose, she said, because Roy knew too much.'

'Why didn't you report it straight away to PC Whitelock, Mrs Sibson?'

'Joyce wouldn't let us. She was too furious. She said women like Mrs Hurst always get off, whatever they do. She said she'd make her pay for what she'd done this time.'

It came into Bowker's mind that he could get Joyce on prints, now he could tell a dabs-team what to look for. She'd been very careful to wipe the neck of the whisky bottle clean, but ten to one she'd left a dab somewhere in the car, getting in, getting out, sitting there talking and being groped by Gavin Fowler.

Maybe she'd left a thread from her clothes on the seat, even a hair or two, or some trace of herself. Bloody Forensic could have a go at proving they were of some use. Stranger things had happened.

'Where's Joyce's husband?' Bowker asked. 'Isn't he here?'

Reg Harris was like the bloody Invisible Man, Bowker thought. He'd never even laid eyes on him.

'He'll be in the Black Swan having a pint with his mates. It's his day off, Saturday.'

Reg would have to be interviewed now his wife had been run in—Jack Knight could look after that. It wasn't likely Reg could tell them anything they didn't know.

'You'd better go and look after your husband,' Knight said as gently as he could. 'He looks as if he's going to fall down in another minute. Get him inside and make him a cup of tea.'

He got in the car and drove off down Orchard Row, leaving her staring after him. When the press heard that Joyce Harris had been run in, they'd mob the Sibson house. They'd be howling questions and taking photos, knocking on neighbours' doors and wanting to know if they'd suspected that a murderess lived at number 23.

Bowker knew them of old. They'd make the Sibsons' life a real misery until another grisly crime happened elsewhere and they went chasing after a new story. He could ask Whitelock to keep an eye on the Sibsons, though there wasn't much a village bobby could do to protect them.

The eight thousand pounds was still missing. Stanhope ought to know where it was; it was his plot to loot the Chalfont. Bowker thought there was every chance he could sweat it out of him. It was going to be a pleasure to put that shifty character through the wringer. Mark James Stanhope was going to find out the hard way what helping the police with their enquiries meant.

And maybe he'd had a hand in other villainies that he could be persuaded to relieve his conscience of by confessing.

Before leaving Long Slaughter, there was an important call to be made, Bowker reminded himself. He had to go 'round to number 6 Yattnall's Rents, wherever the bloody hell that was, and tell Miss Pankhurst her ginger tomcat was alive and on the mend now the vet had stitched him up, no charge. She'd be able to go and fetch Tiger home in a couple of days.

The old dear would be happy about that, Bowker thought. She'd very likely make him sit down and drink a glass of sweet sherry with her, from the half bottle left over from Christmas.